THE BOY
WHO SAW

Simon Toyne is the bestselling author of the *Sanctus* trilogy: *Sanctus*, *The Key* and *The Tower*. He wrote *Sanctus* after quitting his job as a TV executive to focus on writing. It was the biggest-selling debut thriller of 2011 in the UK and an international bestseller. His books have been translated into 27 languages and published in over 50 countries. *The Boy Who Saw* is the second book in a new series of epic thrillers that will span the world and centre around Solomon Creed.

Simon lives with his family in Brighton and the South of France.

simontoyne.net

facebook.com/simon.toyne.writer

@simontoyne

I2844195

Also by Simon Toyne

Solomon Creed
Sanctus
The Key
The Tower

THE BOY
WHO SAW

SIMON TOYNE

HarperCollins*Publishers*

HarperCollins*Publishers*
1 London Bridge Street
London SE1 9GF

www.harpercollins.co.uk

2

This paperback edition 2018
First published by HarperCollins*Publishers* 2017

A catalogue record for this book
is available from the British Library

ISBN: 978-0-00-755165-1 (PB b-format)
ISBN: 978-0-00-824029-5 (PB a-format)

This novel is entirely a work of fiction.
The names, characters and incidents portrayed in it are
the work of the author's imagination. Any resemblance to
actual persons, living or dead, events or localities is
entirely coincidental.

Typeset by Palimpsest Book Production Ltd, Falkirk, Stirlingshire

Printed and bound in Great Britain by CPI Group (UK) Ltd, Croydon CR0 4YY

For my sister Becky, her husband Joe and for little William Quinn Francesco Pingue, born 16/11/16. Who knows what that boy will see?

I

'Three may keep a secret,
If two of them are dead.'

Benjamin Franklin

1

Nothing else smells like blood.

Blood mixed with fear is something else again. Josef Engel had not smelled it in over seventy years – seventy years and he still remembered it like the years had been nothing. And this time the smell was coming from him.

He stared down at his shrunken body, his head too heavy to lift, old skin drooping like canvas over the frame of his ribs. Blood dripped vivid against the white of it, leaking from cuts in his chest that formed the Star of David. Other wounds tickled as they bled, slashes on his back where he'd been whipped, puncture wounds from something that had pinched his flesh together to cause fresh pain when he thought he'd already felt every kind there was. The pain was everything now, burning like fire through flesh that remained oddly slack and useless.

The man had come right before closing, walking into the shop and embracing Josef like an old friend. Josef had embraced him back, surprised by the action of this man dressed all in black like a shadow. Then he had felt the pinprick on his neck and tried to pull away, but the shadow man had held him tight and a cold numbness had quickly spread out from the pinprick and into his whole body. He had tried to call for help but it had come out as a drooling moan and his head fell forward on neck muscles no longer able to support the weight of his skull. There was no one around to hear anyway and the man must have known, for he had not been agitated or hurried as he calmly steered Josef to the centre of his atelier through the headless mannequins. He had slumped to the floor in the centre of the room, his arthritic knees cracking like gunshots, another memory from seventy years ago.

Josef had watched the man's shadow, cast by the skylights above, moving on the polished wooden floor as he removed Josef's shirt. A blade had appeared close to his eyes, turning slowly so the light caught the sharpness of its edge before it moved to his chest and cut through white flesh down to the bone, the blood welling around the blade and dripping down his front to the floor. He had watched it all and gasped at the explosions of pain the blade drew from him, wondering how so much agony could be contained in his old body, and why the drugs that had numbed his muscles did nothing to block the pain. He was a prisoner in his own flesh, feeling everything but incapable of doing anything to stop it. Warmth spread over him as first his blood then his bladder and bowels emptied. When the smell of that hit him he had started to cry because the humiliation was painful too.

Josef had not been this afraid since the war, when pain and death had been commonplace in the labour camps. He had escaped death then but now it had caught up with him. He watched its shadow move away across the polished wooden floor, heard the front door being unlocked and hoped that maybe the shadow man was leaving. But the door was relocked and the shadow returned and something was placed on the floor in front of him.

Tears sprang to Josef's eyes as he read the faded gold

lettering on the wooden sewing machine box – *Pfaff*. It was the same make as the machine he had learned to sew on, before war had come and the world had gone dark, when all he'd wanted to do was listen to the purr of the busy needle and make beautiful things with it. Holes had been drilled in the curved top of the box and a small hatch fitted on one side with a sliding bolt keeping it shut. A faint scratching was coming from inside.

'*Du weißt warum dies dir passiert ist?*'

The man's German was accented and Josef didn't recognize the voice. He tried to look up again but his head was still too heavy.

'You know why this has happened to you?' the voice repeated, and a phone appeared in front of Josef's face, the light from the screen too bright in the evening gloom.

'*Erinnerst du dich hieran?*' the voice asked.

Josef squinted against the brightness and looked at the black-and-white photograph displayed on the phone.

'*Erinnerst du dich hieran?*' the voice repeated. 'Remember this?'

Josef did remember.

A hand swiped the screen and more photographs appeared, stark images of terrible things Josef had witnessed with his own eyes: piles of bodies in mass graves; skeletons behind wire fences, on their knees in the mud, too weak to stand, their bony shoulders tenting striped uniforms, shaved heads hanging forward while men in grey uniforms stood over them with whips and guns or the strained leashes of snarling dogs in their leather-gloved hands.

'You should have died in the camp,' the voice said. 'We should have wiped away the stain of you back then when we had the chance.'

Josef stared into eyes sunk deep in skull-like faces and imagined bony hands reaching out for him across the distance of seventy lost years, and pushing into his chest.

'*Der bleiche Mann*,' he whispered, his numbed tongue blurring the words.

The shadow on the floor moved closer. 'Tell me about him. Tell me about the pale man.'

'*Er kommt*,' Josef replied, his tongue wrapping around a language he had not spoken in decades. 'He is coming.' His mind was drifting now, fogged by the intense pain spreading out from his chest. 'He will save me *und die Anderen* . . . *Comme la dernière fois*. He will come and save us again.'

'*Die Anderen*,' the voice said. 'Tell me about the others. Tell me what happened back in the camp. State your name and give me your confession.'

Josef hesitated for a moment before starting to speak, the words flowing out of him in a steady stream, loosened by the drug and the feeling that as long as he continued to talk he would be allowed to live. 'I kept it safe,' Josef said when he had finished his confession, his hands tingling as the drug began to wear off. He reached up to where the skeleton fingers continued to tear at his heart and pain bloomed.

'What did you keep safe?'

'The list,' Josef gasped.

'Tell me about the list.'

'*Der weiße Anzug*,' Josef clutched his chest and pushed back against the pain. 'The white suit. We promised to keep it safe and we did. All these years we kept it safe.'

Josef managed to raise his head a little and stared up at the outline of his killer silhouetted against the skylights. The man reached down and Josef closed his eyes and braced himself for some new pain, but something touched his face and he opened his eyes again and saw a white tissue in the man's hand, dabbing at the blood around his eyes as gently as a mother cleaning jam from a child's mouth. Josef started to weep at this unexpected gesture of kindness. He could smell disinfectant on the man's hand and saw that he was wearing thin surgical gloves the same colour as skin.

'Remember the camp,' the man asked, 'remember what it was like at the very end, all those bodies piling up and no one left to bury them?' He moved over to the wooden box and twisted the tissue until blood squeezed out between his latex-covered fingers. 'Do you remember the rats?' He bent down and fed the tapered end of the tissue into one of the larger holes and the scratching intensified. 'All those walking skeletons but the rats never went hungry, did they?' The tissue twitched and was tugged inside the box with a flurry of squeaks and scratching. 'I caught these rats near a chicken farm almost a week ago. They haven't eaten much since – only each other. I wonder how many there are left?' He reached down for the bolt holding the hatch shut and Josef felt panicked pain explode in his chest. 'Or you could tell me more about the white suit and I'll keep the box shut.'

Tears dripped down Josef's face, stinging as they salted the wounds on his chest. The pain was unbearable now. He had never escaped the camp, not really. He had carried it with him all this time, and now it was bursting out of him again.

'Tell me about the suit.' The man slid the latch across but held the door shut.

'The pale man,' Josef said, shaking uncontrollably, his breathing shallow. 'We made it for him.' He dragged his eyes from the box and looked desperately over at the door as if hoping he might be standing there. 'He said he would come for it. He said it would keep us safe. We made a deal. He will—'

Pain erupted inside Josef, a jagged explosion of glass and fire that forced all the air from his lungs. His eyes flew wide and he crumpled to the floor, gasping for breath but getting none. He lay on his side and saw a thimble lying deep under one of the workbenches, worn and familiar and bent to the shape of his finger over long years of work, the same thimble he'd had back in the camp, back in that cellar. He had lost it a month or so ago and looked for it everywhere. And there it was. And here was he. The pain was consuming him now. Swallowing him whole. Pulling him down. His killer dropped to the floor, cutting off his view of the lost thimble, and Josef felt a pressure on his neck and smelled rubber and disinfectant as fingers checked for a pulse. Josef's view shifted as he was rolled on to his back and he heard a thud and felt a fist hammer down on the centre of his chest, heard a rib crack but didn't feel anything because the pain inside him was already too great.

Josef looked beyond the silhouette of the man and up to the sky where thin white clouds slid across the deepening blue sky. He had worked in this room for over forty years but this was the first time he could remember looking up. He had never looked at the sky in the camp either, had always found it too painful to gaze up at such simple, boundless beauty when all around him was ugliness and horror.

The man continued to pound on his chest but Josef knew it was pointless. There was no saving him now. The man in the white suit was not coming. He would not cheat Death a second time. He took a last, deep, jagged breath. Stared up at the indigo sky. And closed his eyes.

* * *

8

He stopped pounding on the brittle chest and looked down at the tailor's broken body. He could see the outline of ribs beneath the dark blood and papery skin and watched for a while to see if they moved. They didn't.

He took another tissue from his pocket, balled it up and wiped it around the slashed, wet edges of the star then stood and moved through the silent, headless crowd of mannequins to a blank section of wall on the far side of the atelier. He pressed the bloody tissue to the wall, dabbing it on the chalky surface and returning to the body whenever the tissue ran dry. It was full dark by the time he had finished but he could see what he'd written on the wall. Death was not enough for *Die Anderen*, they also had to know it was coming and feel its shadow on their backs, exactly as it had been in the camps.

He began to search the atelier. No one was due back here until morning, so he took his time, working steadily and searching the main house too, looking for the list and the suit Josef Engel had mentioned. He found nothing.

When he had finished, he stood in the centre of the atelier and looked down at the still figure on the floor, listening to the scratching and squeaking rats and the clock striking midnight in the hallway. He wondered if Josef had wound the clock that morning, not realizing it would keep ticking after his heart had stopped. Time had run out for the old man, like it did for everyone in the end – like it would for him soon enough.

He felt tired and empty and the pain in his head was starting to grow but he wasn't finished here, not quite. He moved over to the wooden box, lifted the hatch on the side and dark shapes poured out, scraps of darkness scrabbling across the polished floorboards towards the scent of blood.

They swarmed over the body, fighting and squeaking as they tugged at the cooling flesh and each other as they went into a feeding frenzy.

The man watched them for a long time. Listening to the tick of the clock and thinking about the list and what he had missed, and everything he had to do before all of this would be over.

2

Madjid Lellouche snicked away another withered vine before looking up. He knew he would be in trouble if he was seen to stop work, even for a moment, yet something made him pause and turn – and then he saw him.

The man was maybe fifty feet away, passing in and out of view between the plane trees lining the Roman road built at the same time as the vineyards. The road was directly behind where Madjid was working and lower down the hill, so no movement could have caught his eye. He was also far enough away that the sound of footsteps could not have reached him, even if the wind had been in the right direction, which it wasn't. There was no wind today anyway, only sunlight and the melting ground mist and the promise of another day of solid heat that would sit like a boulder on his back as he worked, drying the ground to dust between the green lines of vines.

Madjid shielded his eyes against the glare of the morning sun and watched the man pass in and out of view between the trees, moving through the mist that pooled in the lower valley. He was pale and slender and tall and wore a light suit jacket that looked formal and old, and his hair was white though he seemed young, moving with the smooth grace of a dancer and not the stiffness of a man of advanced years. Madjid listened out through the whine of insects for the sound of his footsteps and heard instead the snap of a twig behind him, and the swish of a cane cutting through the air followed by the sharp burn of sudden pain.

'The fuck I'm paying you for?'

Madjid turned and raised his arms against the next blow. '*Désolé*,' he called out, backing away from the man with the stick in his hand. '*Désolé, monsieur.*' Madjid bumped against the vines and a handful of grapes pattered on to the dust, their skins wrinkled and spotted with blight.

'Sorry doesn't get the work done.' The cane sliced back down and Madjid felt the bite of it on his forearm and fell to his knees. He stared up at the large, sweaty figure of Michel LePoux through a gap in his raised arms and saw anger burning in piggy eyes staring out from a bright red face. '*Désolé*, Monsieur LePoux,' he said.

The cane rose again and Madjid closed his eyes against the blow. Heard the swish of it coming back down and the slap of it striking skin, only this time he felt no pain. He opened his eyes and looked up. LePoux was standing right in front of him, silhouetted against the bleached blue sky – and so was the man from the road.

'Ouch,' he said, in a voice that was low like thunder and soft as the wind through the vines. '*Ça fait mal*' – *That hurt*. He stretched the word '*mal*', like the locals did, and it came out sounding more like '*mel*'.

LePoux tugged at his cane, trying to free it from the man's grip but he held on to it with little apparent effort, despite the fact that LePoux was twice the weight of the stranger. LePoux stopped tugging and glared at the man. 'You're trespassing.'

'And you are violently assaulting someone,' the stranger replied, 'which of those crimes is the greater, do you suppose?'

'Crime?' LePoux spat on the ground. 'There is no crime. This man is mine and what I do with *my* property on *my* land is *my* business.'

He yanked the stick again and the stranger let go, sending LePoux stumbling backwards. He grabbed at the vines and more shrivelled grapes pattered to the ground. The stranger dipped down to pick one up. 'Your country banned slavery in 1831.' He crushed the grape, sniffed the pink juice, then licked the end of his finger and looked up at LePoux. 'So how can this man be your property?'

LePoux stood up and pulled his sweat-damp shirt away from his skin. 'I don't know who you are, monsieur. Your accent's local but I know that you're not. I know everyone around here – law, lawyers, judges, everyone – but I don't know you and you're trespassing on my land, so if I want to chase you off it with a stick or a shotgun, no one here would say a thing against it.'

He raised his cane again but the stranger didn't move. 'How long has this land been yours?' he asked.

'My family's been here for five generations,' LePoux replied, puffing out his chest.

The stranger stared at LePoux and shook his head slowly. 'Pity you won't make it to a sixth.'

LePoux's face flushed red and his knuckles whitened. He lashed out with the cane, bringing it down hard on the stranger. LePoux was fast but the stranger was faster. He stepped aside as quick as blinking and the cane smacked on to the ground where he had been standing. LePoux stumbled forward, un-balanced by the force of the blow, and the stranger stamped down on the middle of his stick, breaking it in two with a sound like snapping bone, then twisted and kicked LePoux so hard he flew right through the vines and landed in the next row in a tangle of wire and foliage.

He smoothed his suit jacket down and held out his hand to Madjid and he felt the strength in it as he pulled him to his feet. His hand was solid like marble and strong like a blacksmith's, though with none of the coarseness of work upon it, and he seemed both old and young, his white hair ageing him but his smooth skin making him seem youthful. He could have been any age between twenty and sixty, though his eyes were old and black and deep, like staring into a well.

'The next town,' the man asked in his low voice, 'what's it called?'

'Cordes,' Madjid replied. 'Cordes-sur-Ciel.'

He nodded. 'And is there a tailor there?'

'Monsieur Engel.'

'What about a man or a place called *Magellan*?'

Madjid frowned and searched his memory. He wanted to help this man who'd helped him but the name meant nothing. 'I'm sorry,' he said. 'I've never heard that name.' He felt bad, like he had let him down in some way.

The stranger nodded and frowned. 'Thank you for your time,' he said, then he turned back to LePoux. 'Your land is rotten,' he said, plucking a leaf from a branch and holding it up so the sun lit up the orange and black tiger stripes on the green leaf. 'You have esca in all your vines but, given the sorry state of your land and the way you treat your workers, I would imagine you have neither the funds nor the reputation to get the help you need to cut it out. Your harvest will fail and you will be forced to sell, sooner rather than later.' He dropped the leaf and turned back to Madjid. 'You should leave,' he said. 'There's nothing for you here but pain.' Then he tipped his head in a courtly way and walked away.

Madjid watched him leave, moving through the vines and back towards the road. Behind him he heard crashing and huffing as LePoux scrambled back to his feet.

'Get back to work,' he said, picking up the broken halves of his cane and looking at them before throwing them to the ground.

Madjid looked around at the vines, the tiger-striped leaves glowing orange on almost every plant. The stranger was right, the crop was already lost. And when rot had claimed the whole harvest, LePoux would blame him, call him lazy and beat him as he drove him from the land without pay. He needed to get away from here. It was so obvious he felt like he had woken from a spell. He had been blinded by his lack of options and by his blind faith in hard work. He looked back at the stranger who had opened his eyes. He was almost at the road now. 'What's your name, monsieur?' he called after him.

'Solomon,' the man replied without looking round, his voice as soft as before but carrying back to Madjid as clearly as if he had shouted it. 'My name is Solomon Creed.'

3

Commandant Benoît Amand of the Police Nationale felt the buzz of an incoming call in his pocket. He ignored it, reaching out instead to wipe a finger across the swastika someone had sprayed on the Jewish memorial, the thick black paint dripping on to the names carved into granite remembering those who'd been rounded up and transported to the death camps on the night of 26 August 1942. He heard the crunch of footsteps across the boules court and the slop of water in a bucket.

'You want to take pictures first?' a voice asked.

'No,' Amand said, moving past him and heading across La Place 26th Aout towards Café Belloq on the far side of the square. 'I want you to scrub away all trace of it.'

The breakfast crowd were sitting in the shade of a wide, red awning, drinking their coffee and staring at their phones and newspapers. A few were looking over at him. Jean-Luc Belloq was one of them. He had been polishing the same glass with his apron ever since Amand had arrived.

Amand reached into his pocket, his hand pushing past his now silent phone to the bottle of glycerine pills, and unscrewed the lid one-handed so Belloq wouldn't see. He passed the half-constructed stage, part of the planned celebrations to mark seventy years since the end of the Second World War. The banners weren't up yet, otherwise the vandal might have defaced them too. The rest of the square was deserted, the chess tables and boules courts not yet populated by the old men who used the square as an al fresco social club. He palmed a glycerine caplet, popped it into his mouth under cover of a cough, manoeuvred it under his tongue and immediately felt the tightness in his chest melt away. His phone buzzed again, rattling against the pill bottle, but he let it ring, focusing instead on his breathing like his doctor had taught him as he mounted the stone steps to the café and nodded a greeting to the few diners who weren't tourists.

'Commandant,' Jean-Luc said, polishing the glass like it would never be clean. 'I still can't get used to the way you look. Let me get you a coffee.' He made to turn then stopped and struck his forehead theatrically with his palm. 'Sorry. No stimulants, right? Must be so frustrating to lose all that weight and still have the heart of a sumo.'

The phone in Amand's pocket stopped buzzing and the pill under his tongue continued to dilate his veins. 'What time did you open this morning?' he asked.

'Around six, same as always.'

'Notice anything suspicious?'

'Suspicious how?'

'Like someone over by the memorial plaque spraying a swastika on it?' Jean-Luc shook his head. 'Anyone else around?' He continued to shake his head. 'What about the café, anyone in before you?'

'I'm always first in.'

'When did you notice the graffiti?'

'I didn't.' Jean-Luc nodded at a waitress cleaning a couple

of tables at the rear of the terrace. 'She did. She told me. I called you.'

'Does *she* have a name?'

'Probably. We have a high turnover of staff here and I'm not good with names.'

Amand nodded. Café Belloq was notorious for working its staff into the ground and paying them peanuts. 'Mind if I talk to her?' He started to head over and Jean-Luc followed. Amand stopped and turned to him. 'Alone, if you don't mind.'

Belloq looked like he did mind but the phone started ringing inside the café, the trilling bells like an echo from the past. It was an old Bakelite model, so ancient it had become fashionable again, a result of meanness rather than forward thinking or style.

'Shouldn't you get that?' Amand said. Jean-Luc glanced at the waitress, then turned and marched away. Amand waited until he disappeared inside the café before walking over to the waitress.

'Mademoiselle?' he said, stopping at her table. 'I'm Benoît Amand from the Police Nationale.' She looked up in alarm from the croissant crumbs she was sweeping on to a plate. 'Don't worry, you're not in any trouble. What's your name?'

Her eyes flicked over to the café where Jean-Luc was visible through a window, talking on the phone and looking in their direction. 'Mariella,' she murmured.

'Mariella, Monsieur Belloq says it was you who spotted the graffiti on the plaque.' She gave a tiny nod. 'What time was this?'

'When I was setting the tables out. Six thirty maybe.'

'And when did you tell Monsieur Belloq about it?'

'I told him as soon as I spotted it.'

'And was anyone else around at that time?'

'No.'

'Thank you, Mariella.'

She nodded and scurried away, grateful for the release.

Amand headed into the café, glancing over at the man with the bucket scrubbing away at the memorial plaque, the swastika now concealed beneath thick suds that dripped grey down the stonework.

'He's here,' Belloq said, holding the phone out to him the moment he stepped into the bar.

'Is that clock right?' Amand asked, nodding at the grandmother clock that had kept time in Café Belloq since before the war.

Belloq nodded. 'I reset it each morning when I wind it. Why?'

'Because I'm interested to know why it took you three hours to call us after you first saw a Nazi symbol painted on a Jewish memorial outside your café.'

Belloq shrugged. 'Didn't think it was important.'

Amand took the phone and caught the smell of tobacco soaked into the black plastic over decades. 'Amand.'

'Why aren't you answering your phone?'

Amand stiffened, picking up on the tension in the sergeant's voice. 'What's up, Henri?'

'It's Josef Engel. His cleaner just called. She's hysterical, said that there are rats everywhere. Parra is already on his way to Engel's atelier. She said that he's been murdered.'

4

Solomon's hand stung where he'd caught the cane, a burning sensation that was not entirely unpleasant. He flexed his fingers to feed the ache and let it sharpen his senses as he walked down the road. He could smell hints of the town ahead of him now, like something small and hard buried beneath the softer, blanketing smells of the countryside: stone and concrete; hot tile and cooking oil; sour sweat and hair grease and the underlying sewagey stink of almost a thousand years of human occupation.

His feet were road weary inside the scuffed rancher's boots he'd borrowed from a dead man in Arizona. They had carried him along the interstates and back roads of New Mexico and Texas, clanged on the sheet-metal deck of a container ship out of Galveston, and now trod the same straight road sandalled centurions had built two thousand years earlier. Squares of grey overlapped on the road's surface where intense summer heat and dry frozen winters had split and cracked it again and again until it had become a thing of fragments – like Solomon himself.

The town of Cordes came into view gradually, emerging from the mist like a mountain castle at the end of the patchwork road. Castellated walls circled the summit, the thick stone worn with age and blending into the jagged outcrops of limestone from the original Puech de Mordagne. Stone buildings clung to the side of it like barnacles on a shark's fin and Solomon could read the history of the town's development in its architecture, oldest buildings at the top, youngest at the base, with narrow winding streets and long flights of stone steps linking the different levels. A thin tower rose up at the top, the name of the church it belonged to whispering in his head, prompted by the sight of it: L'Eglise Saint-Michel – the Church of St Michael.

Solomon had seen the town before, in a dream. He slept little and dreamed hardly at all and when he did it was usually the same dream, the one of the mirror that showed no reflection. But once, in his cramped bunk in the galley of the transport ship, he had slipped into slumber and seen this place, misty and indistinct, exactly as it appeared now.

Cordes-sur-Ciel – Cordes on Sky – named for the phenomenon Solomon was now witnessing where the town seemed to float on the valley mist.

The town continued to materialize from the mist as he drew closer, and more facts surfaced in his mind:

Founded 1222 by the Comte de Toulouse . . . Almost ended by plague in 1348 . . . Battered by the Hundred Years War in the fourteenth century and the Wars of Religion in the sixteenth.

Market town. Merchant centre. Textiles and wool, then indigo and Broderie Anglais lace. The small crocodiles on a famous French designer brand had been made here.

Tourist town now, teeming in the long summer months with people drawn by its history and weather and the beautiful stone houses with views over vine-covered valleys.

The information cascaded through Solomon's head, every fact correct but nothing that told him how he might be connected to the place. That part of his memory was gone, along with every other detail of who he was or might once have been. Whenever he focused his know-it-all mind on thoughts of himself, it fell silent – no facts, no memories. It was like staring into the mirror in his dream, the one that reflected nothing. All he had were fragments and questions.

He unbuttoned his tailored suit jacket and looked at the label stitched inside:

Ce costume a été fait au trésor pour M. Solomon Creed – This suit was made to treasure for Mr Solomon Creed.

The gold thread shone in the morning sunlight, spelling out the address where the suit had been made around the edge of the label:

13, Rue Obscure, Cordes-sur-Ciel, Tarn.

He let the flap of the jacket fall back down, the cut fitting the slender contours of his body perfectly. This was the place where someone had measured him and adjusted the cut until it fit him like a second skin. Here someone must have taken payment, perhaps made arrangements for its delivery, noting down an address and a name, tiny fragments of his lost history that might lead all the way back to who he really was, like stones through a dark forest. He was incomplete and so was the story of the clothes he wore.

Ce costume, the label said – this suit – yet he only had the jacket.

He re-buttoned it, the scents of his long journey trapped in the fabric – the salt of the ocean, diesel fumes and rice-wine vinegar, horseradish and tobacco smoke. He flexed his hand and carried on walking towards the town and the tailor he had travelled over five-thousand miles to find. Towards the address stitched in gold on a label. Towards answers.

The scent of the town was stronger now he could see it,

the smell of the people who lived here soaked into the stone over countless centuries and carrying on the misty breeze like pollen. Solomon breathed deeply, identifying each scent as easily as a florist enumerating the fragrance of different flowers. He knew the cause of each too, the emotion beneath each enzyme: fear, regret, happiness, longing . . . and a new scent, an unusual odour, sharp and metallic, that seemed more familiar to him than all the other smells blowing his way on the shifting breeze. It was a smell that made his heart thrum faster and the brand on his shoulder ache in a way that told him it was significant – the smell of freshly spilled human blood.

5

Lieutenant Emile Parra was already at the Atelier on the Rue Obscure when Amand arrived. He parked his fifteen-year-old Citroën, stepped out into the street and looked up at the silent and shuttered house, the single-storey workshop built on the side with a sign above the door saying '*Atelier Engel – Costumier*'.

Amand looked over at Parra. 'Who's been inside the house?'

'Only the cleaner – and me.'

'Where is she now?'

Parra nodded up the street to where a thin, grey woman in a pale blue housemaid's smock sat on the steps of a shuttered-up holiday home, her hands folded in her lap, her eyes fixed on the cobbles in a way that made her look like she was praying. Amand recognized Madame Segolin, a matriarch from one of the older local families. 'Have you questioned her?'

'Briefly.' Parra flipped open a notebook. 'Says she got here shortly after eight because there was a queue in Moulin where she gets Monsieur Engel's baguette. She let herself in, smelled what she thought was blocked drains, went into the atelier and saw Monsieur Engel lying on the floor. Then she saw the rats and ran outside. She called us on her mobile and was sitting there when I got here. She hasn't moved since.'

Amand watched her rocking back and forth slightly, her eyes open but her focus vague. He imagined she was picturing whatever she had discovered lying on the atelier floor and his chest tightened a little at the realization that he was about to see it too.

'Make sure she's OK,' he said. 'See if there's anyone around who can give her a coffee or something stronger.' He stepped past Parra and entered the atelier.

The foul smell hit him the moment he was inside; sewage and ammonia and rust triggering some primal part of his brain, making him want to turn right around and run. His father had told him once that being brave was not about being fearless, it was about being full of fear but doing the thing that frightened you anyway. Papa had spent five years in the Foreign Legion fighting in North Africa and been invalided out after getting shot in the leg, so he knew what he was talking about. Amand reached into his pocket, popped another glycerine capsule under his tongue, and carried on walking forward.

A plastic mop bucket lay on its side with bottles of bleach and cloths spilling out across the floorboards. He imagined Madame Segolin dropping it when she'd seen what was in the room. He moved towards it and looked ahead, but crowds of headless mannequins in various state of undress blocked his view. The rising heat of the day was already starting to stir the first pungent smells of decay into the odour of blood and piss and shit. He reached the bucket and the slumped figure came into view. It was lying in a dark puddle that reflected the light streaming down from the overhead skylights. Amand took another step forward and a slight movement on the body made him freeze. He watched a small pointed snout lift up from behind the old man's head, its whiskers wet, its teeth long and red. The rat sniffed the air for a moment then ducked back down to continue feeding.

Bile burned in Amand's throat. He stamped on the floorboards to try and scare the vermin away and more rats appeared from underneath the body, scurrying away to the safety of the shadows, wet fur and claws leaving trails across the floorboards. One stopped by a small wooden box lying close to the body and looked back. Amand stamped on the floor again but the rat squeaked a challenge, its ragged ears twitching towards him. It turned and started moving towards the body again. Amand felt the bile rise higher. He reached for his service pistol, unsnapped the safety strap and drew. The gunshot boomed in the silence of the workshop and the rat spun away across the floor, a smear of blood and splintered wood marking the spot where it had been. Amand heard running footsteps behind him and turned and held up his hands. 'It's OK,' he said. 'I'm OK. Call La Domial in Les Cabannes, tell them to grab some rat traps and bring them up here. Traps, not poison. These damn things are evidence now.' Parra nodded, reaching for his phone, his wide eyes staring past Amand at the body on the floor. 'And call Albi to get a move on with the STIC team. We need to process this room and bag the body before anything else takes a bite out of it.'

He turned back and stepped further into the workshop, weaving between the mannequins to take a closer look at the body. He swallowed hard when he saw the old man's face. He had known Josef Engel well enough, but he did not recognize the thing now lying on the floor before him.

His face and upper body were red and scourged, thousands of tiny bites showing where the rats had feasted. Amand began to rehearse the conversation he would have with Josef's next of kin, wondering how he could translate all of this into quiet words of condolence.

'Call Marie-Claude,' he said. 'Check she's at home, and if she is, make sure she stays there. Whoever did this might have a grudge against the family. In fact, send someone round, make sure she's OK and tell her I'll be along short—'

The sound made both their heads whip round.

It was music. A piano being played inside the main house.

Amand raised his gun towards the sound and glanced at Parra. 'You said no one was inside.'

'Madame Segolin said . . .'

'You didn't check?'

Parra shook his head. 'I saw the body and called you.'

'Where's your gun?'

'In the car. I could go and—'

'No. Stay here. Watch my back and call the office. Get more people over here fast and send someone to Marie-Claude's house.'

Parra nodded and looked down at his phone. Amand moved towards the door to the main house, leading with his gun. The music continued to play, complex clusters of notes tumbling over each other, and the tightness in Amand's chest grew worse.

Bravery is being afraid of something and doing it anyway.

He reached the door, twisted the handle, and entered the main house.

6

The loud knock on the door made Marie-Claude spill the milk she was pouring on her son's Cini Minis. She glanced at the clock: 8.22 – too early to be a social call.

'Who's that?' Léo asked, his thick, round glasses making his already large brown eyes look even bigger. 'Is it Papa?'

She called this look his *Disney Eyes*, big and wide and filled with all the hope and desire a seven-year-old could muster. But sometimes it was a Bambi look, a look of fear, and this was one of those times.

'No,' she said, and Léo's glasses magnified his relief. 'It's probably a delivery or something. Eat your breakfast, I'll go see who it is.'

Marie-Claude stepped into the hallway and pulled the door almost shut behind her. She could see the dark shape of whoever was standing at her door shifting behind the large pane of frosted glass that let light in. He looked too small to be her husband – her *ex*-husband. It couldn't be him. Only it could. Jean Baptiste had been released from prison three weeks ago, early and with no warning, and no one had seen him since.

She moved down the short hallway, glancing at the base-ball bat buried in the coats and rubbing the scar on her forearm. Amand had offered to get her a gun, but she'd said no. What would she do with it anyway? She couldn't shoot her ex-husband, and she didn't want a loaded gun in the house, not with Léo around. She peered through the peephole, her heart hammering hard. A gendarme stood on the other side, shifting his weight from one foot to the other. Marie-Claude let out a breath she hadn't realized she'd been holding, checked the chain was on properly, then opened the door. The rattle of the chain made the gendarme snap to attention. 'Sorry to bother you, madame. I was told to come and check you were home and make sure you were OK.'

'Why?' She dropped her voice. 'What's happened? Is this about my ex-husband?'

'I don't know. I was only told to make sure—'

'Who told you?'

'Commandant Amand.'

'Did he say why?'

'I didn't actually speak to him, I just got the message to make sure you were here and tell you to stay put until the Commandant gets here.'

'So I'm under some kind of house arrest?'

'No, Amand – I mean, the Commandant, said—'

'My son's due at school in twenty minutes, how's that going to work if I'm not allowed to leave the house?'

'I was only told to . . . I'm sure the Commandant will be here before then.'

'Well, he better be, or I'm taking my son to school regardless.'

She closed the door before he could answer, locked it again and leaned back against the wood, her knees trembling slightly from the adrenaline. She hated living like this, hated the effect her ex had on her. Jean Baptiste. Out there some-where, gone for four years but still casting a shadow over her life. Every knock on the door, every time the phone rang, every footstep she heard following her down the street, all of it making her senses sharpen and her heart hammer harder. It was exhausting. Infuriating.

She had seen a counsellor for a while after it had happened, a lady psychiatrist who'd told her how post-traumatic stress sufferers were in a constant state of heightened alert – fight or flight – all the senses lit up all of the time. She'd also told her how kids healed faster than grown-ups and that she should concentrate on herself and stop worrying so much about Léo. Marie-Claude had stopped seeing her after that.

She moved away from the front door, her legs still shaky, and paused by the open door of her bedroom. She had been logging some interview footage before Léo woke up, and her messy bedroom was lit by the cold glow of her laptop screen and a freeze-frame of a ninety-year-old man with tears shining on his cheeks. She kept her work away from home as much as possible, realizing that what was therapeutic for her was not necessarily the best thing for her son to be exposed to. As soon as he was old enough to deal with it all, she planned on telling him everything: about their family history, about the dark legacy they carried. But for now she shielded him from it, squirrelling her work away in a small unit on the other side of town, far away from watchful eyes.

She closed the door and moved back up the narrow hallway, stopping outside the kitchen door for a moment and watching Léo through the crack. He was eating his breakfast and reading the back of a cereal box. Always reading. She wondered if it was a form of escape for him, a way of zoning out the real world and disappearing into an imaginary, better one. Or maybe he just liked reading and would have been exactly the same if he'd been born into a normal family, whatever one of those looked like.

Léo looked up when she stepped through the door, his curiosity magnified by his glasses. 'Who was it?'

'No one. A friend of Uncle Benny's.'

'Was it about Papa?'

'No.' She picked up the cereal box and moved it over to the worktop. 'Finish your breakfast or you'll be late for school.'

'But the man at the door said we weren't to go anywhere.'

Marie-Claude shook her head. She tried so hard to protect Léo, make sure he had as normal a life as possible, but he picked up on everything. For the first couple of years after it happened he had been totally mute. It was like the trauma of seeing what his father had done to his mother caused him to sink deep into himself. It had made him extra-sensitive, watchful. He saw everything, more than most people, too much, and it made her want to cry because she just wanted him to be a regular kid and she couldn't do anything about it.

'Eat your cereal,' she said, moving over to the sink to keep her back to him. 'I'll decide who goes to school and who doesn't, not you, and definitely not Uncle Benny.'

He watched the gendarme walk away from the house, get back in his car and light a cigarette.

He had parked his own car pointing away from the house, far enough that he wouldn't be obvious and close enough to watch the house using his mirrors. He was waiting for the woman to leave so he could search the house. She would leave soon and maybe drop her son off at school before heading to the Commissariat de Police, or perhaps she would go straight to the morgue to identify her grandfather's body. It all depended on how the lead investigator wanted to run things. Commandant Amand, that was his name, he had picked that up from the police scanner plugged into the car's cigarette lighter. The gendarme smoking in the parked car was far too junior to be him and he had spent too little time talking to the woman to have told her anything much. She hadn't seemed upset either. Maybe he was here to collect her.

She would certainly be upset when she found out what had happened. Someone would sit with her, a grief counsellor or someone trained in dealing with the recently bereaved. The police would have questions they needed to ask:

When did you last see or speak to your grandfather?

Did he have any enemies?

Do you know of anyone who might have wished him harm?

He felt no joy in having caused all this and reminded himself that her grandfather should have died in the war. By rights she shouldn't even exist and neither should the little boy. They were mistakes of history. Mistakes needed to be corrected.

He opened his window a little to let in some air.

He waited.

7

The piano sounded much louder in the main house. It was something complicated and classical, and a vague memory popped into Amand's head of a movie where this same tune had driven a pianist insane. Whoever was playing it now was having no such trouble. It sounded so good that Amand wondered if it was actually a recording, a CD player or something on a timer that had switched itself on automatically. Except a note kept cropping up, muted and flat, that would never pass on a commercial recording. Someone had to be playing it.

Amand followed the music down the hallway, keeping his footfalls soft and straining his ears for any sounds beyond the music. He had never been in the main house before and he peered into each doorway before passing, checking no one was there as he moved closer to the room where the music was leaking through a partially opened door. The house had been searched, he could see that from the mess and all the opened drawers. What they were looking for, he had no idea. Maybe whoever was playing the piano might know. He reached the end of the corridor as the music reached a crescendo, raised his gun and stepped through the door and into the room.

Adrenaline-sharp senses took in the salon all at once – drape-softened windows, elegant antique furniture, bookcases filled with fashion magazines, and more tailor's dummies arranged around the room like headless party guests listening to the recital being given by the tall, pale man sitting at the upright piano against the far wall. This room had been searched too.

'Hands where I can see them,' Amand said. The man at the piano ignored him and continued to play, swaying slightly as his long white fingers coaxed music from the keys. 'Stop playing and raise your hands.' Amand raised his gun and took a step into the room.

The music grew louder in response, building in intensity before the last chord fell and echoed away into silence. 'I wondered if I could play,' the man said, his voice soft and deep. 'I saw the piano and had to know.' The fingers of his right hand rippled up the keyboard, hitting the hollow note at the end of the run. 'The G above middle C needs some attention,' he said, stabbing it a few more times with his little finger. 'But that's not going to happen now, is it?' He turned slowly on the stool and looked up at Amand. 'He's dead isn't he, the tailor?'

He was younger looking than the white hair had prepared Amand for, his pale skin unlined and tight over high cheekbones and a sharp nose. His eyes were dark though. They didn't look at the gun at all. 'What makes you think he's dead?'

'The blood,' the man said in his deep, soft voice. 'I can smell the blood.'

Amand frowned at the odd answer. 'Who are you?'

'I was hoping the tailor might help me answer that. I assume that's him lying dead in the back?'

Amand blinked, his head throbbing with low-level pain. This whole situation was bizarre. The stranger seemed utterly unbothered by the fact that he had a gun pointing at him or that there was a dead man close by. 'Who are you?' he repeated. 'Tell me what you're doing here.'

'I came to see a man about a suit,' the man replied, rising slowly and carefully buttoning his jacket. 'This one, to be precise. And my name is Solomon Creed.'

'How did you get in the house, Monsieur Creed?'

'Through the front door.'

'You just walked in?'

'No, I knocked first. The door was unlocked, so I came in. How did he die? I assume not peacefully. May I see the body?' Solomon took a step forward.

Amand raised his gun. 'No, you may not. What you can do is put your hands on your head and turn around.'

Solomon glanced at the gun for the first time. 'You're not going to shoot me. Not like that rat in the other room. Big difference, shooting a rodent and shooting a man.' He took another step forward.

'I'm warning you, monsieur.' Amand moved back to maintain the distance between them and felt the edge of a chair bang against the back of his leg. There was a blur of movement and a slight tug at his hand and Solomon was gone, darting past and through the open door. It happened so fast it took a moment for Amand to realize he no longer had his gun.

'Parra!' he shouted, and launched himself through the door. Solomon was almost at the door to the atelier. He could see the gun in his hand, his long fingers wrapped around the dark metal of the barrel. The door to the atelier flew open and Parra stood there, eyes wide in alarm. He tried to block Solomon, but he ducked, twisted and was past him and into the room without even breaking stride. Parra lunged forward grabbing at air, and Amand barged past, carried by his own momentum and ready to throw himself at Solomon if he turned the gun on him. Parra stumbled into the room behind him and they stopped in the doorway and stared at Solomon. He stood in the centre of the room, looking down at the body of the old man.

'Give me the gun,' Amand said.

'I will.' Solomon leaned down to study the old man's face. 'There are smears around some of his wounds, like someone was cleaning him.' He looked up and scanned the room.

Amand's eyes flicked to the gun. It was too far away to grab, especially now he knew how quick this man could move.

Solomon breathed in through his nose and turned towards the deep shadows on the far side of the atelier. Amand turned and saw something there. Solomon moved towards it and Amand followed, squinting against the light flooding down from the skylights.

Solomon stepped into the shadows and stopped. 'The killer wasn't trying to clean the body,' he said, his eyes fixed on the writing on the wall. 'They were using Monsieur as an inkwell.'

The sharp sound of metal on metal made Amand flinch and his head whipped round to discover his gun, field-stripped and held out for him to take. He took the pieces and looked back at the wall, reading the words dripping down the white surface where the blood had run, translating the German in his head:

Das zuende bringen was begonnen wurde.
Finishing what was begun.

II

*'. . . though you seek in garments the freedom
of privacy you may find in them a harness
and a chain.'*

The Prophet
Kahlil Gibran

Extract from

**DARK MATERIAL – THE DEVIL'S TAILOR: DEATH
AND LIFE IN DIE SCHNEIDER LAGER**

⁂

By Herman Lansky

I remember the first Nazi slogan I ever saw.

It was painted on the wall of the Great Synagogue in Łódź.

Żyd świnie, it said. Jew pigs.

It had been written sloppily in black paint, the letters dripping down the stonework. I remember being shocked and outraged by the sight of it, but not frightened. It seemed to me the spiteful act of a coward, done in haste in the middle of the night when no one else was around. It was a snipe, not a threat. That's what I thought when I saw it, that's what we all thought, and by the time we came out of the temple it had been scrubbed away.

This was the autumn of 1938, I can't remember the exact date. I remember the chill of winter was already in the air and the leaves of the oak trees on Promenadowa Street were beginning to rust. I remember we walked away talking about what was happening in Germany, our conversation sparked by the graffiti but not about it. Germany was Germany and we were Polish. Polish Jews were too important to the economy for our country to be influenced by the hate-filled anti-Semitism of Hitler.

A full third of the population of Łódź was Jewish. It was our town.

None of us knew that less than a year later, when the leaves turned red again, Nazi troops would march down that same street we were strolling so casually along, or that on the night of 14 November 1939 the Great Synagogue, whose wall had been marked by that splash of black paint, would be set alight, burning for days until all that was left of it was ash and ruin. No one imagined that we would be forced to sew yellow stars on to our clothes, marking us as lesser citizens of Poland, or that all our businesses and property would be taken from us, or that of the quarter of a million Jews living in Łódź at the start of the war, barely ten thousand would be alive by the end of it. We didn't know because none of us had yet seen the true darkness in men's souls.

But now I have.

I have seen how great evil can grow from the seed of a few hate-filled words hurriedly painted on a wall. And that is why those of us who survived and witnessed those dark and terrible things must speak of them. Silence will never defeat words of hate. Only more words can do that.

Words of sorrow.

Words of remembrance.

Words of warning.

⚜

8

Solomon was taken to the Commissariat de Police on the edge of Cordes market square and booked in by a man with a moustache so clipped and waxed it looked fake and a belly that suggested he liked food a lot more than exercise. He asked Solomon to empty his pockets and he complied slowly while checking the building for alarms and cameras. The Commissariat was old and made of stone like pretty much everything in Cordes. It felt more like a castle than a police station. It was unfortunate Solomon had needed to crash the crime scene the way he had, but when he'd seen the police were already there he knew his only chance of seeing what had happened was to go inside. Standing now inside this solid building with its narrow windows and thick walls he wasn't convinced it had been the wisest move.

'No ID?' the man with the belly and neat moustache asked.

Solomon looked down at the small pile of everything he owned: an American quarter he'd found by the side of a Texas road; a shard of antique mirror; a leather string necklace with a cross made from old horseshoe nails. He opened the flap of his jacket and pointed at the label. 'Only this.'

The officer squinted at the name and writing on the label,

copied it all down then swept the items into a large envelope. Solomon was led away down a set of spiral stone stairs into a low, arched corridor in the basement of the building with whitewashed walls and a vague odour of damp and stale air and disinfectant.

'Wait in here,' the sergeant said, unlocking a solid steel door which opened on to a small, windowless room containing a table and two chairs.

Solomon stepped inside and the skin tightened on the back of his neck as the door was closed and locked behind him. The police officer's shoes clipped away across the flagstones and up the spiral stairs, quieter and quieter until all he could hear was the faint buzz of the lights above him and the soft hiss from a small ventilation grille set into the wall above the door. There were no distant phones ringing or murmurs of conversation and it made Solomon realize how solid his prison was and magnified his unease at the feeling of being caged.

He stamped on the flagstones and it thumped dully, no echo, no hollow sounds, only the muffled noise of soundwaves being swallowed whole by dense stone. He made a fist and banged each wall. They all sounded the same. Solid. Impenetrable. The whole room, the entire basement probably, had been carved out of the same dense rock the city was built upon. The only wall that echoed slightly was the one with the door in it, but even that was a foot thick and made up of large stone blocks painted white to bounce the light around and keep the dust down. The door was solid too, oak or ash, with a thick, steel skin held in place by flat rivets the size of coins. There was a small window at head height, small squares of wire running through thick green safety glass. Hard to break through, even if he had the tools to do it. He moved over to the table and pulled out one of the chairs. It was tubular and light, too flimsy to break through either glass or wall. Brute force would not get him out of this room. Only thought could set him free.

He sat on the chair, took off his boots and socks then planted his feet on the cold stone floor and his hands on the tabletop. He closed his eyes and listened to the buzzing light and the silence beyond the locked door. The booking officer with the manicured moustache would be running his name through various French ID databases now. He didn't know how long that would take to process, a while probably, and the lead investigator, the man whose gun he had taken, would be busy too – dealing with the body, processing the crime scene, talking to next of kin. Solomon was low priority for the moment. They hadn't even charged him with anything yet. But the ticking of Solomon's mind told him that under French law they could hold him for twenty-four hours, charge or no charge. He needed to get out of here. He'd already arrived too late, but only just. The tailor's blood was fresh and the person who'd spilled it still close by. They had been searching for something, the upturned state of the house showed that. Maybe they'd found it. Or maybe they were still looking. And Solomon had come too far to be discouraged by the fact that the man he had come to see was dead. On the contrary, he believed that was why he was here. He knew it, deep down in the place where what truth and certainty he could call upon resided, and from the ache in his shoulder that always flared at moments of importance like these.

Solomon closed his eyes and pictured himself back at the atelier. He had discovered during his long sea passage that by concentrating on specific places and moments he had experienced he could recreate them in his mind in photo-realistic detail. All he needed was a remembered object, something solid to anchor his thoughts, and by focusing on that specific thing he could rebuild the whole scene in his mind until it was as real and detailed as if he was standing there. He could then study the memory, walk through it and analyse each object like exhibits in a museum. He could scrutinize people too, recall their conversations, picture what clothes they'd worn, the time displayed on their watches. His mind had provided a word for it – *Hyperthymesia* – superior autobiographical memory, a term that carried a certain degree of irony, seeing as Solomon's own autobiography was somewhat thin. A few times he had tried focusing on his jacket, one of the few objects he possessed from before, to see if it helped him remember. But each time his mind remained blank, like he was on the edge of a seaside cliff, staring into a thick bank of fog and knowing something vast was out there but unable to see it. That was why he had travelled so far to find the man who'd made it and felt honour-bound to find out who had killed him and why.

He took a breath and focused on the memory of the bloody words daubed on the atelier walls:

Das zuende bringen was begonnen wurde.

Finishing what was begun.

In his head the dungeon walls began to melt away and the atelier reappeared, the mannequins, the smell of blood, the scurrying of the rats. Solomon stood in the centre of it all, noticing things he had barely glimpsed before – invoices tacked to the wall by the phone, piles of paperwork stacked on the workbench, names and addresses scribbled on the backs of envelopes. One in particular caught his attention, the brand on his arm flaring in pain when he remembered it. It was written on an invoice for a storage unit in Cordes. It was a woman's name – Marie-Claude.

Solomon rubbed at the ache in his shoulder.

Cherchez la femme, he murmured and studied the memory closer.

Look for the woman.

9

Jean-Luc Belloq was smoothing down a tablecloth and preparing for the early lunchtime crowd when Madame Segolin barged through the door, her face pink above her blue housemaid's smock and her eyes fixed on the bar. She was not a stranger in the café but Belloq had never known her come in this early before.

'Madame,' he said, stepping behind the bar. 'To what do we owe this unexpected—'

'Brandy,' she said, cutting him off and dabbing at her face with a florid handkerchief.

Belloq turned and started to reach for the open bottle of three-star he kept for the regulars then changed his mind and brought down the cognac from the higher shelf instead. Whatever had driven Madame to seek a drink at this early hour had to be something worth hearing and he didn't want to blow his chances by being cheap.

'In honour of your unexpected visit,' he said, placing a small brandy glass on the countertop and pulling the cork out with a liquid popping sound. He poured a generous slosh of cognac into the glass. 'On the house, of course.'

Madame Segolin grabbed the glass, closed her eyes and gulped half of it down like it was medicine. Jean-Luc placed the bottle on the bar and left the cork out, making sure the label was facing her so she would appreciate his generosity. 'You look like you've seen a ghost, madame.'

She shook her head and took another gulp of cognac. 'Not a ghost, monsieur, a dead body.' She leaned in conspiratorially. 'A *murdered* dead body.'

Belloq dropped his voice, though there were no other patrons in the bar. 'Who?'

She drained her glass and placed it on the bar. 'Monsieur Engel,' she whispered.

Belloq's head jerked back in surprise but Madame Segolin didn't notice. 'I clean for him most days,' she said, watching the cognac creep down the inside of her glass. 'This morning I let myself in and he was lying on the floor of his workshop. I thought he may have simply fallen, but there was a terrible smell, and I saw blood, so much blood.' She shuddered. 'And there were rats.'

Belloq felt numb. Josef Engel. Dead. Not just dead – murdered. This was not what was supposed to happen. He would need to report it to the leadership. Tell them what had happened. They would want details. He needed to get some. 'Have you reported it to the police?' he asked.

Madame Segolin glared at him. 'No, I stuffed him in a bag, mopped up all the blood and came here for a brandy! Of course I told the police. I've been with them for the past half an hour, telling them what I saw. Why do you think I needed a brandy?'

Belloq took the hint and refilled her glass. 'It's cognac, madame,' he said. 'A person needs more than brandy at a time like this.'

She picked up the glass and sniffed it appreciatively. 'On the house, you said?'

'You've had a terrible shock. The very least I can do is offer some comfort.'

Madame Segolin nodded as if this was only right and proper then tipped back her head and drank the whole contents of the glass in one.

'Help yourself, madame,' Belloq said, heading towards the back rooms. 'I'll be in my office if you need me.'

He stepped into the small manager's office, closing the door behind him, and snatched the phone from his desk. He dialled a number from memory and shielded the mouthpiece with his hand the moment it connected. 'Tell me about Josef Engel,' he said, his voice low and tight. He listened. Nodded. Frowned. 'Any suspects?'

He plucked a pen from a pewter tankard next to the phone and scrawled *Solomon Creed* on the back of a drinks order and put a question mark by it.

'And who's in charge of the investigation?' He nodded wearily, wrote *Benoît Amand* and underlined it.

'Let us know what he's up to. We need to stay ahead of him on this, make sure he doesn't get too close. You stay where you are for now and keep me up to date with any new developments – I can't rely solely on bar gossip for information. I'll call a meeting of the others.'

He cut off the call and dialled another number from memory.

At the bar, Madame Segolin poured herself a third cognac and shuddered at the memory of rats.

10

The man in the parked car looked up and watched the new arrival in his rear-view mirror. He was walking quickly – a man on a mission, a man with purpose. He stopped to talk to the gendarme.

'Commandant Amand, I presume,' he murmured under his breath, remembering the name the scanner had given him. He paused the video he had been watching on his phone and removed his earphones.

After a few seconds Amand moved away from the gendarme and walked up to the woman's front door. He raised his hand to knock but paused. The man in the parked car knew why. Commandant Amand was carrying a heavy message, the heaviest there was, a death in the family. A violent murder. He felt a sudden rush of sorrow and regret that the woman would have to shoulder the weight of this news. He felt for the boy too, for he would bear his share of the burden by witnessing his mother's grief.

He blinked. Shook his head. Made a fist and hit himself hard in the forehead, hard enough that he felt the dark, solid thing in his skull shift like a burning blob of molten iron.

He breathed through the pain and glanced down at his phone, the bloody image of Josef Engel's face frozen on the screen where he'd paused it. Now was not the time for sentiment. He needed to remain focused on his greater purpose. He had come here to end Engel's long and undeserved life and to find the list that would lead him to the others. But he had not found it at the old man's atelier, nor in the storeroom he kept on the north side of town, which meant his granddaughter must have it. And he needed that list. He was running out of time.

He looked back up at the policeman, standing by the door, hand raised and ready to knock. The Ancient Greeks used to kill those who brought dark news to their door, but the Commandant would undoubtedly be offered a soft seat and a cup of coffee. That was what two thousand years of civilization had achieved. He was deeply suspicious of civilization. He believed in tearing clothes and howling at the sky when confronted with death, not wearing black and trying not to weep whilst people murmured bland words of condolence. The *civilized* practice of forgiveness was unnatural too, unnatural and unjust. It resulted in sub-human animals guilty of unimaginable crimes being allowed to live long lives in comfortable jails while their victims turned to dust and their relatives were condemned to shuffle around in numb prisons of never-ending mourning and loss. Civilization had rendered the death penalty unthinkable in most countries – even in France, where heads had rolled like bowling balls during the French Revolution.

He did not believe in civilization and he did not believe in forgiveness. He believed in justice and punishment. He believed in the Wild Hunt of old where the souls of the damned were relentlessly chased by vengeful gods until natural justice was done.

Over by the front door the Commandant straightened

and knocked, loud enough that he heard it through his open car window. There was a brief pause then the door opened, not on the chain this time. The woman stood framed in the doorway: petite, dark-haired, pretty. She looked up at Amand, her brow creasing as she listened. Her face darkened and a look of disbelief settled on it as Commandant Amand delivered his heavy message. There was something familiar about that look. He glanced back down at his phone and there it was again, frozen on the paused image of the tailor's bruised face, a certain arrangement of creases on the forehead produced by the same DNA and proving her ancestry. He was starting to feel regret again: about what had happened last night; about what he might have to do to get the list from the woman and her son.

He pushed the earphones back in his ears, unpaused the video and listened again to the final words of the dying tailor. He needed to remind himself what this was all for. He needed to stay focused and honest, elemental not sentimental, the vengeful god and not the sentimental man. He needed to continue the Wild Hunt until it was over and the souls of the damned had been reclaimed.

He needed to finish what was begun.

11

Marie-Claude had been all set to lay into Amand but the moment she opened the door and saw his face she realized this was not going to happen.

'It's your grandfather,' he said, in a tone she had heard once before. 'He was discovered this morning in his atelier. He's dead. Murdered.'

She reached out to the doorframe to stop herself from falling and her vision tunnelled so that Amand suddenly seemed like he was talking to her from a long way away.

'May I come in?' he said.

She nodded and pointed at her bedroom door. 'We can talk in here,' she said, closing the front door behind them. 'I'll just go check on Léo.'

She walked back up the short hallway, feeling dazed and numb and thinking about the last time she had spoken to Josef, everything he had said, the warnings he had given her, how agitated he had been. And she had ignored him. And now he was dead and it was her fault. He was dead because of her.

Léo was at the table reading a comic, his wide eyes sucking adventure from the page. He was wearing his maroon school sweatshirt and his Spider-Man socks, his feet dangling below his chair, his legs too short to reach the ground.

Marie-Claude cleared her throat, trying to shake some of the tightness from it. 'You OK here for a minute?'

'Who's at the door?' Léo replied, never taking his eyes off the comic.

'It's Uncle Benny. I need to . . . I have to talk to him about something.'

Léo looked up. 'You OK, Mama?'

She forced a smile. 'I'm fine. Read your comic. I'll tell you all about it after I've spoken to Uncle Benny.'

Then she turned and walked away before Léo could see the tears starting to build in her eyes.

Léo watched his mama leave and heard her go into her bedroom and close the door behind her.

He knew she was sad, he could see it in her colours. He knew why she was sad too because he'd heard what Uncle Benny had said at the door, about Grampy being dead. He heard lots of things he wasn't supposed to hear.

Mama reckoned his hearing was so good because his eyes were weak. It was his special power, she said, his Spidey senses. But it wasn't always a good thing. It meant he heard how sad his mama got sometimes, crying into her pillow at night, though she always acted happy in front of him. He could see when she was sad though, he could see it in the colours that shifted and floated around her like feathers. That was one of his Spidey senses too, only Spider-Man couldn't do it, only him and Grampy could.

It's in the blood, he'd told him one time, *but only in boys, and you have it stronger than me.*

Léo felt sad that he wouldn't have anyone to talk to about it any more. His mama didn't like him talking about it. She didn't have the gift. That's what Grampy called it – his gift.

Léo heard things in colours too. He knew when people were telling the truth because their voices were a different colour from their bodies if they were trying to hide something. That was how he knew when Mama was sad. Her voice was usually a greeny orangey colour, like leaves in autumn or parrot's feathers. Nice colours. Warm colours. But when she was hiding something it became dark grey and purple like a bruise. That's what she sounded like now.

Léo shifted in his chair and leaned towards the door to try and hear what his mama and Uncle Benny were talking about. He liked Uncle Benny because he made his mama happy and did lots of nice things for them. He'd asked her once if she was going to marry Uncle Benny and said he wouldn't mind if she did, and she'd laughed and said Uncle Benny wasn't the marrying kind and that she'd explain it to him when he was older. He could hear his voice now, low and muddy-coloured, the way grown-ups' voices always went when they talked about serious things.

He wanted to go to his mama and give her a hug, tell her it was OK to be sad. Grampy had been old, really old, old enough to have been in the big war, the one where Captain America had fought the Nazis, though Grampy had never talked about it. Léo never understood that. If he had fought against the Nazis he would tell *everyone* about it. His mama said he didn't like talking about it because he'd been held prisoner in a very bad camp where lots of people had died and it was too sad for him to remember it. She'd explained how lots of people had died in those camps, people like them – Jewish people. She'd shown him photos, black-and-white pictures of kids younger than him wearing what looked like striped pyjamas with stars pinned to the front.

When Uncle Benny had gone, he would go and hug her

to help lighten her colours, because his colour was white mostly and he could lighten the darkness in others by hugging them, like when he was painting his comic scenes and swirled a white paintbrush through the murky water in a jam jar. Most kids had bright colours, like most adult colours were murky, but no one was as bright as him.

At first he'd thought maybe he only looked brighter to himself, in the same way his voice sounded louder because he heard it inside his head. Or perhaps it was because there was only him and his mama, so all her love went to him rather than him sharing it with a daddy or brothers or sisters, and this was what made him shine. But Grampy had told him he shone too, and that he had only ever seen one other person in his life who had shone as brightly. It had been the only time he had ever talked about the bad camp and his colours had gone dark when he spoke of it – black with flashes of deep, deep red, like a crow's feathers splashed in blood. He said the pale man had appeared at the end of the war, when most of the guards had gone and the few that were left were liquidating the camp. Léo thought that meant they were washing it or something, but Grampy's colours were so dark he knew it must mean something else – something really, really bad. Grampy told him how everyone in the camp thought they were going to die, then this man appeared dressed in a beautiful white suit, shining as bright as Léo shone, and he'd saved him and his friends when they thought they could not be saved. Grampy had told Léo the man's name, a funny sounding, old-fashioned name, like from a fairy story. And just like in a story, the man had asked Grampy and his friends to make a suit in exchange for saving them. So they did. They made him the finest suit any of them had ever made, according to Grampy. And it must

55

have been something, because even though Léo didn't know much about clothes he could see that the suits Grampy made were special because they always brightened the colours of anyone who wore them, even the greyest people. But the man never returned to collect his suit, and Grampy and his friends decided to divide it between them – the designer, the weaver and the tailor – each keeping a piece of it.

Like a talisman, Grampy had said. *You know what that is, boy?*

Léo knew all about talismans because the comics he read were full of them – magic charms to ward away evil.

It keeps us safe, Grampy said. *We keep the suit and the suit keeps us.*

Léo had asked to see Grampy's piece of the suit, but he had darkened at the question.

Forget about it, he'd said. *Forget about the pale man. Forget the suit. Forget what happened back in the bad camp during the war. Forget everything.*

And he had never spoken of it again. Léo had always hoped, when he was a little older, that Grampy might one day show him the suit and talk some more about the camp. But now he was dead and Uncle Benny had come here all dark and muddy with the news of it, and the suit hadn't kept Grampy safe at all.

He looked back at his comic, one of the earlier Captain America stories when he was fighting the Nazis, the ones Grampy had never wanted to talk about and now never would. The thought made him feel sad and he sensed himself dimming. He needed to stay bright for his mama, so he could stir some brightness into her when she stopped talking to Uncle Benny.

He started to read again, his heavy glasses sharpening the

colours of the drawings while his mind flashed with the colours of the words. Red Skull was nearing completion of the Sleepers, the gigantic Nazi war machines designed to destroy the world if Hitler failed to conquer it. And only Captain America could stop him.

12

Solomon felt the man approaching. He felt the vibrations through the soles of his bare feet like a distant heartbeat, soft and regular and strengthening with each footstep until it smothered all other vibrations – the intermittent rumble of traffic on the road outside, the soft hiss of water through a fracture in the rock deep beneath him, the hum of electricity through thick cables that snaked across the surface of every wall. Solomon put his boots back on and placed his hands on the surface of the table. He could hear the footsteps now, sharp and anxious, like someone in a hurry or someone who was eager or excited. He doubted they saw much in the way of interesting crimes in a small place like this, and there was nothing more exciting than murder. He breathed in, trying to catch the scent of whoever was approaching, but the thick walls and trapped air of the cell returned nothing but dust and hints of his own travels.

Solomon closed his eyes again and the footsteps grew louder then stopped outside the door. He heard the cylinders click in the barrel of the lock and the faint suck of rubber seals as the door opened inward, bringing a puff of outside air and the scent of the man who had opened it. He smelled of coffee and hair wax and stress and Solomon recognized him as surely as if he were looking at him. It was the less senior officer from the murder scene.

'Monsieur,' the gendarme said, and Solomon pictured him standing hesitantly in the doorway. 'Are you OK?'

Solomon took a deep breath and frowned. 'I've been going over what I saw at the house,' he said, keeping his eyes closed, 'trying to remember what I saw.' He opened his eyes and looked up. 'And I did see something. On the steps outside the house where the old man died.'

'What?' the officer said, closing the door with a locking click and pulling out the second chair with a sharp scrape of steel on stone. 'Tell me what you saw.' He laid the envelope containing Solomon's few possessions and a blank witness statement form on the table.

'It's kind of strange,' Solomon said. 'Let me walk you through it. Tell you everything I saw, so you can see what I mean. So you can understand.'

The man nodded, his pupils dilated slightly despite the white brightness of the overhead strip lights, a small physical indication of his willingness to see what Solomon was about to show him.

'What's your name?' Solomon asked.

'Parra,' the man said, then shook his head like he'd made a mistake. 'Emile. Call me Emile.'

Solomon nodded. 'Hello, Emile. I'm Solomon. Let me talk you through everything first, before you write anything down.'

Parra glanced down at the witness statement and Solomon saw his artery pulsing softly beneath the skin. A sudden, violent feeling surged through him. He could leap across the table, throw his arm round this man's neck and press hard against that thin, shivering skin, shut off the blood and airflow until he blacked out. He could keep the pressure on if he chose and ensure he never woke. Or he could throw his arm out, swing straight through his neck like he was striking a baseball, enough speed and surprise to rupture the artery. He would bleed internally, massively –

. . . *subcutaneous haematoma* . . .

– the pressure of all that blood and the rapid swelling of damaged tissue would make him black out too as his brain was starved of oxygen.

. . . *Cerebral hypoxia. Anoxaemia* . . .

The Latin words glittered like jewels in Solomon's mind and his shoulder began to burn in warning. He sucked in air and gripped it.

Parra looked up, drawn by the movement and the vein in his neck was hidden from sight. 'You OK?'

Solomon rubbed at his shoulder where the burning pain was now fading as quickly as his violent thoughts. He could feel the two parallel lines of raised skin through the material of his jacket. 'I'm fine,' he said, massaging away the pain and the scarlet visions that had accompanied it, 'I don't like being confined, that's all.'

Parra smiled. 'Who does?'

'And this place has vibrations, don't you think?' Solomon looked at the white walls he had imagined painted in blood. 'Do you never think about who they kept down here when the cells were fresh cut? Or how dark it must have been? Or about the screams that must have soaked into these walls?'

Parra shivered though the room was not cold. 'There's lots of history here. The whole town is built on it. There's a big mediaeval pageant every summer where we all get dressed up – torchlight processions, knights on horseback, that kind of thing. It's for the tourists mainly, but you can really feel the history of the place. Like it's still alive.'

Solomon nodded. 'Then maybe what I'm about to tell you won't seem so strange. There's a long flight of stone steps behind the tailor's house.'

'The Rue des Chevaliers.'

'Yes, the Rue des Chevaliers. I was walking down it, from the top of the hill and down into the mist. The mist was glowing in the morning sun. You know what that looks like, Emile?'

Parra nodded.

'Good. It's important that you picture it, so you can understand what I saw: the steps and the mist getting thicker as I descended into it. Step by step. One after another. Can you picture it, Emile? Can you see the steps?' Parra nodded. 'That's very good, Emile. Now let me tell you what I saw.'

13

Marie-Claude sat on the edge of her unmade bed and listened in numbed shock as Amand told her in his calm, low voice how her grandfather's body had been discovered. She could tell he was choosing his words carefully, telling her what he could without going into specifics, but she didn't need the detail to know the truth. Her grandfather had been murdered and whoever had done it had made him suffer before he died. And she felt responsible. She *was* responsible.

When she had first told her grandfather she wanted to find the last remaining survivors of Die Schneider Lager and record their memories, she had hoped he might understand and see how she was seeking to honour what had happened there and what had happened to *him*. She had hoped he might even help her. She had been wrong.

Leave it alone, he'd told her, his anger sudden and shocking. *It's old history, painful history. You don't know what you're getting into. It's a cursed subject. A dangerous subject. Remember what happened to Herman Lansky? Remember what happened to Saul Schwartzfeldt?*

She did remember. Lansky's memoir was the only first-hand account of life in the camp and an explosion in his apartment had killed him while he was writing a more detailed follow-up. The fire had destroyed his unfinished book and all his research and Die Schneider Lager had become a footnote, an almost forgotten name lurking in the shadows of other camps whose stories *had* been told, their names now infamous – Auschwitz, Buchenwald, Treblinka.

But as the seventieth anniversary of the end of the war approached, Marie-Claude had begun to feel more and more strongly that the history her grandfather had lived through and the experiences he'd had in the camp needed to be recorded. They did not belong to him alone, they belonged to everyone, to her and also her son. So despite his reservations she had started to search. Lansky's memoir recorded that there were four other survivors of the camp, the ones known as *Die Anderen* – The Others. Her grandfather was one of them. Marie-Claude had set out to track down the other three.

It had been a huge amount of work, sifting through old history trying to pick up the trail of people who had disappeared at the end of the war. But after months of work she had found one, Saul Schwartzfeldt. She had even spoken to him. Once. He had told her to leave the past alone, just as her grandfather had. She had ignored them both and now they were dead. Dead because of her.

She became aware of a silence and realized Amand had stopped talking. 'I'm sorry, did you . . .?'

'I asked if your grandfather had been upset about anything recently?'

Marie-Claude flashed back to the last time they had spoken, two days earlier in La Broderie. Her grandfather had asked if he could store something in the tiny room she used as a studio. She had been surprised by the request, because he had a huge storeroom of his own in the building and had done his level best to ignore her presence in La Broderie entirely, along with her work. She'd thought maybe it was a ruse to take a peek inside her office and her suspicions had been confirmed when all he'd brought with him was one canvas suit-carrier. She recalled the look on his face as he stepped into her office, a mixture of fear and anger as he studied the evidence of her industry displayed on every wall. He had begged her again to abandon her project and stop looking for *Die Anderen*.

There is a great evil and sorrow in our past, he had told her. *Far greater than you realize. I keep it buried for your sake and for Léo's. Please do not dig it up again.*

She had read a lot about survivor's guilt, where those who lived through the Holocaust felt unworthy, but to her the story of her grandfather's survival was miraculous, something to be celebrated and shared. She'd tried to reason with him again, get him to see it from her point of view, but they had ended up arguing like they always did and he had thrown the canvas suit-carrier on the ground and stormed off with the words:

Remember this conversation when I'm dead. Then you'll understand.

She had hung the suit-carrier on the back of her door to give him a reason to return once he'd calmed down, but he never did. And now he was dead, and with the marks of the death camp upon him.

She became aware of silence again and looked up. 'Sorry, I was . . .'

'I said I need you to come with me to the station and make an official statement. You'll also have to identify the body at some point.'

Marie-Claude nodded, only half listening. It hurt that her

last words with her grandfather had been angry ones and that they had never made up. It was uncharacteristic of him. He was usually quick to anger and quick to forgive. It all felt unresolved and unbearably sad. She thought of how the next time she would see him now was when she identified his body and tears sprang to her eyes.

'I need to tell Léo,' she said, rising from the bed and opening the door, suddenly desperate to get out of the room. 'They're very . . . they were close. He'll be upset. I'll come to the station afterwards.'

Amand stood and followed her. 'Of course. Take as long as you need. I'll keep someone posted outside. They can escort you to the station when you're ready.'

'That's not necessary.'

Amand leaned in and lowered his voice. 'I don't wish to alarm you, but whoever killed your grandfather was looking for something. And until we have more information I want to make sure that you and Léo are safe.'

Marie-Claude blinked in surprise. 'What were they looking for?'

'We don't know, but we do have a suspect in custody. Let's see what he has to say.'

'Do you think it's him? Do you think he . . . killed . . .?'

'No. Not really. But he might help us find the killer.' She opened the front door to let him out. 'Let Pierre know when you're ready, OK?'

She nodded and thought about telling him about the suit-carrier hanging on the back of her office door.

Remember this conversation when I'm dead, her grandfather had said, like he'd known he was going to die.

'What is it?'

She could feel a pressure building inside her – anger,

sorrow, and shame. 'Nothing,' she said. Amand had more important things to do than waste time looking into things that were probably more to do with her sense of guilt than anything else. She would mention it in her statement later and they could decide if it was important or not. She smiled. 'I was remembering the last time I spoke to him.'

Amand nodded and kissed her on her cheek. 'Take as long as you like with Léo,' he said, then he turned and walked away.

She closed the door and leaned back against it, staring down the hallway at the kitchen door and thinking about the conversation she was about to have with her son.

How do you tell a seven-year-old boy his Grampy is dead?

How do you begin to find the right words to explain that he was murdered?

14

The man looked up from the red, pain-filled wetness of the video clip on his phone and watched Commandant Amand walk away from the house. He paused briefly to speak to the gendarme in the parked car before heading off in the direction of the Commissariat. The woman watched him leave then shut the door behind him. Amand had not been in the house long enough to have taken a statement, which meant she would most likely follow him soon. The gendarme remained behind in the car, sucking on an e-cigarette and blowing white vapour out of the open window.

Further up the street a woman in a cream linen jacket stepped out of her house and tucked her grey hair under a white sun hat while looking across at the officer in the parked car. Maybe the jungle drums of the town were already beating, carrying the news of the tailor's death to the wider community. Nothing stayed secret for long in a place like this. She finished fixing her hat and glanced up the street in his direction. He was at least thirty feet away and facing in the opposite direction and from her age he imagined she probably needed glasses but was too proud to wear them in public. He doubted she would be able to identify him if it came to it, though her casual scrutiny was a reminder that the longer he stuck around, the more visible he was becoming. He couldn't afford to stay here, but he couldn't leave either, not without the list.

The old woman locked her front door, dropped the key into her shopping basket and walked away down the hill towards Maison Moulin where the morning bread was stacked in warm, crusty piles behind the counter. The gendarme watched her leave, slumped low in his seat, clouds of white vapour rising out of his open window and up into the morning sunlight. He didn't look like he was going anywhere.

He watched him, the wet sound of the tailor's last words playing in his earphones, reminding him what all of this was for as his mind ran through options of how he might get things moving. He reached into his jacket and pulled out two sheets of folded paper containing street maps, local market days, useful phone numbers. He checked the map against a list of houses, the germ of an idea starting to take hold, and copied one of the local telephone numbers into a cheap, pre-paid mobile phone he'd bought at the big E. Leclerc in Gaillac the previous day.

'Police!' a voice answered.

'Yes, hello,' he cleared his throat, over-emphasizing his words to make him sound foreign. 'My dog found something in my garden. A man's shirt covered in blood. I grabbed his collar and locked him in the kitchen before he could start chewing it. Thought I should call you in case it's important.'

'You did the right thing. Could I have your address please.'

'Hang on. I'm here on holiday, let me find it for you.' He looked back at the map and a list of addresses he'd down-loaded from an online holiday lettings agency. He picked one close to his current position. 'It's number 28, Rue de la

Chevalier Noir. When do you think someone will be over? Only my dog is locked up in the kitchen and this is a rented *gîte*, so if no one's going to be here for a while I might have to take him for a walk before he makes a mess.'

'Someone will be with you directly, monsieur.'

'All right. I'll stay put.'

He hung up and looked back at the gendarme in the parked car. The local police would be stretched thin right now because of the murder investigation and would logically send the closest officer to investigate. Or maybe they'd already drafted in extra men from other districts and the gendarme in the car would simply stay where he was and he would be forced to . . .

'*Vingt-sept, come in.*' The scanner crackled.

The gendarme leaned forward, picked up his radio and spoke, his voice sounding scratchy in the scanner's tiny speaker.

'*This is vingt-sept.*'

'*Tourist just called in saying he found a bloody shirt in his garden. I need you to go check it out.*'

'*Amand told me to stay put until further notice.*'

'*It'll take you two minutes.*'

The gendarme glanced back at the house then shook his head and turned on the engine. '*OK, give me the address.*'

The man in the parked car watched the vehicle move away and disappear from sight. He listened to the silence settle on the street then got out of his car and moved towards the boot, stretching the stiffness out of his back as he went. Inside was an old wooden crate containing the relics sacred to his task. He lifted the lid, took out a black scarf and wrapped it round his face, leaving only his eyes visible. It was a ritual with him, this covering up of his real self in order to become something else. The man he was could not do the things that needed to be done, but his other self could.

He took out a black hat next with a short brim and pulled it low over his eyes, feeling his other self beginning to emerge. He looked back down and ran his hand over the different shapes contained in the crate, each wrapped in the grey fabric known as 'death cloth'. He found the long shape of his sword and removed it from the folds. It was a Nazi police dress bayonet with a silver-tipped scabbard and a pommel shaped like an eagle's head. He withdrew the long blade and turned it over in the sunlight, feeling the weight of it in his hand, and his own transformation was complete. He was no longer the man, now he was Wotan and the bayonet was Gram, his sacred sword.

He locked the car and started walking towards the house, the bayonet hidden in the folds of his long, black coat. He was invisible now, featureless and unrecognizable.

Wotan, the avenger.

Wotan, the immortal.

Wotan, the shadow that fell over the hunted as he walked through the sunlight on the Wild Hunt for the souls of the damned.

III

'Some of you say "It is the north wind who has woven the clothes we wear."
And I say, "Ay, it was the north wind, but shame was his loom, and the softening of the sinews was his thread."'

The Prophet
Kahlil Gibran

Extract from

**DARK MATERIAL – THE DEVIL'S TAILOR: DEATH
AND LIFE IN DIE SCHNEIDER LAGER**

⚜

By Herman Lansky

By the summer of 1939 war felt imminent. It hung heavy
in the air like a coming storm and wherever I travelled
on business I saw troops at every station: moving west;
moving east.

The Germans were mobilizing along our western
border and the Russians were doing the same in the east:
ready to come to our aid if the Germans invaded, the politicians assured us, which gave us some comfort. We knew
the Red Army would rather fight the Nazis on Polish
soil than their own and though none of us liked the idea
of our homeland becoming a battlefield we liked the
idea of standing alone against the Germans even less.

The storm finally broke on the morning of 1
September 1939. A million and a half German troops
poured across the border while the Luftwaffe bombed
Polish airfields. I awoke to the distant sound of explosions as the retreating Polish army blew up bridges to
slow the German advance.

The first bombs fell on Łódź on 4 September. They
hit the stations first, cutting a main route of escape. It
was shocking. Unbelievable. Some started fleeing to the

east, away from the invasion. Most stayed. The Polish army was garrisoned in Park Julianów, so we were not entirely defenceless – and there were always the Russians. Only after the war did we discover that Stalin had struck a secret deal with Hitler to carve Poland up, the Germans taking the west and the Russians the east, and that when the Russians headed west across our border it was not to rescue but to invade.

The Germans arrived in Łódź on the eighth, their well-drilled armoured divisions and motorized infantry quickly overwhelming the disorganized Polish army. I was walking down Piotrkowska Street when the first troops arrived, neatly ordered lines of grey uniforms sweeping down the straight boulevard like a river, ethnic Germans lining the way shouting 'Heil Hitler', giving Nazi salutes and throwing flowers like the Germans were conquering heroes. I remember studying their shining faces, shocked by how many there were, and wondering which one was the coward who'd written 'Jew pigs' on the Synagogue wall less than a year earlier. It could have been any of them. Only now they were out in the open and it was us who were about to be driven into the dark.

To truly understand how devastating it was watching the Nazis march down Piotrkowska Street you must realize that Łódź was my city: it belonged to me as much as I belonged to it. My family had helped build it. To give an example, my very first memory of the Great Synagogue was of being introduced to the Rabbi and him shaking my hand and thanking me for the building we were standing in. After he left to lead the tefilah, my father explained that Grandpa Lansky had provided a large portion of the funds for the construction of the temple and that it had been built to accommodate the huge influx of displaced Russian Jews who flooded into the city at the end of the nineteenth century, exactly as my great-great grandfather had done in the early eighteen hundreds.

'We have made this town what it is,' my father whispered as we sat on the Lansky family bench at the front of the congregation, closest to the Torah Ark, the holiest place in the Temple. 'A haven for our kind. A sanctuary that no one will ever drive us from.'

But he was wrong. Within a few short months of the Nazis' arrival, nothing would belong to us at all. In four generations my family had built the largest chain of clothing stores in the country and the biggest textile factory in a city known as 'the Manchester of Poland'. Four generations to build an empire and the Nazis took it all away in just a few weeks. They were incredibly well organized and efficient, like they had been planning it all for years, meeting in secret behind locked doors, drawing up lists of what to take and who to take it from, all that hate so well hidden that all we saw of it before-hand were a few bits of graffiti on the Synagogue wall.

And when their time came they emerged fully formed, a monster made of many faces, some of them people we had considered friends. They blamed us for everything, took everything we had and forced us to live twenty to a room in an overcrowded ghetto in the worst part of a city we had helped build. But after a time even that was too much. They wanted us gone, no trace remaining. That was when the transportations started to the camps, those factories of unfathomable horror where we were to be robbed of the only things we had left – our lives, our souls.

Hell has many names in the Hebrew Bible – She'ol, Abaddon, Gehenna – but to me it will always carry the name of the camp the Nazis took me to, where I existed for four long years. I call it existing because I cannot call it living and in truth it was closer to death.

Hell for me is The Tailors' Camp.

Hell for me is Die Schneider Lager.

15

Café Belloq had emptied out a little by the time the first of the group walked in. Jean-Luc Belloq nodded a silent greeting and watched the man move across the black-and-white chequered tile floor towards the stairs leading to the private room above the bar. A minute later a second person arrived and followed the same path.

'You should go home, madame,' he said to Madame Segolin, taking her by the elbow and guiding her to the door. 'You need rest after the shock you've had.'

She nodded and mumbled something about rats as he led her to the door. Belloq watched her weave away down the street, muttering to herself and steering well clear of the drains. He surveyed the patrons on the terrace, checking to see if anyone was taking any notice, then crooked a finger at Mariella to summon her.

'Watch the bar,' he said. 'If anyone asks for me, tell them I'm out and you don't know when I'll be back.' He passed through the door and went up the stairs to join the others.

The private room above the bar was oak-panelled and intimate with velvet curtains the colour of red wine draped across tall windows, making the room feel dusky. A chandelier dripped crystal over a large oval table, its dark surface burnished by the sleeves of countless diners, though no one had eaten in this room for several months now, not since Belloq had turned it into his command centre. Evidence of its new function lay everywhere, stacked in boxes and piled on the marble-topped bureau running the length of one wall: piles of leaflets and posters, most featuring the smiling face of Belloq himself amid slogans such as – '*La France aux Français*' – France for the French – or – '*LES IMMIGRÉS VONT VOTER . . . ET VOUS VOUS ABSTENEZ?!!*' – The immigrants are going to vote . . . and you're staying at home?!!

A large poster was pinned above the small marble fireplace showing Belloq standing behind his bar, wearing shirt, tie and apron and smiling a welcome. An outline of a black boar surrounded him like a jagged halo with the slogan:

VOTER Belloq – Votez Parti National de la France Libre. Votez pour la France et l'avenir de vos enfants.

Vote for Belloq – Vote National Party of Free France. Vote for France and for your children's future.

Belloq locked the heavy door behind him and turned to face the two men sitting at the table: Edmond Laurent, Michel LePoux. Between them they represented the oldest families in Cordes – their names carved on numerous gravestones as well as the marble war memorial outside the gates of the town cemetery. They were as much a part of Cordes as the stone that made up the walls. They were the town: its past, its present and also, they hoped, its future – and the future of France.

'Josef Engel is dead,' Belloq said. 'Murdered.'

Silence followed and Belloq flicked his eyes from face to face, looking for a reaction.

'Murdered?' It was Laurent who broke the silence, his voice as well cut and smooth as his chestnut hair and dark blue suit. Laurent was in his mid forties, the youngest of the group and also the richest, his family owning more than forty properties in and around Cordes as well as several restaurants and shops. Laurent ran his own successful law practice, continuing a long family tradition of practising law and telling other people what to do. 'Are you sure he didn't die of natural causes? He was quite old.'

'I checked with the Commissariat: it's a murder enquiry.'

Laurent frowned. 'Have you informed the leadership?'

'Not yet. I wanted to talk to you two first. See if either of you knew anything.' He looked at LePoux, who scowled back.

'Don't look at me. Why do you always assume it's me when something bad happens?'

'Well, this is more your area of expertise,' Laurent replied smoothly. 'And you do have a reputation for being somewhat heavy-handed.'

LePoux's face flushed crimson. 'It's not my fault if my workers are lazy and their bones are weak.' He looked up at Belloq. 'I had nothing to do with the Jew tailor's death. Nothing at all. I swear it.'

Belloq nodded. 'Of course. I never doubted it, but I had to ask.' LePoux huffed and shot Laurent a filthy look. 'Nevertheless, the tailor's death poses problems. From what I hear, he was tortured before he died and his house was searched, we have to assume that the killer might have found the list.'

LePoux huffed again. 'I still don't understand why the leadership is so bothered by some old Jew tailor. We should be driving his sort out of the country, not watching over them. I'm glad he's dead. One less dirty mouth to feed.'

'We do not need to understand our orders,' Belloq said. 'All that matters is that we follow them. The tailor is clearly significant for some reason, as is this list. Our job now is to find it. The police already have a suspect in custody . . .' He put on his reading glasses, pulled a piece of paper from his pocket and read the name he had written on it earlier: 'A Monsieur Solomon Creed.'

'I know that name!' LePoux sat forward in his seat, his stomach spilling over the edge of the table. 'He was at my vineyard this morning. He attacked me.'

Laurent turned to him. 'He attacked you?'

'Yes. I was talking to one of my workers and he appeared from nowhere, grabbed my cane, broke it in half and pushed me to the ground.'

'Why?'

'I don't know.'

Laurent shrugged. 'Strangers do not usually go around attacking people for no reason, especially if they're trying to keep a low profile because they're here to commit murder.'

'All I was doing was reprimanding an Arab.'

'With a stick?'

'What business is it of yours how I choose to run my vineyard?'

'Gentlemen, please,' Belloq said. 'I did not call you here to argue.'

Laurent turned to him. 'Do you know if they've formally charged this Monsieur Creed?'

'Not yet. They're currently holding him for questioning.'

'And who's leading the investigation?'

'Benoît Amand.'

Laurent rolled his eyes and pulled his phone from his pocket. 'Let me find out if the *juge d'instruction* has been appointed yet, see if I can't get someone assigned who's a little friendlier to our cause.'

'Wait,' LePoux said, his eyes going wide as he remembered. 'He asked the Arab if there was a Josef Engel living here. It must be him. He *must* have killed him.'

'You're sure?' Laurent said.

'Why would I lie?'

'No reason,' Belloq cut in, trying to calm the situation again. 'But this does shine a different light on things.'

LePoux frowned. 'How?'

'Because,' Laurent explained, 'it means we know this man was here in search of Josef Engel, consequently we can also assume we know what he was looking for.'

'The list?'

'Exactly.'

LePoux's face creased in confusion. 'And how is that useful?'

'Because, if he does have the list,' Belloq said as patiently as he could, 'it means we can get to him and we can take it back.'

LePoux was always the last to understand. He was more of a blunt instrument than a scalpel, a vicious dog you kept on a chain, putting up with the barking because there might be a time when you needed its bite. A time like this.

16

Amand pushed through the large glass door of the Commissariat and headed to the inner offices. 'Where is everyone?'

Sergeant Henri DuBois looked up from his computer. 'Isn't Parra out there?'

'No.'

Henri twisted the points of his moustache and shrugged. 'Maybe he's gone back to the crime scene. Take a look at this. I ran Monsieur Creed's name through the crime database and he popped up on an Interpol warrant. Three weeks ago, practically a whole town blew up in Arizona and the authorities would very much like to talk to him about it.'

Amand stepped up to the screen and studied the report. 'Have you contacted anyone?'

'I called the sheriff's office.' Amand scanned another window showing an article from an Arizona newspaper complete with photographs of a white stone church with a large crack in one wall and bodies lying in the shade of some trees under plastic sheets.

'What did the sheriff say?'

'Nothing. Turns out he's one of the bodies lying under the trees. And look at this . . .' Henri scrolled down to a note at the bottom of the Interpol alert.

Subject is believed to have recently absconded from a private Mexican psychiatric facility run by the ICP (Institute of Criminal Psychology). He is highly intelligent and extremely dangerous. DO NOT APPROACH. If sighted, observe at a distance and alert nearest local tactical force to make the arrest (DEA, SWAT, etc). Any sightings should be IMMEDIATELY reported to this emergency number.

A number was listed beneath that looked like a satellite phone. 'Did you call it?'

'It's a recorded message. I left your name and this number. But that's not all. A few minutes ago we got a call about some tourist whose dog found a bloody shirt in a garden. I sent Pierre to check it out.'

'Pierre!?'

'He was right around the corner.'

Amand grabbed the desk mic that connected to the police radio network. 'Josef Engel's shirt isn't missing, it was folded on a chair in his atelier. Call Parra. Find out where he is.' Amand pushed the call button. 'Car vingt-sept, come in. Where are you, Pierre?'

There was a brief pause before a reply crackled back.

'*This is vingt-sept. I'm on the Rue de la Chevalier Noir, over.*'

'Get back in position right away.'

'*OK. I was heading back anyway. The address Henri gave me must be wrong. That house is shuttered up and there's a thick stack of mail inside the door. No one's been here for a while.*'

Amand glanced at Henri, who was frantically dialling Parra's number. 'Get back to Marie-Claude's house as fast as you can and make sure she's OK.'

He disconnected and reached for his own phone. The

tightness in his chest had returned, a combination of his recent brisk walk and the feeling that everything was drifting away from him. He found Marie-Claude's number and was about to dial it when he heard a slightly muffled sound across the room, like someone plucking a banjo. It was coming from a jacket hanging on the coat stand by the stairs. Parra's ringtone. Parra's jacket. He hadn't gone anywhere. Parra was still in the building.

'Call Marie-Claude,' Amand said, moving towards the jacket and the stairs leading down to the cells. He remembered the words on the Interpol alert:

He is highly intelligent and extremely dangerous. DO NOT APPROACH.

And Parra was down there.
Alone.

17

The sudden sound of the phone ringing in the kitchen made Marie-Claude jump. She ignored it and carried on stuffing comics into a backpack that already contained her laptop and purse. She knew the day ahead was going to be long and painful and wanted to be prepared. She was also avoiding the conversation she needed to have with Léo.

'Phone's ringing, Mama.'

His voice made her jump. She turned and tried smiling down at the little figure standing in the doorway but her heart wasn't in it and she saw in his eyes that it had come out all wrong.

'Grampy's dead, isn't he?' Léo said, taking her by surprise. 'Uncle Benny came to tell you he died.' He stepped forward, arms held out to her, and she sat on the bed and hugged him tight.

She could feel her grief, dark and heavy inside her like a stone laid on top of her heart bringing tears that she tried to hold back.

'It's OK, Mama,' Léo said. 'It's OK to be sad when people die. You don't have to pretend you're happy because of me.'

He returned the hug and she let the tears spill and felt the instant relief of it. 'OK, Léo, I won't. I promise.'

She should have known it was pointless trying to sugarcoat or hide anything from her son. Sometimes she wondered if he was more together and grown-up than she was, the things he seemed to see, the things he picked up about people just by looking at them with those serious eyes of his. He had his great-grandfather's eyes, eyes that looked like they'd seen too much. Maybe that was why she tried so hard to protect him, not wanting to add more sorrow to the sadness already there. Or maybe she was just being a mother.

In the kitchen, the phone stopped ringing. She kissed his hair and pulled away from him a little to look into his face. 'You're right,' she said, holding his face in her hands. 'It is OK to be sad when someone dies. Only Grandpa didn't just die.' She took a breath, pausing at the precipice of what she was about to tell him. 'Somebody killed him.'

Marie-Claude waited for some kind of reaction, tears or anger or fear, instead Léo nodded and turned to look at the rucksack. 'Is that why we're leaving?' he said. 'Because the person who killed Grampy might come for us next?'

'No, *chéri*, no.' She took hold of him and held his small body as tight as she dared. She'd screwed up again. She shouldn't have told him. Not like this. It was too much for a seven-year-old to take on. All the disruption, the visit from Amand, packing a bag with no explanation, then the final flourish of parental genius – the blunt revelation that his great-grandfather had been murdered. No wonder he was confused and scared. She was scaring herself. She was a mess. She should have taken him to school and let him have a normal day while she dealt with everything, like a grown-up was supposed to.

The knock on the door made them both jump and she caught the look of anxiety in Léo's eyes. 'Don't be scared, *chéri*, it's probably Uncle Benny again, or the other policeman.' She stood up and paused by the door. 'Put your shoes on and I'll take you to school, or you can come with me to the Commissariat. Up to you.'

Léo scanned the messy floor for his trainers but couldn't see them. His mama never asked him to tidy his bedroom, not like some of his friends' mothers who seemed to think that toys and books were not meant to be played with. That was why she was such a great mum, though Léo could tell sometimes she thought she wasn't – like now.

He followed her into the hallway and looked past where she had stopped by the hall mirror to dab her eyes with a tissue. His Spidey-sneaks were by the front door, close to where a dark shape shifted on the other side of the frosted glass. Léo felt coldness flowing from it like river water and a deep red flickered through the black revealing a shape at the heart of it, a regular-sized man but surrounded in a dark cloud of feathery blackness as if midnight had come to call.

His mama finished dabbing her eyes and started walking towards the door. Léo's mouth went dry and he leaped forward, all instinct, and grabbed her hand.

'Hey.' She turned to him, saw the fear in his face. 'What's up, Léo?'

He tugged at her hand, shaking his head and trying to pull her back up the hallway and into his bedroom. He raised his finger to his lips and pointed at the shadow. He knew she couldn't see what he was seeing. To her the shape at the door would look like a regular person, but Léo knew it wasn't. He didn't know what was standing on the other side of that door and he didn't want to find out. He tugged at his mama's hand, his mind casting around for the right words to say to stop her from opening the door. She didn't like it when he talked about the colours he saw and all he could think of was:

'Bad.'

'What?'

'Bad,' he pointed up the hallway to where the cold shadow shifted by the front door.

'Look, Léo,' she said, dropping to his level. 'I know this is turning into a bit of a crazy day, but nothing bad's going to happen. I promise.'

Léo stared past her at the shifting shadow. 'It will,' he whispered. 'Don't open the door. There's a darkness there. Something black and red. Please don't open the door.' He was crying now.

She looked at him, her eyes pink from crying and sharp with concern, her colours swirling and mixing to muddiness. He wanted to hold her and stir in some of his lightness, but his own colours were faded with fear too.

He felt the coldness shift and looked past her to see the dark shape moving away behind the frosted glass. He blinked, not quite believing it had gone. It moved along the front of the house and slipped into the passage that ran down the side and continued to move, heading to the back of the house now, not gone, but shifting, looking for a different way in.

18

Amand ran down the spiralling stone steps to the cells, thinking of the bloody mess he'd found in Josef Engel's atelier that morning.

. . . DO NOT APPROACH . . . the Interpol alert had warned.

He is highly intelligent and extremely dangerous . . .

The air grew colder as he descended and the ache in his chest was like a steadily tightening steel band around his lungs. He reached the bottom and burst through the door into the white-painted corridor, the overhead lights head-ache-bright.

The cell where Solomon Creed was being held was at the furthest end of the corridor. Amand moved quickly towards it, his hand resting on the grip of his gun and remembering how easily Solomon had taken it from him last time. He had given it back though. Why would he do that if he was the dangerous maniac the Interpol alert suggested? Parra was probably taking his statement, that was all. Amand listened through his hammering heartbeat for the murmur of voices but heard nothing.

He could see inside the cell through the small window in the door. White-painted walls. An empty chair. An evidence envelope and a blank statement form on the table with an uncapped pen next to it. Then he saw Parra, sitting in the second chair, bolt upright and facing forward, eyes closed, hands placed flat on the table. There was no one else in the room.

Amand ducked below the window and rose on the other side, checking the cell from his new angle. No one there either but the window was small and there was a sizeable blind spot where Solomon would be hidden from view if he was standing close to the wall. And he had to be in there. *Had* to be.

'Monsieur Creed,' Amand called out, his voice sounding too loud in the trapped confines of the corridor. 'Step into view, please. Step into view and sit down at the table.'

Parra opened his eyes and looked around like he had just woken up. Amand watched to see if he might give him a fix on where Solomon was but he seemed confused.

'Parra,' Amand called out. 'You OK?'

Parra nodded slowly. 'Yes, I'm . . . yes.'

He moved slightly so Parra could see him. 'Show me where he is. Look at him now so I can see where he is.'

Parra looked around. 'Who?'

Amand pulled his gun from the holster and pointed it at the floor. 'Listen to me, Parra. I want you to stand up and open the door, OK?' Parra nodded but didn't move. 'Just stand up, open the door, step into the corridor and close the door behind you.'

Parra looked down at his hands on the tabletop. 'I can't,' he said, confusion and panic fraying his voice. 'My hands are stuck.'

He stood and his chair clattered away across the hard floor. He tugged at his hands and the whole table moved, metal legs shrieking against the stone floor.

'You're not stuck,' Amand called out. 'Your hands moved.'

Parra yanked backwards again in panic, dragging the table across the floor into a part of the cell that Amand couldn't see. He dug into his pocket, found the key and jammed it into the lock.

Parra had moved to the right, which suggested Solomon must be on the left. The key slotted home and the shriek of metal on stone escaped through the opening door. Amand raised his gun and ducked his head through the door as another shriek of metal on stone ripped through the air. He swept his gun left and stared at the corner. There was no one there. Solomon Creed had vanished.

19

He raised the bayonet as he neared the back of the house and stopped at the corner to survey the small garden. A child's bike lay on the ground next to a plastic sandpit. Such a small bike. He knew the boy was inside the house and what had to happen if he went inside. The police officer would not be gone long. He would have to be quick. Make the woman tell him where the list was and leave no witnesses.

He looked away from the bike and remembered the video he'd been watching instead, using it to sharpen his nerve in the same way he had sharpened the blade of the bayonet the night before. He knew the Second World War had not ended seventy years ago. It raged still, and there were always casualties in war, innocents sacrificed on the altar of a higher purpose.

He felt the weight of the bayonet. He needed to be like the blade, solid and sharp and clear of purpose – a tool made for war. He needed to be strong, like Wotan was strong – godlike and unrelenting. The woman and her son were mistakes of history. Her grandfather should have died in the war and they should never have been born. He raised the bayonet, the blade angled forward, stepped round the corner and into the yard.

The back door was partially glazed and he caught his reflection in it, black and featureless, a shadow. The kitchen beyond was empty, the remains of breakfast abandoned on the surfaces: a jug of coffee on a hot plate, a bowl by the sink with a spoon in it. He could see the hallway beyond the kitchen and another door on the far side, closed and with superhero cartoons stuck to it and something that made his heart lift. An omen. Showing him the way. Calling him on.

He tried the handle. Locked. Turned the bayonet over, gripped the blade with his gloved hand and swung it hard. The metal eagle's head struck the glass and the window shattered and glass scattered across the tiles. He reached through the jagged hole and unlocked the door from the inside. More glass fell as he pushed the door open and crunched beneath his boots as he marched through the warm coffee-smelling kitchen towards the thing that had spoken to his higher purpose.

He flipped the bayonet over again so the blade was pointing out and entered the hallway. To his left was the front door; a pile of shoes and coats; another door revealing a bedroom. To his right was an empty bathroom. They had to be in the boy's bedroom. Nowhere else they could be.

He stopped in front of the closed door and stared at the omen that had spurred him on. Thor looked back at him, teeth gritted, hammer held aloft with lightning flashing around it. Thor, son of Wotan.

He gripped the bayonet. Held it up. Then kicked open the door.

20

Amand steered Parra back to his desk in the main office and handed him a cup of coffee. 'What happened?'

Parra passed the cup from one hand to the other. 'I can't exactly . . . he was.' He put the cup down and studied his hands.

'Tell me what you remember.'

Parra pushed his hands together. Pulled them apart. Turned them over. In the background, Henri was speaking urgently on the phone, putting out an alert to local and national police and giving them Solomon's description.

'I went to take a statement,' Parra said, studying his hands. 'He said he remembered seeing something.' Parra frowned again, struggling to remember. 'He said he'd been walking down some steps to get to the house, a long flight of stone steps that disappeared into the morning mist, and he asked me to picture them, said it would help me understand what he'd seen. His voice was . . . he was really persuasive, like he was genuinely trying to help. He told me, he *suggested* I close my eyes to help me picture them. So I did. And he was right, I could see the stairs exactly as he described them, a long set of stone steps disappearing into mist.

'He kept talking the whole time, telling me to breathe slowly and imagine myself walking down the steps, said it would help me understand what had happened at the house. I kept thinking I would reach the bottom, that the sun would burn the mist away and everything would become clear.' He shook his head. 'But I never got to the bottom. The steps kept going down, and I kept walking, and the mist kept on getting thicker. And all the time his voice was in my head, talking to me, telling me to relax, asking me things.'

'Like what?'

'About the town. About the cell. How the door was locked. Who else was upstairs.'

'And you told him?'

'It didn't occur to me not to. His voice was so reassuring. It's hard to explain.'

'What else did he ask?'

Parra stared at his hands. Turned them over again. 'He mentioned a name. Asked if it meant anything to me.'

'What name?'

'Magellan. He asked me if there was anyone in town called Magellan.'

'Anything else?'

Parra shook his head. 'He just kept asking about Magellan, if I knew who he was. Said it was important. When I told him I didn't know, it felt like I was letting him down. It was that voice, like it was inside my head, speaking my thoughts. It was almost like he was me. That's why I didn't hide anything from him. Why would I?'

'Do you remember anything else he talked about?'

Parra took a sip of coffee. Shook his head. 'Everything seems vague now. I do remember at one point he told me to place my hands on a wall and I looked down and there it was right in front of me where the next step should have been. He told me to put my hands on it and keep them there so I wouldn't get lost in the mist while he stepped away for a moment. So I did. I placed my hands on the wall and waited for him to come back.' He blinked and looked up at Amand. 'Then I heard you calling my name, and I opened my eyes – and he was gone.'

He looked back down at his hands. Made fists. Opened them again. 'I couldn't take my hands off the table. It was like they were stuck in the dream, or whatever it was. I mean, I could see they were on the table, but I could also feel the wall.' He looked up at Amand with hurt in his eyes. 'I'm sorry. I let him get away.'

Amand smiled. 'Don't worry about it. Not your fault. I should have checked him out first. We'll get him back, don't worry. We'll interview him together. Good cop, bad cop – old school. You can be bad cop, if you like.' Parra attempted a smile but his eyes remained glazed, like he was still in the mist. 'You want to go home,' Amand said, 'maybe get some rest? You've had a hell of a morning, no one would think bad of you if you wanted to take it easy for a few hours.'

'No, I'm fine, honestly. Only . . .' Parra shook his head and stared back down at the floor. 'There's something else he asked me about. Something I can't quite remember . . .'

The desk phone rang, making everyone jump. Henri grabbed it. 'Commissariat de Police. Sergeant Henri speaking.' He frowned. 'Who is this, please?'

He pressed a button to put the call on hold and looked over at Amand. 'You're not going to believe this,' he said, holding out the phone.

Amand took it. 'Commandant Amand?'

'Do you still have the man known as Solomon Creed in

custody?' The voice was deep and the man's French was perfect but accented, American maybe.

'Who am I speaking with?'

'I'm his doctor,' the voice replied, 'his psychiatrist. My name is Magellan. Doctor Cezar Magellan.'

21

Solomon moved down the ancient streets of Cordes, following the street map in his head, keeping to the passageways and the back roads. He was heading to the address he had dredged from his memory while waiting in the cell. The sergeant had confirmed its significance, as had the brand on his arm.

He stopped at a junction and listened ahead for the sound of footsteps or conversation. He needed to be cautious and make the best use of his liberty. They would discover he was missing sooner or later – sooner, most probably – and a stranger like him in a town like this could not hope to stay hidden for long.

The street ahead was silent. He passed into it for a sunlit moment before ducking into the shadows of a narrow alleyway and continuing on his way.

There was something here in this town, something that could help him unlock the mystery of himself. He was here for a reason, he felt certain of it, as certain as he knew that all the facts tumbling through his head were correct. It was tied up with everything that had brought him here: the tailor; the missing suit; the words written on the wall; and Magellan – always Magellan – the word burning in his mind like a red sun with questions spinning round it like planets.

What was Magellan?
Who was Magellan?
And was he trying to find him?
Or was he running away?

22

'Do you have him in custody?' Magellan repeated, his voice rumbling down the phone.

There was a background hiss, like tyres on tarmac that matched the white noise in Amand's head as he tried to process everything he'd just heard.

Doctor Cezar Magellan . . . his psychiatrist . . . the man KNOWN as Solomon Creed.

'Who is he then?' Amand said out loud. 'If not Solomon Creed, then who?'

'I'd rather not go into that. He's very artful, very persuasive. He can extract information from people without them realizing he's doing it, therefore the less you know about him the better.' Amand glanced at Parra opening and closing his hands. 'Anything I do tell you might be accidentally communicated to him, which could be very dangerous. It could trigger his psychosis. You should keep him in isolation until I get there.'

Amand let out a heavy sigh. 'We don't have him.'

'What?'

'He escaped.'

A sigh whispered down the line, mingling with the background hiss. 'How long ago?'

'Not long. Fifteen minutes maybe. He won't have gone far. We'll get him back. He was asking about you.'

'Really?'

'Yes. He didn't seem to know who you were. Kept asking if you lived here.'

'Part of his therapy involves a form of memory control. My team and I have pioneered a technique that enables us to remove certain . . . toxic memories from the minds of particularly disturbed patients, similar to how surgeons remove cancerous cells to protect healthy ones and thereby save the patient. It's a complex and delicate process, a combination of therapy and medication, and has to be conducted in a very controlled, clinical environment. Unfortunately, this particular patient absconded before his treatment was complete. We had managed to remove his old, damaged identity but had not yet reinstated a repaired version of it. Consequently there's a gap in his memory where his sense of self should be, and that's one of the reasons he's so dangerous. Identity is the foundation of the human psyche and his natural instincts will be driving him to try to remember who he is. He'll be feeling vulnerable and confused. He must be found as quickly as possible so I can finish his therapy before he regresses and does something both he and we will regret.'

Amand pictured Josef Engel's broken body lying on the floor of his atelier. 'We may already be too late.'

'I disagree. He has an implant in his arm that releases a controlled dose of antipsychotic drugs designed to suppress the centres of the brain that control his more extreme urges. He is currently incapable of experiencing any of the more vivid emotions that are linked to violence – anger, love, jealousy. At the moment he will be incapable of harming anyone.'

Amand nodded and remembered how Solomon had clutched at his shoulder from time to time. 'How long does this implant last?'

'Twenty-eight days.'

'And when did he escape from your facility?'

There was a pause. More background hiss. 'He's not dangerous, I assure y—'

'How long?'

Another pause. 'Twenty-five days. That's why we must find him quickly. When the meds start to wear off, he'll begin to remember who he is: *what* he is. That is when he will become dangerous, not only to himself but to anyone else around him.'

Amand thought of him now, walking the streets of his quiet little town, heading who knew where, capable of who knew what. 'What kind of toxic memories did you remove?'

A crackle of static cut through the office before Magellan could answer and Pierre's voice whispered through the radio instead.

– Vingt-sept to base.

Henri grabbed the dispatcher's mic and pressed the button to respond. 'This is base. What's up?'

– I'm at Marie-Claude's house. I rang the doorbell but no one answered so I came round the back and found the door wide open and the window broken.

Parra sat up in his chair, his eyes wide with alarm. 'That's it!' He looked up at Amand. 'That's what I've been trying to remember. Solomon Creed asked me if Josef Engel had any relatives.'

'Did you tell him?'

Parra shook his head. Confused. 'I can't remember. Maybe.'

– I'm going in to check it out, Pierre whispered.

'No,' Amand said, taking a step toward Henri and holding his hand up. 'Tell him to wait. I'll be there in five minutes.'

Henri raised the mic to speak but it was too late. They all heard it.

A shout cut short. A crunch like something heavy falling. Then the radio went dead.

IV

'There are but three parts to make up a man:
his shadow behind, the road ahead and the
clothes on his back.'

Traditional

Extract from

DARK MATERIAL – THE DEVIL'S TAILOR: DEATH AND LIFE IN DIE SCHNEIDER LAGER

⁜

By Herman Lansky

My journey to the Hell that was Die Schneider Lager began at Radogast train station a little after dawn on a clear, summer morning in August. It was light enough to see and early enough that the good citizens of Łódź were spared the sight of us marching to the station carrying the single suitcases we had each been allowed. We had no idea where we were going. Many people wore winter coats in case it ended up being somewhere cold.

We were herded together on the platform in front of a line of foul-smelling cattle cars that had been hosed down and disinfected with calcium chloride powder. A sludge of shit and piss and vomit was packed between the boards and in the corners and a single bucket stood by the door, grimed with the filth of those who'd travelled before us.

We were told to leave our luggage on the platform and that we would be reunited with it at our destination. Many people refused. They had concealed gold and jewels in their bags, portable wealth they'd hidden from the Germans. One woman close by me struggled with a guard as he tried to take her leather bag. She was matronly, and elegantly dressed with a long feather swooping away from an expensive-looking grey felt hat. A German officer came forward, drawn by the struggle. I thought he was going to scold the guard for being too rough with such an obviously respectable woman. Instead he drew his Luger and shot the woman through the head.

I still remember the pure shock of that moment, staring down at the lady's grey hat lying on the dusty platform with fresh, bright blood speckling the feather. We all gave up our suitcases after that. I doubt they even left Radogast station.

We were packed a hundred or more into stifling cars built to transport thirty cows. Those who had worn extra clothes now struggled to remove them and had to let them fall to the filthy floor, so scarce was the space available. But nobody complained. Everyone remembered that calm German officer and the blood-jewelled hat on the platform.

The train pulled out of Radogast station and I watched Łódź slip away through a small crack in the wooden wall of the carriage. The last time I had left there I had been in first class on my way to visit one of our larger stores in Warsaw, the morning paper in my hand and a fresh pot of coffee steaming on the table in front of me. This time I was standing and had barely enough air to breathe. Someone used the bucket before we'd even left the city, filling the car with the wet stench of shit and drawing indignant complaints from the rest of us. We had no idea that the bucket would overflow long before we reached our destination, or that, by the end, we would all be pissing and shitting where we stood, trying our hardest with the rocking of the train to get it on the floor instead of on ourselves or neighbours.

Four days we were on that train. Four days with no food, no rest and no water except for when we pulled into sidings and they occasionally sprayed the cars with fire hoses and we would crush each other in our desperation to catch whatever drops we could on our clothes and in open mouths. All we knew was that we were heading west, relentlessly west, through the Czech mountains, into Austria and Germany and across the border into France where we arrived at our destination as night fell.

Mulhouse is something of an orphan of a place, close to the Swiss–German border. It has been fought over and traded between Germany, Switzerland and France for centuries, like an unloved child in a messy divorce. As a result, it has that peculiar, mongrel quality many border towns possess, neither one thing or another, with a strange local dialect like stilted French with German inflections and words embedded in it. It is also a centre for cotton manufacture, which was why we had ended up there.

We were kept locked inside the cattle cars until dark, again to spare the good citizens of the town the unpleasant sight of us in all our ragged filth and squalor. Several people had died in our carriage on the journey and their bodies lay on the floor beneath our feet, spoiling fast in the trapped heat. Some of the people nearest the corpses were becoming hysterical, as if death was a virus that could be caught by proximity to it. Only when night had fallen were the doors finally unlocked.

We spilled out of those stinking carriages and lined

up alongside the railway tracks, breathing our first breaths of clean air while the corpses were carted away. A German officer stood on a flatbed railway carriage looking down on the spectacle of us. Even in my exhaustion and wretchedness I noticed how beautifully his uniform was cut. This was the first time I ever saw Standartenführer Artur Samler, the newly appointed commandant of the work camp designated as 'Mulhouse A' but which came to be known as Die Schneider Lager – The Tailors' Camp.

He was so elegant and civilized-looking that first time I saw him that I naively thought we were going to be all right, that perhaps this place would mark a new beginning away from the casual brutality we had experienced back in the Łódź ghetto. I didn't realize that Artur Samler would turn out to be the most evil and sadistic man I have ever encountered before or since.

Only now, looking back, do I realize that Samler was not a man at all. He was something else, something that looked human but had no soul. A devil in a beautifully cut uniform.

⁜

23

The thin tyres of Amand's old Citroën squealed and bumped down the narrow cobbled streets of Cordes, the underpowered engine whining in protest. Parra was in the passenger seat, bracing himself against the dashboard while Amand kept his foot down, going way too fast and not nearly fast enough. Marie-Claude lived on the far side of the hill, ten minutes' walk from the Commissariat but only two minutes' drive if you took the direct route and didn't bother with the brakes too much.

'Call Magellan back,' Amand shouted, leaning on the horn as they thundered through a large stone arch to warn anyone to get out of the way. Parra dialled the number and put his phone on loudspeaker and held it towards Amand.

'Tell me about Solomon Creed,' Amand said the moment Magellan answered.

'As I said before, I'd rather not go into detail.' Magellan's deep voice mingled with the high-pitched whine of the engine.

'Listen to me,' Amand said, trying to keep his voice calm. 'I'm driving to a house right now with an officer down and possibly a woman and a young boy inside. I have strong reason to believe that your patient may be involved.'

'As I said before his condition is controlled by . . .'

'The magic implant, except he's been missing for twenty-five days. How do you know he hasn't cut it out?'

'It's intra-muscular and implanted fairly deep. It's extremely unlikely he will have managed to remove it.'

'But not impossible?'

'No.'

'OK, let's say he has. What should we expect? What makes him so dangerous?'

They reached the top of the hill and the car lifted high on its suspension before bouncing heavily down as they entered the covered market square and flashed past the thick stone columns holding up the tiled roof. They rumbled past tables spilling out of cafés and on to the street and started to descend the other side of the hill.

'He's not ordinary. Quite the opposite, in fact. I have been working in the field of criminal psychology for over forty years, have had the chance to study some pure psychopaths, subjects so psychologically damaged they could barely be classed as human, and in all that time I have never come across anyone even remotely like him.'

Amand stamped on the brakes and threw the car to the right, sliding into a sharp turn past one of the old garrison towers, the wheels bouncing over uneven cobbles and struggling to grip. 'But why is he dangerous?' Amand shouted over the din of the engine. 'We're almost at the house.'

There was a pause and Amand wondered if they had been cut off, then Magellan's voice answered.

'The man you know as Solomon Creed is a high-functioning paranoid schizophrenic with a partially untreated underlying psychosis. He believes he is a fallen angel on a divine mission to save certain people's souls in order to ultimately save his own. This is not an entirely original delusion but with him it is convincing. His IQ is off the charts and his mind is so powerful that not only does he believe it, he can make others believe it too. He is single-minded in his belief and has proved to be ruthless in its execution. He can out-think you, out-manoeuvre you and he can kill as easily as breathing. That's why you should keep your distance and call in support. Do not approach him alone.'

'Duly noted,' Amand braked hard and threw the wheel to the left before stamping back on the accelerator to slide through the bend, hoping the road ahead was clear.

It wasn't.

A wall of shocked faces stared up at the screaming car, a coachload of tourists lumbering up the hill and filling the narrow street with their soft bodies.

Amand glanced right, past the Horloge with its display window of elegant clocks, to L'Escalier Pater Noster, a broad flight of shallow stone steps meant for pedestrians but thankfully empty. He threw the wheel to the right and stamped on the brakes. The Citroën slewed across the road, the sudden change of direction tipping it on two wheels for a teetering moment before righting itself again with a bang.

Amand fought the car, the tyres slipping and juddering over uneven cobbles. They hit the top of L'Escalier with a thump that almost ripped the steering wheel from his hands and sent a hubcap spinning away down the steps. The front of the car lifted then crashed down, sending sparks flying off the stone steps.

Amand tried to brake but the tyres were hardly touching anything as they bounced down the steps. He dropped a gear and the engine screamed. The road at the bottom of the steps drew closer. Amand hit the horn to warn anything or anyone coming up it. He tried to brake again but the wheels locked and the car started to slide sideways. He steered into it and prepared to make the turn, hoping to God there were no cars and equally aware of a solid stone wall on the opposite side of the road that was not going anywhere, no matter how much he leaned on the horn.

The dusty black road filled the windscreen and they hit it hard, knocking the air out of Amand and almost ripping the wheel from his hands. A front headlight shattered sending shards of plastic skittering across the road. He stamped on the brakes and threw the wheel to the right as the car bounced and his windscreen filled with pale stone wall.

He hit the accelerator, flooring it, feeding power to the wheels and feeling them slip as the wall slid closer. Dust and dirt and bits of broken plastic were thrown into the air. The tyres gripped and the car lurched forward and away from the wall. They fishtailed for a moment and the back end caught the wall with a loud bang before the car surged forward. A smell of burning rubber filled the car and a knocking sound was coming from where bent metal was catching the wheel, but Amand kept his foot down. He could see the street where Marie-Claude lived up ahead. The smell of rubber got worse but he made the turn and screeched to a halt outside Marie-Claude's house. He drew his gun for the third time that day, bundled out of his door and ran towards the passage, heading to the back of the house.

The passage was cold and dark after the glare of the morning sun and Amand blinked to adjust his eyes to the shadows. The tightness in his chest was building and his head felt as if a huge hand had seized his brain and started to squeeze. He heard Parra behind him and vague noises up ahead, the crackle of static, fragments of voices on a radio. He reached the corner and paused, long enough to take a breath and let Parra catch up, before crouching low and peering round the edge of the wall.

A leg lay half in and half out of the doorway, dark blue cotton tucked into a black boot. Police uniform. Amand moved past the edge of the wall, eyes wide and watching for movement. The radio continued to pop and crackle, Henri's voice calling for backup on the same emergency channel Pierre had been using when they'd lost contact. Amand reached the door and peered into the kitchen.

Pierre was lying on his back, blood forming a dark halo around his head, his radio on the floor by his hand with wires poking out of cracked plastic but still working. Amand listened through the crackle and squawk to the house beyond. It seemed silent and empty but that didn't mean it was. He got ready to move and something caught his eye. He jerked his gun down as Pierre's head lolled to the left slightly. He opened his eyes.

'Stay down,' Amand hissed.

Pierre raised his hand to his head and it came away bloody. 'Someone hit me.'

'Did you see who?'

'No.'

'Are Marie-Claude and Léo inside?'

'I don't know. I'm sorry.'

'Don't worry. There's an ambulance on its way.' He turned to Parra. 'Look after him and watch my back. I'll check inside.' He raised his gun and moved forward, past Pierre and into the house, listening through the noise of the radio and his hammering heart.

Keep your heartbeat steady, his doctor had told him. *Avoid stressful situations.*

He reached the kitchen door and looked across the hallway. The door to Léo's bedroom was half open, revealing paintings and posters of superheroes on the walls and a Marvel duvet bunched up on the bed in a way that looked like a sleeping child. Amand crouched low and ducked his head into the hallway. Glancing left and right before switching his attention forward again. He took a breath and surged across the hallway, kicking Léo's door open to catch anyone waiting on the other side. It hit the wall and bounced back. No one there. The room was empty, the duvet just a duvet.

Outside, a siren wailed closer and he spun round and moved down the hallway, checking Marie-Claude's bedroom first. There was no sign of Marie-Claude or Léo, but the room was messier than before, drawers emptied, clothes everywhere, the chair he had sat on earlier was lying on its side, the hessian webbing underneath sliced open and the mattress was crooked too, like someone had lifted it to look underneath before dropping it down again. He looked around for Marie-Claude's laptop. Couldn't see it. It had been here earlier, he remembered the image of the crying man on the screen.

Amand leaned against the wall and took deep breaths to try and calm down. He glanced over at the front door. The baseball bat was there but Marie-Claude's coat was missing and so were Léo's trainers. He took deep breaths, trying to focus and steady his heartbeat. The siren howled to a stop and cut out, blue lights flashing beyond the glazed panel by the front door. The pain in his head was like a slowly twisting knife now and he felt like there was a stone on his chest, weighing him down, making it difficult to breathe. He blinked as the edge of his vision began to blur.

He holstered his gun and started walking back towards the kitchen door, steadying himself against the wall. The door seemed like it was at the end of a tunnel and everything felt like it was moving away from him. He tried to breathe deep and slow, but the tightness in his chest made it impossible. He needed to let everyone know that Marie-Claude and Léo were missing: needed to tell people that they were in danger. If he could just reach the door at the end of the tunnel.

He took a breath to try and call out but no breath came and he felt panic rise up as he struggled for air. His heart hammered harder. The door moved away from him, further and further down the end of the long tunnel. Then the world tilted, and everything went black.

24

Léo had almost made it to the top of the hill in the centre
of town when Marie-Claude finally caught up with him. She
grabbed the back of the rucksack he'd snatched on his way
out the door and spun him round.

'What's got into you?' she said, pulling the rucksack off
his shoulder. 'This has got my laptop in it. You could have
dropped it.'

Léo looked past her and back down the hill. 'I had to
make sure . . . you'd follow,' he panted, trying to catch his
breath.

'Why?'

Léo stared down the road. 'The shadow. You were going
to let it in.'

Marie-Claude looked back down the road. 'Well, there's
nothing there now,' she said, struggling for breath herself.
She smiled and pulled him in for a hug to show that she
wasn't angry with him. If anything, she was worried. Léo
was usually such a cautious child, happier to hang around
at the edge of the playground and check everything out
before tentatively joining in, always on the tamest ride. She
couldn't ever remember him running with no shoes before,
not even on grass, let alone a hard road. She'd grabbed his

trainers as she ran after him but he'd never stopped running, barely even looked back. She knew how he felt. She felt like running too. Maybe that was what her grandfather had been doing all his life: running away from the shadows in his past. She looked over the red-tiled rooftops of Cordes to La Broderie. It was closer than home or the Commissariat. She pictured the canvas suit-carrier hanging on the back of her studio door. Maybe it was nothing. In which case, she should rule it out herself rather than waste police time with it. She picked Léo up, sat him on a wall and started brushing the dirt from his socks.

'Why don't you skip school today?' she said, and smiled at the relief that lit up Léo's face. 'I need to stop by work first, then maybe we'll pay Uncle Benny a visit. Would you like that?'

'Can we stay hidden?'

'What do you mean?' She fitted Spider-Man over his left foot and brushed dirt off his other sock.

'I mean, stay off the main road. Keep out of sight.' He looked back down the road they'd run up.

She wiggled the trainer on to his foot and closed the Velcro fastener. 'OK, if it makes you happy.' She lifted him down and took his hand. 'But no more running off, OK?'

'OK,' Léo said, dragging her away to the side of the road and down one of the shadowy walkways that honeycombed the ancient town of Cordes.

25

Belloq pulled the pay-as-you-go phone from his pocket, cleared his throat and dialled a number from memory. He was in the private dining room above the bar, looking out at the memorial square. He had hoped to have more information before calling the leadership but a journalist had already been in the bar asking if anyone had known Josef Engel and he couldn't let the party executive find out what had happened through the news channels. He listened to the purr of the phone and stared out at the part-built stage.

'Hello?' a female voice answered.

'This is Gaillac. I need to speak with the Leader . . . Yes, he's expecting my call.'

There was a click, a brief blast of a chanteuse singing about a France that no longer existed and probably never had, then a man's voice answered, old and dry. 'Yes?'

'The tailor is dead. He was murdered last night.'

A pause. 'What about the list?'

'We think someone may have been looking for it. We have a man on the inside, part of the police investigation. They have already apprehended a suspect.'

'Do you have his name?'

'Solomon Creed.' Belloq heard breathing and the faint sound of a pen on dry paper.

'It's possible one of our enemies hired him,' the Leader said. 'One of the major parties; the media maybe. I'll see what I can find out about him and pass on any useful information.'

'There's something else. The suspect has escaped from police custody.'

'Escaped!'

'Yes. We are endeavouring to locate him before the police so we might question him ourselves. The tailor's granddaughter and great-grandson have also gone missing. We are searching for them too. Maybe Monsieur Engel gave her the list before he died to assist her in this Jew history project she's doing.'

'No. Monsieur Engel would never have given it to her for that purpose.' There was a pause and Belloq listened to the dry rasp of the old man's breathing. 'However, he may have given it to her without telling her what it was. Find her, find this missing suspect too, but above all find the list. It is imperative it does not fall into the wrong hands.'

'Of course.' Belloq looked across at the Jewish memorial, all traces of graffiti now washed clean from it. 'May I ask – what is this list, exactly?'

'It's a dangerous link to our past and also to the party's origins. It could be disastrous to our cause if the wrong person got hold of it. Locate this missing suspect and Engel's granddaughter quickly, find out what they know, and deal with them. Do you understand? None of this can be allowed to come back to us, not with the election this close.'

'Yes.' Belloq sat down in one of the dining chairs, his body feeling suddenly heavy. 'The woman's son is also missing.

He's seven years old. If we do find her, chances are he will be with her too. Which means we may also have to . . .'

'I understand.' Belloq heard a sigh then the Leader spoke again, softer now. 'Never forget that we are at war here. Sometimes sacrifices must be made in order to secure victory for the greater good. When we are in power, we will have many battles to fight and we must be strong in our leadership if we wish to prevail. It is right that you are troubled by these difficult decisions, it does you credit as a man. But to lead you must look beyond such personal reservations and rise above the ordinary moral and emotional considerations. You must behave not like a man, but as a leader of men. Presidents, kings, emperors – they all face decisions like these, decisions they know will result in the deaths of others: men, women, even children. But it is the security of the many they are thinking of when they make such choices. The country is more important than any one life. Your country needs you to be strong, monsieur, resolute and unwavering. Your country needs you to lead. Can you do that?'

Belloq stared up at his own image, larger than life on the poster with the slogan beneath promising a brighter future and a new France. 'I can,' he said. 'I will find these people and discover what they know. We have someone loyal to the party and close to the missing woman who can help us find her. As for the police investigation, I have already taken steps to lead it in the wrong direction.'

'How?'

'By giving them another suspect.'

26

Madjid took a last look around the dusty hayloft he had called home for the past four years. Four years, and it had taken him less than ten minutes to pack. He had never expected to stay here this long, maybe enough time to prove his worth to the vineyard and be put on the payroll so he could afford a place of his own, but it had never happened. Payment had stayed on the black, cash in hand and subject to random fines and deductions for vague rules broken or displeasures incurred. Even so, he had stuck at it, like a losing gambler at the table, constantly hoping for his luck to change. And now it had in the most unexpected of ways.

This land is rotten – the stranger had said. And he was right.

Madjid pulled the drawstring tight on the canvas backpack he'd carried from Algeria, heaved it on to his back and shifted it until the weight felt comfortable across his shoulders. There was something frightening and exhilarating about embarking on a journey, something pure. He would head west, towards Bordeaux. Plenty of work there, particularly at this time of year. He could walk there in a couple of days, maybe sooner if he managed to catch a ride for some of the way. He stamped hard on the floor by way of a goodbye and watched the dust thicken the fingers of sunlight needling in through the gaps in the roof. No more baking here in the summer. No more freezing in the winter. He listened to the echo of the bang fade away. Then another sound replaced it: the sound of a car engine – some way off, but getting louder. He had wanted to be on the road before LePoux came back but it made no difference. There was nothing LePoux could do to stop him leaving. He did not own him.

Madjid creaked down the loose wooden stairs and stepped out into the sunlight and surveyed the land he had worked for the last four years. A dust cloud was rising above the gently nodding heads of sunflowers, the sound of it drowning out the whine of insects in the fields. It was a smooth sound, not the rattle and squeak of LePoux's battered old Renault. He watched the car emerge from behind the wall of thick sunflower stalks and felt the skin on his neck tighten when he saw what it was. The police car turned a half circle and pulled to a stop directly in front of him in a cloud of dust that forced Madjid to narrow his eyes.

'Monsieur Lellouche?' the driver said, getting out of the car.

'Yes.'

'Madjid Lellouche?'

The other gendarme got out and looked up at the barn. Madjid nodded. 'How can I help?'

'Step up to the car please, monsieur.'

Madjid did as asked. 'What is this about, please?'

'We need to take you in to the Commissariat and ask you some questions.' He pulled Madjid's arms behind his back and produced a set of handcuffs.

'What questions? Are you arresting me?' The officer snicked the cuffs over both wrists and nodded at the second officer, who started walking towards the barn.

'Wait,' Madjid shouted. 'You can't go in there. You need permission.'

'We have permission.'

Madjid watched the second officer disappear into the shadow of the barn. LePoux wouldn't like this, he had a low opinion of the law and generally did what he liked. He glanced over at the track, hoping he might see more dust and hear the rattle of the old Renault. LePoux would throw these men off his land if he found them here. He wondered where he was. Then it dawned on him what was happening. 'What did he tell you?' he said, turning back to the gendarme. 'What did LePoux say that made you come out here to arrest me?'

The officer glanced over at the barn as the second officer reappeared. He was wearing blue gloves and holding something in his hand, a thin length of vine cane that looked like it had been dipped in something dark and wet. He took a bag from his pocket, shook it out and put the stick inside before sealing it.

'This is wrong,' Madjid said, shaking his head. 'I don't know what that is. Whatever LePoux told you is lies.'

'We'll see about that,' the gendarme said, opening the rear door of the car and pushing Madjid inside. He threw his canvas bag in after him, packed and ready for a journey he was not going to take.

27

Marie-Claude stopped by the main road and felt Léo press against the back of her legs. La Broderie was directly in front of her, its roof almost level with the road and the main building below it, all that remained of a much bigger factory complex that had been the town's main industry until the Swiss then the Chinese started producing embroidered goods at a fraction of the cost.

Three cars were parked on the square of gravel where a loom shed had once stood: two belonged to people who lived close by and the other one was hers, an old Peugeot 205 that had been red before a couple of decades of summers bleached it salmon pink. She parked it here because she didn't use it much and the battery was old and often needed a bump start or a jump, which was easier to get here than at home. She looked at it sitting in the shade of a walnut tree, its windscreen speckled with aphid dew, one of the rear tyres looking slightly soft – something else she needed to fix but couldn't really afford. All the shutters in La Broderie were closed; it was too early for most of the artists, web-designers and other creative types who inhabited the building.

'Come on,' Marie-Claude said, grabbing Léo's hand and

heading across the road towards the front door of La Broderie, a huge rectangular slab of studded oak with a cartoon keyhole set beneath a cast-iron handle and a secondary, electronic keypad lock that was a nod to progress. The last person out each night was supposed to lock the deadbolt but no one ever did because the key was huge. Marie-Claude punched the security number into the keypad and pushed the door open to reveal the dark interior of the old factory. Inside it was quiet and still. She glanced behind her one last time then pushed Léo in and closed the door behind them.

Léo listened to the bang of the closing door echo away into the soft gloomy silence of the building.

He'd been here a few times before when he'd been dropped off by a friend's mother after a play date or directly from school, but each time his mama had met him at the front door and walked them straight home, or to Café Belloq for an ice cream or an Orangina. He had never set foot inside before and it felt like being let into some big grown-up secret. He followed his mama, keeping as close as he could without tripping her up. They were in a corridor of new-looking white walls with numbered doors and keypad locks. It looked like he imagined a prison would be like, and he wondered if this was like the one his papa had been in.

They reached a set of wooden stairs and his Spider-Man trainers squeaked on the steps as he followed his mama up them to the first floor. It seemed older up here, like they'd gone up the stairs and back in time. The walls were covered in dark wooden panelling and the doors set into them were old too with writing on them in faded gold paint – *M. Beq – Gérante*; *M. Bouyssié – Directeur Adjoint*. Black-and-white photographs lined the corridor showing men in shirts and waistcoats with big moustaches, and women with their hair piled high on top of their heads, standing by complicated-looking machines. They seemed to be staring out of the pictures and directly at Léo. He didn't like it. He didn't like being on this floor. It was dark and old and empty and he felt as if the shadows were getting thicker, making it harder for him to breathe. He felt like he might drown in this darkness and he hurried after his mother, eager to escape the gaze of these long-dead workers – and bumped right into her.

She had stopped in the middle of the corridor and was staring straight ahead. Léo could feel tension coming off her and saw that her colours were getting darker, which meant she was scared and this made him feel scared too. He peered around her legs to see what she was looking at. The corridor ahead was as gloomy as the rest of the floor, the shuttered window at the end of the hallway allowing little light inside. There were three doors ahead of them, exactly the same as all the other doors. Only one of them was open.

Léo felt a hand on the top of his head and looked up at his mama. She placed a finger to her lips and he nodded. There was no way he was going to make any noise. He wanted to grab her hand and drag her out of this murky building and back into the sunlight. But she was already moving towards the open door, and all he could do was follow. She stopped short, listened again, then moved forward, pushing the door wide open to reveal the room beyond.

The office was smaller than Léo had expected, about the same size as his own bedroom and almost as messy. A dark window filled the far wall, the closed shutters warped slightly and letting in enough light for him to see the tall piles of paperwork on the floor and all around the desk. But it was the walls that drew his attention. They were covered with tiny writing, every surface filled with words that surrounded black-and-white photographs of thin, hollow-eyed people. There was a map of France too that he recognized from school and a piece of paper in the centre of the main wall with thin cotton threads coming out of it like a spiderweb and connecting to different parts of the walls. The paper had some names written on it in bigger letters and Grampy's was one of them. He didn't get a chance to read the others because his mama stepped through the door and started to close it behind her and fear exploded in Léo's chest.

He moved forward, holding his arms out to stop the door from closing, but it opened again as fast as it had closed and his mama reappeared holding something big and white in her hands. She pulled a coat hanger from inside and shook it out.

'Empty!' she said, her colours swirling in confusion. She turned it inside out and shook it again and Léo saw it was one of the canvas carriers Grampy used to protect the suits he made. 'Totally empty.' Léo saw sadness flash across her face. Then she looked up and past him and her eyes went wide, and her colours flashed red, and Léo knew that something awful was standing in the corridor right behind him.

28

Léo leaped away from the unknown horror and hid behind his mother's legs.

'Who are you?' she said, her voice coming out stretched and shrill and all the wrong colour.

Léo clung to her legs and thought of the shadow by the front door of their house and the hollow-eyed people in the photographs. He didn't want to look and see what was there but he had to. He *had* to. He opened his eyes and looked up.

The man in the corridor was tall and thin and his hair and skin were as pale as the unbuttoned waistcoat he was wearing. He held a suit jacket in his hand, pale like the waistcoat but worn with age. But it was his colours that made Léo stare. They were white, as white as Léo's were, and his eyes went wide as he realized who he must be.

'I know you,' he said, the words tumbling from his mouth before he knew he was speaking. The man looked at him and Léo felt the full weight of his dark gaze.

'Who am I?' the man said, his voice soft and low like a stone rolling across floorboards.

'You're the man who saved Grampy from the bad camp.' He searched his memory for the strange name Grampy had whispered to him the one time he had talked about it. 'You're Solomon Creed.'

The man smiled making his colours seem brighter and Léo's mama turned to him, confusion creasing her face. 'You know this man?'

'Grampy told me a pale man came to the bad camp, right at the end, and saved him and his friends. They made him a suit, Grampy and the others, to thank him for saving them.' He looked back at Solomon. 'He said you would come to collect it one day.'

Solomon's eyes bored into Léo, like he was staring right through him. 'What's your name?' he asked.

'Léonardo. But everyone calls me Léo.'

The man closed his eyes and grabbed his shoulder as if a wasp had stung him and his whiteness shimmered with different colours – reds and purples and blues. 'Léonardo Engel,' he gasped.

'Yes,' Léo nodded, amazed that he knew his name.

Solomon gripped his arm tighter and his colours went golden and white. Then the shimmering stopped and he opened his eyes again. 'You are the reason I've come here,' he said. 'I'm here to save you.'

'What?' His mama took a step forward, putting herself between Léo and Solomon like he was in danger. 'Save him from what?'

'I don't know,' Solomon said. 'From whoever killed your grandfather perhaps.' He turned back to Léo. 'What else did he tell you about me, about the suit?'

'He said they shared the suit out. *They kept the suit and the suit kept them* – that's what he told me.' He looked up at Solomon. 'Only it didn't, did it? It didn't keep him safe. Because Grampy's dead. You didn't save him.'

'Léo,' his mama dropped down to his level. 'You're confused, *chéri*. This gentleman is far too young to have known Grampy in the war. That was a long, long time ago.' She looked up at Solomon. 'I don't know what Monsieur is doing here, or why he broke into my office and took something that didn't belong to him.' She held up the suit-carrier. 'That waistcoat you're wearing was in here, wasn't it?' Solomon didn't answer. 'It's mine and I would like it back – please.'

Solomon tipped his head to one side, looking at Léo. 'What was the name you called me?'

'Solomon Creed,' Léo replied.

He nodded and held the waistcoat open to reveal the lining – pale ivory with black stripes woven through it, some thick, some thin – and a maker's label saying:

Ce costume a été fait au trésor pour M. Solomon Creed.

This suit was made to treasure for Mr Solomon Creed.

Léo looked up at his mama, expecting her to be as amazed as he was by this revelation. 'That doesn't prove it's yours,' she said. 'My grandfather made lots of suits for lots of people.'

'But this one fits *me*,' Solomon said opening his arms wide to show how well the waistcoat clung to his slender frame. 'It also matches this.' He slid his arms into the jacket, tugged the sides down to straighten it and opened the left flap, revealing another label identical to the one in the waistcoat – same wording, same name.

'How do I know that jacket wasn't also in the suit-carrier?'

Solomon buttoned the waistcoat. 'Does it look like it was?' The jacket looked dusty and worn and had dark marks on the arms and shoulders like faded burn marks. By contrast the waistcoat was immaculate. 'I promise the only thing I found in the carrier was the waistcoat – and this.' He reached into his jacket pocket, pulled out a small envelope and handed it to Marie-Claude.

Marie-Claude stared at her name, written on the envelope in Grampy's elegant, looping handwriting along with the words:

Only to be read in the event of my death.

She felt something cold and heavy settle on her heart as she realized that her guilty suspicions had been correct. Her grandfather had genuinely been worried about her research bringing danger to their door. And he had been right.

She swallowed the lump that had formed in her throat, opened the envelope and began to read:

My dearest granddaughter,

I know how much you wish to know about my time in the camp, that you feel your own identity is somehow connected to it. Please believe me when I tell you that it is not. You are your own person, a wonderful and strong woman and mother. My past is mine, not yours, and trust me when I say that learning it will only bring you sadness. My continued silence on this subject has always been for your protection and for the protection of others. And it is for the sake of others that I ask you to take this waistcoat to my old friend Otto Adelstein at this address:

Le Métier,
Myosotis-La-Fleur
21000

Do not trust this task to anyone else. You must deliver it yourself. Please tell Otto the pale man did not return to claim

it but he should keep it safe in case he ever does. Ask Otto your
questions too, if you must, though I doubt he will remember much.
I envy him that.

Your generation seems to believe that all knowledge is good and
truth is more valuable than gold. Maybe this is why we fought
the war, so that our children and grandchildren could enjoy the
luxury of such thoughts. Those of us who grew up in the war know
different. We know that knowledge is sometimes a curse. And you
can never unlearn something once it is known.

Your ever-loving Grampy,
Josef

'May I see?' Solomon asked.

She handed the note over, her heart beating fast in a confusion of sadness and fear, and watched him read it, seeing him afresh now she had read her grandfather's words. He couldn't be the man mentioned in the note, the man Grampy had spoken to Léo about, it wasn't possible. But the suit did fit him. And here he was.

'We should go,' Solomon said, handing back the note and tipping his head to one side as if listening to something.

'Go where?'

'Dijon – 21000 is the postcode for a place called Quevillon, close to Dijon. A nine-hour drive, give or take. I assume you have a car?'

'Yes, but – what on earth makes you think I'm going to drive you to Dijon?'

'Because it would appear from your grandfather's note that our pasts are somehow intertwined. You want to learn about where you come from and so do I. I'm also wearing the waistcoat your grandfather told you to take to Monsieur

Adelstein and I'm not going to take it off. Plus, I have a very strong feeling that I'm here to save your son from something, which means we need to stick together.'

Marie-Claude looked down at the note, her brain trying to process it all – *the pale man . . . my old friend . . . ask Otto your questions if you must . . .*

'I know it's hard to believe that your grandfather made this suit for me,' Solomon said. 'I'm struggling with it myself. And if he was still alive we could ask him about it, but he's not, and this Monsieur Adelstein is. So I need to find him and talk to him, and you do too.' He cocked his head to the side again and this time she heard the sirens too. 'But we need to go right now, if we're going.'

Marie-Claude stared at him and was struck by the cold realization of who he was. 'Amand said they had a suspect in custody. It was you.'

Solomon shrugged. 'Wrong place at the wrong time.'

Marie-Claude started backing away and put her hand on Léo's shoulder as she realized the dangerous situation she had put them both in.

Solomon stayed where he was in the corridor. 'I know how this all appears,' he said. 'And if you wish to run from this building and into police protection I will neither stop you nor blame you. I came here seeking your grandfather because of this label in my jacket. I believe I am here to save your son. I can't explain how I know this, or how your grandfather appears to have made me a suit when I have no memory of ever meeting him, but what I do know is that if I stay here the police will most probably lock me up for a long time.'

'Then why don't you run?' Marie-Claude said.

Solomon clutched at his shoulder. 'I can't.'

'Why not?'

'Because if I run, I won't be able to protect your son.'

Outside, the sirens grew louder, but she knew the streets: they were still a good few minutes away. 'But if you stay you'll get arrested.'

Solomon shrugged. 'I suppose I'll have to figure out how I might save your son from inside a prison cell.'

She stared at him and knew he was serious and felt strangely touched that this stranger seemed willing to risk his freedom for the sake of her son.

'I think we should trust him,' Léo said, stepping out from behind her. Marie-Claude looked down at his serious little face. 'Grampy trusted him and the suit he made fits him, so . . .'

Marie-Claude looked at Solomon, the waistcoat and jacket like a second skin on his slender body. The sirens grew louder and she thought of her grandfather's note:

. . . take this waistcoat to my old friend Otto Adelstein . . .

Do not trust this task to anyone else. You must deliver it yourself.

She had ignored his warnings before, not taken them seriously enough, and he had died as a result. And despite all her instincts to run she wasn't going to make that same mistake again, no matter how crazy it seemed.

'Follow me,' she said, hurrying past Solomon and heading for the stairs. 'There's a back way into the building. I'll get my car and bring it round. That way no one will see us leaving.'

V

'Yellow is a light which has been dampened by darkness; blue is a darkness weakened by light.'

Goethe

Extract from

DARK MATERIAL – THE DEVIL'S TAILOR: DEATH
AND LIFE IN DIE SCHNEIDER LAGER

❖

By Herman Lansky

They marched us out of the Mulhouse railroad sidings and into the forest. I thought they were going to execute us but I was already half-dead from the journey and didn't care. It would have been a relief. Night fell as we marched and I remember feeling profoundly sad that I would never see the sun again.

We walked for maybe an hour until we came across a semi-derelict factory complex on the edge of the woods and close to a main road. It had no fences, no guard towers, no accommodation blocks or any of the facilities required to house the six thousand prisoners earmarked for transportation there within the month. Yet this was to be Die Schneider Lager, and it was our job to build it before everyone else arrived.

We slept on the factory floor that first night, huddled together around textile machinery so old my family's factories had scrapped them when I was a boy. It was cold that night and the concrete floor was hard, but we were free from the horror of the train and we all slept for the first time in days. Such a deep sleep. So deep that some never woke up.

In the morning, we were taken out to a large over-grown field beyond the main factory building and ordered to clear it and put up old army tents left over from the Great War to serve as temporary dormitories until we had built permanent accommodation blocks. We were tailors and seamstresses, shopkeepers and mothers, we barely knew how to put the tents up, let alone construct buildings of brick and wood.

I remember that first day, struggling with the old and broken tools we had been given, exhausted from the train journey and the heat of the summer sun. It took everything I had just to stay standing, but I did. I stood and I worked. I had to. Anyone who faltered or fell to the ground was shot and dragged into the forest where a fire burned, sending greasy smoke drifting across the field. The message was clear: you work, you survive; you don't work, you die. It should have been written above the camp gates as a warning to all the thousands who came there.

Die Schneider Lager had not been set up as a death camp, but that is what it became. The records show that it only had enough allocated rations to adequately feed three thousand prisoners a month, and there were already double that before the camp had officially opened. With no guarantees that these already inadequate supplies would be maintained, Artur Samler decided to abandon any hope of improving the situation; rather than request more food supplies, he asked for more prisoners.

Less than a month after the first transportation of six thousand, two thousand more Jews arrived from Poland, another thousand from Germany, a thousand from France. The chronic overcrowding helped nurture and spread disease; typhus and cholera were as much a part of camp life as the random executions. And so it went on: the population grew, disease and starvation worsened, the population reduced again. Expansion followed by contraction, like the camp was some hellish organism, breathing in life and breathing out death.

To the Nazi High Command, Artur Samler was a hero and Die Schneider Lager a great success, providing an efficient solution to the twin problems of cheap manufacture and management of the Jewish population. It was the first of the Nazi camps to use a crematorium to dispose of the dead, and in a horrible twist of ingenuity, Samler had his engineers run water pipes through the furnaces and used the heat to create steam to drive the ancient looms in the factory. We called the cloth we made on those looms *Tkaniny śmierć* – Death Cloth. Some believed the spirits of the dead were woven into it, and in the damp shivering darkness of the accommodation blocks we had built, where we were packed in so tight it was impossible to see where one person ended and another began, we would pray to God that the souls of the dead would curse the cloth, and that all the soldiers, airmen and seamen who wore the uniforms made from it would know only defeat and death and the cloth would be soaked in the blood of the enemy. But as more Jews arrived and the crematorium fires continued to burn, it seemed God was not listening. The factory roared on, powered by the burning dead, operated by the damned, and policed by demons in human form.

And in the midst of this hell, Samler thrived. For as long as the uniforms kept rolling out and Jews kept pouring in through the gates, no one interfered and no one asked questions. He was a king in his own domain, killing and mutilating whomever he wanted, raping and brutalizing whomever caught his eye, feared by the prisoners and his own men alike. If Die Schneider Lager was Hell, then Samler was the Devil. And Death was his to command.

29

Amand woke to a sharp burn of ammonia at the back of his throat. He twisted away. Tried to get up.

'Whoa there.' A strong hand held him down. He squinted up into the concerned face of François Verbier, his friend and also his doctor. Then he remembered where he was and why he was here and tried to get up again, which made his head feel like he'd been hit with an axe. He lay back down. Took a breath. 'How long have I been out?'

'About five minutes. Parra called me.'

'How's Pierre – have you checked him over?'

'SAMU got here just before me. They say he doesn't have a concussion so he's probably OK, though he'll need to go to Albi for further tests.'

'What about Marie-Claude and Léo?'

'We're still looking,' a new voice answered. Amand glanced over at Parra, standing by the kitchen door. He could hear the squawk of an emergency radio and murmur of voices behind him. 'Have you checked Léo's school? The Commissariat?'

'He's not at school and they're not at the Commissariat either.'

Amand raised himself up slowly and leaned on one elbow. 'She's got an office at La Broderie, check there too. And put an alert out on her car, it's an old Peugeot – a 205, I think, red but faded-looking. Get Henri to pull the registration.'

'I'm on it.' Parra walked into the kitchen, already dialling a number.

Verbier pressed a finger into Amand's neck. 'How many tablets have you taken today?'

Amand shook his head and something sharp and jagged seemed to roll around inside his skull. 'I don't know – a couple.'

'A couple, like "two"? Or a couple, like "more than two"?'

'Two.'

Verbier checked his watch. 'Not yet eleven and you've already popped two pills.'

'I've had a bit of a morning.'

Verbier nodded. 'I saw your car. Looks like bears have been humping on it.' He glanced at the kitchen door and lowered his voice. 'You can't be running round like this, raising your blood pressure and chewing pills to bring it down again. It puts too much strain on your heart. Keep it up and I'll sign you off work and tell everyone why.'

'Don't.' Amand sat upright and the room swam a little but the jagged thing in his head stayed put.

'I'll have to. I'm your doctor first and your friend second. The only reason I agreed to keep your condition quiet was because you assured me you'd be better off staying active and you *promised* to take things easy. This is not taking things easy.'

'Josef Engel is dead – he was murdered.'

'I know.'

'Pierre was attacked, in this house, and Marie-Claude and Léo are now missing.'

'I know all of this, Parra briefed me when he called to tell me you'd blacked out.'

Amand frowned. 'How come he called you?'

'Because I asked him to. I told him your blood pressure was a little high and I'd put you on some mild meds to manage it, but that he should call me immediately if you became unwell for any reason. Listen, Ben, I'm telling you this as your friend more than your doctor. You need to let someone else take over this investigation.'

'No.'

'I know how you feel about Marie-Claude, and I understand why you might feel more responsibility towards her and Léo than to most, but that is exactly why you should step aside. Your personal feelings, your history with this family, all of it is going to cloud your judgement and potentially compromise not only your health but also the investigation.'

'It won't. I'm quite capable of separating personal feelings from professional duty.'

'Really? Try telling that to your car.' Verbier screwed the cap back on the smelling salts and slipped the bottle into his pocket. 'You can still be part of the investigation, but on a level that is more conducive to your health. No more car chases. No more running about. You can't piss around with cardiomyopathy. Too much strain and you'll need more than smelling salts to wake you up again. You may not wake up at all.'

Amand nodded. 'OK. As soon as Marie-Claude and Léo turn up safe and sound, I'll step aside. I promise.'

Parra reappeared at the door, holding his hand over his phone. 'Henri's putting the details of Marie-Claude's car on the wire now and dispatching someone to check out La Broderie. He also said to tell you we have a suspect in custody.'

'Solomon Creed?'

'No. Someone new. A migrant worker from one of the vineyards.'

'OK, tell Henri we're on our way.' Amand stumbled to his feet and reached out a hand to steady himself against the wall.

'Step away from this or I'll make you,' Verbier murmured. 'I'm serious.'

'I know you are,' Amand said. 'No more car chases, I promise. I'll even sit down while interviewing this new suspect and get someone else to beat him up if he doesn't cooperate. How's that sound?'

30

He listened to the drama unfolding on the police scanner as he drove away from Cordes, sweating heavily despite the chilled air blowing out of the vents. He should never have taken such a risk, going into the house that way. It had been reckless and undisciplined and when the officer had returned sooner than anticipated, had so nearly ended in disaster.

He was tired after the long night, not thinking straight, his head throbbing with the thing growing inside it. He opened the glove compartment and rummaged through pill bottles until he found the one he needed and fumbled at the cap, desperate for the relief inside. He glanced down for a moment and a long blast on a horn made him look up again. A large truck had appeared round the corner, lights flashing and an angry driver. He yanked the steering wheel, dragging the car back to the right side of the road and his wheels caught loose dirt on the verge and the car shimmied and slipped as the truck roared past in a long mournful wail. This was no good. He was panicking. Losing control. He needed to calm down. He needed to *think*.

He spotted a gravelled lay-by up ahead by an ivy-clad water tower, slowed down and eased the car to a halt by a row of bins. He left the engine running to keep the air cold and pressed a button to open the boot so it would look like he was dumping trash. He needed to stop anyway to stay in range of the local police scanner frequencies. There were things he could learn by staying close, like the name of the new suspect, or a fresh lead on the old suspect who was still missing. But first he had to get rid of the pain exploding through the centre of his head.

He unscrewed the lid of the pill bottle, tipped a pale green tablet into his hand and swallowed it dry. He closed his eyes and listened to the scanner for a while, feeling the cold air chill his damp skin.

A car drove past and he opened his eyes and watched it moving away across the vine-covered hills. A short-toed eagle swooped down from a power line and landed on the edge of the road, its pale feathers ruffling in the breeze. It hopped forward and started to peck at what looked like a length of rope. He realized what it was and smiled. Eagles were good omens and the sight of this *Jean-de-blanc* tearing at the flesh of a dead snake cheered him. It was a physical manifestation of good triumphing over evil and it reminded him of his greater purpose.

The scanner squawked as a unit headed over to La Broderie to check out the Engel unit. The police were wasting their time. He knew because he'd already searched it. He had learned about it from his background research on Josef Engel and broken in the night before his visit to Monsieur Engel. He liked the idea that Engel might suffer more, believing that his silence was protecting the low filth he called his friends, only to discover at the death that he had suffered for nothing because the list had already been found. But in the end, all he had found in the storeroom were old invoices and moth-balled clothes, the same things the police were about to find. The key to locating the list was the granddaughter, he felt sure of it. She had to know something, why else would she go missing so suddenly in the shadow of her grandfather's death?

The scanner squawked again.

– Commandant Amand. Come in. Over.

– This is Amand.

– We're at La Broderie now but we can't work out which unit belongs to Marie-Claude, her name isn't on the floor plan. Over.

He jerked forward in the car seat and the pain in his head expanded again. He had not known Engel's granddaughter had a unit there too.

– It's on the first floor. She sublets off some web-design company called WebWeaver or something. It's the last door on the right at the end of the corridor. Over.

– OK, got it. Stand by.

What an idiot he had been. He could easily have broken into her unit and searched that too and the list could well have been his now.

– Looks like someone's been here. The door's wide open. There's no sign of a struggle and there's some computer gear in here, which rules out a burglary. If she did come by here she must have been in and out fast. She didn't even close the door behind her.

In and out. And why was that? Because she was after something specific, something small and portable and easy to collect – something exactly like the thing he had wasted hours looking for the day before in the wrong place.

– Is her car there? Over.

– Negative.

– OK, thanks. Secure the room and ask around in case anyone's seen her. Out.

The radio clicked and he looked up to see the great wings

of the eagle spread and flap and lift the bird into the air, his good omen deserting him.

– Henri, this is Amand. Put out the details on Marie-Claude's car again. Looks like she's in it and we need to find her, fast. Out.

He watched the eagle gyre up into the air in a lazy circle around the bloody meal it had abandoned on the road below and heard the sound of a car approaching from behind.

– All units, all units.

The scanner crackled again through the hiss of the air-conditioner.

– Please be advised to be on the alert for missing vehicle registration 585 ADP 81. Vehicle is a 2001, red model Peugeot 205, owned by one Marie-Claude Engel. Urgently sought in connection with a homicide. Over.

He put his car in gear and waited for the approaching car to pass. He needed to move before he was spotted by one of the units now looking for the missing girl.

Up in the blue summer sky the eagle waited too, eager to return to its meal, just a hungry bird, not an omen at all. Then the car drove past and he realized he was wrong. The eagle *was* an omen, an augur of change and fortune. He stared after the faded red Peugeot – registration *585 ADP 81* – a young woman driving, a small boy with glasses sitting in the back next to a pale man dressed in a white suit and waistcoat. Then he put his car in gear and eased back on to the road, flattening the head of the dead viperine snake with a gentle bump as he drove over it.

31

Solomon remained hidden from view until they were clear of town then sat up, wound down the window and sucked in deep lungfuls of warm air like a swimmer breaking surface after a long dive. The car smelled fusty and vinegary and it all added to his general feeling of nausea.

'You OK, back there?' Marie-Claude glanced at Solomon in her rear-view mirror.

'I don't like being in cars.'

'Well, that's a shame because you're going to be in this one for the rest of the day. Here,' she tossed her phone into the back seat, along with the note from her grandfather. 'Put Monsieur Adelstein's address into Google Maps to see exactly how far it is. And see if you can find a number so I can try calling him.'

Solomon glanced down at the phone, felt nausea ripple through him and looked out of the window again, recalling the address in Dijon and studying the map that appeared in his head. 'It's six hundred and twenty-eight kilometres away,' he said, plucking pieces of information from the torrent of facts now tumbling through his mind. 'Around seven hours' drive, depending on which route we take and how many times we stop.' He concentrated for a moment and shook his head. 'And there isn't a phone number for Otto Adelstein at that address. There is a number, but not for him specifically.'

Marie-Claude studied Solomon in the mirror. 'You haven't even looked.'

'I don't need to. I have a peculiar mind, full of information, most of it useless, sometimes not.'

She frowned. 'And knowing a phone number at some random address in Dijon is one of those things?'

'Yes.'

She shook her head in disbelief. 'Léo, you look it up, but make sure you hold the phone up or else you'll barf.'

Léo took the note and the phone and held them above his head while he copied the name and address into Google.

'What's it say?' Marie-Claude asked. 'Is Monsieur Adelstein listed?'

'No.'

She glanced at Solomon. 'OK delete the name and try the address on its own.'

Léo's little fingers tapped the screen again, his face tight with concentration. 'I got a number.'

'Great. Hand me the phone back, *chéri*, I'm going to call Monsieur Adelstein, tell him who we are and that we're coming to see him.'

'The number is for a private residential facility,' Solomon said. 'I doubt they'll confirm Otto Adelstein is even living there.'

Marie-Claude took the phone, dialled the number and put it on speakerphone. It rang twice then a stern-sounding woman answered.

'Myosotis-La-Fleur, can I help you?'

'Yes, I'm hoping you can. I'm trying to get in touch with

a Monsieur Otto Adelstein. Do you have someone by that name staying with you?'

'I'm sorry, I can't give out any information about residents.'

'Not even to confirm if they're resident or not?'

'I can't give out any information, I'm sorry. This is a strictly private facility. If you wish to contact a resident, you can leave your name and number and somebody will call you back.'

Solomon waved to catch Marie-Claude's attention, shook his head and placed a finger on his lips.

'Oh wait,' Marie-Claude said, 'I'm about to go into a tunnel. I'll have to call you back.' She hung up and looked at Solomon. 'You knew that would happen. How did you know?'

'Educated guess.'

She continued to look at him, her forehead creased into a frown. 'OK, what do we do now?'

'We drive to Dijon.'

'But what's the point? If they won't tell me anything over the phone, they're hardly going to let us talk to him if we just show up at the door.'

'It's a private facility.'

'So?'

'So there will be fences to climb and locks to pick. You get us there, I'll get us in. There's a left turn about a kilometre ahead. Take it.'

Marie-Claude's frown deepened. 'That road takes us south. Dijon is north.'

'We're not heading to Dijon,' Solomon replied, 'not directly.'

'Then where *are* we going?'

'Toulouse.' Solomon settled back in his seat and closed his eyes.

The car swerved suddenly and they crunched to an abrupt

halt on one of the tracks leading into the vineyards. A cloud of fine grit filtered in through Solomon's open window and a black car drove past, blowing in more. Marie-Claude twisted around in the driver's seat.

'Toulouse!? Why the hell are we going to Toulouse? Just so you're absolutely clear, I'm already having serious regrets about being in a car with you and my seven-year-old son and I've half a mind to throw you out right here and call the police on my way back to town. The only reason I'm not is because Léo trusts you and he's generally a much better judge of character than me, and because my grandfather asked me to take that waistcoat you're wearing to an old friend of his, which is a crazy thing to do in the circumstances, but I feel like I owe him that much and I should probably have my head examined for all of it, and if I could leave Léo with someone, anyone, I would, but I can't, so don't give me any bullshit. Tell me, right now, why we're going to Toulouse and not Dijon.'

Solomon looked at Léo, strapped into a booster seat beside him, a nest of superhero comics scattered in the footwell below his seat. 'I like your mama,' he said.

'Me too,' Léo said.

'I like that she swears in front of you.'

'She does that all the time.'

'I do not.'

Léo leaned in closer. 'Mostly it's when she thinks I'm not listening. Mama swears a *lot*.'

'Well, Mama has a lot to swear about. You should be grateful I don't beat you too.' She glared at Solomon. 'And stop trying to change the subject.'

Solomon looked in her eyes and saw the fire inside her, burning with the intensity of a protective mother and a grieving granddaughter. It made her look fierce and beautiful. 'We're going to Toulouse because we need to switch cars,' he said. 'Yours will be registered in your name and I imagine they'll ramp up the search for you pretty soon. So if we want to stand any chance of getting to Dijon without being stopped, we need to swap this car for one that has no ties to you and is less distinctive – hopefully one that's also a tiny bit less fragrant. The turn up ahead will take us to Toulouse by the back roads and we need to stay off the péage for now because there are cameras at the toll booths linked to registration recognition software. Unless you want to get pulled over and spend the next few hours explaining exactly why you were driving away from Cordes with me in the back, I suggest you put the car in gear, and drive.'

Marie-Claude held his gaze for a long few seconds. 'I could say you kidnapped me.'

'You could, but I'd deny it because it's not true, and you'd be bogged down in witness statements. You would also be making it much harder for me to protect your son. So drive if you're going to, or call the police if you've changed your mind. I wouldn't blame you at all if you have. But I hope you haven't.'

Marie-Claude looked over at Léo. Solomon could see she was weighing things up, having an internal debate about whether to dump him by the side of the road or not.

'I think we should throw him out and call the cops,' Léo said, his face creased in seriousness.

'Really?'

Léo's face exploded into a smile. 'Only kidding. I say we go to Dijon and find this friend of Grampy's. I'd like to ask him about the bad camp and I figure if we have Monsieur

Creed with us wearing his waistcoat, he might not mind talking about it.'

Marie-Claude shook her head slowly and softened. 'Well, aren't you your mother's son?' She looked back at Solomon and stiffened again. 'Don't get too comfortable, it's a long way to Dijon.' She faced front and forced the car back in gear. 'And my car smells fine.'

32

Amand's battered Citroën limped back to the Commissariat, something loose knocking against a wheel every time they turned a corner. Verbier glared at Amand each time it happened as if to say, *This is what you're doing to your body*, and Amand did his best to ignore him. They rattled to a halt outside the Commissariat and Verbier leaned in.

'Don't forget what I said. Slow down or I'll slam the brakes on for you.'

Amand nodded. 'Understood.' He opened the bent car door with a screech of metal against metal and something fell off the front and shattered on the cobbles when he slammed it shut again.

'What was that about?' Parra murmured as they entered the Commissariat.

'Nothing,' Amand replied, pushing through the door to the main office.

The room was noisy with ringing phones and conversations between people in uniform that Amand mostly didn't recognize. Henri stood in the centre of it all, phone clamped to his ear, frown on his face.

'Where's the new suspect?' Amand asked him.

Henri covered the mouthpiece with his hand. 'Down in the cells.'

'Anyone talked to him yet?'

Henri shook his head and held up a booking sheet. 'Only just signed him in.'

'What about the potential weapon they found?'

'It's on your desk in a bag.'

Amand frowned. 'You didn't send it over to the PS lab at Albi?'

'Figured you might want to see it before the Police Scientifique got their hands on it.'

Amand was annoyed that it hadn't been fast-tracked but Henri was up to his ears so he let it slide and headed to his office instead, closing the door behind him to muffle the din of the outer office.

The evidence bag lay on his desk in a nest of Post-it notes. Inside was one of the bamboo poles the *vignerons* used to support younger vines, about a metre long and as thick as a man's finger. It was splintered and bent, and a dark, sticky, reddish brown substance covered half of it. Amand pictured the straight wounds he had seen on Josef Engel's back and frowned. He picked up his desk phone, pushed a button to speed-dial a number and scanned the Post-it notes on his desk. The phone connected.

'Could you connect me to Doctor Zimbaldi please, coroner's office . . . I'm calling about a homicide victim currently being processed.'

He was placed on hold and a scratchy Debussy recording filled the silence. The Post-its were filled with the names of people to call back and numbers to ring – none of them were Marie-Claude.

The Debussy cut out and a woman answered. 'Zimbaldi?'

'Doctor Zimbaldi, this is Benoît Amand from the Commissariat de Cordes. I know you're in the process of examining the body of Josef Engel, but there has been a development. We found a cane with blood on it. I'm sending it over now for analysis, but I'm also about to interview the suspect whose home we found it in and it would be useful to know if, in your opinion, a bamboo cane might have been the weapon, one of the weapons, used on the victim?'

'Monsieur Amand, I have barely even begun my examination, so I can hardly . . .'

'The cane is about the thickness of a man's index finger, maybe a centimetre and a half in diameter. Your opinion might give me some leverage in the interview.' There was a pause. Amand imagined her looking down at the battered and bloody corpse of Josef Engel on an examination table, studying his wounds. The thought made him shudder.

'That sounds too thick for the lash wounds I'm seeing,' Doctor Zimbaldi said.

Amand nodded. 'That's what I thought too.'

'That's only an observation. I'd need to properly measure . . .'

'Of course. I'll get the cane sent over right away. Let me know what you think when you've had time to consider it. Any information gratefully received, as and when you have it. You can always get hold of me here. Thank you, Madame Doctor.'

Amand hung up, grabbed the evidence bag and headed into the noise of the outer office.

'I need this to go to Albi right away,' he said, dropping the bag on Henri's desk. 'Drive it yourself if you have to and fast-track the shit out of it. Doctor Zimbaldi is expecting it. Who tipped us off about the suspect?'

'Michel LePoux. The man is one of his workers. He said he'd overheard him talking about the Jew tailor a few times and when he found out what happened this morning he thought he should report it. Suspect's name is Madjid Lellouche. Algerian. Muslim, no doubt. That'll be the cause of all this.'

'What!?'

'You know what these migrants are like. They're all thick as thieves and they hate the Jews. That's what it will be about, I'd bet money on it, some kind of Jew-Arab thing.'

'I don't want to hear that again. It's dangerous speculation. Has LePoux even given us an official statement about what he heard?'

'No, he just called it in. We went out to investigate, found a weapon, arrested the Arab, that's where we are now.'

'So at the moment we have nothing to suggest this is a religiously motivated hate crime. Get hold of LePoux, tell him to come in and give us a proper statement. If this Monsieur Lellouche is our man we'll need a solid chain of evidence, not idle speculation.'

Henri flushed red. 'I'll give him a call.'

'You do that. What about Marie-Claude and Léo? Solomon Creed? Any news on them?'

'Nothing yet, but there are alerts out everywhere: physical descriptions, details of her car, everything.'

'Let me know as soon as you get any new information. I'm going down to have a preliminary talk with Monsieur Lellouche. You find LePoux and get him in here as quick as you can. We can't interview this suspect properly until we know exactly what LePoux heard.'

33

Michel LePoux's phone rang as he turned his battered Renault 4 on to a track running between his vineyard and Chateau Montels. Belloq was in the passenger seat smoking a thin cigarillo and blowing smoke out of the open window. He picked up the phone and recognized the number. 'Cops.'

LePoux fidgeted uncomfortably in his seat. 'You think I should answer it?'

'No. They'll want you to make a formal statement about the Arab and we don't want to help their investigation, we want to hinder it. You're a busy man with many hectares to tend and a harvest looming. Let them chase you.'

The phone rang a few more times, *La Marseillaise* filling the interior of the car, before falling silent.

'There might not be a harvest this year,' LePoux grumbled. 'Look at my vines, this fucking esca comes back as fast as I cut it out. I swear those bastard Arabs brought it with them and are infecting the vines to make more work and laughing behind my back the whole time.'

Belloq blew a thin stream of smoke out into the dry air. 'The esca has been here since Roman times,' he said. 'Not everything is the fault of the Arabs.'

'Well, the Romans were immigrants too,' LePoux snorted.

'The Romans were invaders, not immigrants. They brought law and order, and roads, and wine. Not like these modern immigrants with their empty pockets and their hungry mouths. These people are nothing but parasites, sucking the country dry like the esca.'

'Esca isn't a parasite,' LePoux muttered, 'it's a fungus.'

'Whatever,' Belloq waved his hand and sent a shower of ash floating down to the floor, 'the principle's the same.'

They were bouncing along a rutted track between a field of yellow sunflowers and one of vines. The sunflowers were vibrant and bright, the vines were squat and gnarled, their leaves streaked brown. Belloq didn't know much about vineyards but he could see that LePoux's vines were in a bad state. The clusters of grapes dangling in bunches beneath the discoloured leaves were small and shrivelled and he couldn't imagine the wine produced from them would be either plentiful or tasty. But his politician's brain, always searching for a strong image to dramatize the peril his country was in, seized on it and he began to compose a speech in his mind:

'The other day I was driving through a vineyard . . .'

No, not 'driving' – too passive, too detached.

'. . . I was walking through a vineyard and I saw how a disease – an ugly disease – was taking hold of the sturdy old vines: brown streaks creeping across green, healthy leaves to slowly poison the sweet grapes from within.'

It was a great image. Nothing was more French than a vineyard and he liked the way he could demonize the colour brown as something rotten. Muslims didn't even drink wine, which told you everything you needed to know about them.

They reached a fork in the track and turned away from the bright sunflowers and headed deeper into the blighted vines. In the distance, Belloq could see a squat stone building, nestled in the lowest part of the valley, a single, shuttered window on the upper floor and a small door beneath a rickety porch. A thin tendril of smoke curled up from a chimney.

Belloq drew deeply on his cigar and realized he was feeling a little nervous. He'd had to ask people for all kinds of things – trust, money, support – but he had never had to persuade someone to risk their freedom or potentially kill someone before and he felt anxious and honoured at the prospect. It was as the Leader said: one of the biggest tests of leadership was the ability to persuade a person to do your bidding, and he was about to be tested.

They pulled to a halt outside the barn in a cloud of dry dust and the Renault coughed and spluttered like an old smoker before it shuddered and fell silent. Belloq got out and felt the heat of the day wrap around him. He listened to the sounds of the place – the buzz and whirr of insects in the fields, the distant clang of a church bell carrying across the fields, and the dull, wet thud of something coming from inside the barn. He could hear a voice too, someone saying things in German then repeating them in French.

He took his handkerchief from his pocket and wiped the back of his neck. The heat seemed greater here, like it had pooled in the bottom of the valley, yet he shivered at the sight of a hare hanging on a hook in the shade of the small porch, its eyes bugged out in surprise or horror or both. LePoux marched towards the barn, hitching up his trousers as he went. Belloq opened the back door of the car, retrieved a small cool box and a heavy-duty supermarket bag from the floor, and followed him.

Stepping through the door of the barn felt like climbing

into an oven. A small window on the far wall let in some light and air, but the building was stifling and smelled of blood and cooking meat. A rough ladder led up to a half-timbered hayloft with a bedroll spread out on it. The ground floor was mostly taken up by a large oak table with something large and dark and bloody lying on it. A man stood next to it, stripped to the waist, his skin mired with sweat and blood. He raised a cleaver high above his head and brought it down hard, making the noise Belloq had heard outside.

'*Sanglier!*' LePoux exclaimed, moving round the table and inspecting the thing lying upon it. The cleaver came down again with a sound of splintering bone and the entire leg of the wild boar came away in the butcher's hand. An old CD player on the window ledge continued to fill the stifling barn with a steady murmur of German phrases and French translations.

'You're learning German, Monsieur Baptiste,' Belloq said, stepping forward and offering his hand out of habit before remembering the hand he would shake was currently holding a bloody leg.

'It passes the time,' the man replied, and threw the leg into a large bowl along with some other lumps of meat.

'English would be more useful,' Belloq said.

'I already learned English while I was inside,' the man replied. He placed his cleaver on the table and moved over to a large cauldron of blood bubbling on the stove and stirred it, his thick forearms so wet with dark smears of blood that it looked like he'd washed in it.

'Big bastard,' LePoux said, his large head nodding approval at the dead boar on the table. 'Where did you kill it?'

'Up on the southern slope. I saw it moving around in the trees and went up there last night. It made a change from snaring rabbits and birds, and there's not much else to do out here. Take what you want, I can't use all this meat and it will spoil in the heat.'

Belloq smiled. 'I'm sorry you've been feeling under-employed out here.' He held up the cool box and carrier bag. 'I've brought some cold beers and something else you may be interested in. Why don't we step outside and talk. You look like a man who could use some refreshments.'

34

Amand descended the stone spiral stairs into the basement for the second time that day. This time Parra was behind him, a witness processing pack in one hand and a small digital voice recorder in the other. He stood aside to let Parra unlock the door then stepped into the cell. The man inside looked up at the sound of the unlocking door. He was sitting at the table, hands clasped in front of him; he watched the two men enter the room and lock the door behind them.

'Monsieur Lellouche,' Amand said, pulling out a chair and sitting opposite him, 'my name is Benoît Amand. I'm the lead investigator in the murder of Monsieur Josef Engel. This is Lieutenant Parra.' Parra sat next to him and laid the paperwork and recorder on the table. 'Anything you can tell us that helps with our investigation may also help you in the long run, do you understand?'

Madjid nodded, eyes wide, shoulders slumped. Parra set the digital voice recorder running and recorded the time and date as well as the names of the three men present. He uncapped his pen and prepared to take notes.

'Perhaps we can start by establishing your relationship with the victim, Josef Engel.'

'I don't know him.'

'You never met him?'

'No.'

'Ever heard his name before?'

Madjid hesitated, his eyes dropping to his hands. 'Yes. I heard the name.'

'Do you remember when?'

He shrugged. 'I hear many names – from other workers, from the market. I knew Monsieur Engel was the tailor who lived in Cordes, just as I know Monsieur Arnaud is the Notaire and Monsieur Moulin is the baker. None of these things are secret.'

'But you never had any dealings with Monsieur Engel.'

'No.'

'This morning, when the two police officers called on the vineyard where you work, they found you in the process of leaving. They also found a cane hidden in the barn where you live. Do you want to tell me about that.'

Madjid shook his head. 'I know nothing about that. That stick is . . . I don't know what it is. I don't know why it is there.'

'Why were you leaving?'

'The harvest is failing. The land is no good. Disease in the vines. Why stay and watch it all die?'

'But why this morning? Why not at the end of the week?'

Madjid glanced down at a raised red stripe on the nut-brown skin of his forearm. 'It was time to go.'

'How did you get that mark?'

Madjid covered it with his hand. 'A scratch. From the vines.'

'Can I see?' Madjid reluctantly removed his hand again and Amand studied the mark. 'You know the name Laveyron?'

'Like the vineyard? Chateau Laveyron?'

'Exactly.'

'Yes, I know it.'

'I went to school with Patrice, the youngest boy. Well, old man Laveyron liked to use those bamboo canes you train vines with to train his children too. I'd see marks on Patrice sometimes when we were changing for swimming or rugby. They looked exactly like that mark on your arm.'

'It's nothing,' Madjid said, hiding the mark again with his hand.

Amand nodded. 'Listen, Monsieur Lellouche. If you have anything to tell me about how you got that mark on your arm or who put it there, now would be the time. Because if you're not prepared to tell me the truth about something small like this, it makes me wonder if you're telling the truth about bigger things as well.'

Madjid looked up at him, a mixture of anger and defiance in his eyes. 'Ask Monsieur LePoux about it. If he wants to tell you, he will. You won't hear anything from me.'

Amand nodded. He didn't need to ask LePoux about the mark because he knew he was as fond of swinging the cane as old man Laveyron had been; it was clearly a hallmark of the *vignerons*. 'Did you know that it was LePoux who tipped us off about you?' he said, hoping to shake whatever strange loyalty Madjid was bound by. 'He said he heard you talking about Monsieur Engel last night.'

Madjid shook his head. 'Monsieur LePoux is mistaken. The only time I spoke about Monsieur Engel was this morning, when I was talking to the stranger.'

'What stranger?'

'The tall man in the suit jacket.'

Amand exchanged a glance with Parra. 'Did you catch this man's name?'

Madjid looked up, his brown eyes so dark they almost seemed black. 'Yes,' he said, his voice no more than a whisper. 'He said his name was Solomon Creed.'

35

Solomon breathed deeply, focusing on the fresh smell of the countryside rather than the vinegary smells of the car. The vineyards had disappeared now and the hills had flattened into huge fields of maize as they drew closer to Toulouse. He felt a faint tickle on his skin and glanced across to meet the gaze of Léo, sucking on a sippy cup, a small bead of liquid hanging beneath it, bulging and ready to drop. Solomon watched it stretch, then fall and extended his arm to catch it on the tip of his finger.

'Whoa!!' The boy's voice sounded slow, like an old record played at the wrong speed. 'How come you can move so fast?'

Solomon touched his finger to his tongue and tasted apple juice, which explained the cider-vinegar smell of the car from previous drips soaked into the seat fabric and fermented in the hot summer sun. He winked at Léo. 'I can move faster. If I need to.'

'Cool. Can you teach me?'

Solomon considered the question. 'I don't think so. I'm not entirely sure how I do it myself. I just concentrate on something hard and everything else slows down.'

'Like Quicksilver in X-Men?'

'Something like that.'

'Are you some kind of a mutant?'

'Léo, don't be rude,' Marie-Claude said sharply from up front.

'It's OK,' Solomon said, looking down at the comics littering the floor beneath Léo's seat – Marvel, Manga, DC – 'I think it's a compliment.'

Léo nodded. 'Mutants are cool.' He continued to stare at Solomon, who stared back. The shutter had not come down on him yet or brought the guarded look he saw in most adults' eyes, like they were peering out from their walled-city selves as the world lay siege around them. 'How come you're so white?' Léo asked.

'I don't know. How come you're so short?'

He shrugged. 'I'm seven.'

Solomon smiled. 'Good answer.' He turned back to the window and spotted a plane ahead, dropping lower in the sky. He wondered whether he could get into a plane, a sealed metal tube with no chance of escape. The thought made him shudder.

'You get sick in cars?' Léo asked.

'A little.'

'Me too. Mama says if I read in the car, I mostly puke.'

Marie-Claude's eyes flicked in the rear-view mirror. 'That's right, no reading – and look straight ahead, don't look down, like you were . . .'

'. . . walking on a tightrope or climbing a mountain, I know, I know.' Léo turned to Solomon, adding in a whisper, 'Only it's not the same because I'm not going to fall and die, all I'm going to do is puke.'

'Yeah, and who'll have to clean it up?'

Léo rolled his eyes. 'OK, OK – I got it.'

'Who's your favourite?' Solomon asked, nodding at the pile of comics.

'Iron Man, maybe.'

Facts tumbled through Solomon's head, the usual white noise of everything and nothing. 'Tony Stark,' he said, plucking a single scrap from the river of information.

'Yes.' Léo sounded impressed.

'Why Tony Stark?'

'I think it's because he's normal. He doesn't have super-strength and he can't fly or anything – at least, not on his own, he needs the suit for that. But he built the suit. He's really smart and he can fix anything. That's why I like him. You're smart too, aren't you? You know all kinds of stuff.'

'Doesn't make me smart.'

'I think you're smart. I bet you can fix things too, can't you?'

'I hope so,' Solomon said. 'I'm going to try.' His shoulder started to ache a little at the thought of this and he rubbed at the pain.

'Did you hurt your arm?'

'I'm not sure. There's a burn there, like a brand. Do you know what a brand is?'

'Like the mark they put on cows using a red-hot poker.'

'Exactly.'

Léo's eyes flew wide. 'Someone did *that* to you? What is it, is it like a shape or something?'

'*Chéri*, don't keep asking Mr Creed questions. It's not polite.'

'It's fine,' Solomon said, leaning forward and slipping his jacket off. 'Focusing on something helps with travel sickness, so he's doing us both a favour – you too, if it means you won't have to clean up any puke.' He unbuttoned his waistcoat and the top few buttons of his shirt and slipped them over his shoulder to reveal the raised welt on his skin, two red lines running parallel to each other.

'Whoa,' Léo said, studying the symbol. 'That must have hurt.'

'Still does, from time to time.'

'It's important, isn't it?'

Solomon nodded. 'Yes, I think it is.' He put his shirt back on and studied the boy. 'What makes *you* think it's important?'

Léo glanced at his mother then leaned closer and whispered. 'Because your colours change when you rub it. They go green, sometimes a little red, but green mostly and green is a good colour, though not as good as white. Mostly you're white – like me.' He glanced forward again, caught his mama's eyes in the rear-view mirror and sat back down like he'd been caught doing something wrong.

'If green is good, what about red?'

Léo pulled a face.

'Not so good?'

He shook his head.

Solomon finished rebuttoning the waistcoat. Whenever the mark started to ache, he felt an odd mixture of euphoria and pain, and the boy had sensed it. He had *seen* it. 'You have synaesthesia,' he murmured. He turned to Léo. 'Does everything have a colour?'

Léo shrugged. 'It's people mainly. People and words. The colour is different, depending on what sort of person they are or if it's a nice word or not. Nice people have bright colours and bad people have muddy colours, like different birds have different feathers. The colours look like feathers to me too, soft and downy. Except they can change depending on how someone's feeling.'

Solomon's mind hummed with information and he smiled in happy recognition that something very rare had happened – he had discovered something new about himself. 'I have it too,' he said.

'Really?'

'Yes. Only I don't see colours. Synaesthesia comes from the Greek words meaning *together* and *sensation* and can describe the mingling of any of the senses. With me it's smell. I can smell emotions the same way you can see them.'

'Cool. What do I smell like?'

'At the moment you smell like the car, but beneath that you smell like lemon zest and cotton and sea salt.'

'Is that good?'

'It's the smell of curiosity and eagerness.'

'What's eagerness?'

'Enthusiasm.'

'Cool.'

'What about me?' Marie-Claude asked, drawn into the conversation. 'Actually, forget it. I don't want to know what I smell like. Probably dirty laundry or something.'

'Ash and stone,' Solomon said, 'and a little smoky.'

'What's that? Despair? Tiredness?'

'Anger,' Solomon replied. 'Anger and guilt.'

The sound of the wind blowing through the open window filled the silence that followed until Léo broke it. 'I always thought there was something wrong with me.'

'No,' Solomon told him. 'Having synaesthesia makes you different.' He leaned down and picked up an X-Men comic from the floor. 'You're like these guys. You have a special power too.' He handed the comic to Léo and his face lit up. 'Plenty of great men have had your gift. Have you ever heard of Jean Sibelius?' Léo shook his head. 'Franz Liszt? Duke Ellington? They're all famous musicians, geniuses. They all had synaesthesia too. Rimsky-Korsakov was another one. He was friends with Liszt and they used to argue about the correct colour of different musical keys. What about Vincent van Gogh?'

'I've heard of him.'

'Dutch painter; he had a thing called timbre synaesthesia, which means he heard sounds when he looked at colours or pictures. Some people's paintings sounded like violins to him and others like nails on a blackboard. What about Nikola Tesla, I bet you know him?'

'He's the Night Machine in the SHIELD comics.'

'Yes, but he was also a real person. A genius inventor and physicist. Master of electricity. He had spatial synaesthesia, which allowed him to see numbers and words in three dimensions. It meant he could analyse and manipulate them in a way normal people couldn't. He saw the world differently and it helped him to change it. Exactly like you.'

Léo beamed and looked out of the window as if he expected the world to be transformed in the light of what he had learned. Solomon caught Marie-Claude staring in the rear-view mirror and he smiled at her to try and gauge whether she was angry with him or not. Léo had been reluctant to talk about his abilities and he imagined that came from his mother. She probably wanted him to blend in, play down his differences, not be the weird kid at school, and Solomon had encouraged him to do the opposite. He held his smile but she didn't return it and the scent of ash and stone coming off her held steady.

Anger and guilt – now where did that come from?

Anger about what? Guilt about what?

'We'll be in Toulouse in ten minutes,' she said, looking back at the road. 'You might want to hide yourself again when we get there. Plenty of cameras at the airport. Plenty of police too.'

36

Belloq placed the cool box and carrier bag in the shade of the porch while LePoux dragged two chairs outside and turned a crate over to serve as a table. Baptiste stood off to one side, washing himself in a bucket drawn fresh from the well, the water running red off him and staining the dirt. Belloq opened the cool box and pulled three beers out, ice-water dripping off them as he twisted the tops off. He gave one to LePoux, kept one for himself and set the third down on the up-ended crate. He sat down and watched Baptiste dry himself, solid muscles moving beneath sun-darkened skin that made his tattoos writhe as if they were alive. He had a large black boar on his right shoulder, a rough impression of the same animal now lying in bloody pieces in the stifling dark of the barn and symbol of their party, the PNFL – National Party of Free France. The smudgy ink suggested Baptiste had acquired it in prison along with his bulked-up physique. The boar was also the sign of the white supremacist gangs in the French prison system. Baptise finished drying himself, slipped his arms through the sleeves of his shirt and walked over to join them in the shade.

Belloq raised his bottle. 'Your health, monsieur.'

Baptiste walked past him and disappeared back into the dark of the barn. The man speaking German was suddenly silenced and Belloq looked at LePoux, who shrugged and gulped his beer greedily, finishing most of it by the time Baptiste reappeared with a tin cup in his hand. He leaned down and filled it with ice-water from the cool box. 'I don't drink, Monsieur Belloq,' he said. 'Not any more.'

Belloq nodded. 'Of course. I'm sorry, I should have thought to bring something else.'

Baptiste drank the iced-water in deep gulps. 'You did,' he said, and refilled his cup.

'Such a tragedy,' Belloq lamented, 'the direction your life has taken. So much taken from you, even the simple pleasure of a cold beer on a hot day.'

Baptiste ran the chilled cup across his forehead. 'I am grateful for your hospitality and also for your help, messieurs. I do not need your pity.'

'Good,' Belloq said, 'because that's not why we came.' He pointed at the remaining chair. 'Please. Sit.'

Baptiste wiped a smudge of blood from the back of the chair and sat down. LePoux swapped his empty beer bottle for the one Baptiste had refused.

'You may not want pity,' Belloq said, 'but your situation is worthy of pity nevertheless. You committed a crime, yes, but you have paid a far greater price for it than most. You are still paying the price, are you not?'

Baptiste drank his water and said nothing.

'I can only imagine how hard it must have been for you in prison, an ex-policeman amongst all those criminals. It must have taken all your courage, all your willpower to survive. And for such a long time. Too long. Much too long.' Belloq raised his bottle. 'I know you don't drink but, nevertheless, I will drink a toast to you. I drink to your courage and to your patriotism.'

Baptiste shook his head. 'It was not my courage or my patriotism that put me in prison. It was my anger.' He pointed at the bottle in Belloq's hand. 'And it was that.'

Belloq placed his bottle down on the crate and looked at Baptiste. 'You blame yourself. Your temper. Alcohol. But I blame a country that has lost its way. The country our party would build would not seek to blame you for what you did. I know your story, everyone in town knows it. I cannot imagine how betrayed you must have felt when you discovered that the woman you loved, the mother of your child, had lied to you about what she really was. Some may say you over-reacted when you discovered the truth, but you paid the price and more. How long was your initial sentence?'

Baptiste stared into his cup as if his lost years were inside. 'Eighteen months.'

'Eighteen months. With good behaviour and time served, you should have been out in six. But good behaviour was never an option for you, was it? How long was it before you were first attacked?'

Baptiste ran a finger along a pale scar visible through his dark beard. 'The second day.'

'Your second day inside and someone tried to kill you. You had no choice. It was dog eat dog. Kill or be killed. What was your sentence for killing the Arab who gave you that scar?'

'Eight years.'

Belloq spat in the dust and wiped his mouth with his handkerchief. 'Eight years for manslaughter. Eight years when what you slaughtered was no better than that wild boar you were butchering – less even. At least a pig you can eat. What can you do with a dead Arab? Nothing. Celebrate one less in the world, maybe.'

LePoux snorted in agreement and downed the rest of Baptiste's beer.

'All of this injustice you have suffered, all these trials, and yet you survived. With the help of the Brotherhood, you survived. I saw the tattoo on your shoulder. The Brotherhood became your family, didn't it? And families look after each other, as we have looked after you. Did you not wonder how you managed to attain such an early release from a near ten-year sentence?'

Baptiste looked up and surveyed the green valley all around. 'I am grateful for all you have done. But being here, keeping out of sight. It's another form of prison.'

'I agree, it's intolerable you should have to live like this. But things are changing, not only for you but for all of France. We have party members in every strata of society and France is finally waking up, along with the rest of Europe. Our party is stronger in the polls than it has ever been. We are challenging for power – real power – and real power will enable us to make real changes.

'And when those changes come, anyone who helped the party can expect to be rewarded in the new society we will build from the ashes of the old. I cannot promise to give back everything you have lost, but I can give you back your home. I can give you back your position within the community, maybe even your old job.'

Baptiste looked Belloq squarely in the eye. 'What about Léo?'

Belloq smiled. 'Yes,' he said. 'We can give you your son.'

Baptiste spat into the dust. 'Then why don't you stop making speeches and tell me what it is you want me to do.'

37

Amand re-emerged into the noise of the Commissariat and moved over to Henri's desk.

'No news,' Henri said, without even being asked. 'Did he confess?'

'No. Did you send the cane to Albi?'

'It's on its way now.'

Amand nodded. Part of him wanted it to be as simple as it appeared: the cane would match the wounds on Josef Engel, the blood would match too and they might even find a few fingerprints to seal the deal. But another part of him didn't buy it. Madjid Lellouche did not strike him as the sort of man who would carve a Star of David into an old man's flesh, or bring rats to gnaw at his corpse. Solomon Creed, however, the man Madjid had spoken to and who had asked about Josef Engel, the man who had taken Amand's gun and field-stripped it without even looking, and walked out of the Commissariat in broad daylight, he imagined he was capable of all of it.

'I'm going to take a look at Marie-Claude's studio at La Broderie,' he said, heading to the door.

'I'd go out the back way, if I were you.'

Amand looked through the entrance and saw a couple of

news reporters smoking cigarettes and talking on phones. One was studying his dented car bleeding oil on to the cobbles. He needed to call the garage and get it towed and fixed or written off for the insurance, but that all seemed far too mundane, given the day he was having. He turned around and headed to the back door.

Amand emerged into the alley running along the rear of the building, found Marie-Claude's mobile number, dialled it and listened to her voice asking him to leave a message.

'It's Ben. Call me when you get this. I'm worried about you. You need to call me.'

He hung up and glanced over at the Tabac. A few tourists sat under the awning, drinking coffee or glasses of chilled rosé or beer because they were on holiday, so what the hell, but none of the locals had claimed their spots yet and LePoux wasn't there.

He cut across the cobbled street, sticking to the shade in order to dodge the heat and make it easier to see the screen of his phone. As a town councillor, he had contact numbers for all the other members, including LePoux. He found his home number, dialled it, listened to it ring out then tried his mobile phone next. He rang it three times in case he was ignoring it, before giving up and leaving a message.

'Michel, this is Amand from the Commissariat. I need to talk to you urgently regarding Madjid Lellouche. Please call me back on this number as soon as you get this message.'

He hung up and scrolled through the other councillors' names until he found an entry for Jean-Luc Belloq. If LePoux wasn't in his vineyard or the Tabac, he could usually be found in Belloq's café. He dialled the number and imagined the bell of the old phone tinkling behind the bar.

A woman answered, her French accented.

'Is Jean-Luc there?' Amand asked.

'No.'

'What about Michel LePoux, has he been in this morning?' There was a pause.

'Mariella, isn't it?' Amand said, dragging her name from his memory.

'Yes.'

'We met earlier. I'm Ben, from the Cordes Commissariat. Monsieur LePoux isn't in any kind of trouble, Mariella, and neither is your boss. I just need to get hold of Monsieur LePoux and I thought he might be there. So if you do see him, could you tell him to call me.'

'He was here,' Mariella said, in a tiny voice he had trouble hearing. 'He came in a car to pick Monsieur Belloq up and they drove away. I don't know where they went.'

'How long ago was this?'

'Maybe half an hour.'

Amand nodded. Henri had been trying to get hold of him for longer which meant he was deliberately avoiding them.

'Thank you, Mariella, you've been very helpful.'

He hung up and felt annoyed and hot. He found Belloq's mobile number, dialled it and listened to it ringing.

'Come on, you pig, you always have your phone on you,' he muttered.

It went to voicemail, Belloq's smooth, smiling voice apologizing for not being available and assuring him his call was important and to please leave a message. Amand didn't bother. Instead he found LePoux's number, dialled it again and continued on his way to La Broderie.

38

La Marseillaise mingled with the orchestra of insects in the vines. LePoux looked at the screen and held up his phone for Baptiste to see. 'It's your old friend Amand.'

Baptiste spat in the dust. 'He's no friend of mine.'

The trumpeting tune played on for a while then fell silent, leaving only the sound of insects and tick of the heat.

Belloq turned to Baptiste. 'Actually, what the party would like you to do involves Amand to some degree: helping us will also hinder him.'

Baptiste nodded. 'So much the better.'

'Josef Engel is dead,' Belloq said. 'Murdered, and in such a way as to make it appear that we, or someone sympathetic to our cause, might have done it.'

Baptiste glanced over at LePoux. 'Did you?'

'No. But the party did have an interest in Monsieur Engel and his sudden death presents certain problems for us. The leadership believe he had a list of names in his possession: survivors from the camp he had been interred in during the war. We have been asked to find this list, but it appears someone else may have got there first. Josef Engel's house and workshop had been searched and this morning the home of his granddaughter was also broken into.'

Baptiste looked up.

'Don't worry. Marie-Claude was not there and neither was Léo. However they are now both missing, as is a suspect who escaped police custody this morning. They may be together, they may not, but we would like you to find them.' He picked up the carrier bag and handed it to Baptiste. 'In there is a laptop with the entire, up-to-date case file on the Engel murder loaded on to it.'

'How did you get that?'

Belloq smiled. 'We have friends everywhere. You'd be surprised how much the party has grown since you've been away. The person who furnished us with the police file will also keep you updated on every new development, and there are people like him in every Commissariat across the country who will also be feeding you information if you need it. These are all people like us, true Frenchmen, sick of the constant spending cuts and increasing expectations that they keep the peace in a country that is letting them down and being overrun by people who wish to see the end of us and everything we believe in.'

Jean Baptiste pulled the laptop from the carrier and set it on the upturned crate. The screen lit up when he opened it and asked for a password.

'It's *prodigal*,' Belloq said, 'all lower-case. It seemed fitting, the prodigal son returning home.' He smiled and nodded at the barn. 'You even slaughtered a fatted beast.'

Baptiste tapped *prodigal* into the box and the laptop unlocked. He clicked open the single folder on the desktop and scanned the large directory of files inside: witness statements, crime scene photographs, everything.

'There's also a smartphone in the bag, so you can connect to the internet wherever you are, and a set of clothes back in the car in a travelling case with everything else you might need. We realize this might take some time. There's something else for you in the carrier bag.'

Baptiste reached inside and pulled out a small biscuit tin about the same size as a hardback book. He shook it gently and something heavy shifted inside.

'Our man in the Commissariat managed to secure it and keep hold of it for you after you were . . . dismissed. He was hoping to give it to you in person, and a great deal sooner than this. Anyway, there it is for you now. You may find it useful.'

Baptiste prised open the lid and lifted out something loosely wrapped in oil-stained newspaper dated four years earlier. Underneath was his old police ID card, the photograph showing a much younger, clean-shaven, unhardened version of himself. He unwrapped the newspaper and stared down at his old service weapon, an SP 2022 semi-automatic, the matt black polymer surface dulled with age.

'I brought you some ammunition,' LePoux said, gazing at the gun the way an addict stares at drugs, 'also some gun oil and some cloths to clean it. They're in the car.'

'You know what kind of trouble I'll get in if I'm discovered with a concealed weapon?'

Belloq shrugged. 'Then don't get caught. Or don't take it with you, though I think we can assume that whoever killed Josef Engel might also be looking for Marie-Claude, if they haven't found her already. And if they find her, they will also find Léo.'

Baptiste closed his fingers round the grip, his trigger finger curling into the firing position. It felt comfortable and familiar and made him feel something else he had not experienced for a long while. It made him feel powerful.

'You know she's bringing your son up as a Jew,' Belloq said, his voice low like he was sharing something shameful. 'She takes him to the synagogue in Toulouse and he's been seen wearing a little Jew cap on Fridays. Is that what you want for him? You want to let his mother ruin him, or do you want to take your son back and raise him right?'

'I never knew she was a Jew when I married her.'

'I know. She tricked you. She tricked us all. But that's what they do. They're like the disease in these vines: do nothing and the rot will spread and the vine will die. But catch it early and cut it out and the vine survives. Tell me, did you ever dream, while you were marking off all those months and years in prison, that you might one day get your son back?' Baptiste turned the gun over in his hand and shook his head. 'Of course you didn't. How could you, with your prison record and a conviction against his mother hanging over your head. But this is your chance, your only chance maybe.'

Baptiste placed the gun on the crate next to the wet circle where Belloq's beer bottle had stood and took his ID card from the tin. 'I'll need a car and some money. And I want to see Marie-Claude's house.'

Belloq pointed at the laptop. 'I'm sure there some pictures on—'

'Not pictures. I need to see for myself. To start a hunt, you need a good scent of the prey, then you follow whatever tracks have been left behind. There are always tracks. Get me into the house. I'll find them.'

39

Amand stepped through the open front door of La Broderie and headed to the stairs, listening to the morning hum of activity in the building. He'd been here before, after Marie-Claude first got her grant from the Shoah Foundation and sublet the tiny office from a web-design company moving to a bigger unit. He'd hauled a desk, a chair and a computer up to the small office for her but not been back since. He'd asked her about her work but she'd always been evasive and he hadn't wanted to pry. He knew she spent a lot of time here because her car was always parked outside, but he wasn't prepared for what lay beyond the door to Marie-Claude's office.

He stood in the doorway for a moment, staring into the gloom. The desk and the computer were exactly where he'd put them, but the desk was now swamped with paper and books and a printer/scanner lay half-buried in paperwork. But it was the walls that made him stare. The last time he'd seen them they were blank and unremarkable, now they teemed with tiny writing. Names, hundreds of names, thousands even. Many had been crossed out but some had red threads of cotton connecting them to a piece of A4 paper pinned to the centre of the wall beneath a photocopied page from a book.

He moved into the room and studied the photocopied page,

a handwritten note in the margin identifying that it was: *From the diary of Private John Hamilton, liberator of Mulhouse A.*

The photocopied text was faded and hard to read in the gloom. Amand crossed to the window, opened the shutters to flood the office in sunlight and turned back to read the entry:

There were thirty-four men inside that cellar, locked up and left to die by someone whose evil I cannot begin to fathom. Maybe the explosions that had part-demolished the buildings had been deliberately set to collapse the cellar on top of them, murdering and burying them at the same time. If so, they had failed. But only just. Thirty-four men had been buried in that cellar and only twelve of them were still alive. A day later, despite the best emergency medical care we could give them, there were four.

Four men out of thirty-four and God knows how many countless thousands before them. These were the men who came to be known as Die Anderen – The Others.

Amand studied the sheet of A4 next.

MULHOUSE A
DIE SCHNEIDER LAGER
Artur Samler
Josef Lansky

DIE ANDEREN
1) Saul Schwartzfeldt
2) Jacob Engel
3)
4)

The red cotton threads all converged on two empty spaces at the bottom of the page. Marie-Claude had been looking for the survivors.

Amand took out his phone, snapped a photograph of both pages then opened a Notebook app and started methodically working his way round the room, following each red thread to an individual name before carefully noting it down. When he'd finished, he counted them. There were fifty-eight. Fifty-eight names from a list of thousands. He looked at the list again. He had known Josef had been a prisoner during the war, that had all come out around Baptiste's trial, but he had never known exactly where.

He sat at the desk and switched on the computer, glancing through the stacks of paperwork while he waited for the hard drive to boot up. An open pack of memory sticks lay next to a pile of envelopes with La Broderie's address written on them, stamped and ready to be sent out. A smaller pile of returned envelopes lay next to them, their tops ripped open and correspondence visible inside. Amand picked one up and read it:

Dear Mme Engel,

Thank you for your letter regarding my late grandfather Thomasz Edelmann. Unfortunately, I cannot help you in your enquiries regarding Die Schneider Lager except to say that we believe my grandfather died in Bergen-Belsen after being transferred out of Mulhouse A towards the end of the war.

I wish you well in your continued research and applaud your efforts in commemorating this chapter of history that, sadly, many now seem happier to forget.

Sincerely Yours,
Erik Edelmann

Amand put the letter back in the envelope and turned his attention to the piles of paperwork. They were made up of printouts of PDF files, screen-grabs from various archived web pages, and page after page of the same kind of neat columns of handwritten names that covered the walls around him. There were copies of death certificates too, Nazi transport and prisoner manifests with swastikas stamped across them, ghetto census lists from both Łódź and Warsaw, and several bundles of paperwork relating specifically to Mulhouse A. Hundreds of thousands of names, many of which had been crossed out in various coloured pens.

Amand marvelled at the amount of time it must have taken Marie-Claude to not only track down all this information but also meticulously sort through it all. He wondered why she hadn't just asked Josef for the names, but realized she must have done. Josef had always been something of a spiky individual, cold and withdrawn, and relations between him and Marie-Claude had been difficult. Maybe this explained why.

The computer finished booting up and a password box flashed up. He typed in marieclaude. The screen shook and 'Incorrect Password' appeared. He tried capitalizing it, then tried Léonardo and Léo, upper and lower case, but they all came back incorrect and a new message popped up telling him he had one more attempt before the computer locked itself for thirty minutes.

Amand stared at the flashing cursor, trying to think like Marie-Claude, searching for a word that would be significant enough to use as a password. He thought of one but hesitated to type it, half hoping he was wrong but also keen to unlock the computer and discover what it contained. He left the Caps Lock on, typed 'BAPTISTE' and hit *Return*. The screen shuddered and locked him out and a timer popped up starting a thirty-minute countdown.

He sat back in his chair, and blew out a long breath of relief. It was worth waiting half an hour to know Marie-Claude had not used her ex-husband's name to keep her documents safe.

He turned his attention to another pile of paperwork, more lists of names, more crossings out, but at the bottom, standing like a foundation for the whole enterprise were two books, each with numerous yellow Post-its bursting out of the pages. Amand picked up the first and read the title:

Freeing the Dead: The Nazi Death Camp Liberators

He turned to the first page marked with a Post-it and read the chapter heading: 'Extract from the Diary of Private John Hamilton, 2nd Royal Wessex Infantry, on the Liberation of Nazi Labour Camp Mulhouse A – known as Die Schneider Lager'.

It was the book the photocopied page had come from. The full entry was ten pages long and marked with numerous Post-its. Amand flicked through it then picked up the second volume:

Dark Material – The Devil's Tailor: Death and Life in Die Schneider Lager by Herman Lansky

Lansky's name was on Marie-Claude's list. Amand glanced at the timer on the computer screen. Twenty-five minutes left to wait before he could try another password. Maybe he would find something in these books that would give him a clue as to what that password might be. He leaned back in the chair, turned away from the window slightly so the sunlight fell on the pages, and started to read.

VI

'Who by water and who by fire?'

**From the 'Unetanneh Tokef',
traditional Jewish prayer**

Extract from

DARK MATERIAL – THE DEVIL'S TAILOR: DEATH AND LIFE IN DIE SCHNEIDER LAGER

✠

By Herman Lansky

It is impossible to know where to start when chronicling the heinous crimes of Standartenführer Artur Samler. Whenever I think of Nazis now I see only him, as if all the darkness and evil of the Third Reich has crystallized into this one person. He was all of the things you would imagine a Nazi camp commandant to be – cruel, brutal, sadistic – but there was also something stylish and civilized about him, which made him seem all the more inhuman. Even when beating people to death with the swagger stick he always carried he remained placid and calm.

He used to walk around the camp like a king, stick under one arm and his other hand resting on the silver eagle's head handle of the ceremonial bayonet he always wore on his belt like a sword. I saw him behead a prisoner with it once for accidentally splashing mud on his uniform, but mostly he used it to disfigure people: castrations; slicing the breasts off women; cutting the Star of David into people's flesh, hacking away their humanity piece by piece while the guards held them down. And all of these things he did with the same quiet, detached calm, like he was simply cutting down weeds on an evening walk.

The only time I ever saw Samler show any form of human emotion was when his dog Brutus died. A group of us were ordered to construct a tomb for him in Samler's garden, and I was part of the burial detail. We hid in the bushes to spare the ceremony our wretched presence and appearance, but I saw Samler weeping as he carried his dog into the tomb in a specially made cherrywood coffin. All those people dead with nothing to remember them by and that dog got a marble shrine and fresh flowers every week. Samler loved his dogs more than people. I know it to be true.

I once saw two of his dogs tear a young girl to pieces. She can't have been more than fourteen or fifteen. She slipped on the icy mud on our way to the factory one morning and struggled to get up, half-starved and frozen as she was. A few of us went to help her but Samler ordered us to leave her and go to work. We heard the snarls and screams as we trudged into the factory. None of us looked around. Afterwards I was asked to tidy up the yard, a euphemism for clearing away what was left of the girl. While I was shovelling bones and mud and bloody rags into a bucket, I heard Samler remark to a guard how it was a shame that he loved his dogs too much to starve them enough to finish jobs like these properly. How does a man become like that? Was he even a man at all?

After the war, when I was preparing to write this memoir, I tried to find out something of Samler's background and upbringing, as if something there might explain what had turned him into the creature I knew.

What I discovered was banal in its ordinariness – a string of unremarkable jobs, from selling sewing machine parts to managing an abattoir – before he became a campaign advisor for the fledgling National Socialist party. This was rewarded with a commission in the rapidly expanding German Army when Hitler became Chancellor in 1933. I don't know what I was expecting to find by digging into Samler's past. Maybe some early trauma that might explain what had made him what he was. But there was nothing, no easy explanation, and that was even more chilling than discovering some sad story of a blighted childhood. It suggested to me that men like Samler simply exist, a splinter in evolution perhaps, a branch of the human species that is either more primitive or possibly more evolved than the rest of us, doing whatever they want without the burden of conscience or emotion to hamper them. His son served as a guard too towards the end of the war and he was the same: a prince in his father's empire, a spoilt brat cut from the same dark cloth whose childish tantrums resulted in executions and torture. Samler encouraged it. He seemed proud. What kind of a father would do that?

The best way I can describe it is to say that Samler did not appear to possess a soul. Maybe he never had one, or maybe, as many of us in the camp believed, he had sold it to the Devil in exchange for the awful power he enjoyed as Commandant of Die Schneider Lager, a king in his own domain. Maybe he was the Devil himself. Whatever he was, I believe men like Samler are around us still. I fear it. And this is why I write this memoir and revisit these awful memories. It is to warn others that these creatures exist, co-existing with us, looking like us but not like us. They are there in the shadows, harbouring their hate, scratching slogans on walls, and waiting for the right circumstances to come howling back into the light.

⊹

40

Jean Baptiste stood in the sun and stared at his reflection in the broken tractor wing mirror wedged into a crack in the stone wall of the barn. The man who looked back was a stranger: black hair grown long; Jesus beard; hard eyes. He tilted his head and traced the white, ragged line where the hair didn't grow, starting in his beard and ending at his left eyebrow, a souvenir of that first time he'd been attacked in Lannemezan after the judge decided to make an example of him.

– *Given the nature of your job as a police officer . . .* he'd said during sentencing . . . *a figure of trust, a man expected to uphold the law, not break it, the court views your crime as greater than if an ordinary civilian had committed it. And though the court's hands are tied by statute in terms of length of custodial sentence it does have some leeway in deciding where you will spend that time.*

He had sent him to Lannemezan for twelve months, a bleak, concrete compound in the Midi-Pyrénées filled with lifers and violent career criminals. It was a bad enough place to be sent if you were a con but for ex-police it was practically a death sentence.

His attacker had been a small-time pederast named René

Ibrahim looking to make a name for himself with the Da'esh contingent who ran C-Block. Ibrahim had attacked him in the dinner queue with a prison shiv – a toothbrush with the handle worn to a point – stabbing at his throat, aiming for the neck but catching his face instead.

Baptiste leaned in to the cracked mirror and tried to cover the scar with his beard but it only made him look more like a vagrant. He dipped the dirty sliver of soap he'd found by the stone *evier* into the bucket of cold water and started to work up a lather.

There had been blood everywhere when Ibrahim had cut him. Face cuts bleed almost as bad as arteries and blood had poured into his eyes, blinding him. He'd raised his arms and planted his feet apart to try and stay upright, but someone had kicked him in the side of the knee and he'd gone down and curled into a ball, feeling like that was it, that was how he would die. He remembered bracing himself for the kicks and when none had come he'd looked up, blinking away the blood to see two huge figures standing over him like tattooed angels, staring out at the dinner queue and daring anyone to make another move. One had waved the guards over – the guards who had been looking the other way – and stood over him until they came and took him away to the infirmary. The prison medic who stitched him up had been shaking so badly Baptiste could still see the tremor in the jagged line of his scar. He took his razor, rinsed it in the cold water and started scraping away his beard, starting at the site of his scar and working out.

They'd kept him in solitary until the stitches came out. He had never in his life felt more alone or scared. In prison, a man's standing is dictated by the calibre of his enemies. The fact that a prison low-life like Ibrahim had confronted him in broad daylight showed how low he was in the pecking order. He was nothing, less than nothing. Even the guards had been prepared to stand by and let him die, and he knew as soon as he healed he'd be out there again. Only the silent giants with the tattoos had seemed to care one way or another if he lived or not. He thought about them a lot, about why they had saved him and what it would cost when he was released.

Baptiste rinsed the razor in the bucket again and shaved the beard down his neck, stopping short of where his tattoos started.

The first thing he'd done when he was released from solitary was walk straight through the middle of the recreation yard. There was nowhere to hide anyway, so he decided to turn it into an act of defiance that screamed *Here-I-am-motherfuckers-come-and-get-me*. He wanted everyone to see him, and, more importantly, who he talked to.

He found the two giants in the weights room where most of the muscle monsters hung out. One was bench-pressing what seemed like every weight in the room while the other stood over him, guiding the bar back to the rests between repetitions. Baptiste had stood watching them, not quite knowing what to say or whether it was rude to interrupt someone while they were lifting the equivalent of a small family car. The giant finished his reps, grabbed a towel and walked straight past Baptiste. The other one followed. Neither spoke. Neither acknowledged him, but he followed too. He didn't know what else to do.

He remembered that walk, back across the rec yard, into A-Block and up the stairs to the third-floor gantries. He felt eyes on him the whole way and registered the silence, like the whole prison was watching. The giants stopped at the end of the upper landing, stood aside and gestured for him to pass. There was only one cell left on the floor. The door was open and some kind of music leaked out, violent and angry. He hadn't known what might happen to him inside that cell but he knew what would happen if he turned and walked away, so he squeezed past the two giants and went in.

Baptiste finished shaving and stared at himself again in the cracked mirror. The scar seemed less obvious now it was no longer framed by the beard. He should probably come up with a story about how he got it in case anyone asked: a motorcycle crash, maybe, or a sporting accident – something that didn't involve prisons and home-made knives. He towelled himself off, tipped the soapy water on to the ground and headed back into the barn.

The kitchen table was clean and scrubbed, the carcass of the wild boar removed to LePoux's cold store. A black suit jacket was draped over the back of a chair and a pair of black jeans and a white shirt lay folded on the table, the same clothes he had worn every day to work for years. He stripped and started to put them on, feeling like he was piecing himself together again. LePoux would be back soon with a car, ready to head off in search of more lost pieces of his broken life.

The cell on the third floor of A-Block had belonged to a man called Marcel Marrineau. He was head of a prison gang of extreme nationalists and white supremacists known as the Brotherhood. Ironically, they were the minority in the predominantly Muslim prison population. Marrineau was a lifer serving his time for an exotic cocktail of convictions – murder, race hate, possession of illegal firearms and materials related to bomb-making – though all these charges seemed like smaller planets circling the central shining star of his main crime of burning down a mosque with a large crowd of people inside. His arms and chest were as big as the guys' outside but his legs were withered and strapped together in the wheelchair that turned when Baptiste entered his cell. Marrineau looked him up and down before leaning over to turn down the angry-sounding music – Rammstein, Baptiste would find out later, Marrineau's favourite group. 'You know why you're here?' he'd asked.

'Because of you,' Baptiste said.

Marrineau nodded and smiled. 'Because of me. You may have been police on the outside but in here you're nothing, less than nothing. Only now I have made you into something. Something new. I know why you're in here. I know what you did. And my enemy's enemy is my friend. Which makes you my brother. And now everyone out there knows it too. That don't mean you won't get bothered, but you won't get hassled by small-time *beurs* with sharpened toothbrushes like Ibrahim.'

And he was right. When Baptiste walked out of that cell and back across the yard, no one looked at him, or at least they pretended not to. And no small-timers came after him any more. Mostly they left him alone. Mostly. He had other scars too, but nothing like the one on his face.

Outside he heard the faint sound of a car engine, the hum of it carrying a long way in the stillness of the valley. He picked up his service weapon from the table and detached the magazine. It came out cleanly, everything smooth and oiled, and he opened a box of shells and started filling it. He glanced over at a photo pinned to the wall showing a small boy with big glasses standing at the edge of a play-ground and staring tentatively at the rides. It was slightly blurry, taken secretly with a zoomed-in camera. It was the only recent photograph he had of his son. Monsieur Belloq had sent it to him a few months before he was released.

He wondered now if it had all been planned, and those acts of kindness – the photo of Léo, being protected by the Brotherhood inside, the offer of somewhere to stay when he got out – all of it had been simply grooming him for this.

He slid the magazine back in place and felt the new weight of the gun. It didn't really matter what had brought him to this point, all that mattered was that he was here. The past was irrelevant. There was no point in dwelling on it, he had learned that inside. All there was was today, right now. You didn't think about the future because it made you weak. Except now Léo represented a future. And the thought of that didn't make him weak, it made him strong and determined.

The car crunched to a stop outside and the engine stayed running.

Time to go get his life back.

41

Marie-Claude's rattling Peugeot reached the outskirts of the city and she followed the signs for Toulouse–Blagnac Airport past the Stade Toulousain, where the locals worshipped rugby like a religion, and on to the grey steel and glass of the terminal building.

Solomon reluctantly wound his window up to make it harder for the security cameras to see inside and watched an orange-and-white plane rise up from behind the main terminal building with a deep rumbling roar, its wheels tucking up as it climbed into the air. He pointed to a sign with '*P5* & *P6 – Eco*' written on it. 'Head to the long-stay car parks.'

Marie-Claude fell in behind a large, black Audi SUV with tinted windows and a tow-bar on the back. 'What's the plan?' she said. 'I mean, if we've come to hire a car, I hope you've got money, because I don't and my credit cards are pretty much toast.'

'We're not going to hire a car,' Solomon said.

Ahead, the Audi turned off the road and entered a vast tarmacked field of multicoloured metal and glass. 'Follow that car and park as close to it as you can.'

'Are we gonna steal a car?' Léo whispered.

'Not exactly.' Solomon pulled the worn quarter he'd found by the side of a Texas road out of his pocket, rolled it back and forth across his knuckles, flicked it into the air then caught it and slapped it down on the back of his hand. 'We're going to make one disappear.' He removed his hand and the coin was gone.

Marie-Claude took a ticket at the barrier and followed the Audi into the heart of the car park, parking a row along from it between a dusty blue Volkswagen and a polished silver Porsche.

'How about that one?' Léo said, pointing at the gleaming car. 'Can we make that one disappear?'

Solomon smiled. 'I admire your sense of style, but we need something a little less showy.' He looked over at the black Audi, where a stormy-faced man was hauling cases angrily out of the back and thrusting them at his waiting wife and two children.

'Wait here,' he said, leaning forward to talk to Marie-Claude. 'Collect together everything you want to bring and keep out of sight.'

'Hey, wait! Where are you—'

But it was too late. Solomon was already gone.

He watched the tall, pale man walk away from the faded red Peugeot and frowned when the woman and boy didn't follow. Maybe they were waiting to make it look like they were travelling separately.

A plane banked over the car park, the noise of its engines like the sound of the sky ripping apart. He felt it rumble inside him and a sudden, blinding pain rapiered through the centre of his skull. He gripped the wheel, closing his eyes against the agony of it. It felt like something inside him, trying to split him open and escape. One day it would. One day soon. Episodes like this were getting more frequent, more painful. The thing inside him was getting stronger. He tried to breathe through the pain, his hand fumbling across the dashboard to the glove compartment and the relief that lay inside.

Outside the sound of the jet engines began to fade but the pain in his skull did not. It was like a great pressure, pushing up and out like lava through rock. He found the catch to the glove compartment and twisted it open, his hand sending pill bottles clattering as he fumbled for the metal hip flask containing the only thing that could cool this heat and calm the beast inside him. His hand closed round the cold metal and he dragged it out, sending more bottles rattling to the floor. The pressure in his head was like an explosion now, a huge, hot expansion of air in something too small to contain it. He unscrewed the lid, lifted the flask to his mouth, and sipped the bitter liquid.

The relief was instant, like water tipped on a fire. The liquid was morphine sulphate, the brand name Roxanol, but he knew what it really was. He took another sip, seeking the sweet aftertaste of the honey he mixed in to try and soften the bitterness of the liquid. It didn't really work, the bitterness was too profound, but he had come to associate the taste of honey with relief from the pain and continued to add it. Honey also held significance for the thing he was becoming, because honey was the taste of mead, the drink of Wotan, the liquid of poetry and knowledge.

He opened his eyes and the colours of the world burned around him, the sun reflecting off the windscreens in blades of light. He looked over at the bus stop and the world drifted and stretched like something not quite solid. The shuttle bus was there and he wondered how much time had passed since the pain had engulfed him, because it had not been there before. People crowded the doors, waiting for others to get off. Not long then.

He switched his attention back to the car. He could see the woman inside, along with the boy. No one else around. If what he sought was inside the car, he could easily take it. Seize the boy, put the blade to his throat, and his mother would do whatever he asked.

He leaned forward in his seat, looked up to make sure there were no cameras nearby, took a deep breath and felt the pressure shift a little in his head. The pain was gone but the thing that had brought it was still there – the thing that would soon overwhelm him and complete his transformation. He screwed the cap back on the flask, scooped the spilled pill bottles into the glove compartment and locked them away.

Outside, the colours were beginning to fade and the world seemed a little less dreamy. Over by the bus stop the passengers were streaming away into the car park, searching for their keys and their cars. He looked back at the faded red Peugeot. He would wait until the bus had gone and the passengers had found their cars and driven off. Then they would be alone in the car park, no cameras bearing witness: just the woman, her son – and him.

42

The screen beeped and Amand looked up. He had been immersed in the book and was surprised to discover a new command box had appeared in place of the countdown.

Three attempts remaining. Failure to input correct password will result in computer being permanently locked.

He leaned forward, his head humming with what he had read and what Marie-Claude might have used as a password. He typed in '*DieSchneiderLager*' and the screen shuddered.

Incorrect Password. Two attempts remaining.

He typed it again, in capitals this time. Another shudder.

One attempt remaining.

He sat back and stared out of the window. He knew he should give up and leave it to the Police Scientifique, but if he turned it over to them it could take days to find out what the hard drive contained, and it wasn't like the computer was going to self-destruct if he got the password wrong. He imagined the techies could probably hack a locked computer as easily as a password-protected one. He thought of Marie-Claude and Léo, still missing, maybe in danger. What the hell. If there was something locked inside this computer that might help track them down, he needed to try and get it out now, not wait for some teenager in a lab coat and a Star

209

Wars T-shirt to dig it out a week from now when it was too late.

He leaned back over the keyboard and tried to think like Marie-Claude. He thought about what he had read, the thousands of names on the wall and the red cotton threads converging on the piece of paper. All of it about one thing. He took a breath, typed '*Die Anderen*' and hit *Return*.

The screen blinked, the command box disappeared – and the desktop loaded. It was as neat and tidy as the desk was messy, with five named folders on display arranged on the screen like dots on a dice:

Herman Lansky   *Saul Schwartzfeldt*
                     Josef Engel
Artur Samler   *Die Anderen*

He opened Lansky's folder. It contained four sub-folders labelled – *Early Years, War Years, Post War, Death.* Amand opened the last one first and a new window opened, filled with a variety of documents – Word files, PDF files, JPEGS. He opened a PDF and an article from *The Hampstead Gazette* filled the screen. It was dated 16 June 1949 with the headline:

Death Camp Survivor Gassed in Own Flat

Amand scanned the article, his English just about good enough to glean details of how Herman Lansky's remains had been found in a burned-out flat in the London Borough of West Hampstead. He was described as a Polish Jew who'd resettled in London after the war and had achieved a small degree of celebrity following the publication of a memoir describing his time in a Nazi death camp run by the now notorious Nazi commandant, Artur Samler. A photograph accompanied the article showing Samler looking arrogant in his tailored Nazi uniform. There was no photograph of Herman Lansky.

Amand opened another file, a copy of the coroner's court report dated six months after the newspaper article, and scrolled down to the closing statement:

> The partial skeletal remains of a male adult were found in the embers of the flat. The intensity of the fire makes it impossible to positively identify the body but it is consistent with the age and sex of the known resident – Mr Herman Piotr Lansky – who has been missing since the fire.
>
> *Verdict:* Death by misadventure.

There were no documents in the folder relating to the police investigation and he made a mental note to look them up when he got back to the Commissariat.

He checked through the other folders, scanning the documents they contained, then opened the folder labelled *Saul Schwartzfeldt*. It contained the same four sub-folders and Amand spent a few minutes in each, working chronologically to build up a thumbnail sketch of the man and his life.

The *Early Years* folder was almost empty: a blurry, black-and-white photograph of a dark-haired child and a copy of a Nazi identification document dated 24 DEZ 1938 and stamped with a large red 'J' for '*Jude*' – *Jew*. It had a head-and-shoulders photograph of a young man and listed his name as Saul Israel Schwartzfeldt, along with *Geburtsort* – birthplace – Frankfurt, and *Beruf* – profession – *Schneider*. Schwartzfeldt had been a tailor, like Josef Engel.

The next folder – *War Years* – contained records of Jewish transportations from Frankfurt to Łodź and Warsaw. The name Saul Schwartzfeldt appeared multiple times on different lists and was highlighted in green marker each time. Again Amand marvelled at the amount of work Marie-Claude had done to find these lost people in history, these tiny needles in seventy-year-old haystacks.

The *Post War* folder contained various documents from the end of the war right up to the previous year and told the story of a full life lived, mainly through civic records gleaned from the archives of a town called Colmar. Amand recognized the name; he had visited it once and remembered a mountainous and woody place, more German in character than French. Maybe Monsieur Schwartzfeldt had chosen it as a kind of compromise, an ersatz German town where he could make a fresh start instead of returning to an old life in Frankfurt that the war had undoubtedly destroyed.

There were two marriage certificates in the folder, thirty years apart, and birth certificates for three children, all boys, as well as various newspaper articles showing photos of an increasingly older and fatter Saul, opening a school gym his textile-printing company had helped pay for, receiving the key to the town on the occasion of his retirement, campaigning for various local council offices and ultimately being elected as Mayor of Colmar. The photograph of his investiture, with his grown-up family and second wife surrounding him, was a portrait of success, a record of a full life well-lived and a man well-loved. All of which made the contents of the last folder all the more shocking.

Saul Schwartzfeldt's *Death* folder was by far the fullest. It consisted mainly of newspaper reports dated six months ago, where the same local papers that had borne admiring witness to his charmed life now reported his brutal death with equal shock.

Amand opened one of the longer articles and scrolled past the headline '**Shocking Murder of Ex-Mayor**' to a photograph of a small cottage by a wide river with a group of gendarmes standing around it. The man in the centre was identified as Commandant Gilles Rapp, lead investigator in the murder case. He scrolled back to the top and had started to read when his phone buzzed suddenly, making his heart twinge with a sharp stab of pain. He snatched it up to answer it. 'Amand?'

'It's Henri. Where are you?'

'Still at La Broderie.'

'Well, get back to the Commissariat. There's someone here you need to talk to.'

'Who?'

'Magellan.'

'Solomon Creed's psychiatrist?'

'He just arrived here. Says he needs to talk to you about his missing client. Says it's urgent.'

'OK, stick him in my office and give him a coffee or something and I'll be right there. And run a background check on him, we only called him an hour ago. This could easily be a journalist posing as him to try and get information about the case.'

'OK: coffee, background check. Got it.'

Henri hung up and Amand looked at all the information he had yet to go through. There was too much and it was too important to skim-read. He reached over to the open pack of memory sticks, took one and fitted it into a USB port at the back of the computer. The icon for the stick appeared and he highlighted all five folders on the desktop and drummed his fingers on the desk as the hundreds of files Marie-Claude had meticulously accumulated were copied to the drive.

He looked at the headline again, '**Shocking Murder of Ex-Mayor**', and thought about what Magellan had told him earlier, about Solomon having certain toxic memories removed. He wondered again what those memories were and what exactly Solomon had done to end up in Magellan's facility. Perhaps he had been in France; his French was certainly good enough. Maybe he had visited a little town on the German border called Colmar. He would ask Magellan about it when he saw him. He would ask him a lot of things.

43

There were no seats left by the time Solomon reached the bus and he had to squeeze through people to stand where he needed to be, up front and facing backwards. The bus smelled of deodorant, bad breath and the rusty, metallic smell of stress that had oozed from the pores of everyone who'd ridden on it to board planes they didn't want to catch. The doors closed with a hydraulic hiss and Solomon felt the usual tightening at the back of his neck at being confined. The bus lurched into motion and Solomon rode it, his feet planted apart like a seasoned sailor on a rolling deck.

The family from the Audi were next to him, the father scowling at his phone and the two boys glaring impatiently at their mother, who was busily pulling various electronic devices and tangled earphones from a large shoulder bag. She seemed harried and tired, the lone servant in a retinue of emperors. She was also the only one standing, her husband and two boys having claimed three of a group of four seats and filling the fourth with the large case the man had been carrying. The bus took a corner and the mother stumbled into Solomon.

'*Pardon, monsieur,*' she said, looking up but keeping her head tilted down in a way that showed how accustomed she was to submission.

'Not your fault, madame.' Solomon looked at her husband. 'Monsieur. Do you think you might move your case so your wife can sit down?'

The man looked up from his phone and his skin reddened. 'It's too heavy to move,' he said. 'We'll be there in a minute. She doesn't mind standing.'

'But I mind,' Solomon said. 'And she's not the only one having to stand. Here,' he grabbed the handle of the case. 'Allow me.' He hoisted it from the seat and across the aisle to an empty space high on the luggage rack opposite. 'Madame,' he said, indicating the vacant seat. 'No point in standing now.' She looked at the empty seat as if it were a trap before slowly sitting in it.

The man grunted and returned his attention to his phone. His wife smiled nervously at Solomon then resumed her frantic mission to provide electronic amusement to her children. She had managed to furnish them with iPads and earphones when the bus pulled up at the terminal.

Solomon stood aside to let other people off first, trapping the family in their seats behind him.

'You going to let us get off or do we need your permission?' the man huffed behind him.

'Just letting the people off,' Solomon said, turning to him with a broad smile. 'I have a thing about good manners. Here, let me help you with your luggage.'

He turned and lifted the case clear of the high shelf as easily as he had put it there and carried it down the steps to the pavement. The mother shepherded her boys after him, carrying their cases while they clutched their screens. The man followed, taking his time, making it clear he was not being ordered around by anyone. He stepped on to the pavement and drew himself up to his full height. He was as

216

tall as Solomon and twice the size, something he had clearly noticed too. He tilted his head back, jutted his chin out and looked down at Solomon as if deciding whether to punch him or not.

'Sorry if I offended you,' Solomon said, offering his hand. The man glanced at it and smiled. 'I'll shake your hand,' he said, loud enough that everyone around would see him being the big man. Then he took Solomon's hand – and he crushed it.

Solomon saw the glint in his eye as he gave him his best locker-room knuckle-breaker. He took the pain for a second, allowing the man his moment of satisfaction as he ground the bones in Solomon's hand. Then he squeezed back. The victory glint in the man's eyes vanished and was replaced by surprise. Solomon continued to squeeze, his long, pale fingers wrapping fully round the man's fist and tightening steadily. A fork-shaped vein swelled in the man's temple and he snorted, an involuntary noise in his throat, the closest he could allow himself to acknowledging the pain he was experiencing. He was trapped in the handshake now, snared in his own locker-room rules. He couldn't pull away, that wasn't how these things worked, he couldn't yelp or plead with Solomon to stop either. All he could do was suck it up and stay quiet until Solomon released him. Solomon leaned in, using the handshake to pull them close enough that their chests were touching and his mouth was right by the man's ear. 'Thank you for accepting my apology,' he whispered. And let go.

The man almost jumped backwards, flexing his hand but trying not to show it hurt. He nodded, still acting as if he was the big man, but his chin was down and when he glanced at Solomon he was effectively looking up at him. He grabbed the handle of his wheelie case with his uncrushed hand and hurried away, snapping at his wife and kids to keep up. Solomon watched him leave.

'Bravo, monsieur.' He turned to the voice and looked through the open doors of the bus at a man somewhere in his sixties with a thick moustache that made him seem mournful. 'I drive this bus back and forth, four days a week, six trips an hour, eight hours a day, and there's not one day yet I haven't gone home at the end of a shift wanting to strangle some kid or punch some guy for being rude. The women aren't much better, talking on their phones and cursing like sailors.' He shook his head and smiled at Solomon. 'If I wore a hat, I'd take it off to you, monsieur, for what you just did, but they cut the hat from the uniform about ten years back. We don't even have to wear a tie any more, but I do. Just because the world's going to hell in a hurry doesn't mean I have to go along for the ride. But today you restored my faith a little. I'm sure tomorrow I'll go right back to hating everyone, but thank you for giving me a rare day off.'

Solomon smiled. 'When are you due to return to the car park?'

The driver checked his watch. 'Five minutes. Why?'

Solomon held up the key to the Audi he'd lifted from the man's pocket while he'd been distracted by the pain in his hand. 'I left something in my car.'

The driver looked in his mirrors to check how many people had got on the bus and see if anyone else was coming, then hit a button to close the middle and rear doors. 'Jump on,' he said. 'I'll take you back right now. Compliments of the house.'

218

44

Marie-Claude stared down the line of parked cars, waiting for the bus to return, wondering if Solomon would be on it. She ran through everything that had happened that morning, from the first knock on her door to sitting here waiting for a man she knew almost nothing about to return.

When he'd appeared from nowhere and said he had come to save her son, it had touched something in her. Maybe because she wasn't used to having someone prepared to make sacrifices for her or her son. And Léo had trusted him too, and he *never* trusted new people, not after everything he'd been through and the way he saw people so clearly. She didn't fully understand how Léo's gift worked, the way he could read people like he could. Sometimes she wished he didn't have his gift because he saw more than a seven-year-old should and it made him withdrawn and odd when all she wanted was for him to fit in and be normal. But it had been her decision ultimately to drive them here and she had been carried along by adrenaline and curiosity, always her curiosity, blinkered by the prospect of finally discovering something of her family history. The psychiatrist she had seen for a while had identified it as her tendency to obsessively focus on only one perspective and react emotionally to it instead of rationally. She had done it again today, jumping in the car when she should have stayed in Cordes. It was only now, in the calm of this moment, that she could see things differently. She closed her eyes, dropped her head down and shook it slowly.

'What's up?' a small voice piped up from the back.

'I'm sorry, Léo.'

'Why?'

'For dragging you all the way to Toulouse with a stranger.' She shook her head again.

'Monsieur Creed isn't a stranger. Grampy made the suit for him.'

'Honey, he *can't* be the same man.'

'But his hair is all white, like Grampy's, and he talks like an old person. He knows loads of stuff too. And he came for the waistcoat and it's got his name in it, so it must be him.'

Marie-Claude opened her mouth to speak then realized something.

The suit – Solomon had it: jacket and waistcoat. Maybe he wasn't planning on coming back at all. Wasn't this what con men did: win your trust to make you drop your guard before walking off with your credit cards? She had been too trusting. *Far* too trusting. She looked in the back seat. The note from her grandfather was there, with Otto Adelstein's address inside it.

'Listen,' she looked over at Léo, 'why don't we head to Dijon ourselves, just you and me?'

Léo's face clouded. 'What about Monsieur Creed?'

'He'll be fine. You heard what he said: he can make cars disappear. Anyone who can do that doesn't need us to drive him around. We've brought him this far, but I think maybe we'd be better off on our own from now on.'

220

Léo looked out of the window towards the empty bus stop, the last place they'd seen Solomon. 'I think we should wait for him to come back. I think Grampy would want us to stay with him. He said if we kept the suit safe for him, Monsieur Creed would come for it and he would look after us. And he did come. If we go now and leave him, how can he keep us safe? What if the shadow comes back?'

'He won't come back, honey. There's nothing to worry about.'

The man wrapped the black scarf around his face, tucked it under his hat then stepped out of his car. He moved to the boot, removed the bayonet from the folds of grey cloth, locked his car and moved away, keeping the Peugeot in his peripheral vision. The bayonet was long and unwieldy, not the best weapon to use in a confined space like the interior of a car. He would use it to smash the rear window and grab the kid without running the risk of fumbling at a locked door. All that flying glass, the sound of the window breaking, followed by the sight of the big heavy blade against her son's throat – the woman would tell him whatever he wanted to know, give him whatever he asked for. If she had the list, he would take it. Once he finally had the names of *Die Anderen*, the Wild Hunt could continue to its end.

Das zuende bringen was begonnen wurde – Finishing what was begun.

He reached the end of his row and cut through the lines of parked cars, closing the distance between himself and the Peugeot. The woman was twisted round in her seat, talking to the boy, her focus all on him. He gripped the handle of the bayonet and tasted honey and bitterness in his mouth.

Then he saw movement beyond the car.

'The bus!' Léo shouted, pointing across the car park.

Marie-Claude spun round, saw the shuttle bus coming down the access road and experienced a moment of sudden panic, like she was running out of time. Maybe they should wait. She glanced in her mirror and saw a dark figure moving between the cars in the row behind her. It was only there for a second then slipped from sight but it made her mouth go dry. She twisted the key in the ignition and the engine of the Peugeot turned and coughed but refused to catch.

'Shouldn't we wait for Monsieur Creed?' Léo said.

She looked in the mirror, searching for the shadow and saw nothing but cars. She stamped her foot on the clutch to free the gearbox up, pumped the accelerator pedal a few times and turned the key. 'I don't think he's coming back,' she said, twisting the key again. She didn't want to tell Léo about the shadow. She wasn't even sure now she'd seen it herself. 'I think Monsieur Creed has gone and it's time we went too.'

She twisted the key again and the car shuddered into life. She rammed it into gear and lurched out of the parking spot, glancing in her mirrors to try and catch a glimpse of the figure but seeing nothing. It was probably only a passenger on their way to the bus. She was jumpy, that was all. It didn't matter, she was committed now. They were leaving and that was that.

She pulled up at the barrier as the bus reached the stop and searched around for her ticket. She thought she'd tossed it into the passenger seat but it wasn't there now and she started frantically sifting through the snowdrift of receipts and wrappers on the floor.

'Look,' Léo said.

She sat up and looked in her mirrors, convinced that the dark figure had appeared behind them again. But there was no one there.

'He *did* come back,' Léo said. She realized he was looking forward at Solomon, who was walking towards her with a neutral expression that could have been surprise or disappointment or any number of things. She sat back in her seat, feeling like a kid who'd been spotted sneaking out of school, and waited for him to arrive. He stopped by her window, his expression as unreadable close up as it had been at distance. He held up a small white card and Marie-Claude's mild shame flared into anger when she saw what it was. 'You took the ticket!'

'I borrowed it.'

Marie-Claude snatched it back from him. 'Why – to make sure we couldn't go anywhere?'

Solomon shook his head. 'I wanted to make sure you were here when I got back so I could give you this.' He held out an electronic key fob with an Audi logo on it. 'You really won't get very far in your car, especially now your registration plate has been picked up by the barrier cameras. I also wondered if you might be having second thoughts about travelling with me.' He looked at the car parked by the barrier. 'Clearly you did. I don't blame you. This whole situation is . . . unconventional. I don't want you to feel compelled to continue travelling with me if you don't want to. So take the keys and go, if that's what you want.'

'What about the waistcoat? Will you hand that over too, if I decide to leave?'

223

Solomon smiled. 'No.'

She glanced in her mirrors, looking for the figure that had spooked her earlier, but saw nothing except Léo's eyes staring back at her, wide and imploring. She knew what he would say on the subject. She looked again at Solomon, the waistcoat snug on his slender frame, and remembered what her grandfather had written:

. . . take this waistcoat to my old friend Otto Adelstein . . .

Do not trust this task to anyone else. You must deliver it yourself.

She owed it to him to do as he asked; it was the least she could do. And if that meant delivering it with a person inside it, well, that was what she would do.

'Get in,' she said, and forced the car into reverse with a harsh grinding sound that exactly matched her mood.

45

Amand was sweating and his chest felt tight by the time he made it back to the Commissariat. He entered by the rear entrance to avoid the journalists and found the office had quietened considerably. Henri looked up as he entered.

'Where's Magellan?' Amand asked.

'In your office drinking the finest stewed police coffee, as requested. You also had a couple of messages . . .' He peered at his notebook: 'The court has appointed a *juge d'instruction* and he wants to see you.'

'Who is it?'

'Jacques Laurent.'

Amand groaned inwardly. He didn't know Laurent senior particularly well, but he knew his son Edmond. He was a member of the PNFL and was heavily involved in Jean-Luc Belloq's political campaign. Rumour had it that the apple hadn't fallen far from the tree. Amand had hoped to get a more liberal judge, particularly given the nationality of the new suspect. 'Can't I just call him?'

'He said he wants to see you. You also got a call from Madame Zimbaldi.'

Amand took out his phone, found the number for the morgue and dialled.

A woman's voice answered after the first ring. 'Zimbaldi!'

'Madame Coroner, it's Benoît Amand at Cordes.'

'Oh yes, thank you for getting back to me. I looked at the wounds as you requested and there is something odd about them – not only the lash marks, all of them.'

'Odd in what way?'

'It would be easier to show you. I'm sure you probably don't have time but—'

'I'm on my way to Albi to see the *juge* anyway. I'll be there in twenty minutes.' He hung up and glanced out of the window at his Citroën, looking even more battered alongside the gleaming black Range Rover parked next to it. 'Is there a spare car I could use?'

'They're all out looking for Marie-Claude and Solomon Creed.'

'What about yours?'

'I walked in today.'

'Great.' He looked over at the door to his office. 'Did you check Magellan out?'

Henri angled his screen so Amand could see it. It was filled with a series of overlapping documents, academic articles mostly. The top one was from a French psychology journal detailing advances in the field of criminal psychology. It carried a photograph of a distinguished-looking man with long silver hair swept back from a widow's peak and a matching full beard that gave him a leonine appearance. The caption identified him as Dr Cezar Magellan of the ICP – Institute of Criminal Psychology. 'Is that him?'

Henri shrugged. 'Either him or his identical brother.'

Amand scrolled through the article, skim-reading about Magellan's work in the field of psychopathic studies and rehabilitation. Towards the bottom of the article, another photograph showed what looked like a nuclear bunker surrounded by high fences and desert and dusty mountains. According to the caption, it was the main, high-security facility of the ICP in the Sonoran Desert, Mexico. There was also an impressive list of the criminals being treated there, a rogues' gallery of monsters whose crimes had been exotic enough to afford them a macabre kind of international celebrity. Amand had heard of all of them and reminded himself that Solomon Creed had been one of Magellan's patients too and was probably out there somewhere with Marie-Claude and Léo.

'Do I pass?' a deep voice rumbled behind him.

Amand turned to discover the man from the photograph standing behind him wearing a slightly crumpled, grey linen suit. 'We have to confirm you are who you say you are.'

Magellan smiled, showing neat American teeth. 'Of course.' His low, therapy-smooth voice sounded deeper than it had on the phone. 'Thank you for agreeing to see me.'

They shook hands. Magellan's grip was strong and firm and he studied Amand with eyes that had some sparkle in them, like he was amused at something. Amand had a thought. 'You wouldn't happen to have a car, would you?'

'Yes, why?'

'I need to go somewhere. If you drive me, we could talk at the same time.'

'Of course.' Magellan pointed out front at the black Range Rover parked alongside Amand's wrecked Citroën.

Amand headed to the door. 'Don't say anything until we're in the car,' he said, then stepped through the front door and into the sun. One of the journalists spotted him and surged forward holding his phone out. 'You've arrested an Arab,' he said. 'Do you think the murder was racially motivated?'

'No,' Amand replied. 'And if you print that I'll arrest you.' He got into the car and slammed the door shut. Magellan got in too and the engine purred to life.

'Drive,' Amand said, 'straight up here then take a left.'

They rumbled away across the cobbles and Amand took in the dark leather interior, the walnut dashboard, the whisper of the powerful engine. 'The psychiatry business has clearly been kind.'

Magellan shrugged. 'I have a lot of extremely wealthy clients who pay me obscene amounts of money to help them with their banal, self-induced ailments. It's a perfect symbiotic relationship: I help them cope with the psychological fallout of their ridiculous lives, drug addiction and the like, while they help fund my more serious research. They also grant me access to their resources, if I need them. I flew to La Rochelle on a private jet, for example – small compensation for having to listen to their grotesque, first world, privileged problems. Where are we going?'

'Albi. It's a twenty-minute drive, plenty of time to talk. Let's wait until we get off these cobbles and on to the main road. Then I want you to tell me everything you can about Solomon Creed.'

46

Marie-Claude parked the Peugeot back in the space she had recently vacated and the car shuddered and coughed before falling silent.

'Anything you want to bring, grab it,' Solomon said, scanning the car park. 'And switch off your phone and take the battery out.'

Marie-Claude took her phone from her pocket and stared at it. Right now she could drive home with Léo and say she'd gone for a drive to clear her head if anyone asked where she'd been. But if she switched off her phone, took the battery out, and drove away in someone else's car, she would be crossing a line.

'You can go home, if you like,' Solomon said, picking up on her hesitation.

Marie-Claude nodded. The mother in her was telling her to return home and let the police deal with everything, but the granddaughter part felt that all of this was her fault, that if she hadn't started digging into her family's past her grandfather might still be alive. But it was too late now. She couldn't undo what had been done, all she could do was try to find out who did it and why. She owed him that.

'OK,' she said, prising the back off her phone and pulling

the battery out. 'But I'm driving – and I warn you, I'm going to hound you with questions the whole way down.'

'Fine.' Solomon handed her the keys. 'In truth, I'm not sure I can drive.'

Marie-Claude stared at him. 'You don't know if you can drive or not?'

'There are lots of things I've forgotten about myself. Maybe if I get behind the wheel it will come back to me. Maybe it won't. Now is not the time to find out. So you drive, and ask your questions as we go. But first, you both need to do exactly as I say.'

He watched the Peugeot and the pain in his head shifted and moved. He had been so close until she'd seen him in her mirrors and he'd had to hide. Or maybe she hadn't seen him at all. No matter. They were back in the car now. Waiting for something. He could wait too.

The shuttle bus departed and returned again, and he prepared himself to move if they went to catch it. But they didn't. The passengers disembarked, found their cars and drove away. The bus left again. The car park was silent.

A plane took off and banked overhead, the roar of its engines like the ominous growl of something big and wild coming his way, like another omen. Everything seemed to be an omen to him now, the ordinary stuff of everyday life shining with fresh colour and meaning as he saw things through different eyes, Wotan's eyes. The plane climbed higher, disappearing into the clouds, dragging the sound of thunder with it.

When the bus came a second time he began to suspect that the sound of thunder *had* been an omen – one he had failed to heed. More passengers emerged from the bus, dragging their wheelie cases behind them, hard wheels rumbling across the concrete like a reminder of the thunder.

They reached their cars and started to drive away. He joined them, easing out of his spot and heading for the space where the Peugeot was parked. He drove past slowly, head tilted down, eyes straining to look left. When he saw the car was empty, he turned his head and looked properly. He pulled to a stop, the pain in his head expanding as he got out of his car, the bayonet heavy in his hand. They had to be in there. He had never taken his eyes off it. They had to be ducked down, keeping out of sight. The woman must have seen him after all; maybe this was a ploy to lure him out into the open. If that was what they had in mind, they would be sorry. Because here he was – not the man but Wotan – striding towards them with his sword in hand.

He reached the car and felt the boiling rage of the angry god inside him as he moved from front to back, not believing what he was seeing. They had gone, vanished. Another plane took off, filling the world with thunder. He turned and stumbled back to his own car and the flask in the glove compartment with the bitter, honeyed water that would ease the growing pressure in his head, wondering who the pale man was, and what other kinds of magic he might be capable of if he could make people disappear in broad daylight?

47

'His real name is James Hawdon,' Magellan said, 'though I would suggest you continue referring to him as Solomon Creed, if that's the identity he has adopted. Some of what I'm about to tell you are my own observations and deductions, the rest comes from case notes and anecdotes related and independently verified by either James Hawdon's family or by individuals who have known him throughout his life.'

He took a deep breath like he was about to dive into a dark ocean, then started to talk, his voice blending with the hum of the tyres along the Albi road.

'James John Huffam Hawdon is the only son and heir of an extremely wealthy, very powerful and – between you and I – dangerously dysfunctional family. The Hawdons are old money, European aristocracy who moved to the New World when their fortune began to fail and succeeded in making a new one, bigger than the one they had lost.

'They started by leasing, then building slave ships and used the profits to buy land: sugar, cotton and tobacco plantations in Louisiana, Georgia and South Carolina. They still own most of those estates, and tobacco and sugar prices are booming.

'In accordance with their European aristocratic heritage,

they tended to marry within their own narrow social circle and became cursed over time with what might be described as "weak blood". This manifested itself in congenital health problems such as haemophilia, as well as psychological peculiarities often exacerbated by the excessive lifestyle and opportunities of the idle rich.

'Jefferson Hawdon, James's father, is a case in point. He has a long history of psychosis that has been significantly worsened by addictions to both alcohol and narcotics, which was how I first became acquainted with the family. I'm not breaking client confidentiality by revealing any of this to you; it's been well documented in the tabloid press. I tell you only to give some context about the world James Hawdon was born into.

'James John Huffam Hawdon was born on 29 February 1980, the only son of Jefferson Makepeace and Honoria Bellefleur Hawdon. He was remarkable from the moment he was born, partly due to a total lack of pigment in his skin – a result of his "thin" bloodline – but also because of his extraordinary intellect. Every single person who knew him as a child – nannies, tutors, school friends – they all said the same thing: James Hawdon was the smartest person they ever met. He started talking when he was only a few months old, had learned to read by the time he was one, and was reading the newspaper and whole books shortly thereafter. He surprised his mother one morning by greeting her in Spanish – he'd picked it up from a Mexican maid. By the time he was four, he was fluent.

'When he was five they tried to measure his IQ, but all existing tests proved too easy for him. He was beyond the measurable scale. Of course, having a high IQ is one thing, applying it is another. I have treated many incredibly bright people who totally lack any kind of meaningful focus and consequently embark on self-destructive behaviours. James Hawdon was not like this. His interests were boundless: languages, art, science, medicine, physics, philosophy. In a time before the internet, he was like a human Wikipedia. Reading everything. Remembering everything. He was physically gifted too, possessing an extraordinary form of eidetic kinaesthesia, meaning he can see a movement or action once and mimic it perfectly, allowing him to pick up new disciplines as fast as his many private tutors could teach him, everything from ballet to martial arts.

'His mother encouraged him in everything – the best teachers, unfettered access to the extensive library in the main Hawdon family estate in England, no subject barred, no age-restriction on the material he was allowed to read. Maybe some of his problems started here. Just because a child is able to read anything doesn't mean they should. And a boy like James Hawdon, with such a ferociously vivid and powerful mind . . .' Magellan shook his head. 'I wonder what he made of such things such as Nietzsche's nihilism, or Dante's *Inferno*, or the works of the Marquis de Sade, or any number of books fathoming the darkest and more venal facets of the human animal? I fear such works would inevitably leave marks on the developing mind. I believe they did.

'As part of his education, he was taken to see all the great wonders of the world, both ancient and modern, always accompanied by his mother, often staying with distant relatives from the European branches of the Hawdon family. It was like an old-fashioned Grand Tour – all the great cities, all the best sights, all the greatest museums and galleries – and young genius James at the centre of it all, absorbing everything with his loving mother his constant companion.

'Jefferson Hawdon was having problems of his own during most of this time, managing all the family interests as well as developing and battling his own addictions. It is not generally the custom of the rich and privileged to look after their young anyway, or at least not the men, not when they can pay other people to do that for them. His mother could have done the same, of course, handed her son over to a succession of nannies and tutors, but she didn't. Honoria was utterly devoted to her son. Besotted. Which makes what happened to her all the more inexplicable.

'When James Hawdon was twelve years old there was an incident. Police were called to the Hawdon estate after a housekeeper found James's mother bloody and unconscious on her bedroom floor. She had been badly beaten – broken ribs, cracked skull, a dangerous swelling on the brain. She was in a coma for several weeks. When questioned by the police, Jefferson Hawdon told them his son James was responsible. The boy had always been close to his mother, but on reaching puberty the relationship had developed into something more sinister, a sexual obsession as well as a growing hatred of his father – classic Freudian, Oedipus complex stuff. He said his wife had confided in him that she felt increasingly uncomfortable around their son, that his demands for attention were becoming insistent and inappropriate. He claimed she'd been trying to distance herself, redraw the boundaries and make their relationship less intense, but this had only served to anger and confuse James even more, until she had become afraid of him.'

Amand looked across at Magellan. 'You keep saying "claimed". You don't believe him?'

Magellan shook his head. 'When Honoria eventually came out of the coma, she refuted everything her husband had said. Though she claimed she didn't know who had attacked her, she insisted it wasn't James. She denied there was anything inappropriate about their relationship. Her husband said she was hysterical and confused and only doing what any mother would do to try and protect her son. While she had been in her coma the doctors had found historical evidence of physical abuse: unexplained scars, cracked finger bones that had healed. Jefferson said it proved his son's abuse had been going on for a while and that his wife had clearly been too afraid to tell anyone. He argued that things would only get worse if his son remained in the family home and that his priority was to protect his wife. He had James committed to a juvenile psychiatric facility.'

'Did no one suspect the father?'

'Maybe. But the Hawdon family wealth and name clearly carried more weight with the police than the urge to follow correct procedure. So James was committed and his mother, utterly inconsolable at the loss of her son, was released into her husband's care and removed to the Hawdon estate where a private medical team was hired to look after her and nurse her back to health.'

'How long did James Hawdon remain in the institute?'

'Well now, there's the real tragedy. You'd probably think, given James's privileged background, that he would have been committed to some country-club facility, something that resembled a health spa, but he wasn't. The place his father sent him was called Bethlehem Hospital, a bleak and backward institute on the north-eastern coast of England, built in the nineteenth century by a Victorian philanthropist and family friend of the Hawdons. It was modelled on the hospital in London of the same name. Bethlehem Hospital is where the word *bedlam* comes from, meaning chaos and uproar – and that was exactly what was recreated on the Northumberland shoreline. It was a truly horrible place.

'I visited it once as a student, long before James was incarcerated there, and Bedlam was the right name for it. This was no place for getting well, it was a place to suffer and get worse. I saw patients wandering through the grounds and white-tiled wards, lost in delirium, their white gowns making them appear more like ghosts than people. I don't know if James was genuinely psychologically disturbed when he arrived there – we only have his father's word on that, along with the paid-off quacks who committed him. What is certain is that he did become genuinely disturbed once he got there. Who wouldn't? There he was, this unworldly, delicate boy genius in possession of a colossal intellect and vast knowledge of the world in the abstract, but with almost no real experience of it. He had travelled, of course, but always in his privileged bubble and with his mother as his constant companion and confidant. Being removed from her must have been extraordinarily traumatic, like having a limb torn away.

'James's notes record a predictable reaction from the moment of admission: paranoia, terror, anger. I imagine he thought it was all a terrible mistake and that someone would come along to rescue him. But nobody did. People were not sent to Bethlehem Hospital to be cured, they were sent there to be forgotten. And as days became weeks, James slipped into a deep despair. Without his mother, he would have felt frightened, abandoned, betrayed – not only by her but also by his father. And if he was innocent, as I believe he was, he would also have burned with the injustice of it all.

'But survival is a powerful and primal instinct, and the human mind will try to make sense of even the most nonsensical and unbearable of situations. James Hawdon's mind, marinaded in all that classical learning, began to create a narrative to explain what had happened to him. He believed that the hospital was in fact Hell and his father was God who had cast him out from the heaven of his life and into this hellhole populated by other lost souls like him.

'Delusions such as these often come hand in hand with strategies for potential salvation, and in James Hawdon's case this took the form of a redemptive quest. He began to believe the only way he could save himself was by saving others, and that each "soul" saved would take him a step closer to his own redemption. Had he been my patient, I would have worked with this delusion and attempted to steer him back to a more solid sense of reality through therapy and medication. Unfortunately, at Bethlehem Hospital the favoured treatment was sedation and electro-shock therapy, which only made him worse.

'He began to believe he could see the dead and that they were there to help guide him on his quest. He interrogated other patients about their own delusions, searching for people to save. He was probably the only one in the place who took any real interest in the patients and the act of listening is powerful medicine. As a result, this pale, charismatic, genius kid became a figurehead for the inmates of Bethlehem Hospital. Someone who would listen to them when no one else would. A kind of prophet of the abandoned and the damned. And all of this fed into James's growing delusions that he was some kind of Messianic figure, sent to save the damned so that he might ultimately find his way back to God, his father – and also his mother. The tragic irony, of course, was that his deepening delusions made a return to his family impossible. As far as his father was concerned, it merely proved what he had always claimed:

that his son was a dangerous lunatic who needed to remain in full-time, high-security psychiatric care.

'And he did. James Hawdon grew up in that facility. He became a man there, or more accurately he became a more grown-up projection of his delusions. He shifted through different names to identify his proliferating identities – Adam, Zachariah, Solomon – and began to hold sermons in the main hall, predicting a coming day of resurrection when he would walk through the walls, be reborn in the world outside and begin his journey towards salvation.

'Then one day, just over a year ago, he did exactly that. He orchestrated a mass riot, used the chaos to slip away from the hospital and turned up a few days later at the Hawdon family estate, having walked the whole way there. Whether he was looking for a reconciliation with his father or not is unclear. What he found was his mother, home alone, playing with her eight-year-old son Henry – James Hawdon's brother.

'One can only begin to imagine the shock James must have felt when he discovered, after all those years of clinging to the hope of one day being reconciled with his adoring mother, that she had effectively replaced him. It must have broken his heart. It certainly broke his mind.

'Jefferson Hawdon came home later that day to discover that his family had finally been united – but only in death. His wife had been eviscerated, her entrails wrapped around the bloody corpse of his young son, as well as James, who was lying naked on the floor, curled up in the foetal position as if attempting a form of rebirth. I think if Jefferson had realized that James was still alive, he would have killed him. As it was, he went into his office, called a close friend at the justice department to come and deal with it, and began a narcotics and alcohol binge that is ongoing. I was treating Jefferson for his addictions by this stage, so knew the family and its history. That's how James came into my care.

'Bethlehem Hospital had burned down during the riot James had started, so a return there was impossible. His father also wanted to remove him from England, and put physical distance between him and the family, so he sent him to my facility in Mexico, a maximum-security hospital set up to study and treat the most dangerous criminals in the world.'

'And this is the place he escaped from three weeks ago? The place where you removed his memory?'

'Not removed, subdued, by using a combination of therapy and a subcutaneous implant of antipsychotic drugs here –' He pointed at a spot on his shoulder.

'The implant that's about to wear out?'

'Indeed. I believe you are also looking for someone other than James in connection with the recent murder, correct?'

Amand nodded. 'A woman and her son.'

'I hardly need point out the dangerous symbol a mother and young boy might represent to James Hawdon, given the history I have told you. I'm not saying he would harm them, but I can't say he wouldn't either. And if he is travelling with this woman and her son, then you and I must find him before that implant runs out, or we will both have to live with the consequences.'

48

Baptiste stayed low in his seat as LePoux drove them into Cordes, his face covered by a cap so anyone glancing in the car would see someone sleeping instead of Jean Baptiste, disgraced local son, skulking back to town after four long years away. He had imagined his return many times while staring at the concrete ceiling of his cell, though never like this or in these circumstances.

He could see fragments of the town now, the underside of trees, the tops of stone houses, corrugated red-tiled roofs and the blue sky beyond. He smiled as the bell tower on the Rue D'Horloge struck the hour, marking time even though time stood still here. Every day the shadows shifted and the sun slid across the sky, but the town stayed the same.

The car turned, the view shifted and they started to slow. 'We're here,' LePoux grunted.

Baptiste synchronized his watch with the one in the car. 'Check there's no one around, then drop me off and drive away. Come back in twenty minutes.'

'But what if someone comes along?'

'I'll be fine. Just make sure you get back on time.'

They pulled to a halt and LePoux looked around in a way

that was so unsubtle he might as well have been leaning on the horn. 'There's no one here,' he said.

'That's lucky,' Baptiste muttered. He opened the door and stepped back on to a street of his home town for the first time in four years.

La Rue des Lices was one of the less pretty side roads, lined with hundred-year-old workers' cottages that were practically new in Cordes terms. Most had been split into apartments. Marie-Claude had a ground-floor garden flat, which made things easier for Baptiste. He moved towards the passage that ran between her address and next door, and disappeared into it, listening ahead for any sound, and slowing as he neared the rear of the house. He peered round the edge of the wall, swallowed at the sight of the kid's bike lying on its side, then moved forward, keeping close to the house.

The back door was locked but one of the panes of glass in it had been broken. He looked through it into the kitchen beyond, saw a dark pool of something like blood on the kitchen floor and felt a rush of anger at this evidence of violence in his son's home.

He reached through the broken glass, unlocked the door and went inside. Everything was still and silent, no sign of anyone at home. He looked around the kitchen and pictured his son here, sitting at the table, getting a glass of water from the sink. The breakfast things were out: a bowl with a puddle of milk and a red-handled spoon next to a box of Cini Minis, which angered him further. She shouldn't be giving him sugar-filled crap for breakfast.

He looked at the bloodstain, the broken glass on the floor. Who else had been here? What had they been looking for?

He spotted a pile of unopened letters on the worktop

next to the toaster and some unpaid bills stuck to the fridge alongside drawings of action scenes and hero figures: men flying, men fighting, some wearing armour, others wearing capes. One looked like an ordinary guy apart from the knives coming out of his fists. The drawing was good, the snarl on the man's face angry and convincing. It looked a little like him. Baptiste freed it from the rest and traced the name scrawled in the corner in pencil – Léo. He folded it, put it in his pocket, and moved deeper into the house.

He spotted the superhero drawings and cut-out images covering the partly open door opposite and Lego and comic books scattered across the floor beyond it. He could see the corner of a bed too, and a rumpled duvet cover with more superheroes on it. He imagined that Léo was curled up in it, unaware that his father was standing on the other side of the door. He pictured the slow rise and fall of his chest as he slept, his long eyelashes on his cheek, and felt a pricking at the back of his eyes. He turned away to check the other rooms first, putting off for a little longer the moment when he would push the door open and see that he wasn't really there.

He checked Marie-Claude's bedroom first and felt a twist of disgust when he saw the mess inside – the unmade bed, the underwear. She had always been untidy. Living alone had seemingly made her worse. And she did live alone, he could tell that as he quickly tossed the room. There were no men's shirts or boxer shorts mixed in with her clothes, and that made him feel happy. He was an alpha male: territorial, like all dominant male animals. Just because he had rejected Marie-Claude did not mean he wanted someone else to have her, and he did not like the idea of someone else playing daddy to Léo either. He noticed the upturned chair, the mattress out of place. Someone had searched the room before him. Cops? Someone else? The man who had broken the window? He thought about Josef Engel's murderer coming here to where his son lived, bringing this violence. He *would* kill him if he found him. *When* he found him.

He checked his watch. Ten minutes left before LePoux returned. He walked back to Léo's bedroom, pushed open the door of superheroes and stared down at his son's empty bed. It was unmade and in disarray, like Marie-Claude's had been, but Baptiste could see the ghost of Léo in it, an indentation in the middle of the pillow and a creased outline in the centre of the sheets where he'd slept.

Baptiste moved over to the bed, picking his way through comics and clothes, and sat gently on the edge of the mattress, like he was checking on his sleeping son or preparing to read him a bedtime story. The dent in the pillow was perfectly head-shaped and he bent down and buried his face in it, breathing in the faint smell of his boy lingering on the cotton. It was a puppyish smell, like hair and soap, earth and hay. He picked up the pillow and pressed it to his face, breathing in the scent and swallowing a painful lump that appeared in his throat. He put the pillow to one side and moved down to the sheet, breathing in the same sweet, musky smell, and pushed his face deep into the mattress to muffle his sobs. He wanted to lie down, pull the duvet around him and fall asleep, breathing in the smell of his lost boy. He had spent a lot of time in prison imagining what his son might be like – what he sounded like, the things he might be interested in, the things he might be good at. But he had never considered his son's scent and the sudden, raw reality of it had caught him off guard and left him sobbing.

He stayed like this for long minutes, clutching the duvet and pillow to his chest and pressing them to his face, as if he was holding Léo. Then he sat back up, wiped his face with the back of his hand and arranged the bed in a semblance of how he had found it.

He stood and looked around the room, searching for anything that might tell him something new about his son, something that might help find him. There was a heavy duty case for spectacles on the bedside table; there was a small plastic tag and hook attached to the zipper, presumably so it could clip on to a bag or a coat. Baptiste picked the case up and opened it. The glasses weren't there but the soft cloth to clean them was. He put the case back and moved over to the small wardrobe in the corner of the room. The smell of his son escaped as he opened the door. There were one or two empty hangers, but most of the clothes were still there, spilling from the shelves in a jumble of cotton and colours as though they had been searched, or his wife and son had packed for a trip in a hurry.

He stepped back out into the hallway and looked over at the front door. A row of hooks was fixed to the wall, clogged with coats and hats and caps in various sizes and colours. There was no empty hook, nothing obvious missing. A pile of shoes and boots lay on the floor beneath them, but there was too much inherent chaos and mess to tell if anything was missing. He moved over to it and went through pockets, finding receipts and sweet wrappers but nothing useful. He took Léo's coat off the hook and held it up, trying to imagine the boy inside it. He heard a car approaching and saw the dark shape of it moving behind the rippled glass by the front door.

He pressed Léo's coat to his face and breathed the sense of him again like a bloodhound getting the scent before the hunt. The zipper had a small plastic tag attached to it, exactly like the one on the glasses case. It was made of heavy-duty white plastic and had the word 'tile' embossed on it.

Baptiste smiled when he realized what it was. He unclipped the tag and headed to the kitchen, grabbing the stack of mail on his way out and dumping the Cini Minis in the rubbish.

'Find anything?' LePoux asked as he got in the car.

'Maybe.' Baptiste held the small white tile up.

'What's that?'

'An opportunity.' He slid down in his seat and pulled his cap back over his face.

'Where now?' LePoux asked.

'Anywhere I can get free Wi-Fi,' Baptiste replied. 'And a decent cup of coffee.'

49

'This car is cool,' Léo said, running his hand along the leather seats of the Audi.

'Don't get used to it,' Marie-Claude said. 'We're only borrowing it.'

Marie-Claude liked the car too. They were driving north out of Toulouse, using the péage now they'd switched cars, and the Audi purred along the road in soft comfort. She'd always thought these luxury SUVs were pointless, four-wheel drive on a car that was only ever going to travel on roads, but now she was driving one she was starting to get it. The engine hummed smoothly and they flashed past the other traffic as if it was crawling. It felt luxurious and solid and made her realize how ratty and shabby her own car was. There was no mess inside either and she felt a pang of guilt because this was a family car too, with *two* children to mess it up, yet it looked and smelled like it was fresh out of the factory. It was so nice, such an unexpected bubble of luxury in the general struggle of her life, that she was already feeling anxious at the prospect of having to give it back. She turned to Solomon. 'How long can we keep it?' she murmured.

'The owners are on holiday for the next week at least,'

Solomon said, angling his head and checking behind them in the passenger mirror.

'How do you know that?'

'Because they had too many cases for a short trip.' He twisted round and scanned the road behind them. 'And all the flights leaving Toulouse in the next few hours are long haul, apart from one to Brussels and one to Frankfurt.'

'They might be going on a mini-break.'

'Would you take your kids with you on a mini-break, or pick Frankfurt or Brussels as a family destination?'

Marie-Claude shrugged. 'I've no idea. Mini-breaks are not really on my radar.'

'They'll be gone for a while, I think.'

'You *think* but you don't know.'

'Everything is relative. We, for example, are relatively safe. Safer than we were ten minutes ago.'

'Why?'

'Because we are no longer being followed.'

'What?! Who's following us?' She jerked her gaze to the mirror.

'There was a black Toyota on the road behind us heading out of Cordes and an identical car in the airport car park. That's why I asked you to stay low when we switched cars. Anyway, the car's gone now.'

'Did you see the driver?'

'No. He may not have been following us at all – an airport is a fairly obvious destination point and black Toyotas are common. I didn't see the registration plate.'

'Mama doesn't like those cars,' Léo piped up from the back.

'Black cars?'

'Toyotas. She calls them devil cars.'

Solomon looked over at Marie-Claude. 'Bad experience?'

She shrugged, embarrassed by the revelation. 'It's the symbol, the two ovals interlocking: they look like horns. Like the devil. I don't like them.'

'I don't really like any cars,' Solomon said, pressing the button to open his window a little more. 'They all seem evil to me.'

'Bad experience?' Marie-Claude echoed.

'Maybe. They just seem unnatural. All closed up and confined.'

'Maybe you escaped from a prison,' Léo suggested.

'Possibly,' Solomon conceded.

'Or you're a dangerous criminal who escaped from a dungeon,' Léo added, warming to his subject.

'A dangerous criminal who has a phobia of cars,' Marie-Claude muttered.

Solomon shrugged. 'Napoleon was afraid of cats. Hitler was afraid of dentists. You can't judge a man by his fears.'

'I'm afraid of shadows,' Léo said.

'I'm afraid of you reading and barfing all over this nice car,' Marie-Claude said, glaring at Léo in the rear-view mirror.

Léo tried to hide the comic. 'But I don't feel sick.'

'Well, let's keep it that way. Put it back.'

Léo rolled his eyes and put it in the backpack.

'Zip it up too, and don't try to sneak another one out.'

'OK,' he said. Then he grabbed the white tile on the zipper and pulled it shut.

VII

'... yet from those flames
No light, but rather darkness visible.'

Paradise Lost
John Milton

Extract from

DARK MATERIAL – THE DEVIL'S TAILOR: DEATH
AND LIFE IN DIE SCHNEIDER LAGER

⚬

By Herman Lansky

Living in hell is one thing. Escaping it is something else.

Liberation came on the night of 23 November 1944. We heard it coming for days, like a storm rumbling, and saw flashes in the western sky, getting louder and brighter. We had heard the sounds of distant battles before, but never this close and never so constant, and we knew it was serious when the guards ordered us to start burning all the factory records, the first time the incinerators had ever been used for something that mundane.

A fight broke out between two guards at the main gate and we all stopped and watched, shocked that these cold, inhuman creatures were displaying such raw, human emotions. I thought the bigger one, a Lithuanian sadist called Aras, was going to kill the other, until Commandant Samler appeared and calmly ended it by putting a bullet in his ear. Death was common in Die Schneider Lager, but I had never witnessed the death of a guard before. Samler ordered the other guard back to work but his face was bloody from the fight and he coughed as he got up and some blood went on Samler's uniform so he shot him too. Right in the face in front of us all.

Looking back now, we could have killed him then. Samler had a gun but he was alone and there were hundreds of us. We could have overpowered him, but we didn't. We watched him pick up the rifles of the dead guards and walk away to the officers' quarters. I am still tortured by this memory. I wonder, if we had killed him at that moment, whether we might have prevented the slaughter that followed.

After the death of the guards, the day continued as normal. We went to the factories and made the cloth and cut the patterns and stitched the uniforms. We were making our own uniforms by then; the striped material for all the camps came from the looms of Die Schneider Lager. The sheer amount we produced gave us an idea of how many other camps like ours there were out there.

Every day the sound of shelling grew louder until we could see flashes in the daylight sky and feel the ground tremble like something huge was coming. On the last day, a British plane flew overhead, low enough that we could see its markings. The guards looked afraid when they saw it. There were very few of them at the end, a skeleton crew left behind to run the factory, most of them new, brought in to replace the original guards who had been sent to new battalions to help defend the Reich. A lot of these new guards had been drafted in from essential industries and were either old or very young. Some had been sent to Die Schneider Lager because they had been tailors or apprentices who'd been working in textile factories. They were not much different from us – terrified they might die with the end of the war so close.

Those last few days were the longest and hardest, I

think. Until then I had lived entirely in the moment, existing from breath to breath, from shift to shift, measuring my days in mouthfuls of stale bread. Survival was a simple case of luck and keeping going, living merely a habit I couldn't seem to break. But now, with the sudden prospect of a future, I wanted to live more than I had ever wanted anything. And I became terrified of dying.

I knew a man in camp, Janusz Kryński, a marathon runner who had been part of the Polish athletics team in the 1936 Berlin Olympics. He said it was the last few miles of a marathon that were the hardest. Everything that went before, the miles already run, the training you had done, all of it meant nothing. Those last few miles were all about character and luck, and you either had it or you didn't. That's what it felt like for me during those last few days at Die Schneider Lager. Staying alive became an act of defiance, each new heartbeat an act of rebellion. Stamping out that rebellion was the last order Artur Samler ever gave, if indeed it was him who gave it. Because there was someone else there on that final day, someone I only glimpsed through the window of the factory. He walked right in through the main gates with such command that the guards let him pass unchallenged. He wore a beautiful pale suit, perfectly cut, and I remember thinking he must be some high-ranking officer and that his arrival must mean the end was close – either surrender or evacuation. It was neither.

About an hour after I saw this pale man, the doors to the factory opened and more prisoners flooded in. It was not time for a shift change and those of us already working stayed at our posts. There were murmurs that we were being gathered together to be transported out. Prisoners continued to file in, so many that we shut down the looms for fear of someone falling into them. We were expecting angry shouts to come from the guards, ordering us to turn them back on again, but none came. That was when we realized there were no guards in the shed and the doors had been locked.

I don't know what made me do what I did next – maybe some kind of sixth sense, a premonition of what was coming. Or maybe it was that thing Janusz Kryński had told me about – the unknown instinct that carries you over the line.

My job was to package the bolts of cloth and send them to the machine shops or load them on to lorries to be transported to other facilities and my work area was at the back of the factory, close to the delivery bays. We had been producing cloth at the same rate as always but the transports had stopped and on that last day the storage area was piled high with bolts of Tkaniny śmierć – the Death Cloth – with narrow tunnels between the stacks of cloth to let people move between them. As soon as I realized we were locked in, I ran into one of these and had almost reached the end when the first explosion sent a wall of heavy cloth tumbling down on top of me, plunging me into a stifling, airless dark. I was hardly able to move or breathe, but I could feel the vibration of more explosions and hear screams muffled by the thick material. I tried to push forward, towards the factory, but the way was blocked and the only progress I could make was backwards, towards the wall of the factory, so I kicked and squirmed like a swimmer tangled in seaweed until I finally hit the wall and cut my hand on a twisted steel strut where a row of shelves had collapsed. I could smell smoke now and hear the patter of what sounded like rain on the roof. And the screams. Such screams.

Something primal takes control of you when you smell smoke, something hard-wired into our desire to survive. Trapped there in that suffocating darkness, I turned to the wall and started clawing at it with my bare hands, the old plaster crumbling beneath my fingers. I could feel the pain as my nails split and my fingertips bled, but I didn't stop, I couldn't stop. I would have worn my fingers to stumps rather than let the fire claim me, but a small part of my brain that was still rational recalled the twisted shelving I had cut my hand on and I found it again in the dark, wrenched a piece free and used that as a tool to attack the wall instead.

The poor quality of the factory and the cheapness of its construction was what saved me that day, that and my fortunate position within the factory when the slaughter started. I don't know how long it took me to break through – it seemed like hours but it can't have been more than a few minutes – but when I did, it felt like I was breaking out of hell.

Outside, the guards were preoccupied with the slaughter, machine-gunning anyone who managed to break out of the factory. A large wooden garbage container was stationed by the delivery bay and this had concealed my own escape, or I would surely have been shot too. I knew if I tried to make a run for it I would be seen, so I climbed into the container and buried myself under all the stinking rags and filth.

I lay there for a long time, listening to the shouts of the Germans and the screams of the dying and the roar of the flames amid the rattle of machine-gun fire. Eventually the screaming stopped and so did the shooting, but the roar of the fire remained. Ash rained down from the sky like grey snow and the smell of burning bodies grew stronger than the smell of the rotting garbage that concealed me. A plane flew over-head, an Allied reconnaissance plane drawn by the fire. They were closer now, closer than they had ever been, and bringing liberation with them – but it was too late. All too late. Everyone was dead. Everyone except me.

One hundred and twenty-five thousand Jews and other enemies of the Reich had been transported to Die Schneider Lager over the three years of its existence and I was the only one who had survived. The only one. Or so I thought.

⁙

50

Magellan pulled the Range Rover to a halt in front of L'ancien Hôpital d'Albi where the body of Josef Engel now lay in the same subterranean morgue that had housed corpses from the Black Death, the Revolution, the Napoleonic and two world wars.

'Would you like me to wait and drive you back?' Magellan asked. 'Or perhaps . . .'

Amand turned to him. 'What?'

'Well, maybe I could come in with you and give you the benefit of my expertise.'

'You're not assigned to the case, which means anything you say would not be admissible.'

'Yes, but my opinion may be useful. You don't have to use anything I say in evidence, but I might be able to help profile your killer.'

Amand remembered Josef's ritually mutilated corpse and the rogues' gallery of killers listed in the articles on Magellan. He nodded. 'Follow me.'

They entered the building, signed in, walked down the stairs to the basement and headed down a white-tiled corridor towards the examination room. Amand knocked once and entered.

Doctor Evie Zimbaldi stood at the examination table focusing a camera on the brightly lit remains of Josef Engel. She was almost sixty years old but looked forty and had a quiet, cold beauty that made junior doctors stammer and drop things. Her black hair, dark eyes and pale, smooth skin had earned the nickname *La Reine des Morts* – The Queen of the Dead – though nobody called her that to her face.

'Madame Coroner,' Amand said, his voice echoing off the enamelled walls. She looked up, her eyes resting on Magellan. 'This is Doctor Magellan, a visiting criminal psychologist from the United States. Doctor Magellan, Doctor Evie Zimbaldi, Chief Coroner for the commune of Albi.'

'Doctor Cezar Magellan?'

'Indeed, madame. Delighted to meet you.'

'I read your paper on the Electra complex and female serial killers.'

Magellan smiled. 'Ah yes, that ruffled some feathers at the ICP.'

'I can see why. I disagreed with most of it.'

Magellan held his smile. 'Well, it would be a dull world if we all agreed, would it not?'

'Doctor Magellan has treated a man who is a suspect in this case,' Amand said, handing Magellan a surgical cap and a face mask. 'I thought it might be useful for him to consult and see if any of the evident psychopathology matches with his patient.'

'As you wish.' Doctor Zimbaldi turned back to the body.

Amand pulled on his own surgical cap and joined her at the table. Josef Engel was on his back, a single piece of gauze draped across his waist. She had not started cutting yet, which Amand was deeply grateful for, and the blood had been cleaned away leaving his skin shining bright and blood-less under the examination lights and the wounds looking dark and violent. 'Jesus,' he said, confronted by the stark evidence of the old man's suffering.

'All these wounds are ante-mortem,' Doctor Zimbaldi said, pointing at the Star of David sliced into his chest, 'which means he suffered a great deal before he died. However, the things I want you to focus on are the rat bites.' She pointed at the hundreds of tiny puncture marks peppering the old man's skin. Some were small and some larger where the rats had feasted, which they had done everywhere, even on his face around his staring eyes. Amand wondered why Doctor Zimbaldi had not pulled the eyelids down, then saw the ragged edges of skin and realized the rats had made a meal of these too. 'Is it usual for rats to do this?'

'Not usual, but not unknown either. I often receive bodies with animal bites on them. Rats are scavengers, opportunists, they'll always sniff out an easy meal if one is available and take a bite or two out of a body, but not like this. This is more like a frenzy.'

'What would make them behave like this?'

'Hunger,' Magellan said. 'The rats that did this were starving.'

Doctor Zimbaldi looked up at him. 'Exactly.'

Amand felt the tightness grow in his chest. 'We found a container at the scene, a wooden box lined with metal sheeting and with air-holes drilled into the lid. It's been signed into evidence, but it looks like rats had been kept inside it, which suggests the killer brought them with him, maybe as part of some premeditated torture routine.'

'Except the rat bites are all post-mortem,' Doctor Zimbaldi

said. 'Which suggests to me that, if the killer did intend to use them, the victim died before he got the chance.'

'Any idea yet about cause of death?' Magellan asked.

'My hunch is AMI.'

AMI – *Acute Myocardial Infarction* – Amand knew all about that. François Verbier had warned him that was what he was heading for if he didn't slow down.

'See the mottling of the skin on the upper body and around the neck?' Doctor Zimbaldi used a pencil torch to point out the areas. 'Also the redness in the face and that slight bluish tinge at the extremities – fingers, nose. That's all consistent with a massive heart attack. And look at his chest. See this bruising around the sternum?' She reached out and pressed the old man's chest lightly with her blue-gloved fingers. 'See that rib moving?' Amand nodded, mildly nauseated by the way it bulged beneath the loose skin. 'It's broken. That, plus the mild bruising and lack of swelling, suggests it probably happened at around the time of death. My guess is that the killer saw he was going into arrest and attempted CPR.'

Amand frowned. 'But why torture him almost to death, then try and save his life?'

She shrugged. 'My job is only to tell you what happened. The "why" is your department.'

'If I might suggest something . . .' Magellan moved round the table. 'All of this suggests to me that your killer had a script, a specific order of what he wanted to do to the old man. The heart attack messed up his plans and the CPR was an attempt to get things back on script. Maybe the rats were supposed to be the grand finale. I think your killer is very controlled, very organized. Look at the hands.'

Amand looked. Josef Engel had the hands of a much

younger man, lithe and nimble. A rat had gnawed away the tip of the little finger on his left hand and there were a few other bites, but other than that they were untouched. 'What am I looking at?'

'Nothing,' Magellan replied.

Amand looked again and nodded. 'No defence wounds.' He switched his gaze to the old man's wrists. 'No signs of ligature bruising, either. Why didn't he fight back or try to protect himself? Was he unconscious, maybe?'

'That's what I thought,' Zimbaldi replied, 'until I saw this.' She pointed at a mark on the old man's neck, a red spot with a ragged-edged hole in the middle, like a wasp sting. 'It's a needle mark. A dose of the right drug administered there would take effect instantly. Lots of blood flow, up into the brain, down into the heart.'

Magellan nodded. 'Some killers like to immobilize their victims. It's a cat-and-mouse power dynamic; they like to toy with their prey before the kill.'

Doctor Zimbaldi nodded. 'I've sent off blood and tissue samples to toxicology. I should get the results back in an hour or so. Now look at this.' She twisted on her penlight and shone the light along Josef Engel's side. It was covered with two distinct types of cut: long, deep slashes and circles of puncture marks. 'The straight cuts are the lash marks,' Zimbaldi explained. 'They're clean, no splinters, so I doubt they were made by your bamboo cane. The force and repetition of these lashes would have splintered any cane thin enough to make them, therefore I would suggest they were made by something thin and springy, something that doesn't shed like leather or plastic.'

'What about the blood on the cane, does that match?'

She looked up and Amand noticed redness around her

eyes, like she'd been crying. 'I haven't seen it,' she said. 'I thought you might be bringing it with you.'

Amand felt a surge of annoyance. 'I specifically asked for it to be . . . I'll chase it up.'

'OK, as soon as I get it, I'll fast-track the bloods and fingerprinting, but I'm sure that will only help rule it out. Now, take a look at this.' She moved the torch beam across to one of the other marks, a rough circle made up of different-sized puncture holes.

'Dog bites,' Magellan said.

'Yes. Have you had any reports of dogs barking last night at the crime scene, Commandant?'

Amand shook his head. 'We're continuing to knock on doors, but nothing thus far.'

'But when a dog attacks they generally bark, yes? First a warning, then the attack.'

'Usually.'

'And it's ferocious, more barking, snarling, growling, and that doesn't even include whatever noise the person they're attacking makes. When dogs attack, they go all in and you have to drag them off. Dogs don't savage someone in silence. Yet no one heard anything. Take a look at this.' She turned to the instrument stand next to her, tapped the space bar on a laptop and the screen lit up with the photographs she had been taking. She selected a couple and enlarged them. 'What do you see?'

Both photos were red and lurid, taken as part of the initial examination before the body was washed. The first showed the Star of David, bloody and ragged. The second was the bite she had just shown him. 'Blood,' Amand said. 'I see lots of blood.'

'Exactly.'

'The wounds were inflicted while he was alive.'

'Correct. All that blood shows that the heart was still pumping. And look at the direction of blood flow from the bites. He was upright when they were inflicted. Some anaesthetics can paralyse the muscles but leave neural activity largely unaffected. Which means this man may well have been fully aware of everything that was happening to him but incapable of doing anything about it, hence the lack of defensive wounds or any signs of a struggle.' She turned to Magellan. 'Does any of this match your patient's profile?'

Magellan shook his head. 'My patient doesn't really have a pattern of behaviour. The nearest thing he has to a pattern is the lack of one. He is more a creature of chaos and impulse. I would suggest that whoever did this is the exact opposite. Your killer is meticulous and controlled and acting out a careful ritual. Everything they did has meaning.' He turned to Amand. 'I wouldn't be surprised if he hasn't done this before. Possibly several times, perfecting his routine each time.'

Doctor Zimbaldi nodded. 'I agree.' She turned to the laptop and clicked open a new file. 'Look at this.' More photos opened, bright blood made vivid by the flash of the coroner's camera. 'This was a case I processed three years ago. The deceased was a thief who broke into a warehouse guarded by a pack of Rottweilers trained to attack anyone they didn't recognize. They didn't recognize this man, so . . . Anyway, look at the bite pattern.'

She selected a photograph and enlarged it. It showed a close-up of one of the bites, the teeth marks clear and deep, the flesh around them ragged and torn.

'See how messy these bites are and how deep the teeth went? Dogs are carnivores, they don't have side-to-side jaw movement like herbivores, they bite on to something and thrash their heads around to tear the flesh away.'

Amand looked back at the body of Josef Engel. The bites on his back were neat, no tearing, no sign of any trauma at all, just neat circles of shallow puncture marks. 'So what happened here?'

'I don't believe he was attacked by a dog. That's a fairly decent-sized bite radius, similar to the Rottweiler, but narrower, which suggests a different breed, one with a more pointed snout.'

Amand remembered what he'd read in the memoir. 'An Alsatian?' he suggested.

'Yes, or a Doberman. And any dog this big has a powerful bite, it's their primary weapon, their main means of feeding and hunting in the wild. These bites should be much deeper and more violent, but they are controlled, which matches Doctor Magellan's suggested profile of a meticulous and organized killer. I found some residue in a couple of the bites, tiny fragments of tooth or bone; I sent them to the lab along with the bloods and marked it all as urgent. I'll have the results by the end of today. The thing that strikes me about all of this – the rats, the drugged subjugation, the Star of David cut into his chest, the dog bites – is that none of it is accidental, everything here is deliberate. Everything has a meaning and a reason.'

Amand felt as though a hand had grabbed the back of his head and started to squeeze. He knew the reason, the killer had written it on the wall in Josef Engel's own blood.

Finishing what was begun.

51

The McDonald's in Gaillac was busy with the late-morning, pre-lunch trade, though not so busy that they couldn't get a four-person booth. Baptiste had asked for somewhere with decent coffee and free Wi-Fi and LePoux had brought him here. He was sitting opposite, drinking a beer straight from the can and ogling the students ducking school and taking selfies with their burgers. It was a different world from the one Baptiste had known before prison. The dark-skinned girl who'd served him had such a thick accent he'd barely understood her. France was disappearing and no one seemed to care. He prised the plastic lid off his paper cup and took a sip of thin, bitter coffee. Hopefully the Wi-Fi would make up for it.

He opened his laptop and while it searched for a signal, he sorted through the stack of mail he'd taken from Marie-Claude's kitchen. Most of it was junk, a letter from the *Mairie* about planned roadworks, a water bill, a phone bill. He studied this one. It listed services for a landline, internet, TV and a mobile phone, the number was included in the breakdown, showing what calls Marie-Claude had made and how much data she'd used. She was a pretty heavy user, which was good. The more she used her phone, the more likely it was that Baptiste would be able to find her.

A connection window opened on the laptop asking for a name and email address. Baptiste typed in 'Thomas Martin' and a Gmail address with the same name. It was the most common name in France, someone was bound to have the address. Sure enough, the window reloaded with a welcome message. He Googled 'DARKLE', hit *Return* and clicked on the top result.

A new window opened with a download icon in the centre. Baptiste clicked it to start downloading and picked up the white plastic tag he'd taken off Léo's coat. He ran his finger over the raised lettering, spelling the brand name of the device – *tile*. It was a Bluetooth tracker, a small, localized device with a unique identity code that paired with a nearby transmitter, a phone or a computer to keep tabs on valuables using geo-location. They used them in prison to keep tabs on the inmates because they were cheaper than ankle brace-lets and more efficient than having some bored guard staring at TV screens all day. They were worn on the wrist, sealed inside plastic hospital bracelets – easy to put on, impossible to remove without it looking like it had been tampered with. Anyone who strayed too far from the central transmitter would be detected, an alarm would sound and the guards would come running. Cheap and effective. Except a guy inside had figured a way round them.

His street name was Le Serpent, another member of the Brotherhood, doing ten years for robbing banks using laptops instead of shotguns. He'd figured out a way to hack the Bluetooth security tags and had written a piece of software that cloned their signals. He'd also introduced Baptiste to the Dark Web.

The download finished and Baptiste installed the DARKLE software. A new search window opened that looked like a black version of Google. He typed 'GeoLocate' into the search box and a new window opened with a map of the world on the right and a search box on the left with two option buttons next to it – a phone icon and a Bluetooth symbol. He highlighted France on the map and copied the mobile number from Marie Claude's phone bill into the search box and clicked the phone icon.

The cursor arrow turned into a hand with drumming fingers as the app searched for the phone's GPS records and cross-referenced it with coordinates on the map. Le Serpent had once explained how it worked, but it was too technical for him. It worked, that was all that mattered.

Baptiste drummed his fingers in time with the icon. Back in his police days, he would have had to jump through all kinds of hoops in order to run a trace like this: drawing up a warrant with clear legal reasons justifying why the search was necessary, presenting it to the *juge d'instruction*, who may or may not have signed it. If his time inside had taught him anything it was that his previous life as a policeman had been largely pointless. It didn't matter how well resourced the police were, the criminals were always way ahead: better tech, better information, more money, and no bureaucracy to waste their time or hold them back. Law enforcement in its current state was like a Band-Aid on an arterial wound. You needed a police state and a strong hand. A dictatorship. Democracy didn't work because most people were stupid. You only had to spend five minutes in a place like this, watching the students with their pouty poses taking pictures of their fries, to see just how stupid. There was no democracy in prison. It was survival of the fittest, human nature stripped down to its purest form. And he *had* survived. Now he wanted his reward – a new life, for him, for his country and his son.

The screen flashed and the map reloaded, showing where Marie-Claude's phone had last been detected: Toulouse–Blagnac Airport, somewhere to the northwest of the terminal building. The time stamp said the signal had been lost over an hour ago, which meant she'd either turned her phone off or the battery had died.

Baptiste picked up the white tile and pressed the 'e' with the end of his wooden stirrer to activate its connectivity. He clicked the Bluetooth symbol next to the search box and the phone number was replaced by a sequence of numbers showing the app had acquired the tile's signal. The map reloaded, showing a blue dot at the edge of Gaillac, roughly where the McDonald's was, then the map began to widen as the app searched for other tiles with the same signal.

The downside of Bluetooth devices, Le Serpent had explained, was that they were designed to be used in a very localized network, up to a hundred feet maximum. Which was fine if you were trying to locate a lost phone or a set of keys in your house, not so great if you were trying to track down a missing person somewhere in France. Baptiste knew this particular brand of tile, however, was the most popular and offered a 'Find my Tile' option that allowed users to tap into its large and growing network so other phones and devices running the app would automatically look for missing tiles and send a locater if they found one. The company's website contained several testimonials from people who'd recovered property using the function. Baptiste was hoping he could now do the same thing to locate Marie-Claude and Léo.

The map continued to expand and he nursed his thin coffee but no new dots appeared. He knew that locating them this way was a long shot. It assumed that Marie-Claude or

Léo had one of these tiles with them and that they would pass close enough to a device running the same app and for long enough for the signal to be acquired. The laptop beeped and a cluster of new blue dots appeared. Baptiste frowned. They were in Cordes, clustered around Marie-Claude's house. For a moment he wondered if they'd doubled back, then realized that the GeoTracker had picked up the tiles he'd already seen in her house. At least it proved the search app was working. He watched it for another five minutes but no new dots appeared. He switched back to the phone search and studied the map. Toulouse airport was less than an hour away, quicker if the traffic was good. He could run the search again when they got there. He'd find her. He had to.

52

Marie-Claude rolled her shoulders and pushed her hands against the wheel to try and squeeze out some of the tension the hours of driving had put there. Léo was asleep in the back. Solomon had his eyes closed, his head tilted towards the open window. She took her hand off the wheel and squeezed her left shoulder, her thumb working at the knot of scar tissue above her crooked collarbone.

'Does it ache before the rain?' Solomon murmured.

Marie-Claude looked over at him, his eyes remained closed. 'Did you say something?'

'Your fused clavicle. Does it hurt whenever a storm is coming?'

'Sometimes.'

He opened his eyes and looked ahead at the road. 'It's air pressure. It drops before rain and any inflammation in your body worsens. Old people feel it in their joints, young people around the sites of old injuries. You can smell it coming too. Or I can, at least. It even has a name – petrichor. Was it a person?'

'Was what a person?'

'The cause of your broken collarbone?'

All the tension returned to her shoulders. 'What makes you think that?' Her eyes darted to the rear-view mirror to see if Léo was awake.

'He's asleep,' Solomon assured her. 'I can hear his breathing and heartbeat, slow and steady. I waited until he was sleeping before asking. It was Léo's father, wasn't it?'

'What!? Jesus, you're . . . what makes you think . . .' She stared ahead, eyes fixed on the horizon. 'Things didn't work out between us.'

'But why is he totally absent from your life. Is he dead?'

'No, he's . . . What makes you think he's absent?'

'In your grandfather's house there were photographs of you and Léo on the wall but no one else. You also said earlier that you would leave Léo with someone if you could, but there wasn't anyone. Therefore you're on your own and I'd like to know why.'

'Why do you want to know?'

'Because I'm here to save your son but I don't know how or what from yet, so I'm trying to identify potential areas of threat.'

Marie-Claude opened her mouth then closed it again. She had been trying to convince herself that Baptiste wasn't a threat, that he wouldn't come and cause trouble again, not after everything that had happened. But deep down she knew that he was a threat. Because of Léo, he would always be in her life and he would always be a threat. 'Yes,' she said. 'It was my husband who broke my collarbone. He also cracked my skull, broke two fingers, a rib and burst my eardrum. His name is Jean Baptiste.'

'How long ago was this?'

'Almost five years.'

'And where is he now?'

'Up until three weeks ago, he was in a prison in the Midi-Pyrénées.'

'And now?'

'I don't know. He was released early.'

Solomon studied the horizon. 'Could he have killed your grandfather?'

Marie-Claude had been half avoiding and half asking herself the same question. The person she had fallen in love with couldn't have done. But that person wouldn't have beaten her bloody in front of their son either. And Baptiste had spent almost five years in a tough jail since. 'Maybe,' she said. 'I don't know. I don't know him any more.'

'Does Léo remember him?'

She glanced in the mirror at her sleeping son. 'He was tiny when it happened. Just turned two. He was there when . . . when Jean Baptiste – flipped. I remember in the hospital afterwards, Benny – that's Commandant Amand – he said when the medics found me, I had pieces of ripped tissue all over me, like confetti. They didn't know what it was at first, then they realized that . . .' She turned away as tears came with the memory. 'They realized Léo had been trying to put plasters on me. He had been trying to make me better.'

'Amand is the man in charge of your grandfather's case.'

'Yes. He's a friend too. He was my husband's best friend. They worked together.'

'Your husband was a gendarme?'

Marie-Claude nodded. 'It was Benny who arrested Baptiste. I think it broke his heart.'

'What made your husband flip?'

Marie-Claude took a deep breath and blew it out slowly. 'Because he found out that I'm Jewish.'

'Did he not know?'

'No. I didn't even know myself. My background is . . . complicated. I was never brought up Jewish. Never had any idea. My mother died giving birth to me, my grandmother brought me up. I have no idea who my father is. My mother was pretty wild, by all accounts. A bit of a rebel. She was eighteen when she . . . when she had me. My grandfather was around when I was growing up, but he was always a distant figure, always working in his atelier. This was my family, until Léo came along.'

'Tell me about Jean Baptiste.'

'Jean Baptiste was history repeating itself, I think. My own rebellion. I'd known him since school and he was always a bit of a bad boy. He was captain of the rugby team, which is a big deal round here. All the girls liked him. But the girl he liked best was me.

'I was kind of geeky and awkward and felt weird because my grandparents were bringing me up and they seemed ancient compared to everyone else's parents. I was flattered that this hot boy was interested in me and we had a kind of teenage fling, which was . . . wonderful, actually. I had no expectations it would lead anywhere because I was determined to leave Cordes and do something with my life. I broke up with him when I was about to go to university, telling him I couldn't spend the rest of my life hanging off the back of his motorbike and drinking *vin en vrac* while watching the sun go down from the top of Cordes. So off I went to university in Marseille and I thought that was it.

'But Jean Baptiste had other ideas. He came to see me most weekends, five hours down the péage on his motorbike each way. I think me going away opened his eyes too, showed him that there was something else out there apart from rugby and joy-riding and getting drunk with his wild friends. He had one sensible friend who was quieter and more thoughtful than the rest who'd joined the police straight from school. Baptiste decided to do the same. That friend was Benny Amand.

'By the time I graduated, Baptiste was a changed man and rising fast through the ranks of the police force. I came back to Cordes and worked for my grandfather to save up enough money to go and live in Paris, and we all hung out again, doing the things we'd done before – me, Jean Baptiste, Benny Amand and a few others from school. Then I fell pregnant, total accident. I expected Baptiste to be freaked out – I was freaked out – but instead he cried and asked me to marry him. The money I'd been saving to move to Paris went on a small ceremony instead. We didn't need the big church wedding because we were happy and we had Léo on the way, what more proof of love did anyone need?

'Baptiste put in for more work so we could start saving for a place of our own, and he got a placement in Toulouse, which meant staying over with friends a few nights a week because of the shift patterns. That was when he started to change. I don't know if it was the pressure of work or becoming a father, but he started drinking again and ranting about all the filth he was seeing on the streets, the *beurs* flooding the suburbs with their swarming families and ruining France, the Muslims, the blacks, the Jews. This was when he joined the PNFL – *Parti National de la France Libre*. He said it was a career thing, networking with the right people to help him climb the greasy pole. But it wasn't only about that. The PNFL was a marginal party back then, but they were starting to grow, catching people young to slowly build their power base. I wonder how many people like Jean

Baptiste they courted: ambitious, well-placed young men on the rise, whose patriotism they harnessed and twisted to help drive the party forward. It worked, because now the PNFL are serious contenders, riding a toxic wave of nationalism and fear along with far-right parties all over Europe. They certainly got their hooks into Jean Baptiste. They turned his head until I hardly recognized him any more. He was so full of hate, for anyone who was different. Then I discovered that I was Jewish.'

'How did you not know?'

'Because I wasn't brought up Jewish. I had no idea. Engel is a fairly common German name. I knew my grandfather had moved to France from Germany after the war, but I didn't know the real story. He didn't want me to know. He didn't want anyone to know. But when Léo was two my grandmother was diagnosed with breast cancer. It was too advanced to treat, so she came home to die. I looked after her right to the end, which didn't take long, and I was with her the night she died. That was when she told me about Die Schneider Lager and how my grandfather had been imprisoned there and was one of only five men who had survived it. She knew she wasn't going to be around for much longer, and I think she was trying to help me understand why my grandfather was like he was, always so withdrawn and distant. But I think she could also see what Jean Baptiste was turning into and wanted me to know who I really was. She had spent her life denying her own Jewish ancestry for the sake of her husband, who wanted to turn his back on that whole side of himself. She said he was afraid of being defined as Jewish, like it was a curse, and had been forced to do the same. But she wanted me to have a choice. She wanted me to know who I really was. She told me all this in a rush, like a confession, then went to sleep and never woke. I hope she felt at peace for having passed on the family secret. And I'm glad she didn't live to see what happened next.

'I waited until after the funeral before I told Baptiste. He hadn't been around much anyway; I think he knew my grandmother didn't approve of him and had kept his distance while I nursed her. A couple of days after the funeral he came home late from work and I told him. He didn't say anything, he just looked at me for what seemed like a long time, then turned and walked out of the house. I didn't know where he'd gone or when he'd be back and eventually I went to bed. He came back late. Drunk. I heard him crashing around in Léo's room and I went in to find him stuffing Léo's things into a carrier bag. He said he was taking him away. Said I'd lied to him. Tricked him into mixing my dirty blood with his. He said he was taking Léo so he could . . .' Marie-Claude swallowed and blew out a long breath. 'He said he was going to bring him up "pure", away from his Jewish whore of a mother.

'Léo was awake the whole time. Crying. Scared. I was scared too. Baptiste picked him up, but I stood in the doorway and wouldn't let him pass. That was when he hit me – a hard slap across the face that made my ear bleed. But I wouldn't move. Then he got really angry. I don't remember much after that.

'Benny told me afterwards that someone heard the screaming and crying and called the police. I think Baptiste must have heard the sirens coming and panicked. He ran off, leaving me on the floor and Léo tearing up tissues to try and make me better. They sent him to prison to make an example of him, and I thought that would be that. But a few weeks ago I found out he'd been released early. I don't know where he is now.'

She wiped her eyes with the back of her hand and nodded at a line of grey clouds on the horizon. 'You were right,' she said. 'There's rain ahead. We should stop and get some fuel before the storm breaks.'

53

Amand emerged on to the street and took deep breaths to try and flush the smell of the morgue from his nose. Magellan followed him out and headed over to his car. 'You still think Solomon Creed didn't do it?' Amand asked him.

'Absolutely,' Magellan replied. 'His implant would have stopped him doing any of what we witnessed in there. He simply wouldn't have been physically capable of conducting a sustained, controlled attack like that.'

'Why not? What does this implant do exactly?'

'When the body commits violence it undergoes a rapid and complex chemical change. Adrenaline and noradrenaline flood the body, inhibiting insulin and promoting glycolysis, leading to an increase in blood glucose and fatty acids. More energy is produced, the heart rate increases, blood vessels contract and air passages dilate. In the brain, the amygdala, the part that deals with emotions, becomes hyperactive. It wants to *do* something, the instinct we call fight or flight. All of this happens within two seconds. That's why counting to ten is used in anger management, because it allows this surge of adrenaline to pass. The implant in James's . . . Solomon Creed's arm is an artificial count-to-ten strategy. It's loaded with a cocktail of drugs and hormones such as acetylcholine, which are triggered when spikes of adrenaline are detected in the bloodstream. They counteract all the potentially violent stimuli by dumping neural inhibitors into the bloodstream, causing acute pain and making the muscles cramp and weaken. You found Solomon at the crime scene, correct?'

'Yes.'

'And what state was he in?'

'He was playing the piano.'

Magellan smiled. 'Brilliantly, I would imagine.'

Amand shrugged. 'He was OK.'

'Well, if he *had* killed your man, you would have found him curled up on the floor in acute pain.'

'Unless he cut the implant out.'

'As I said before, it's implanted deep – very hard to remove.'

'People are capable of almost anything if they put their mind to it, especially if they're delusional – you of all people must know that.' They stopped by the Range Rover and Amand looked up at the red-brick monolith of Albi Cathedral. 'A few years back, when I was working a street beat in Toulouse, I arrested a young kid out of his mind on PCP. Said he had the evil eye and kept threatening us with it unless we let him go. We locked him up to calm him down and he started screaming. Said he didn't want to be left alone with the evil eye. When I returned to the cell with the duty psychiatrist about forty minutes later, we found him sitting on the floor with blood all over him and a huge grin on his face. He'd clawed his own eye out and never made a single sound while he did it. So let's assume that Solomon Creed *might* have removed the implant. Could he have killed Josef Engel?'

Magellan waited for a young woman to walk past and move out of earshot. 'No,' he said. 'I don't believe he could.

Whoever killed Monsieur Engel is very controlled, whereas the man you know as Solomon Creed is chaotic. Impulsive.'

'Is he, though? When he killed his mother and brother, you said he arranged the scene. That sounds pretty controlled to me.'

'Yes, but he had a personal connection to his victims. The violence was spontaneous and the narrative underpinning it was pre-existing. There was nothing planned about it. I don't believe he went to the house intending to kill his mother. It was only the shock of discovering a brother that triggered his rage and violence. When he killed them, he was improvising; whereas Josef Engel's killer brought hypodermic syringes loaded with anaesthetic and starved rats and specific tools to inflict distinct wounds. He must have spent time watching the victim, learning his routine and figuring out the right moment to strike when no one would disturb him. It must have taken weeks to prepare, and Solomon Creed has only been in France for three days. He must only have arrived in Cordes this morning.'

'You know this for a fact?'

'Yes. I've been tracking him since he escaped my facility twenty-five days ago. He surfaced in a small Arizona town almost three weeks ago, which was how I discovered the name he's travelling under.' Magellan unlocked the car, reached into the back and pulled a file from his briefcase with Solomon's mugshot clipped to the front. 'The police in Arizona had him in custody for a while.' He removed a bundle of police evidence photographs and handed them to Amand. The top one showed a detail of the label in the pale suit jacket Solomon wore, the address of Josef Engel's atelier embroidered on it in gold thread. 'This is why I thought he might be heading here.'

'Why didn't you call to warn us?'

'I thought I might be able to intercept him. I travelled east from Arizona and managed to track him to a Hong Kong container vessel that had sailed out of Galveston on its way to the Far East, stopping at La Rochelle. I flew there, hired a car, drove to the port and showed his photograph around. He'd passed through there two days ago. I hoped I would get here before him because he was travelling on foot. I was wrong.'

Amand flicked through the rest of the photographs, the dappled sunlight from the trees lining the street making them seem alive. 'I don't see a passport. No credit cards or cash either. How did he manage to get passage on a ship without those?'

'I imagine he agreed to work his passage for no pay and no questions asked, or maybe he got hold of some money and bribed his way aboard. He's extraordinarily resourceful and slippery, as you know from your own experience. Incidentally, how did he escape from your custody? It would be useful for me to know the details.'

Amand stared at his reflection in the dark, tinted window of the Range Rover. 'It was my fault. I left a junior officer with him to take a statement and when I went down to check on him, Solomon Creed was gone and the officer was in some kind of trance and convinced his hands were stuck to the table.'

Magellan nodded. 'Hypnosis. Autosuggestion. All part of the therapy regime we use to rehabilitate our patients.'

'You taught him hypnosis?'

'No, but the man you know as Solomon Creed has a remarkable mind. He can master things as fast as they're explained and recall things in intricate detail after seeing them only once. He picked up hypnosis techniques along with every other therapy we practised on him. His mind is quite extraordinary – broken, but extraordinary.' He shook his head. 'You're right, I should have contacted you the moment I knew he was in France to inform you that he might be heading your way and warn you about how slippery he can be. It's not your fault he escaped, it's mine.'

Amand's phone buzzed and he frowned when he saw the message.

'Problems?'

'Only unavoidable ones. I'm being chased by the secretary of the *juge d'instruction* assigned to the murder case. I need to brief him on where we are with the case.'

'You have to report to a judge already?'

'It works like a District Attorney in the States: they issue any warrants and help guide the investigation to make sure everything is legally robust if it comes to court. At least, that's the theory.'

'Do you need a lift?'

Amand shook his head and pointed at a white stone building beyond the trees. 'His office is right there.'

'I'm happy to wait and drive you back to Cordes afterwards, if you like.'

'Thanks, but I might stick around here for a while.'

Magellan nodded and produced a thick white card with his name and contact details on the back. 'Well, if you change your mind, give me a call. And please let me know as soon as you have news of Solomon Creed. We've both let him slip through our fingers once. Maybe together we can find him again and keep hold of him this time.'

Amand pocketed the card and held out one of his own. 'Likewise, if anything occurs to you about where he might be heading, don't keep it to yourself.'

Magellan smiled and took the card. 'Deal.'

Amand turned away and crossed the street, heading for the white building that housed the judge's chambers and mentally preparing for his briefing. He had four possible suspects now and he arranged them in his mind based on what he knew and what he believed, starting with the one he thought least likely to have killed Josef Engel and ending with the one he believed the most. Four suspects:

Madjid Lellouche

Günther Samler – Artur Samler's son

Solomon Creed

and Jean Baptiste.

54

Jean Baptiste walked into the main airport building at Toulouse and looked around. The last time he had been here they had been knocking down the old buildings to make way for the airy steel-and-glass hangar he now stood in. He spotted the departure board and counted the different airlines listed on it. There were eight. If Marie-Claude and Léo had taken a flight, it would require a lot of legwork and smiling and flashing his out-of-date badge to check every desk and passenger manifest. He checked his watch. Thanks to LePoux's driving, they had got here in under half an hour, making up some lost time. But he still had to find them.

He walked over to the escalator and headed down to the check-in desks. There were even more carriers down here, different logos and names, most of which he'd never heard of. Some desks were empty but most had uniformed staff manning them, chatting to passengers or each other. As he scanned the hall, trying to decide where to start, he spotted a sign on a pillar that gave him an idea.

He pulled the laptop from his satchel, moved over to one of the empty desks and searched for the Free Wi-Fi the sign advertised. It had been thirty minutes since he'd last checked the GeoTracker and something new may have popped up that could spare him the legwork. He waited for the laptop to connect, launched the GeoTracker and clicked the Bluetooth icon.

The unique code of the tile was still in the search box and the map refreshed when it picked up the signal of the tile in his pocket and showed it as a blue dot at the centre of the main terminal building at Toulouse–Blagnac. The map began to expand, looking for matching signals from other tiles. It beeped as it found the cluster in Cordes and continued to zoom out.

Baptiste looked across at the Air France desk, trying to gauge which member of staff might be the best one to approach. He noticed one of the women was wearing a head scarf in the Air France colours and felt a wave of disgust. They should be enforcing the uniform, not relaxing it to accommodate immigrants.

The laptop beeped again.

A new dot had appeared, way up at the top of the map. It was lying on the thick orange line of the A20, the main highway that ran north to south through almost the entire country. Baptiste zoomed in on it and place names appeared on the map, showing the nearest towns and cities. The new dot was about twenty minutes south of Limoges and, given the way LePoux drove, about a two-hour journey from Toulouse.

Baptiste studied the map, tracing the route Marie-Claude had taken, southeast to Toulouse before heading north. Why hadn't she gone directly north? Taking this detour must have added an hour to her journey. He ran a search on her mobile phone number again in case she'd turned it back on, but the map returned to the same place as before, slightly to the northwest of the building he was now standing in. He zoomed in, studied the large expanse of tarmac with tiny dots lined up on it and realized what it was and why Marie-Claude had taken this detour.

She had not driven here to catch a plane. She'd come here to change her car.

55

The service station was noisy and bright and smelled of fuel and sweat and burnt coffee, and Solomon was glad to escape from it. They had gone inside separately but everyone was far too preoccupied with themselves or their phones to notice anyone else. Marie-Claude was buying snacks for the onward journey. Solomon wanted air.

He stopped under the shade of an acacia tree and looked down at the grass. It was dry and yellow and littered with cigarette butts, but even in its sorry state he still contemplated taking his boots off to connect with the earth for a moment. He laid his hand on the trunk instead, feeling the rough contours of the sun-warmed bark flexing gently in the exhaust-laced breeze. This was a nowhere place, a place of permanent transit, limbo. The tree was the only thing that lived here, the only thing with roots, and Solomon drew a measure of calm from touching it.

Marie-Claude emerged from the service station holding a bag in one hand and Léo's hand in the other. He looked around, the thick lenses of his glasses amplifying the way his eyes lit up when he spotted Solomon. Solomon reluctantly broke contact with the tree and stepped up to the car, opening the doors for both Marie-Claude and Léo.

'Wow. An old-fashioned gentleman,' she said.

'Manners are the glue of civilization.' Solomon winked at Léo. 'And the ladies will love you for it.'

'Will they, now?' Marie-Claude shook her head and got in the car.

'Oh yes,' Solomon murmured.

They rejoined the péage and Solomon lowered his window.

'You know the air-con works better with it closed,' Marie-Claude said.

'Yes, but I work better with it open. Do you actually like being in a car?'

She looked around at the soft, leather interior. 'I like being in this one.'

Solomon held his hand out and felt the air rushing through his fingers, the speed of the car making it feel liquid. 'So why don't you have a car like this?'

'The kinds of jobs I want to do don't pay the kind of money that would get me one of these, and the hours are too long. I've got Léo to think of.'

'I wouldn't mind you working long hours if we could have a car like this,' Léo said.

'Thanks. I'll bear that in mind.'

Solomon pulled his hand back inside and turned to Marie-Claude. 'What is your job exactly?'

'This is. Tracking down survivors of Die Schneider Lager. Collecting their stories.'

'You get paid to do that?'

'Kind of. I got a grant from the Shoah Foundation. You know what that is?'

Information shimmered through Solomon's head in response to her question. 'It's a charity set up to archive the oral history of Holocaust survivors. Funded by profits from the Hollywood movie *Schindler's List.*'

Marie-Claude nodded. 'Of course you know. You know everything – except useful stuff like how to drive a car. Anyway, to tie in with the seventieth anniversary of the end of the war, the Foundation set up a fund to collect stories that hadn't been told before. My proposal was to tell the story of my grandfather and the other survivors of Die Schneider Lager. The only thing that's ever really been written about the camp is Herman Lansky's memoir. It's one of the great untold stories.'

Solomon waited for the usual torrent of information but none came. 'Who's Herman Lansky?'

'You don't know? I thought you knew everything.'

'Not everything, and the things I don't know are usually significant. Tell me about Herman Lansky.'

'I can do better than that.' She reached into the back and pulled a book from her backpack. 'You can read his book.' She handed it to him, leaned over and pulled a second book out of the bag. 'You should read this one too. It's an account of how the camp was liberated. Those two books are the foundation of all my work.'

Solomon read both titles:

Freeing the Dead: The Nazi Death Camp Liberators

– and –

Dark Material – The Devil's Tailor: Death and Life in Die Schneider Lager by Herman Lansky.

He opened Lansky's book and tried reading the first page,

but the low-level nausea he'd been enduring since leaving Cordes welled up and forced him to look at the horizon and take deep breaths instead.

'You OK? You want me to pull over?'

'No, it's OK. Keep going. I'll read it next time we stop.'

'That won't be for a while,' Marie-Claude said. 'Still a looong way to go.'

'That's why car rides are boring,' Léo muttered in the back. 'No reading.'

'That's right,' Marie-Claude said. 'No reading and no barfing. And that goes for both of you.'

56

Amand was kept waiting for almost twenty minutes before Jacques Laurent – his appointed *juge d'instruction* – finally emerged from chambers, immaculate in a gun-metal grey suit the same colour as his hair. 'Walk with me,' Laurent said, heading away down the oak-panelled corridors. 'I have to be in court in five minutes. Tell me about the new suspect. Or has this one escaped too?'

Amand let the comment slide. 'His name is Madjid Lellouche. Migrant worker. I interviewed him before coming to see you.'

'I don't suppose he confessed?'

'No, sir. He says he's innocent.'

'Don't they always.'

'Yes, but in this case I think he's telling the truth.'

'Based on what evidence?'

'I've just come from the morgue and the weapon we found at the suspect's home does not appear to match the wounds on the victim.'

'Does not *appear* to match?'

'At the moment, it's only a preliminary observation.'

'What about the blood on the weapon?'

'Hasn't been tested yet.'

'Well, perhaps you should hold judgement until you have all the facts. What about the other suspect, the one you let go?'

'We believe he may have absconded with the grand-daughter and grandson of the murder victim.'

'Any idea why?'

'No. They may have been coerced.'

'*May* have been.'

'We don't know for certain.'

'You don't seem to know very much, Commandant. Any other leads?'

'We're considering two other possibilities. Josef Engel was a death camp survivor and the nature of his murder suggests his killer might be connected to his past.'

'Any idea who?'

'I'd like to look into a man named Artur Samler, the commandant of the camp Monsieur Engel was incarcerated in. It's possible that he or someone connected to him may be carrying out some long-standing vendetta.'

'Sounds tenuous. How old would this man be now – a hundred?'

'Yes, but his son also worked at the camp for a time and he would only be in his eighties.'

'*Only*. Sounds very unlikely.'

'Maybe, but the victim was chemically subdued before he was tortured and killed, which would suggest his killer was not physically strong.'

'You said there were two other leads, I hope your second one is better.'

'We're also trying to locate Monsieur Engel's ex-grand-son-in-law, Jean Baptiste.'

Laurent stopped walking and turned to face Amand. 'Jean Baptiste.'

'Yes.'

'Why?'

'Because he has a history of violence against the Engel family, was recently released from prison and has since disappeared.'

'He was released early, which means he was a model prisoner. A reformed character.'

'A model prisoner who killed someone whilst inside.'

'In self-defence, and he paid a heavy price for it.' Laurent dropped his voice as a couple of sober-suited lawyers walked by. 'Given your role in Jean Baptiste's arrest and incarceration and the sense of responsibility you must feel towards his ex-wife, your concern is understandable. However, if your personal feelings are going to cloud your judgement, perhaps you should step down from the investigation.'

Amand nodded. So that was what this summons had been about. It was difficult and unusual for a judge to remove someone from an investigation, but an officer was perfectly free to recuse themselves.

'I think that until we have more evidence we should pursue all lines of enquiry,' Amand said as calmly as he could. 'That includes known offenders with a history of violence against the victim's family. That is not personal feeling, that is common sense.'

Laurent stepped closer, so close that Amand could smell his cologne and see the white foam in the corners of his thin-lipped mouth. 'Leave Jean Baptiste alone,' he said. 'Go back to Cordes and get me some hard evidence. Go talk to the Arab again and try to sweat a confession out of him, that will be the best use of your time, not chasing Nazis or pursuing personal vendettas.' He turned and walked away. 'And the moment you have some *proper* evidence, let me know.'

Amand watched Laurent marching away, the sound of his expensive leather shoes echoing down the grand corridor. He forced himself to breathe deeply for a moment, then headed to the basement where the Albi Commissariat kept an office. Some of his irritation came from being told what to do by someone he didn't respect, but some came from knowing that Laurent was partly right. Because he did feel responsible for Marie-Claude and Léo. He *was* responsible. He had been instrumental in taking away Marie-Claude's husband and Léo's father. And though he had tried to do his best to fill the hole in their family he had helped create, he had never managed it. And now they were missing and he needed to find them and make sure they were safe – and he was failing at that too.

He pulled his phone from his pocket and dialled the Cordes Commissariat. Henri answered after the second ring. 'How was the morgue?'

'Not great. Where's the cane, Henri?'

'It should be there.'

'Well, it's not.'

'But I . . . I'll chase it up.'

'What have you found out about those other two murders – Herman Lansky and Saul Schwartzfeldt?' There was a pause and he heard a muffled conversation with what sounded like Parra.

'Calls have been placed to London about Lansky, but due to the age of the case it's unlikely we'll get anything back on that soon, if at all. And we're waiting to hear back from Colmar about Saul Schwartzfeldt. Hopefully I'll have something by the time you get back.'

'I'm not coming back. I'm going to stay here until that cane shows up. I'll be on my mobile if you need me.' He hung up and pushed through a door into a small office containing three desks and an ancient sergeant. 'Any chance I can borrow a desk for half an hour?' He showed the sergeant his ID and the man's bushy eyebrows shot up as he recognized the name.

'You're the guy who caught the murder over in Cordes.' Amand nodded wearily. 'Good news travels fast.'

'Help yourself,' the sergeant said, gesturing at the empty desks.

Amand nodded his thanks and plopped down at the tidiest one. The only item on the desktop was a framed photograph of a kind-looking woman with two dark-haired girls, all smiling for the camera. It was like a window into the kind of life he might've had: wife, kids – normal. But that had never been on the cards for him. He had been an outsider his whole life and people like Jacques Laurent only made that feeling stronger. He thought about what he'd said, about finding more evidence and trying to make the murder stick to Madjid Lellouche. But he was an outsider too. Maybe that was what made Amand feel sympathetic towards him. The cane would help prove it, one way or another. He checked his watch. Still only mid-morning.

He leaned forward, logged on to the computer using his network ID and password, checked his email and opened a search engine. He would give himself until the cane finally turned up to explore other leads. After that, he would return to Cordes armed with the results and either talk to Lellouche again or let him go. He typed 'Artur Samler' into the subject box and hit *Return*. A whole raft of results came back, topped by a Wikipedia entry showing the same picture he'd seen in Marie-Claude's research notes of Samler looking immaculate in his Nazi uniform. The short biography said he was believed to have committed suicide at the end of the war.

Believed – but not confirmed.

He clicked on the main link and started to read.

57

Patrice Boudy was pretending to look at his computer screen but secretly reading a detective novel when he became aware of someone approaching his desk. He looked up, saw the police badge and his stomach did a somersault.

'I need to talk to someone about security cameras,' the man with the badge said. 'The ones covering the car parks.'

'I can help with that.' Boudy sat up in his seat, his eyes pausing at the scar on the man's face. 'Do you have a warrant?'

'Well, here's the thing,' the man said, tucking the ID into his pocket. 'I'm investigating a murder case and this is more of a hunch than a solid lead. I don't really want to bother the judge with it only to find out it's a dead end and was wondering if I might have a quick unofficial look and if we find anything useful I'll get the proper paperwork in place and we can find it again, officially.' He glanced at the detective novel lying face down on the desk. 'I'm sure you understand how these things work, Monsieur . . .?'

'Boudy. Patrice. Yes, I . . . yes.' Boudy was feeling flustered and excited. His morning had been the usual dull parade of giving people directions and replacing lost parking tickets. Now he was being asked to help in a *murder* investigation.

'Thank you, Patrice. I really appreciate it. And if anything useful comes out of it, I'll be sure to mention you in my report.'

Boudy's stomach did another flip. He had a half-filled-in application form to join the Police Nationale in his flat. He'd abandoned it at a section asking for any relevant experience. If he could put something in about helping in a murder investigation that would be way cool.

'Follow me, monsieur.' Boudy rose from his chair and headed through a door into a dark, dimly lit office with a desk, a computer, and a wall of flat-screen monitors showing various fixed views of the airport. Boudy dropped into the seat and typed in his username and password. 'Which car park do you want to check?'

'The big one to the north.'

'That's long-stay.' He tapped *P5* into a command box and the screens changed to all the feeds from that car park. 'What are we looking for?' Boudy said, excited at the prospect of doing real police work.

'A red Peugeot 205.'

'Any idea what time it entered the car park?'

'Around an hour and a half ago, maybe two.'

'Registration number?'

Baptiste recited it from memory and Boudy copied it into a search field.

'Bingo!' He hit a button to zoom in on a freeze-frame of the registration plate. 'The barrier cameras picked it up entering *P5* at 10.42.' He checked the parking log and frowned. 'Wait a second.' He tapped in a new number and the screen changed to an image of the same registration plate from a slightly different angle. 'Another barrier camera picked it up fifteen minutes later, only it didn't leave. It's still in the car park.'

'Do you have a wider angle of that?'

Boudy tapped more commands and the screen changed to show the Peugeot parked at the barrier. He hit the space bar and the image unfroze and started to play forward in real time. Baptiste leaned in, eyes fixed on the partial profile of a boy in the rear window of the car. Then the man appeared: tall, pale, white hair. He held something out and a hand reached through the driver's window and took it. The man got in and the car reversed away from the barrier. Baptiste watched on a wider feed as the Peugeot backed up until it came to an empty spot and parked. 'Do you have a closer angle on that?'

'No, but I can make that one bigger.' Boudy tapped keys and the whole wall of screens filled with the same camera feed.

Baptiste stared at the pixellated image of the car, shifting slightly as the recording moved on. After about a minute, one of the doors opened slightly and a small, blurry figure emerged, keeping low. Baptiste moved forward a little, wishing the resolution was better so he could see Léo's face. The tiny figure moved out of the way and two larger figures got out. All three stayed low as the door closed again, then they moved into the line of parked cars and disappeared from sight. After a few seconds the indicators of a large black car parked further along from the Peugeot flashed, the driver's door opened and Baptiste caught hints of movement in the car as the three figures crawled inside. There was a brief pause before the car pulled out of its spot and headed away to the barriers. Boudy waited to see where it stopped and switched the cameras again.

'Freeze it there,' Baptiste said, reaching for a pen to copy down the registration.

'I can do a screen-grab, if you like.'

'Let's wait for the warrant before we do that,' Baptiste said. 'For now I'll just make a note and put out an alert. What make of car is that?'

'Looks like an Audi. One of those four-by-fours, like a Q3 or something.' On the screen, the barrier lifted and the car drove away.

'Thank you, Patrice,' Baptiste said, already heading for the door. 'Keep this under your hat until I come back with that warrant, OK. I'll definitely mention you when I write it up.'

Boudy watched him leave then turned back to the screen with a big grin on his face. This was what he'd always hoped police work would be like, like it was in the crime novels he read. He tapped a new command into the computer to access the Police Alert database, wondering if he could figure out what murder investigation he'd helped with. Ever since the Belgian airport bombings, airport security networks had been linked directly to the police, which meant he could access alerts relating to any new and ongoing investigations.

A new window opened on the screen, filled with information, every alert for all the investigations currently active. There was a search command to filter the results and Boudy thought for a moment, trying to think like a cop would think. He smiled and set the camera feed running backwards. He watched the black Audi reverse away from the barriers, park back in its space, then the Peugeot did the same, stopping at the barrier as before. Boudy froze the image, copied the Peugeot's registration into the search field and hit *Return*.

The solid mass of information vanished and was replaced by a single alert, issued by the Cordes Commissariat. Boudy read it eagerly, sucking up the details of how the owner of the car (Marie-Claude Engel – 29) was missing with her son (Léo – 7) and was possibly travelling with a man (Solomon Creed – age unknown) wanted for questioning in connection with the murder of Josef Engel (89). There were also contact details for any new information. Boudy stared at the phone number and email address. The cop had said to wait but this alert meant he didn't need a warrant. Boudy could easily have picked the alert up during the normal course of his work. Surely that would demonstrate initiative and alertness and would also look good on his application to join the Police Nationale.

He reached for the desk phone to dial the contact number and paused. If he spoke to someone he would probably have to lie to cover up for the cop – what was his name? He had seen his ID but had been too flustered to take it in. Either way, he didn't want to get him in trouble and jeopardize the good word he said he'd put in for him. He stared at the frozen image of the licence plate. There was a better way to do this, one that did not require him to speak to anyone or have to come up with a lie.

He took a screen-grab of the registration plate then worked through the footage, taking more screen-grabs and building up a photo montage of what had taken place in the car park earlier that day. When he'd finished, he put all the images in a folder, compressed it, and attached it to an email addressed to the Cordes contact email from the alert. In the subject line he wrote the reference number and added a note:

Dear sirs,

I spotted your alert, ran a routine registration check and got a hit. I believe your subjects switched cars and are now

driving a black Audi. I have attached photos as evidence,
along with the registration of the Audi. I hope this helps.

Yours,

Patrice Boudy – Blagnac Security

He re-read it twice before pressing *send* and watched the
large file upload then go.

He smiled and reset the system, restoring all the real-time
camera feeds before heading back out to the desk to give
more people directions and help them with their lost tickets.
He couldn't *wait* to tell his girlfriend about this later.

58

Amand glanced up at the soft ping announcing the arrival of a new email. He had spent the last fifteen minutes trawling through reports of Artur Samler's supposed suicide and making a list of all the unconfirmed sightings there had been of him since, of which there were many. Most of them were posted on Nazi discussion forums dedicated to remembering the 'heroes' of the war and keeping the flame of Nazism alive. There were whole sections dedicated to Samler and his son, Günther, who had also worked as a guard at Die Schneider Lager, also been reported as killed at the end of the war, and also been spotted numerous times in the post-war years. There were pages and pages dedicated to sightings of Hitler and all the other Nazi leaders too, and Amand wasn't taking any of it at face value. But still, they were leads that needed following up and he felt tired at the thought of how much work lay ahead, so the email came as a welcome distraction. It was addressed to the general information account but Amand recognized the alert code in the subject line and opened it. He read the note and clicked the attachment.

A series of photographs appeared in a new window and his skin went cold when he saw the first one. Marie-Claude's

Peugeot. Parked by a barrier. Solomon Creed standing next to it. His biggest fear confirmed. They *were* together.

He scanned the rest of the photos, looking for any sign that Marie-Claude and Léo were in any distress, while everything Magellan had told him about Solomon came screaming back to him. The final image showed the registration plate of the car they were now driving. Amand picked up the desk phone and was halfway through dialling Henri's number when the photos vanished from his screen. He checked his inbox. The email had gone too. Panic rose up at the thought that this slender thread connecting him to Marie-Claude had snapped. He remembered it was an Audi but he hadn't written down the new registration number. He refreshed the inbox. Checked the trash. Nothing.

His heart started to race and he reached into his pocket, took out a glycerine tablet, popped it under his tongue and forced himself to calm down and think. He couldn't remember the details of the email but he remembered where it was from. He opened a new window, found the website for Toulouse–Blagnac Airport and a number for Parking Services, dialled it and opened up his personal Gmail account while it connected.

'Blagnac Stationnement?'

'Hi, my name's Commandant Benoît Amand from the Cordes Commissariat. I need to talk to whoever's in charge of the security cameras that cover the car parks.'

'I can help with that.'

'Did you send an email with some photographs of a missing car – a Peugeot?'

'Yes . . . that was me.' Amand detected a hint of suspicion in his voice.

'Great, I was hoping to get hold of you. Your message

was very helpful but I wondered if you could send it again to another email address. We're having a few issues with our servers today and the attachment isn't downloading.'

'OK, sure. Where do you want me to send it?' Amand gave him his own Gmail address and listened to the tap of fingers on a keyboard. 'It's gone. Let me know if you have any more problems.'

Amand refreshed his Gmail account and the email appeared. He opened the attachment to make sure the photographs had come through and stared at the grainy image of Solomon standing by the car again. 'Got it. Thanks.'

'Pleasure. And if you need hard copies, I can print them off and give them to the other guy when he comes back.'

Amand froze. 'What other guy?'

'The cop,' he sounded defensive again.

'Did you get this guy's name?'

'No . . . he showed me his badge, but I didn't catch his name . . . He said not to make it official until he came back with a proper warrant, but I saw the alert on the police database and figured he wouldn't need one. That's why I sent the email. I hope that was OK.'

'Absolutely. You did the right thing.' Amand's mind raced with this new information. 'Actually, hard copies would be helpful. What did this guy look like? I might be able to figure out who it was and get him to swing back to pick them up.'

'About medium height, quite fit, like a boxer or something. He had black hair and a scar on one side of his face.'

Amand felt like someone had punched him in the stomach. 'OK,' he said. 'I know who that is. I'll call him right now. Thanks again.'

He hung up and stared at the screen. He had been worried

about Marie-Claude before: now he was terrified. Not only was she travelling with a known killer who was most likely becoming increasingly unstable, but her ex-husband was actively looking for her too. He started to redial the Cordes number to inform Henri and get him to upgrade the alert, then stopped. The email had been sent to Cordes and it had vanished. The cane had vanished too. Two key pieces of evidence, both now missing. There was probably a simple explanation for it – the bamboo cane was held up in transit, there was some kind of glitch in the mail server – but there was also another possibility, and Amand felt sick at the idea. There was a way to test it, though.

He dialled the number for the Commissariat and Henri picked up on the second ring. 'Henri, it's Ben. How're you getting on with the bamboo cane?'

'Someone at the morgue's gone in search of it, in case it's in dispatch or something.'

'So it hasn't arrived.'

'No, but I'm on it. It'll turn up.'

'What about the Lansky and Schwartzfeldt cases?'

'Still waiting for people to get back to me.'

'OK. Anything else?'

'Nope.'

Amand let the silence stretch, giving Henri the chance to say something about the email, anything. He must have seen it, he was the dispatcher, everything went through him. He'd known Henri for years. Respected him. But the silence continued to stretch.

'Anything else you need?' Henri said finally.

'No,' Amand said, and hung up. He stared at the phone, thinking back through all the things he'd asked Henri to do that morning, wondering now if any of them had been done.

His head felt like his brain was swelling inside his skull, and he forced himself to breathe deeper. Verbier had warned him to take it easy or he would force him to step down, but he couldn't, not now. Who would look out for Marie-Claude and Léo then? He wondered who else might be involved. LePoux, Belloq, the Laurent family too most probably, senior and junior. The local mafia, closing ranks, but for what? Had they killed Josef Engel? Had their right-wing nationalism evolved into murder now? He thought of the swastika on the Jewish memorial that morning and how Herman Lansky's memoir had talked about the same thing happening right before the Nazis seized power. That was how it started. Words of hate written on a wall. He had to keep everyone thinking he was still in the dark and gather evidence himself. Find Marie-Claude before they did. At least she was out of the area. The Belloqs and Laurents might own Cordes, but they did not own France.

He opened the internal directory on the computer, found the number for the Gendarmerie Nationale, the division in charge of traffic, and dialled it.

'Dispatch!'

'Hello, I'm calling from the Cordes Commissariat. We're urgently looking for a suspect in relation to a current murder investigation and have received information that they're driving a black Audi Q3 out of Toulouse–Blagnac Airport. Can you run the registration through the péage camera database and see if any of the barrier cams have picked it up?'

'Sure. Go ahead.'

Amand read the registration number from the photograph and listened to keyboard taps.

'That car passed through the Porte de Montauban heading

north out of Toulouse on the A20 a little over an hour ago. There are no other hits.'

'So it's still on the motorway?'

'Has to be. They'd have to pass through another barrier to get off. I would say they're somewhere around Souillac by now, if they haven't stopped.'

'OK, thanks. Can you put out a level one alert for me. There are three people in the car – a man, a woman and a seven-year-old boy, I'll forward you photos and details. The man is potentially extremely dangerous and the woman and child are in immediate danger. They *must* be apprehended and approached with extreme caution.'

'I'll issue the alert now and put your name as contact. Who am I speaking with?'

Amand paused. If he gave his own name, they'd know he was operating independently of the investigation. 'DuBois,' he said. 'Sergeant Henri DuBois. I'll give you my mobile number and email the additional information. Our phone system is playing up, so that's the best number to get me on.'

'OK, sure. I'll wait for your email and add your details to the alert.'

'Thanks.' Amand hung up and opened a new window. He created a Gmail account in Henri's name and copied the photos from Blagnac into a new message, attached the Interpol alert for Solomon and added a few lines about Marie-Claude and Léo, then sent it.

Somewhere near Souillac, the dispatcher had said.

He opened Google Maps and studied the thick orange line of the A20 snaking up through the middle of France. Marie-Claude was on it somewhere with a killer in her car and Baptiste on her tail.

59

Jean-Luc Belloq was serving coffee to a group of Dutch tourists when the cheap mobile phone buzzed in the pocket of his apron. He moved into the café, checked the number and summoned Mariella. 'Watch the bar,' he said, and headed into the small back office, closing the door behind him before answering.

'Tell me you have good news.'

'I have news, but I wouldn't call it good. That guy Baptiste spoke to at Blagnac emailed screen-grabs from the security cameras to the Commissariat. Fortunately, I was at my desk and deleted it as soon as it appeared. I don't think anyone else saw it.'

Belloq fished a skinny dark cigarillo from the pack on his desk and fitted it into his mouth. 'What about Amand, is he still being a pain in the ass?'

'He's over at the morgue in Albi, checking in on the autopsy and forensics results.'

'And where's the bamboo cane?'

'In my locker, but Amand is chasing it hard. I can probably hold it back for a few more hours, that way the test results won't come back until tomorrow.'

'Good. Keep hold of it as long as you can.' Belloq lit the

cigarillo and breathed in smoke. 'As soon as they realize it's pig's blood on that cane they'll have to let the Arab go and all efforts will be refocused on Solomon Creed. We need to get to him first and find out what he—'

'Shit!'

'What?'

'A new alert just popped up from the central traffic division.' Belloq heard tapping on a keyboard. 'It's got the Engel case number on it and the screen-grabs from Blagnac.'

Belloq blew out smoke. 'Can you delete it?'

'No. It's on the national database. Every commissariat in France will have got it. Wait a second. They've already got a hit on the Audi too, it passed through the péage barrier at Montauban an hour ago heading north on the A20.' There was a pause and more keyboard clacking. 'The next toll booth is at Vierzon, so unless they pull off beforehand, that's where they'll get picked up.'

'OK, keep watching. Do your best to keep it contained and let me know as soon as anything new crops up.'

He hung up, unlocked his computer and input Vierzon and Montauban into Google Maps while dialling LePoux's mobile. The map loaded, a thick blue line joining the two dots. The distance between them was four hundred and sixteen kilometres – three hours and forty minutes' driving time – but Marie-Claude had already been on the road for an hour. The phone clicked and LePoux answered, the hiss of motorway in the background.

'Where are you?'

'We just passed Montauban.'

Belloq shook his head. 'Then we have a problem. Put me on speakerphone and I'll explain.'

LePoux obliged and Belloq ran through the new information he'd received.

'We can still catch them,' Baptiste said.

'They're more than an hour ahead of you.'

'Yes, but they're bound to stop for lunch, and they've got Léo with them so they'll probably have to stop a few more times. He gets car sick. We can catch them.'

'But what if they don't stop? What if they turn off before they get to Vierzon? It's too risky. We need to pick them up before the police do. I'll call the leadership. They'll have someone local they can trust. Stand down, Jean Baptiste, this is no longer your responsibility.'

'Léo will always be my responsibility. I want to continue. I think we can catch them.'

Belloq stubbed his cigarillo out in an overflowing ashtray. 'Carry on if you want to, but I think you're wasting your time. I'll call the leadership now and see what they say.'

He hung up before Baptiste could object any further and dialled the direct number the Leader had given him earlier. 'We have a problem,' he said, the moment he answered.

'An insoluble one?' the desiccated voice replied.

'Depends. Does the party have anyone in the Vierzon area?'

'Of course. We have soldiers suited to every task in every corner of France. What kind of person do you need?'

Belloq thought about what needed to be done. 'Someone serious,' he replied.

60

Thommé Terrau, known as Bull for reasons obvious to anyone who met him, knocked on the battered blue door for the second time. He was on the third floor of an ugly apartment block in the centre of Vierzon. He knew someone was home, he'd seen movement through the rippled glass door panel when he'd first arrived. He also knew they weren't going to open the door because if they were, they would have done it already. But he knocked a second time anyway because that was his ritual, something he'd started after one of his longer stints in jail where an American cellmate had taught him the rules of baseball and the notion of 'three strikes and you're out'. Bull liked the neatness and fairness of that: first chance, last chance, then no chance at all.

'We doing this or not?' Roberto said behind him, his voice tight with the same energy that made him twitch and fidget as he wound himself up for what was coming. This was another reason Bull liked the three strikes rule. It enforced a degree of discipline. Any idiot could go charging into a place and start breaking heads. That was what he used to do himself, which was why he'd ended up in jail learning the rules of baseball from a crazy American. Now he stuck to his ritual.

'Three strikes,' Bull said, raising his size fourteen boot. 'You're out!'

He kicked the door so hard that the lock broke free and smashed a mirror hanging on the opposite wall. Bull charged through the door and into the cheap, rented flat, ducking to avoid the lamps that always hung too low for him in these crummy, low-ceilinged dives. The place was sparsely furnished with the kind of shitty, mismatched stuff you bought at the Troc. Some people never had anything, no money, no taste and no common sense either, or they wouldn't take out street loans and neglect to keep up the repayments.

Bull headed to the bathroom because they always went to the bathroom, and that was always next to the kitchen because it was cheaper to put the plumbing all in one place. He spotted a Baby Alive doll on the floor next to a closed door, surrounded by bits of toilet paper folded into nappies. He picked it up and raised his boot again. No three strikes when you were inside, that let them know you were outside and you risked getting shot through the flimsy door or walls. He kicked hard, too hard, and his boot went straight through the door. Someone screamed inside and he drew his foot back, kicked again and this time the door broke in half.

'He's not here,' a woman screamed.

Bull barged through the wreckage of the door and stared down at the scrawny woman cowering in the bath, hugging a terrified young girl in her heavily tattooed arms.

'He's not here,' she screamed again.

'I'm not interested in him,' Bull said, 'only in what he owes.'

'He's getting it. He said he'd get it and bring it to you later.'

'That's not the way it works.' He held up the doll, twisted off its head and tossed it into the bath. The little girl started crying and Bull looked at the mother. 'You know these things are harder to pull apart than real babies.' He grabbed an arm and yanked that off too. 'You wouldn't think it, but it's true.' He tossed the arm into the bath next to the head.

'Rent money,' the woman screamed. 'I can give you the rent money.'

'It's only rent money if you give it to your landlord. Until then it's just money. Where is it?'

'Microwave.'

'Microwave!' Bull shouted and he heard Roberto clattering around in the kitchen.

'Eighty euros,' Roberto called out.

Bull shook his head. 'What else you got?'

'That's it.'

Bull pulled a leg off the doll with a pop and tossed it into the bath. The little girl was sobbing now.

'You got a phone?' The mother nodded. 'Where?'

'Handbag. Bedroom.'

'Handbag in the bedroom!' Bull called out and there was a loud crash as Roberto pulled something on to the floor in the kitchen on his way out.

Bull held up what was left of the doll and looked at the little girl. 'You gonna be a good Mummy and make her all better?' She was having trouble breathing now, her snotty sobs ragged and desperate as she held the mutilated remains of her baby. Bull dropped the doll into the bath and she hugged it while her mother hugged her. She had at least a thousand euros' worth of ink on her skin and that was only the bits he could see.

'You got any piercings?' Bull asked. She hesitated. Nodded.

Roberto appeared behind him with a fake Louis Vuitton handbag in one hand and assorted items in the other: 'Driving licence, passport, iPhone 4.'

Bull nodded. 'OK, you can keep your jewellery for now. We'll take your bag and give it back when your boyfriend pays what he owes. See you later.' He winked at the little girl and left.

Outside on the street, Bull opened the boot of his BMW with the button on his key fob and dropped the handbag inside next to several others. The bags were all fakes but their contents had value. Phones were like cash cards now, you could pay for all sorts of things with the credit on them or sell them to the dealers, who always needed phones. Passports and driver's licences could be sold for identity fraud. He dropped the cash into a shoebox, along with the rest of the day's take, and added eighty euros to the running total in his notebook. They were already at almost three thousand – not bad for a weekday. He closed the boot, got into the passenger seat, took his phone from the glove compartment and checked his messages. He had one and he frowned when he read it and dialled a number from memory.

'I got your message,' he said. He listened and jotted some things in his notebook: *Solomon Creed, Marie-Claude, Léonardo. A20. Heading north.*

'Where are they now?' He listened some more. Nodded. 'OK, send me the details. I'll let you know when it's done.' He hung up and turned to Roberto. 'You feeling patriotic?'

Roberto shrugged and unwrapped one of the aniseed sweets he'd become addicted to since giving up smoking. Bull's phone buzzed again and he opened the message and studied the attached photographs of the people whose names he had written down. He lingered on the woman. She was dark-haired, fine-featured, pretty. At the bottom of the text was a sequence of numbers and he leaned forward and copied the coordinates into the satnav. The map on the display changed and plotted a course from their current position. They were forty minutes away, but the target was heading north, coming towards them. Bull studied the map, working out the best place to intercept. 'Head to the péage,' he said.

'What we doing?' Roberto asked, the aniseed lozenge clacking against his teeth.

'Our duty for a free France,' Bull replied, pointing at the tattoo of the black boar on his arm. He'd got it in prison when he was young and stupid and the Brotherhood had taken him in and protected him and made him one of their own.

61

Solomon smelled salt and turned to Marie-Claude. Her cheeks were glossed with tears, showing she had been crying for a while, though she had not made a sound. She noticed Solomon looking and turned away, wiping her face with her hand.

'Do you want to stop?' he asked.

'No,' she said, her eyes flicking to the mirror and the sleeping form of Léo. 'I want to get to where we're going, find out what the fuck all this is about, then go back home and get on with my life.'

He could smell her anger beneath the salt – ash and smoke – as well as the solid stone smell of her guilt, like the foundation upon which she had built herself. 'You may not get answers,' he said. 'Or they might not be the answers you want.'

She nodded. 'I know.'

'Is that why you're upset?'

She shook her head. 'I'm crying because I'm tired, because I'm angry, because my grandfather was murdered and it might have been my fault, and because I'm afraid that I've put my son in danger. And I'm crying because the only way I can see to possibly explain any of this is by driving halfway across the country in a stolen car to talk to a man I'm not even sure will tell me anything. Frankly, if Léo wasn't asleep I'd be screaming right now.' She turned to Solomon and he felt the heat of her gaze. 'How can you stay so calm? If this Otto Adelstein doesn't know you, you'll have wasted your time too.'

Solomon stared at the road ahead. 'I stay calm because it's the best place to think from – and because calm feels safe.'

'Safe? What do you mean?'

Solomon rubbed his hand across the brand on his arm and felt the raised skin beneath the fabric of his jacket. 'Whenever I feel things too strongly, something stirs inside me, something painful and dark and powerful. It's deep down and locked away and I want to know what it is, but I'm afraid of it too. I feel that maybe, if I know more about myself, I could let it out – like wanting to know what kind of creature is inside a box before deciding whether to let it out or not. At the moment, I don't know enough, so I keep calm and I keep it contained. But I'm also afraid of what it might reveal about who I am. Knowledge is not always power. Remember what your grandfather wrote in his note to you? "... *knowledge is sometimes a curse. And you can never unlearn something once it is known.*" That stands as a warning for both of us, because we both potentially have monsters in boxes. You want to know yours and crystallize your sense of identity by learning about your grandfather's past. But what if this man we're driving to see tells you something awful, something that your grandfather did in the camps to survive? You've read the stories. You know the lengths people had to go to, the depths they had to plumb just to stay alive.'

Marie-Claude shook her head. 'Things were different in

the camps. Normal laws and morality didn't apply. My grandfather was not a bad man and even if he was forced to do bad things, I know that's not who he was and I will not judge him for it.'

'But what if he didn't only kill one person, what if he killed thousands? They used the prisoners to run the ovens, you know that, the *Sonderkommandos* who serviced the death machine under threat of their own execution. What if your gentle grandfather was one of these, reassuring the new arrivals and telling them everything was going to be fine as he led them to the gas chambers? What if he only survived because he killed hundreds of men and women, and children like Léo? Would you want to know that? Would that help inform your sense of self? Would you tell Léo that he was only born because thousands of others exactly like him died? Or would you rather not know? Because right now, you have a choice. You can choose not to know because this knowledge is not your truth. You are removed from it, and perhaps that is how it should stay. It's different for me. I'm afraid of this rage inside me but I know I must face it and own it one day because it's part of me. But you don't have to. Maybe that's why I'm here. Maybe that's how I can save Léo.'

Marie-Claude glanced in the mirror again, checking Léo was still asleep. 'You keep saying that. Why do you think you need to save Léo? Save him from what?'

'Have you ever heard of Sin Eaters?' She shook her head. 'It's a tradition dating back to the Aztecs and beyond, but found in many cultures where a person assumes the sins of the dead. Sometimes this is by a verbal process of confession and absolution, as in the Catholic Church, and sometimes it is a physical thing. In Scotland there is a tradition of placing a piece of bread on the chest of a dying person. The bread is believed to absorb the sins of the dying and is consumed by someone known as a Sin Eater. This person is often an outcast, a pariah in the community. Jesus Christ was a Sin Eater of sorts. Maybe I'm one too.

'I can't tell you how I know that I'm here to save Léo – some things I just know. But it seems that the unknown story of your grandfather's past is my story too. And I *have* to know mine, I have no choice. But you do, and perhaps this is how I can save Léo: by taking on the story of his past so that he may never be tainted by whatever it is we discover. Maybe that's why I'm here, right at this moment, taking this journey with you. Because I'm your Sin Eater.'

62

Amand found a notebook in the desk, tore out a blank page and made a list of all the things he'd asked Henri to do:

1. *Search alerts for Marie-Claude / Léo / Solomon*
2. *Bamboo cane to Albi morgue*
3. *Look up Saul Schwartzfeldt murder and check details against Josef Engel's*
4. *Ditto Herman Lansky*

There was the scrape of a chair against floorboards and the ancient sergeant rose to his feet. 'I got to head up to the courtroom for ten minutes. Could you answer the phones while I'm gone?'

Amand nodded. 'No problem.'

He waited until the sergeant had gone before turning his attention back to his list. He put a tick next to the first item and a question mark by the second. Henri had said someone at the morgue was looking for the cane, but he now doubted it. He would head over and check it out for himself. For the third item he took out his phone and opened the notes he'd made in Marie-Claude's office and opened the National Police directory on his borrowed computer. He typed

'Colmar' into the search field and dialled the number that came back.

'Commissariat de Colmar,' a woman answered.

'Hello, this is Commandant Benoît Amand calling from Albi. Could I speak with . . .' he checked the notes on his phone, 'Commandant Rapp, please.'

'Can I say what it's regarding?'

'It's about Saul Schwartzfeldt.'

There was an intake of breath and a short blast of Alpine music before a man answered. 'This is Rapp. I understand you wish to talk about Monsieur Schwartzfeldt?'

'Yes. I'm investigating a murder and believe that my victim was a survivor of the same Nazi camp as Saul Schwartzfeldt. I'm calling because the manner of his death was unusual. I apologize if you've already spoken to someone in my office about this.'

'No. This is the first I've heard of it.'

Amand wrote 'Henri' at the bottom of his notes and drew a heavy circle round it.

'You said the manner of death was unusual,' Rapp asked. 'How exactly?'

'Well, none of this is being made public but – he was tortured before he died.'

'Tortured how?'

'A Star of David was cut into his flesh, for one.'

'Oh, Jesus, not another one. Were there rats too? Starved rats?'

Amand felt as if the blood had drained from his head. 'Yes.'

'It's the same. Monsieur Schwartzfeldt was the same.'

'Could you send me a copy of your murder file so I can compare them?'

'Of course.'

Amand gave him his Gmail address, along with the same excuse about a faulty server.

'Please, monsieur,' Rapp said. 'Find whoever did this. Saul was a good man, everybody liked him. My town has not been the same since his death. People used to leave their doors unlocked, now there are houses with bars on the windows. I feel I let my town down by not catching this monster, this . . . devil. Good luck, monsieur. Anything you need that will help with your investigation, just ask.'

Amand hung up and looked down at his notes. He drew a line between Saul Schwartzfeldt's name and Josef Engel. Magellan had been right. Josef had not been the killer's first victim. He switched his attention to the last name on the list – Herman Lansky. Lansky had died in London almost seventy years earlier and it had not been classed as a murder, so he doubted the files would have been kept. But there had been a police investigation, he had seen the verdict of the coroner's inquest, which meant there was a chance.

He opened the contacts on his phone and started scrolling through, looking for the name David Munroe, someone he'd met a few years back at an international crime symposium in Toulouse. Munroe had worked for the Metropolitan Police in London. Amand hoped he still did. He found his number and hesitated. He had meant to call him many times over the last few years but had always changed his mind. The English detective represented a side of his life that he'd been forced to keep hidden because of where he lived and the small-town attitudes that prevailed there. He'd often wondered if that was why he felt such empathy with Marie-Claude. They both had secret identities. They were both outsiders. He took a breath and dialled the number, hoping

Munroe might recognize the name and answer. It started to ring, a foreign-sounding tone that went on for a long time before someone answered.

'Benny?'

Amand smiled at the sound of that familiar voice. 'David. Long time.'

'Too long. How's France?'

'Lots of bread, lots of wine – the same. Listen, David, I'm ringing for a favour.'

'Personal or professional?'

'Police business.'

'Always with the business,' Munroe sounded a little disappointed. 'What do you need?'

'Any information you may have relating to an old case, a death in London.'

'Name and date?'

'The name is Herman Lansky. The date is June sixteenth, 1949.'

'Whoa, when you said "old" I didn't realize you meant prehistoric!'

'I know. That's why I called you instead of going through the channels. There's probably nothing, or the files will be in a box in some huge warehouse somewhere.'

'They won't be. The Met sold off the old Scotland Yard archive building a couple of years back. What was once a huge warehouse in Docklands is all luxury flats now. There are no boxes full of old files any more.'

Amand circled Herman Lansky's name and put a question mark next to it. 'I thought it was a bit of a long shot. It was nice to talk to you again, David.'

'Hold your horses.' He heard typing. 'Just 'cause there's no boxes doesn't mean there's no archive. Part of the deal when they sold the old warehouse was that the money had to be used to update everything, so all those old documents were digitized. No more rooting through boxes. All the files were indexed and archived, which means they're now search-able from any terminal. I'm looking at Herman Lansky's file right now. Death by misadventure – some kind of fire. Give me your email and I'll send it over.' Amand gave Munroe his Gmail address and heard the whooshing sound of an email being sent. 'And what do I get in return? You should come over to London and take me out. The scene here is a bit more lively than yours.'

Amand remembered the drunken nights of the conference. The freedom of being away from Cordes and everyone he knew. The freedom to be himself. He had been carrying some extra weight back then but Munroe hadn't minded. He hadn't minded at all. 'I will,' he said, and he meant it. 'As soon as I've squared away this case I'll take some time off and come to London. I promise. Be great to see you again.' He wanted to see what Munroe would make of the new, slimmer him and felt a sudden, strong urge to get away from Cordes and all the small-town eyes filled with curiosity and judgement at anyone who was different.

'Deal,' Munroe said. The email appeared in Amand's inbox as he hung up.

The Lansky file was fairly small and consisted mainly of PDF scans of old documents. There were a couple of black-and-white photographs showing a burned-out flat, a copy of the same coroner's court report he had already seen, and a whole load of handwritten notes from the beat cops. Amand struggled to read the old-fashioned handwriting that looped and swirled across the lined pages, his rusty English not helping either. It seemed to be mostly witness statements from neighbours saying the usual things about how Herman Lansky had kept himself to himself and seemed nice – despite being foreign. One resident said she'd heard raised voices in Lansky's flat on the night of the fire and had thought it odd because she'd never known Mr Lansky to have a visitor before, but no one else had heard anything and that line of enquiry had not been followed up.

Amand struggled through the statements, looking for anything that might prove useful. He was about to give up when he turned a page and saw something that sucked the breath right out of him. It was a note from one of the beat cops who'd spotted some graffiti written in chalk on an alley wall at the back of Lansky's apartment building. The policeman noted that he'd served as an infantryman in the war and knew the language as well as its unpleasant meaning. He also noted that he'd scrubbed it out because Herman Lansky was Jewish and he didn't want to risk stirring up bad memories of Nazi evil that people were still trying hard to forget in 1949. But first he had copied it down:

Das zuende bringen was begonnen wurde.

Amand sat back in his chair. He had not expected to find the Lansky files, let alone something in them that might link his death to the murders of both Josef Engel and Saul Schwartzfeldt almost seventy years later. He knew now that Jean Baptiste could not have killed both Engel and Schwartzfeldt, because the Schwartzfeldt murder had happened six months ago when Baptiste was locked up in Lannemezan. That left two other possibilities. He pulled a business card from his pocket, dialled the number on it and Magellan answered on the second ring. 'Commandant. How can I help?'

'Six months ago, where was Solomon Creed?'

'In my facility in Mexico.'

'You're sure?'

'Positive. The ICP is a maximum-security facility with the same level of security as a penitentiary. James Hawdon broke out twenty-five days ago. Why do you ask, has there been a new development?'

Amand paused before answering. After the vanishing email, his instinct was to trust no one, but Magellan was an outsider who only seemed concerned with the well-being and safety of his patient. 'Yes,' he said. 'I no longer consider Solomon Creed a suspect.'

'Good. Have you found him?'

'Not yet. Let me check a few things out and I'll call you back.'

He hung up and closed all the emails and windows until the only one left was the Nazi discussion forum he'd been reading when the Blagnac email had come in. He scrolled down the page until he found a photograph he'd seen earlier of two men standing by the barbed-wire fence of Die Schneider Lager. They were the same height, but one was thin and wore a guard's tunic whereas the other wore the uniform of an officer.

Amand studied the two faces staring back at him across seventy years of history, the same pale grey eyes, cold and unreadable: *Standartenführer* Artur Samler, Commandant of Die Schneider Lager, and Günther Samler, his son. He must have been a teenager in the photograph, a skinny apprentice hoping to one day take over his father's kingdom until the war ended and took away any chance of that. Or maybe not. Günther Samler's death had never been confirmed, he had simply vanished along with scores of others fleeing the crumbling ruins of the Third Reich. And he and his father were the only ones with a personal link to all three victims. Maybe he was following in his father's bloody footsteps after all:

Das zuende bringen was begonnen wurde – Finishing what was begun.

63

The car pulled off the péage and into one of the rest areas, coming to a halt beneath a large ash tree that spread its shade wide. He switched off the engine, wound down the windows to let in some air and sat listening to the cheep and caw of birds overhead and the distant hiss of the motorway. His head ached from caffeine and his mind was foggy from the honey-laced morphine that kept the worst of his pain at bay.

He opened the door and his joints cracked like gunshots as he unfolded himself from his seat. He shuffled round the car, stretching gently and breathing deeply for three full circuits that felt like laps of a running track, then sat on the bonnet and felt the heat of the engine through the steel. He was tired and the world around him shifted and flexed like it was starting to come apart. Sometimes he saw things that he knew were not there, strange creatures lurking in the shadows, watching him with hollow eyes.

The doctors said these visions were a symptom of the tumour in his occipital cortex, the part of the brain that controlled his visual imagination, but he knew the truth. When Saul Schwartzfeldt's identity had been revealed to him, he understood what these visions really were: not things to be feared, but augurs of what was to become, of what *he* was to become. He realized that the tumour was not death growing inside him but a new life, an egg from which his new self would hatch, reborn as something divine and eternal and righteous. And the Wild Hunt was his journey towards it.

He looked up at the great ash tree creaking and whispering above him, the sunlight flashing yellow through shimmering leaves of bright green. There was a rope tied high in its branches, swaying slightly with the movement of the tree, the noose looped into the end of it wide enough for a neck to pass through. This was no ordinary tree he was standing beneath, it was Yggdrasil, the great tree that grew through all the worlds, the gallows upon which he would sacrifice his human self in order to be reborn as Wotan.

He stared up at the rope swinging like a beckoning arm and wondered how he might climb high enough to reach it, tired and weak as he was. Movement shook the tree and leaves fluttered down as two scraps of black tore away from the green, cawing hoarse as they flew away. Two ravens, Wotan's birds, Huginn and Muninn – thought and memory. He watched them flap and glide, weaving in and out of each other's path as they headed north, following the line of the motorway. He looked back up at the ash tree and the rope had gone, nothing there now but sunlight and shifting green shadows. Maybe he had imagined it all. He found it increasingly difficult these days to tell the difference between what was really in the world and what was only in his head.

Nine months, the doctors had given him. Maybe a year. That was six months ago. He looked down at the ground, saw a spot of black in amongst the leaves and bent down stiffly to pick it up. He rolled it between trembling fingers, watching the green and blue play across the surface of the black feather like petrol on water. He *had* seen the ravens. They had been sent to remind him that the Hunt was not yet over. He rose and walked slowly back to his car. He needed to follow the birds north, back to his home where he could rest, and refill his flask with the bitter honey water, and prepare for the final part of the Wild Hunt. He collapsed into the driver's seat and glanced at his pale eyes in the mirror – old and bloodshot and so, so tired.

He opened the glovebox, tucked the black feather in among the bottles of pills and pulled his phone from the back of the compartment. He needed some darker fuel to drive him forward and chase away the bone-weary urge to close his eyes and sleep. He fitted the earphones in his ears, crunched a couple of painkillers and swilled them down with the last drops of sweet coffee from a Thermos flask. He opened the video player application on his phone. There were three files in it. He selected the middle one and started it playing.

An old man appeared on the screen, head bowed and on his knees in the same position Josef Engel had been in only this morning. The Star of David was cut into flesh made loose by the cancer this man had recently battled. He touched the screen and dragged his finger along to shuttle through footage showing the man getting bloodier and more wretched. He stopped before the end and found the part that always worked best for him in low moments like these when he needed a boost. He pressed *play* and felt a mild buzz as the sugar and caffeine hit his bloodstream.

I am the man known as Saul Schwartzfeldt . . . the wretched man on the screen said, his voice syrupy from pain and the drugs that had incapacitated him.

. . . I wish to record my final confession before Death claims a debt that should have been paid a long time ago in Die Schneider Lager . . .

This was the thing that always worked for him, the reason for the Hunt and why he had to continue it to the end. The revelation of truth.

64

The ancient sergeant returned to the basement office and Amand immediately headed out. He still had calls to make and things to check and didn't want anyone listening to his conversations. He stepped out on to the street and headed into the breeze towards the red brick monolith of the cathedral. He looked up 'Die Schneider Lager Museum' on his phone, found a contact number and was almost at the cathedral before someone answered.

'Mulhouse Museum.' The voice sounded old and weary, as if the phone had dragged him up a long flight of stairs or out of bed.

'This is going to sound like a bizarre question,' Amand said, 'but have you had any break-ins at the museum in the last year or two?'

'Who is this?'

Amand hesitated, but since no one else would be likely to call up and ask these questions, he answered: 'My name is Benoît Amand, I'm Commandant at the Cordes Commissariat in the Tarn.'

'My grandson recently joined the Police Nationale. Shitty pay and terrible hours.'

Amand smiled. 'That sounds about right, Monsieur . . .?'

'Carrièrre. Guillaume Carrièrre. What were you asking?'

'I was asking if the museum had been broken into recently or if anything has been taken, particularly items relating to Artur Samler.'

'Well, it's funny you should ask, because there was an incident at the Commandant's house about six or seven months back, but it's hard to say if anything went missing. The museum is run by volunteers, you see, and it's a real struggle to keep track of everything. Most of us are retired and it gives us something to do, and we think it's important to tell the younger folk about the war and what happened – a warning from history kind of thing.'

'Monsieur Carrièrre – the break-in?'

'Oh yes. Well, in the Commandant's house we have a room set up as Artur Samler's study. It's been recreated from photographs and is filled with items that have been donated over the years, lots of things that were actually his.'

'And something was taken from there?'

'Well, like I said, it's difficult to say for sure. We add and take things away from the room all the time because we have so many items in storage. Only we're not exactly systematic about it and things don't always get written down. What I'm saying is, we don't know precisely what was in Samler's house at the time of the break-in, so it's hard to know if anything is missing from it.'

'What about something small, like a cane or a swagger stick, something like that?'

'Well, it's funny you should ask, because that's exactly what I wondered at the time. Samler kept a stand full of sticks by his office door, because he used to beat the prisoners with them and the sticks often broke. We've got a stand there too, but as I said, we can't be certain one was taken because none of us could remember how many canes were supposed to be in the damn stand. The only thing we know was taken beyond a doubt was from the Brutus mausoleum.'

Amand felt the skin tighten on the back of his neck. 'What did they take?'

'Well, it's the damnedest thing, but they went and took the dog's skull. We didn't report it because there's no real value to it as far as insurance goes, though I bet if you went on eBay and did a search for "Nazi dog skull" you'd find some crazy person trying to sell it. There's quite the growing market out there for Nazi memorabilia, particularly stuff that belonged to someone infamous like Samler. Isn't that a sorry state of affairs? You'd think people would want to avoid anything touched by such evil, but no, quite the contrary. That's why we're forced to spend money we don't have on extra security, otherwise the whole damn museum would end up on eBay.'

'Apart from the skull and maybe a swagger stick, nothing else was taken?'

'Not as far as I know.'

'And this was around six months ago?'

'Autumn of last year.'

'Thank you for your time, Monsieur Carrièrre. If we recover anything, I'll make sure it's returned to the museum.'

He hung up and stared at the pigeons flocking around the cathedral tower like all the new information buzzing inside his head. He imagined the killer, holding the skull of Samler's dog against Josef Engel's skin and squeezing the jaws together until they drew blood, a symbolic recreation of a dog attack because the real thing wasn't practical. Starving rats made no sound but a hungry dog would. That's why there was no tearing around the shallow bites, because a dog had not bitten him. The killer was recreating the death camp and making his victims die as if they were still there – weak, beaten, brutalized. *Finishing what was begun.* Could it really be Artur Samler? He would be a centenarian now, if he was still alive. Even his son, Günther, would be in his eighties. Or was it someone else, a relative, a crazy person obsessed with the death camps and carrying on the Samler legacy?

He felt frustrated that he couldn't share his new information and push the investigation forward, but after watching the email from Blagnac vanish from the police server, he didn't know who he could trust. His theory about the dog needed proof. They would have to extract DNA from the remaining bones in the mausoleum and hope they matched the tooth chips Evie Zimbaldo had found in Josef Engel's wounds. All of that was time-consuming and expensive and there was no way Laurent would sanction any of it.

The tightness in his chest was beginning to build again, so he headed over to one of the tourist cafés that surrounded the cathedral, ordered a coffee and a chocolatine, and sat for a while, trying to calm his breathing and think. He felt like he was swimming upstream, fighting against the current while Marie-Claude and Léo were being swept away towards jagged rocks. He opened Maps on his phone and entered 'Vierzon', the place the dispatcher at the Police Nationale said she was most likely heading. A blue line appeared, stretching north from his current location, revealing that Vierzon was a four-and-a-half-hour drive away. Too far. Much too far.

Verbier's warning about slowing down sounded at the back of his mind, but there was too much to do, too much at stake, and too many things stacked against him. Even the judge in charge of the case was opposing him, telling him not to investigate Jean Baptiste, dismissing his theory about the death camp connection, even suggesting he should step down. He would have to burn valuable time and energy persuading him to reconsider, energy he would much rather spend finding Marie-Claude and making sure she was safe. It made him feel tired just thinking about it and the tight feeling in his chest grew worse. He looked up and watched a pigeon flapping furiously as it tried to land on the top of the cathedral, fighting against the high winds before giving up and swooping away with easy speed as its wings caught the wind. So much easier to go with the flow than against it. Amand frowned at the simplicity of this and opened his contacts, found the number for Jacques Laurent's office and dialled it. 'I'd like to leave a message for *Juge* Laurent,' he said when the secretary answered.

'He's in court right now.'

'I know. I don't need to speak to him. Just say Commandant Benoît Amand called and that I've thought about what he said and he's right, I am too closely involved with the Josef Engel case. I am therefore officially recusing myself from the investigation.'

'The Josef Engel case?'

'That's right.'

'OK, I'll let him know.'

'Thanks.' Amand hung up and felt a lightness, like the pigeon on the breeze.

He looked back at the map on his phone, a thought starting to crystallize in his mind. He zoomed in on Vierzon and the map reloaded, filling with more detail – road names, knife and fork symbols for cafés, bed symbols for hotels. The waiter arrived with his order and he emptied a paper tube of sugar into his coffee for the energy and continued to study the map, widening it until he saw what he was looking for south of the town. He tapped the aeroplane icon and a website opened, giving him more details and a name. He pulled Magellan's card from his pocket and dialled the number, taking a bite of his chocolatine and washing it down with coffee as it connected. He hadn't intended to call Magellan back because it wasn't policy to use outside agencies in murder investigations. But since he wasn't in charge of the investigation any more, that no longer applied.

'Magellan?' the deep voice rumbled out of the phone the moment it connected.

'Hi, it's Benoît Amand from Cordes. We've found Solomon Creed.'

'Where?'

'In a car heading north with quite a head start. You said you flew to France on a private jet. I was wondering, do you still have it at your disposal?'

'Yes.'

'Where is it?'

'In the air, on its way to Albi. There's a private airfield outside the city called Le Sequestre. Where's Solomon?'

'Heading to a place called Vierzon, about four hundred and fifty kilometres to the north of here. I checked and there's a private airport in the region called Vierzon Méreau. How quickly do you think we could get there?'

'We?'

'I'd like to come too, if I may. I can help smooth things over with the local police if Solomon ends up in custody or if we need their assistance in other ways.'

'Of course. The jet's due to land in five minutes. Tell me

where you are and I'll come pick you up. Assuming there are no hold-ups on the ground, I would imagine we can turn around and take off straight away. We should get to Vierzon in less than an hour.'

65

Bull stood by the side of the A20 and felt the wash of traffic whooshing past. He was standing ten metres back from the BMW, close to the barrier and next to a small reflective triangle he'd placed on the road. His phone was clamped to his ear and his attention was focused down the road, like he was watching for a breakdown truck to arrive. Roberto was bent over the engine though his attention was also on the road. If the police came by they would say they'd over-heated and were letting the car cool down. That was the backup plan. In the end, they didn't need it.

Bull spotted the black Audi and watched as it passed. Three people inside. A woman, a child, and a guy who looked like you could snap him in two with a strong sneeze. He picked up the triangle and headed back to the car. Roberto was already in the driver's seat with the engine running.

They caught up with the Audi and sat back in traffic, keeping a safe cushion of cars between them. The next toll stop was almost an hour ahead, but reaching it was not an option. Bull was hoping they'd pull off soon for a break or to refuel; that way they could catch them out of the car with a minimum of fuss. If they didn't stop, he would call a friend of his called Iron Mike who owned a scrapyard south of

Vierzon. Mike would intercept the Audi in his breaker-truck, get in front of it and slam the brakes on to cause a crash. First on the scene would be Bull and Roberto, full of concern:

We saw everything.

Are you OK?

Why don't you come sit in our car while we wait for the cops and the ambulance?

Then – Boom. Gagged and bound and on their merry way. The Audi would have airbags up the ass, so they wouldn't get hurt, not in the accident at least. A bit of whiplash maybe, some bruised ribs.

He'd give them twenty minutes, maybe twenty-five before he called Iron Mike.

Bull settled back in his seat and stared ahead at the Audi, and the road, and dark grey clouds on the horizon.

66

Marie-Claude glanced in her mirror and instantly knew something was wrong.

'You OK, Léo? You don't look too good.' He was pulling a face and swallowing. 'Are you going to be sick? Hang on. There's a rest stop up ahead, I'll pull over.'

Solomon glanced at him. 'He looks like how I feel in cars.'

'Not helpful.' Marie-Claude indicated right and shed speed. 'Look, Léo, I'm turning off. Hang on for two minutes.' She pressed a button and Léo's window slid down. 'If you need to barf, do it out the window.'

They followed the curve of the slip road up past a couple of parked long-distance lorries with shades over the windows and a car with bikes on the back parked by a picnic table covered with fruit and bread and with a family of six circling it and helping themselves. Marie-Claude pulled into a space, cut the engine and was out of her door and helping Léo out of his seat in a smooth and well-practised move that suggested to Solomon she was well-drilled in the manoeuvre.

'Are you going to be sick?'

Léo screwed his face up like he tasted something bitter. 'I don't think so.'

'OK, good. Go to the toilet and splash water on your face. You want me to come with you?'

'No, I'm OK.'

Solomon got out of the car, grateful to be free of it. He watched Léo wander off towards a grey, squat toilet block with a wide gap between the top of the concrete walls and the roof providing the cheapest form of ventilation.

'Not wishing to sound like your mother,' Marie-Claude said, 'but you should make use of the facilities yourself. This will probably be the last chance you get before we hit Dijon.'

'Thanks,' Solomon said, retrieving the two books he'd been unable to read earlier from the car. 'But I think I'll stay here and do some nausea-free reading instead.'

Marie-Claude nodded. 'You don't eat, you don't drink, you don't even need to go to the bathroom. Is this going to be like in one of those movies where it turns out I've been imagining you the whole time?'

Solomon picked up one of the bottles of water from the carrier bag and took a sip. 'Ghosts don't drink water.'

She nodded wearily. 'The mother and sane person in me is happy to hear it.' She turned and walked away towards the other end of the toilet block, rubbing her pink-edged eyes.

Solomon moved over to a tree and leaned against the trunk, feeling the same, comforting reassurance he'd felt earlier. He studied the two books, Lansky's memoir and the anthology of Death Camp Liberation stories. He opened Lansky's memoir and read that first, soaking up the words and story as fast as he could turn pages and experiencing occasional jolts of déjà-vu, like he recognized some of what was being described. He paused at the mention of the man in the white suit who'd appeared on the final day, searching his lost memory for some stronger recollection. When none came, he read the rest of the memoir then opened the second book, turning to the marked page where the story of Die Schneider Lager's liberation had been recorded by different eyes. He was so immersed in what he was reading that he didn't notice the storm clouds blot out the sun, or the picnicking family hastily gathering their lunch together, or the BMW drive slowly past and park up by the grey slab walls of the toilet block.

VIII

'Sometimes war dreams of itself.'

Carl von Clausewitz

THE DIARY OF PRIVATE JOHN HAMILTON, 2ND ROYAL WESSEX INFANTRY

⁜

On the Liberation of Nazi Labour Camp Mulhouse A – Known as Die Schneider Lager

We were about a mile outside the camp when we smelled the burning bodies. We all knew what it was because the day we landed in Normandy we'd had to double past a burning Panzer beyond the beach with the German tank crew still inside. Once you smell something like that you never forget it, and we smelled it on the road into Mulhouse.

A reconnaissance plane had spotted some kind of camp complex ahead but no one had fired on the pilot so we expected minimal resistance. Most of the German forces were either north of us or south at Altkirch. Our job was to plug the gap and flush out any pockets of German resistance that might cause problems on the flanks, a footnote to the Battle of the Bulge and lucky to be away from the main fight – or so we thought.

The main building was a smouldering ruin when we reached it and our approach was cautious. The camp was set back from the main road and surrounded by a high, barbed-wire fence but there were no guards in the towers and when a unit went forward to open the gates they found them unlocked.

We set about securing the place and found plenty of evidence of a hurried exit: dormitories with the beds made; laundered shirts hanging on rails; offices with paperwork strewn everywhere and empty filing cabinets lying on their sides.

I was part of a team tasked with investigating the charred mass where the main building had been. There were a couple of partially demolished buildings to the rear of it, which led me to assume that the factory had been hit by stray bombs or long-range shells, killing the workers inside and burning the building to the ground. But as we approached the smouldering pile of rubble I saw the bones, thousands of bones in the ashes, skulls, leg-bones, skeletal hands, so many that the building must have been filled with people when it caught fire.

There were fire tankers parked around the ruins and I couldn't understand how there could be that many bodies in the wreckage when they had been fighting the flames. It was only when we inspected the trucks that we realized the Germans had not been spraying water on the fire, they had been dousing it with diesel.

We found a bulldozer in one of the other buildings and used it to scratch a grave in the frozen earth. There's a memorial there now, a big block of marble with thousands of names carved on it. If we'd known they were going to do that, we would have taken more care where we dug the hole. But this was December 1944, ground frozen solid, so we dug where it seemed easiest and when the hole was deep enough we set about shovelling the dead into it. That was when we found Herman Lansky.

He was buried in garbage in a large wooden crate by

a scorched wall. We thought he was dead, bones sticking out of his skin, eyes sunk so deep that his head looked more like a skull. It didn't seem possible that a man who looked that bad could be living. But when we dragged him out of there the company medic found a pulse and he was carted off to the infirmary. We doubted he would make it through the night, but he was tougher than anyone thought. Within a day he had recovered enough to talk. That's when they called for me.

I'd been studying languages before enlisting. My mother was Polish and I'd grown up speaking Polish and English at home. She'd taught me some Russian too and I'd learned French at school. I'd lied about my age to join up because I was worried the war would be over by the time I finished my studies and it would be hard in post-war Europe to visit all the countries I wanted to see. If I'm honest, I also wanted to see what war was like. I was fifteen and had never been outside of West Sussex before landing in Normandy.

I remember listening to Lansky talk, shifting between Polish and French, telling us all the things that had happened in the camp, about the Commandant, Artur Samler, and the grotesque things he'd done. You have to remember that the liberation of Bergen-Belsen and Auschwitz and all those other camps had not happened yet, so we had no comprehension that anything like this could even exist in the modern, civilized world – a death factory producing murder on an industrial scale. It was like a dark fairy story, one that couldn't possibly be real, except we had seen the bodies, all those bodies.

We continued to clean the place up, burning rubbish, burying the dead and waiting for the order to move out.

351

None of us wanted to stay there. It wasn't only the cooked flesh smell that hung in the air, there was something eerie about the camp, as if the stain of evil clung to the fabric of the place.

Two days after we liberated Mulhouse, an American battalion came through and took Lansky away with them. They had better medical facilities than us and more resources so we were happy to hand him over. He left. We stayed.

The Battle of the Bulge continued to wage, the Allies pushing forward, the Germans pushing back. Our mission had been to secure the camp and await further orders, but its position close to the main road between Mulhouse and the Rhine made it tactically valuable and more units moved in to bolster the flank and our temporary position became semi-permanent. The factory complex became a supply yard filled with fuel tankers, munitions trucks and pallet loads of food rations.

Christmas came and went, 1944 turned into 1945.

One night in early January, waking in the middle of the night and unable to get back to sleep again, I decided to go for a walk. There was fresh snow on the ground and a half-moon behind thin, shifting clouds that made the snow sparkle. There was no artillery that night, no bombardments, no distant rifle fire, just a kind of soft, tinkling silence as frost formed and fell to the ground. It was probably the first time since England that I had heard silence, a proper, deep silence as if someone had simply flicked a switch and turned off the war.

I walked deeper into the camp towards the two

partially demolished buildings that lay slumped beneath a blanket of fresh snow. There's something pure and beautiful about snow at night. It carries light into the darkest of shadows and removes any horror you might imagine there. I stood in the softly twinkling dark and felt a contentment and a calm I had forgotten even existed. I remember turning my face up to the sky and feeling the kiss of the cold flakes on my skin.

That was when I heard the sound, metallic and faint, like the clink of a wedding ring on a beer bottle. I remember holding my breath and listening out until I heard it again, so faint – three short taps, three with pauses, then three short again – Morse Code. An SOS coming from beneath my feet.

I shouted for the guard and men appeared, pulling on uniforms as I breathlessly explained what I'd heard. We couldn't risk the bulldozer because we didn't know what state the cellar was in; instead we formed a human chain and began shifting rubble by hand. We had been there for twenty-six days by that time, and we all knew whoever was underground had been buried for at least that long.

We unearthed a concrete stairwell filled with rubble and broken brick and started digging it out while I called out in French and Polish, letting whoever was down there know we were coming. After long minutes of shifting rubble we uncovered a door, the bent key jammed in the keyhole, showing that it had been locked from the outside. Someone fetched a fire axe, handed it to me and I broke through. The smell that escaped from that splintered hole was evil – rotten and human and animal – like I had broken through the door to hell.

And when I shone my torch through the gap and saw what was inside, I felt sure we had.

There were bodies everywhere, piled up against each other, all mired in filth and dust and wearing the same striped uniform Lansky had been wearing. The cellar was barely bigger than a hotel bedroom, but thirty or more men were crammed into it. I saw movement on the body closest to me and watched a rat crawl from a gap in the striped fabric, sniff the air with a snout made dark from something I don't even want to think about, before scurrying away into the cellar.

Then I heard the sound again, metal on metal – three short taps, three long, three short – and followed it with my torch to one of the revenants propped against the wall. He had his eyes closed and his head tilted to one side and looked as dead as the rest, except his finger was moving, twitching as if it was the only part of him living. There was a tailor's thimble on the end of it and it tapped against a water pipe, the SOS I had heard in the silent night. This was Josef Engel.

We cleared out that cellar as quickly as we could, slipping on a concrete floor mired in ordure and vomit and the various secretions that had leaked from the many corpses. There were thirty-four men inside that cellar, locked up and left to die by someone whose evil I cannot begin to fathom. Maybe the explosions that had part-demolished the buildings were supposed to collapse the cellar on top of them, murdering and burying them at the same time. If so, they had failed. But only just. Thirty-four men had been buried in that cellar and only twelve were still alive when we carried them out. A day later, despite the best emergency medical care we could give, there were four.

Four men out of thirty-four and God knows how many countless thousands before them. These were the men who came to be known as Die Anderen – The Others.

⁜

67

A raindrop smacked on to the open page of the book and Solomon looked up into the flat grey sky. Some of what he had read felt so familiar, like his own memories written down, but there had to be more. Josef Engel had never told his story, but Otto Adelstein might. Solomon wanted to look him in the eye and watch for the flicker of recognition as he asked him who'd locked them in that cellar, and about the man in the pale suit.

The rain grew heavier, pattering on the dusty ground and hissing in the leafy canopy overhead. Solomon closed the book and looked up to see Marie-Claude running toward him, head down against the rain. She glanced at the closed book. 'Finished already?'

'I'm a fast reader.'

'Both books?' He nodded. 'No way. OK, what regiment was John Hamilton in?'

'Second Royal Wessex infantry.'

'That was easy.' She moved to the driver's door and opened it. 'What month was the camp liberated?'

'December 1944, snow on the ground. Hamilton thought they were going to be a footnote to the Battle of the Bulge. He was wrong. Ask another.'

Marie-Claude dropped into her seat to escape the rain then turned and looked in the back. 'Where's Léo?'

Solomon stared at the empty booster seat. 'I don't know.' He looked across at the concrete toilet block, saw the BMW parked next to it. It bothered him that he'd not noticed it arriving. There was no one inside and that bothered him too. 'Maybe he's waiting for the rain,' Solomon said. 'I'll go tell him it's time to go.'

He closed the door and moved towards the block, breathing deeply and smelling ozone from the storm, garlic and yeast from the picnic table and the astringent burn of toilet disinfectant. There was something else there too, something feral and predatory, testosterone mixed with adrenaline and the faint smell of aniseed. He listened through the rapidly building hiss of rain and heard the faint drip of a tap inside the toilet block, the thrum of raindrops on the roof – nothing else. He breathed in again and caught the cidery apple scent of Léo mixed with the metallic tang of fear. Solomon unbuttoned his jacket to allow movement then stepped out of the rain and into the building.

Léo stared right at him, the fear in his eyes made huge by his glasses. A dark whip of a man crouched behind him, one hand clamped over Léo's mouth, the other holding a six-inch hunting knife to his throat. A bigger man stood by the sinks, inspecting his teeth in the mirror. 'About fucking time,' he said. 'How long do you normally wait for a little kid to take a piss?'

Solomon shrugged. 'I don't hang around toilets as much as some.'

The man turned and smiled. 'Funny guy.' He was huge. A foot taller than Solomon and twice as wide. 'Turn around, cross your hands behind your back and don't try and be a hero. My orders are not to hurt you, but I'm happy to improvise if you piss me off.'

'Whose orders?' Solomon said.

'You see now, questions are exactly the kind of thing that piss me off. Turn around, give me your hands. You get two warnings, then it gets painful – and not necessarily for you.'

Solomon smiled at Léo, winked at him, and turned. He felt air displace as the huge man moved up behind him. Something hard and thin looped over his wrists and bit into them with a plastic, ripping sound.

'Good boy,' the man said, slapping the side of his face with a hand the size of a tray. 'Stand over by the sinks. Don't move. Don't speak.'

Solomon did as he was told and turned to face the room again. The big man moved over to Léo next and lifted his glasses off his nose with a daintiness his thick fingers did not look capable of. 'I'll just go have a word with Mama, show her these to make sure she doesn't get nervous and start calling anyone. Then we can all go quietly on our way.' He moved to the door and stepped outside, his heavy footsteps rapidly dissolving in the hiss of rain.

Solomon studied the man holding Léo. He was in the corner by the cubicles, ten feet away, too far, even if his hands were free. He looked at Léo, his eyes seeming smaller without his glasses. 'Can you see me, Léo?' Léo nodded as much as the hand across his mouth would let him. 'And are my colours still white?' Another small nod.

'No talking,' the man with the knife said.

'You know Ant-Man?' Solomon continued. 'You know what he does in order to become strong?' Léo nodded. 'When you see my colours turn red, I want you to be like Ant-Man. Do you understand?'

'I'm warning you,' the man holding Léo said. 'One more word and I'll hurt him.'

Solomon nodded and smiled. He didn't say anything. He didn't need to.

68

Marie-Claude was studying the screen of the satnav when she became aware of someone approaching. She had been checking the distance to Mulhouse, where the Die Schneider Lager museum was situated, and looked up expecting to see Solomon and Léo. Instead she saw a huge figure heading towards her car and instinctively reached for the central locking button. There was a syncopated clunk as all four doors locked.

The man kept coming and held something up when he heard the locks activate. Marie-Claude peered through the rain-streaked windscreen and her heart stopped when she saw what it was. He made a gesture, an upward flip of the finger, and she hesitated then unlocked the doors as he reached the car.

The passenger door opened and he dropped into the seat, making the car rock on its suspension. 'No one's been hurt,' he said in a calm reasonable voice that made her want to scream and start hitting him. 'And as long as you do as I say and don't try anything stupid, that's how things will stay. Understand?'

Marie-Claude stared at Léo's rain-splashed glasses, tiny and fragile in the man's huge hand.

'Do you understand?' the man repeated, a harder edge to his voice.

She nodded.

'Good. Now you take these little things before I break them.' He handed her the glasses and she felt like screaming again. 'When I give the word, I want you to sound your horn once to give my colleague a signal that everything is fine. Then you and I are going to get out of this car, walk to that BMW over there, your son and your skinny white boyfriend will join us and we'll drive away together, safe and sound. All right?'

Marie-Claude nodded. 'Then what?'

'Let's deal with one thing at a time, shall we? Now, that family in the car with the bikes on the back are about to drive away. Soon as they're gone, you hit the horn, just a quick sharp stab, OK?'

She nodded and looked out through the rain.

At the BMW.

At the family car with the bikes on the back.

At the concrete toilet block where her son was being held prisoner.

69

Solomon cleared his mind and focused all his attention on this moment. This place. The people within it. The man and the boy.

The sound of the rain drumming on the roof slowed until he could hear the boom of each individual drop and the light sharpened until everything shone clear and in focus. He concentrated on Léo. He could hear his heartbeat, soft and fast, scampering over the deeper heartbeat of the man who held him. He had to see that Léo had understood before he let go of the rage that boiled deep in the depths of himself like the molten core of a planet. But Léo looked at Solomon and did not seem to see him, his dancing eyes showing fear and panic.

Solomon dropped down a little, relaxing the muscles in his body until he felt as fluid as the rain gurgling in the gutters. Time stretched long in his heightened state and he watched the boy, waiting for the sharpening of understanding, but seeing only continued confusion. He could feel his anger rippling through him, a hint of the locked-down heat that simmered deep inside him and pain twitched in his arm where the mark was.

Léo's world was a blur and bad colours shifted above the hand clamped over his mouth, muddy browns and slimy greens, like the feathers on a drowned bird. He could see Solomon, the whiteness of him standing out against the grey, and wondered why he wasn't doing anything to save him. He'd said that was why he was here, but he hadn't even fought the men, he'd just let them tie him up, and now he was standing over by the sinks doing nothing.

He'd told him to be like Ant-Man when his colours changed but he didn't understand. Ant-Man had a suit that made him go really small and gave him super-strength. But Léo was already small. Small and weak. How would getting smaller help?

He stared at the bright spot where Solomon was, his neck hurting from where the man held it tight. Then he saw it, a flicker of red in Solomon's whiteness, the same colour he'd seen in the shadow outside his front door, and Léo understood.

The smaller Ant-Man got, the stronger he became. So Léo drew up his legs and dropped his head down, and made himself as small as possible to get out of the way of the red that was coming.

Solomon saw Léo shrink in languid slow motion. He heard the creak of sinew in the man's arm as it tensed against the extra weight. Saw the knuckles glow white around the handle of the blade. And he let go.

He uncoiled and twisted and cracked across the room like a whip, his fury exploding out of him, his leg stretching out and up and catching the man full on the side of his throat where Léo's head had been a fraction of a second earlier. The head snapped back, thrown by the savage force of the kick;

the hand holding the knife jerked away from Léo's throat. Léo continued to drop, making himself smaller, becoming Ant-Man. The man staggered back, fighting for breath and balance, trying to haul Léo in front of him like a shield.

Solomon landed, pivoted, sprang again, the pain in his arm screaming and the room now red in his eyes. He kicked upward, aiming for the wrist of the hand holding the knife, and felt the soft crunch of compacting bone as his foot connected and the hand turned to jelly. The knife spun away, struck the wall and clattered to rest on the concrete floor. The man tried to scream but his throat had been crushed. He fought for breath that wouldn't come and Léo squirmed free from his slackening grip and scampered away across the floor.

The man was on his knees now, his mouth opening and closing like a beached fish, his hands clawing at the swelling on his throat like he was trying to loosen a knot. Solomon felt a surge of pain as he looked down upon the dying man – and he *was* dying. He would pass out soon, fall asleep and never wake up. Pain burned through the mark on Solomon's arm at the thought of it. He wanted to grip it and squeeze the agony away but his hands were cable-tied behind him, the thin plastic digging in his flesh.

'The knife,' he said, nodding at where it had come to rest on the concrete. 'Fetch the knife and cut me free.' Léo peered at the floor, his eyes struggling to see without his glasses. 'By the wall,' Solomon said, biting down on the agony in his shoulder. Léo stepped around the man, found the knife and skipped back across the room. 'Slip the blade between my wrists and hold it steady.'

Solomon felt the cold edge of the blade touch his skin and slide slowly forward until it pushed through the tightly pressed flesh. He began sawing his wrists back and forth. He was feeling weak from the pain now. Nauseous. He had hurt the man, killed him probably, and the agony that was spreading through his body was a result of it. The cable-tie snapped and Solomon's hands sprang free, fresh pain lancing through his arm at the movement and drawing a cry from his lips.

Léo grabbed his hand and tugged him towards the door. 'We need to help Mama.'

Solomon squeezed his burning shoulder and looked down at the man, eyes closed, body twitching slightly. A short blast of a car horn cut through the thrum of rain and his eyes flickered but did not open.

'We need to help Mama,' Léo repeated.

And they did. But not yet. Solomon dropped to his knees and patted the unconscious man down, running his hands over the pockets of his trousers and jacket. He found a wallet, a handful of small black sweets in wax-paper wrappers, a set of car keys, a small notebook and a pen. The pen was a cheap plastic Bic with a clear hollow tube and a chewed blue cap.

Solomon handed it to Léo and took the knife from him. 'Pull that apart for me,' he said. 'And look away.'

Solomon knelt beside the man and positioned the point of the blade in the centre of his throat, right below the swollen larynx that was blocking his airway. Having checked Léo wasn't looking, he banged his fist on the end of the handle, driving the point into the man's throat with a pop. The man twitched in response but remained unconscious.

'Give me the clear plastic tube from the pen,' Solomon said.

Léo handed it to him, eyes wide and staring at the knife sticking in the man's throat. 'You killed him!'

'No,' Solomon said, taking the tube and positioning the narrow end by the blade. 'I'm saving him.'

He withdrew the knife and pushed the tube into the incision at the same time, turning it and keeping a finger over the exposed end to create pressure in the tube and stop it getting blocked. He pushed until he felt resistance then withdrew it a little and removed his finger from the end. There was a whistling, sucking sound as air was drawn in through the tube and the man's chest expanded.

Solomon felt the relief of it too, the pain in his arm melting away like a glowing coal had been removed from his skin. He turned to Léo and smiled. 'Thank you,' he said. 'You were very brave back there.' A thought struck him. 'What are my colours like now?'

'They're white again,' Léo said. 'They were red and black but they went all white again as soon as you put the pen in that man's neck.'

Solomon nodded. 'That's what it felt like,' he said. 'It hurt when I had to hurt him and it stopped when I decided to make him better.'

'Maybe you're not supposed to hurt people,' Léo suggested.

Solomon nodded, rubbed his shoulder and looked out at the rain. 'Sometimes you don't have a choice. Now let's go save your mother.'

70

Bull stared at the toilet block through the rain.

Maybe they hadn't heard the blast on the horn. The rain was loud on the roof of the car; it would be loud in the toilet block too. He could see spray coming off the tiles and there was a gap between the roof and walls to let air flow through the building, which would make it even louder inside.

'Hit it again,' he said.

Marie-Claude leaned on the steering wheel and stared ahead through the rain, desperate to catch a glimpse of her son and feeling anxious with every second she didn't.

The rain fell. Time ticked. No one came out of the toilet block.

'Where's your phone?' Bull said.

'In the bag,' Marie-Claude pointed in the back.

Bull reached around and grabbed the rucksack, his eyes fixed on the concrete building. 'Give me your keys.'

She handed them over and Bull opened the passenger door. 'Stay here. Don't move. Don't do anything until I come back.'

He stepped into the rain, slammed the door and locked it as he walked away.

The rain was solid and heavy and made the canopy of leaves above him sound like a round of applause. He placed the rucksack with Marie-Claude's phone by the trunk of a tree to keep it dry, checked to make sure no new vehicles had appeared then reached into his jacket and pulled the gun from his shoulder-holster.

He moved forward, gun pointing down, eyes fixed on the toilet door. He stopped short of the building and listened through the drumming rain for the sound of voices or movement or anything.

'Bobby?' he called out.

A door banged inside the building and a shape darted from the entrance and ran away across the grass. Bull jerked his gun towards it and saw it was the boy. The horn sounded behind him, long and loud and mournful, a desperate attempt by the mother to distract him from her fleeing son. Bull ignored it and saw fresh movement in the shadow of the entrance. Roberto emerged slowly on his hands and knees, head tilted back and blood all over his shirt and neck. Bull's gaze shifted to the boy, small and skinny like the doll he had pulled apart in the flat.

Fucking people, he thought as he raised his gun and centred on the running figure, *I warned them not to do anything stupid. Three strikes and—*

There was a splash and a flash of white and something hit him so hard it spun him completely round and sent him staggering across the wet grass. He hit a tree, which knocked the breath out of him but stopped him from falling. He heard the splashing again, close and to his left, coming fast through the trees. He tried to bring his gun round but was hit again, hard on the inside of his wrist where the tendons and veins are packed together. As he felt his hand go loose, the gun slipping from it, a foot flashed out of nowhere and caught him hard on the side of the temple, driving right through his head and sending his brain rattling violently from side to side in his skull. He staggered away from the tree and took a few shuffling steps before his balance went completely.

The last thing he heard was the car horn cutting out.

He was unconscious before his face hit the grass.

71

Marie-Claude saw the big man fall and threw open her door.

'Léo!' she hollered, sprinting across the tarmac towards the spot she'd last seen him. 'Come back.' She splashed through puddles and felt the sting of rain on her face. 'It's OK, Léo.'

She ran past the picnic table where the family had been and spotted him squatting down behind a tree, shivering and squinting at her through the misty veil of rain. She skidded to a stop, grabbed him, and squeezed him so hard she had to stop in case she hurt him.

'I'm OK, Mama. I had to run.' She put his glasses back on and brushed rain from his face. 'Monsieur Creed told me to stay where I was, but when the other man woke up and started crawling over to me, I ran. He saved me, just like Grampy said he would. He moved so fast. You should have seen him, Mama.'

Marie-Claude looked back to where Solomon was crouched down by the big man. 'I did,' she said.

Solomon looked up as if he'd felt her gaze upon him and waved them over. She stood and carried Léo, unwilling to let him go again, squelching back through the rain. She glanced over at the other man as she drew closer, sitting inside the entrance and out.

'We need to go,' Solomon said.

Marie-Claude looked down at the unconscious man who had sat in her car and calmly talked about kidnapping them. She looked at the other man, slumped in the entrance of the toilet block, back to the wall and legs splayed out in front of him, one hand on the ground and the other clamped to something sticking out of his throat. This was insane. All of it was insane. She clutched Léo tighter. 'We need to call the police.'

'No,' Solomon said, rising up from the ground and heading over to the BMW. 'We need to take their car and go.'

Marie-Claude grabbed her rucksack from beneath the tree and hurried after him. 'No way. I'm not stealing another car. This has gone too far.'

Ignoring her, Solomon unlocked the boot of the BMW with the key he'd taken from the driver and started sorting through the bags and wallets he found inside.

'Stop this,' Marie-Claude said. 'You're only going to make things worse. We need to call the police and tell them everything that's happened.'

'They already know,' Solomon said, handing her the Police Nationale ID card he'd taken from the man sprawled by the toilet block with blood on his shirt. 'They are the police.'

72

The jet began its descent into Vierzon Méreau Airport and dropped into grey cloud. Amand looked out of the window and saw lightning flicker around the wings. He was sitting in a ridiculously soft leather chair that was more like a sofa while a cabin attendant tidied fresh fruit and pastries from the low table in front of him.

'Should I buckle up?' he asked her.

'Up to you,' she smiled, then swept away past a mahogany bar containing bottles of whisky that were older than him.

'Who does this plane belong to?' Amand asked.

Magellan looked up from a copy of the *Wall Street Journal*. 'I can't say,' he said. 'Patient–doctor privilege. Let's just say there are plenty of Arabian princes who are very grateful to anyone who can cure their feckless, dissolute children from the addictions and excesses only great wealth can facilitate and keep secret. I could write a book on the toxic nature of immense wealth.'

'You don't seem to mind it too much.'

Magellan smiled. 'One doesn't necessarily have to be wealthy to enjoy the fruits of it, any more than you have to believe in God in order to admire a cathedral. I'm like the jester in a medieval court – part of the tableau but also apart. An observer. I provide a service, my clients are grateful, they offer me tokens of appreciation. I'm not going to turn them down.'

'And what will Solomon Creed's family give you for returning their son?'

'I'm sure Jefferson Hawdon would pay me more to keep him locked up forever, but I'm not looking for any kind of reward. My interest is personal. As I said before, he's extraordinary. Like an evolutionary leap – sidewards, forward, I'm not sure which. He's special.'

The wheels bumped on the tarmac and Amand looked out of his window. 'That was quick.'

'Another perk of private travel, no circling until a runway becomes free. There's also a car waiting for us; I got the pilot to radio ahead. Where do we need to go?'

Amand pulled his phone from his pocket, dialled the Cordes Commissariat and tensed at the familiar voice that answered. 'Hey, Henri,' he said. 'Is Parra around?'

'Ben! Where are you? I heard you recused yourself from the investigation.'

'I did.'

'But why didn't you tell us first?'

Amand wanted to tell Henri to go fuck himself. 'It was a pretty quick decision. Jacques Laurent suggested my personal history with the Engel family might cloud my judgement and I decided he was probably right.'

Henri grunted. 'Not sure I agree, but never mind. They've put Parra in charge now.'

'Good for him. Is he there?'

'I'll find him for you.'

The phone went silent and Amand looked out of the

window as the plane taxied to a standstill beside another black Range Rover with tinted windows.

'Benny!' Parra said. 'I hear you're off the case.'

'You heard right.'

'That's a shame, where are you now?'

'Still in Albi.' Amand followed Magellan to the door. 'Should be back this afternoon, but I'm on my mobile if anyone needs me.'

The hostess opened the door and the white noise of rain and jet engines flooded into the cabin. 'Sounds noisy,' Parra said.

Amand moved back into the soft, insulated interior of the plane. 'A street sweeper went past. I'm checking to see if there's any news about Marie-Claude and Léo? Last I heard, they'd been spotted driving north in a black Audi.'

'Yeah we found it.'

'You found— Are they safe?'

'No, I mean, I don't know – we didn't find *them*, only the car. It got picked up by the barrier cams leaving junction 8 of the A20 with two men inside. One had been badly beaten. He's on his way to hospital now.'

Amand gripped his phone so hard it creaked. 'Where's the car?'

'Impounded at the toll booth, I think. This is all fresh in.'

'OK. Let me know if you hear anything about Marie-Claude – I may be off the case but that doesn't mean I'm not worried.'

'Of course.'

'And, Parra – Keep your eye on Henri.'

'Why?'

'Just keep your eye on him. If anything important needs doing, do it yourself.'

'OK, I will. You want to tell me about it?'

'Later.' Amand hung up and emerged from the plane into the rain and noise of cooling jets and hurried down the steps to the Range Rover where Magellan was waiting, engine running and satnav menu open. 'Where to?' he said.

'Junction 8 of the A20,' Amand said. 'They found the car. One of the guys driving it had been so badly beaten he was hospitalized. Still think your boy isn't dangerous?'

Parra put the phone down and got up from his desk.

'Going somewhere?' Henri said, peering at him over his glasses.

'For a smoke,' Parra replied and headed to the back door. He stepped into the passage and pulled a Marlboro Light from a pack and his phone from his pocket. He lit the cigarette, dialled the private number for Café Belloq and listened to it ring.

'You have news?' Belloq answered.

Parra blew out a long stream of smoke. 'Maybe. I just got a call from Amand. I think he might still be a problem.'

'How so?'

'He was asking about the case. Casually, but he was definitely interested. He said he was in Albi, but it sounded to me like he was at an airport.'

'OK, try and find out where he is. Good work, Parra.'

Parra smiled and took another deep drag on his cigarette. 'That's why I'm here.'

73

Marie-Claude stared ahead through the rain and the wind-screen wipers, her knuckles glowing white on the wheel of the BMW. Solomon was in the passenger seat, sorting through the bags they'd found in the back of the car, taking deep breaths to combat his nausea while spray blew in through his open window. She felt detached from herself, like she was in a dream, a really bad dream, because none of what was happening could be real and if it was she couldn't see a safe way out of it. 'We're fucked,' she said.

'We're not.'

'But that was the *police* back there.'

'Only one of them, and he wasn't there on police business.'

'You don't know that. How do you know that?'

'Police don't tend to take kids hostage and hold knives to their throats.'

She stared at him, shocked at the revelation that Léo had had a knife to his throat. Solomon rubbed at his shoulder as pain lanced through it at the memory of the fight.

'Are you hurt?'

'No.'

'You're acting like you are.'

'I'm in pain, there's a difference. Visiting pain upon others doesn't agree with me.'

'But you're awesome at it!' Léo said, leaning forward from the back seat. 'You should have seen him, Mama – he kicked the knife right out of the man's hand and stuck it in his throat.'

'Jesus!' Marie-Claude shook her head. 'You shouldn't be watching people have knives stuck in their throats.'

'It was a *cricothyroidotomy*,' Solomon said, 'an emergency opening of the airways. His throat had been crushed and he couldn't breathe. If I hadn't done it, he would have died. And I made Léo look away when I made the incision.'

'Oh, well that makes it OK. As long as Léo wasn't looking when you jammed a knife into the windpipe you'd crushed, everything's fine. Jesus, put that away!'

Solomon checked the magazine of the gun he'd taken from the big man, put it on *safe* and dropped it into Marie-Claude's rucksack, which he started to root through.

'Hey, what are you doing? That's my stuff.'

'I'm making sure your phone is off.'

'It's off. I took the battery out, like you said.'

'They still managed to track us. What about your laptop?' He picked it up and checked it was turned off.

'It's Wi-Fi enabled, but that won't tell anyone where we are unless I go online, and we haven't been anywhere to do that since we stopped for fuel.'

'And you didn't turn it on?'

'No.'

'Léo?'

'I never touched it.'

Solomon put the rucksack back on the floor and took deep breaths of rain-filled air. 'It had to be the car. They must have figured out the switch and got the registration number from the airport, which means the legitimate police might be looking for us too.'

'Why don't we turn ourselves in? We can explain everything that's happened, show them the ID of that guy so they know we're telling the truth.'

'And which police do you think we should turn ourselves over to?' Solomon said. 'The good police, or the ones who hold knives to children's throats? If we turn ourselves in they'll put me in a cell and send you back home, back to where your grandfather was killed. Can you trust the police in Cordes? Your husband was police.'

She thought back to that morning, sitting in her bedroom with Amand as he'd told her the terrible news about her grandfather. Maybe if she'd gone with him, none of this would have happened. But then she might never have found the note her grandfather had left for her and his killer might have found it instead, putting Otto Adelstein in serious danger. She thought about Amand and whether she trusted him. She wanted to but she couldn't, not entirely. She found it hard to trust anyone.

She turned to Solomon. 'We need to get to Dijon and warn Otto Adelstein.'

'Agreed.'

'He might know who's doing this and why. Once we know that, we can decide who to tell and what to do next. Either way, we need to warn him, make sure he's safe. I don't want anyone else to die. I can't be responsible for any more pain.' She shook her head and Solomon saw the shadow of pain darken her face. 'But what do we do? We're in a stolen car and the police are looking for us.'

'Pull off at the next junction,' Solomon said, sorting

through the collection of passports they'd found in the boot of the car. 'Find somewhere to park – somewhere busy where we can hide this car.' He opened one of the passports and studied the photograph of a young woman inside. 'I have an idea.'

74

'Over there,' Amand said, pointing at a fenced-off area beyond the péage barrier. The Audi was parked under a canopy next to a low office building. 'Park in front of the office and let me do the talking. Once we're at the car, I want you to distract whoever's chaperoning us.'

Magellan parked the Range Rover and they entered the building. Two men and one woman in white shirts and dark-blue trousers were standing behind a counter, talking over each other excitedly and pointing at the Audi. Amand smiled and held up his police ID badge. 'Who's in charge here?'

'That would be me,' the eldest, fattest man replied, squinting at Amand's ID card.

'What's your name, sir?'

'André. André Gaudin.'

'Monsieur Gaudin, my name is Benoît Amand. I'm the investigating officer in a murder that took place in the Tarn earlier today and this is Doctor Magellan, a consultant criminal psychologist helping us with the case. That vehicle you have parked outside is wanted in connection with my investigation. Mind if we take a quick look?'

The man looked hesitant. 'The other police officers said no one was to touch anything.'

'Quite right, and no one will. We only want to take a look. There are certain items that may be in the car and it would be helpful if I could check.'

The man's gaze shifted to Magellan then back to him. 'Just a look?'

Amand smiled. 'That's all.'

He nodded uncertainly. 'OK.'

They stepped outside, the rain thrumming on the canopy like a slow drum roll. Amand peered through the tinted windows of the Audi. 'Is it unlocked?'

'You said no touching.'

'I'm not going to touch, but these windows are making it hard to see.'

After a moment's hesitation, Gaudin dashed back to the office and returned almost instantly with a black key fob in his hand that made all the indicators flash and a solid clunk sound inside the door panels when he pressed it.

Amand pulled the sleeve of his jacket over his hand and used it to open the driver's door. There was blood on the dashboard and pooled in the leather of the passenger seat, a couple of torn Marvel comics on the floor in the back.

'Tell me about the men who were in the car,' Magellan said, stepping in front of Gaudin. 'What did they look like? The more detail you can give, the better.'

'Well, the driver was huge, like a wrestler or something. The other guy was the injured one . . .'

As soon as he saw that Gaudin was distracted, Amand leaned in and switched on the car's satnav. A map appeared. He selected *Recent Destinations* and a list filled the screen. Amand read the last entry, deleted it, switched everything off and stood up.

'You can lock it up,' he said, already walking away.

'I can't see anything obvious. Let's hope the tech guys have more luck. Thanks for your help, Monsieur Gaudin.' He got into the Range Rover, eager to leave before someone else showed up.

Magellan climbed into the driver's seat and closed the door against the rain. 'Anything?'

'A destination,' Amand replied. 'Has this thing got satnav?'

Magellan pressed a button and a map appeared. Amand typed MULHOUSE into the search field and the map redrew, showing the smudge of a town near a thick blue line marking the German border.

'They were heading here,' Amand said, pointing at a small icon north of the town that looked like a mini Roman forum.

'What's that?'

'A museum,' Amand replied. 'It's called Die Schneider Lager.'

The satnav plotted a route from their current location – a five-and-a-half-hour drive. Magellan tapped the screen to zoom into Mulhouse and looked around for an aeroplane icon but couldn't see one. 'Private airfields don't always show up on regular maps,' he said, and started the engine. 'I'm sure we can get close. Close enough to get there before anyone else does, at least.'

75

Bull paced around the table in the interview room, keeping his head tilted back to try and stop the blood leaking from his broken nose. He couldn't believe this had happened. He had vowed he would never see the inside of a cell again and yet here he was.

He wanted to break something or punch the wall, or even better, batter the skinny white fucker who'd somehow managed to kick him unconscious and break his mother-fucking nose. How had that even happened? He was as much embarrassed as he was angry. At least the fucker had done him a favour by taking his gun. If he'd been caught with that it would have been much worse. As it was, they seemed more interested in the Audi and the people who should've been in it, but he wasn't telling them anything and they were giving him shitty looks because of it.

He knew they had nothing on him, nothing serious. They'd have to let him go sooner or later. And when they did he would go after them because he wanted his car back and he wanted a rematch with the Thin White Duke. He stopped by the mirror and examined his nose. He knew it was a two-way and someone was most likely watching him on the other side but he didn't care. Let them look. He tilted his head and inspected the damage. It was swollen and red and the bruising was starting to come around his eyes, making him look like a panda. Fucking guy. A lucky shot is all it was.

He heard a click and turned as the door opened and a uniform stepped inside and placed a plastic cup of water on the table. 'Compliments of the house,' he said. 'You need anything else – coffee, something to eat?'

'Depends how long you're going to keep me here.'

'A while I think.' The door closed behind him and he made no move to leave.

Bull stared at him. 'What do you want, a tip?'

'Information,' he said, unbuttoning the sleeve of his shirt. 'Maybe you want to tell me something about the car the woman is now travelling in?' He rolled his sleeve and Bull saw the tattoo of a wild boar on his wrist. He glanced at the mirror. 'There's no one listening,' the gendarme said, rolling his sleeve back down.

'You're looking for a black BMW three series. Two years old. Top of the range.'

'Registration?'

'I can do better than that. It's got a V-Rec unit attached to it. Vehicle Recovery. Download the V-Rec app, put in a user code and GPS will show you exactly where it is on Google Maps. Let me out of here and I'll go get it for you.'

The gendarme smiled. 'Can't do that, I'm afraid, but the leadership is grateful for your help.'

'I don't want gratitude, I want a favour.'

'What's that?'

'When you find my car and the dude who's driving it, I want you to fuck him up. Fuck him up real bad.'

76

The Leader sat in his private office and wrote down the details of the BMW and the user code. Having thanked the gendarme for his good work, he hung up, opened his laptop and downloaded the V-Rec app. Within five minutes a red dot on a map showed that the BMW had doubled back from its previous direction and headed south on a road running almost parallel to the A20 but was now stationary.

He looked at the towns closest to where the car was, trying to remember what assets and resources he had there. There was a time when he could recall every name and location of his secret army, but it had grown too big and his mind had grown old and forgetful.

He picked up the laptop, rose slowly from his chair and moved across the polished parquet floor into the empty outer office. He had dismissed his secretary for the day because there was too much going on and she was oblivious to most of it and he wished for it to stay that way, for now. By necessity, he led something of a double life, the private and the public, and it took careful balancing and separation to maintain. He looked forward to a time soon when these two halves could merge and become whole once again. And it *would* happen. He was not prepared to let some nosy

Jewish bitch ruin everything by raking up things he'd spent almost a lifetime keeping secret.

He moved into the hallway and walked past rows of softly lit display cases containing mannequins dressed in iconic suits and gowns from his company's long history. He had personally designed each one, even made some of the earlier ones too, every stitch. Some people wrote their lives in words and ink, others in paint or in the stones of buildings, his was made from cloth and cuts and stitches.

He climbed into the small lift he'd installed when the stairs started proving problematic for his ageing knees and hips, hugging the laptop to his chest as he descended into the basement. When the lift doors opened, he shuffled along a corridor to a solid, featureless door and entered a code into the keypad made up from his real date of birth and his birth name, a name no one knew but him.

There was a click as the door unlocked and lights blinked on as he entered, illuminating display cases containing more mannequins and other items laid out like exhibits in a museum. The Leader closed the door and walked to the far end of the room where a desk sat in front of a huge map of France with leaflets pinned all around it alongside campaign posters for the PNFL, the party he had built from nothing. The desk was identical to the one upstairs in his public office, a desk for each person he had to be. The upstairs desk brought the money in and the desk in the basement paid most of it out again, routed through a myriad of shell companies that rendered it impossible to trace. This little room was the foundation upon which the party had been built and the work he did here was about making far more than clothes. Down here, he was weaving history.

He opened the laptop and studied the red dot. The BMW

had stopped on the edge of a town called Massay. The name rang no bells. He reached for a large leather-bound book and opened it. Inside were lists of names with locations and occupations next to them, every man, woman and child loyal to the cause of making France free again. He called it the Ledger of the Loyal and kept it locked away along with his other great secrets. Computers could be hacked, but you could not hack a book.

He flicked through the pages, pondering who he could send to intercept the quarry now his first choice had failed him. The gendarme who had forwarded the information about the BMW was one candidate, but he wasn't close and the Leader was reluctant to use another police officer after the first had been arrested. Better to keep things isolated. He glanced up at the map of France and the posters of the various smiling candidates poised to seize power and snatch France back at the elections. His eyes found Belloq, hands on hips, apron tied around his waist, his café in soft-focus behind him. He located his number in the ledger and dialled it.

'Those men of yours,' the Leader said, as soon as Belloq answered. 'Where are they now?'

'They're heading north on the A20. I decided not to recall them until I was sure our problem had been dealt with. When I last spoke to them fifteen minutes ago, they'd passed junction 11. Should I call them off?'

'No,' the Leader said, widening the map on the laptop and finding junction 11. 'They switched cars and changed direction. Your people are close. Ten minutes away, twenty at most.' He gave Belloq the location and description of the new car. 'Let me know when they have them.'

He hung up and smiled. This was why they were going to reclaim France, because of good people like Jean-Luc

Belloq, people who could think for themselves and were not afraid to lead. He had an army of them in every department across the country. He rose from his chair and walked over to a display cabinet containing a ragged uniform, neatly folded, the stripes on the rough material picked out by the glow from the overhead light. He stared at the yellow star stitched to the front of it, looking almost like a flower to his age-blurred eyes. It reminded him of how far he had come.

77

Baptiste pulled off the péage, following the directions on the satnav. Belloq had sent them the coordinates in a text, along with details of the car they were looking for.

'Must be in there,' LePoux said, pointing at a large car park in front of a row of superstores. 'Needle in a fucking haystack.'

They entered the car park and started cruising up and down lanes looking for the black BMW. They finally found it after a couple of false alarms, parked in the middle of a row, right in the centre of the car park. LePoux backed into a space close by and switched off the engine. They sat for a moment with their windows open slightly to stop them steaming up, watching the car and listening to the soft drum of rain.

'You think they're in the supermarket?' LePoux said.

Baptiste shook his head. 'I think they've gone. Look at the windows – no steam. The car's been here a while.'

He opened his door, stepped into the rain and breathed in air that smelled of tarmac and earth. He moved towards the BMW, scanning the wider area in case Marie-Claude was heading back with a few bags of groceries, but the rain had emptied the car park. He reached the BMW and walked around it, checking there was no one inside. The interior of the car was spotless: no clutter, no empty wrappers, not even a loose parking ticket. He moved to the front, put his hand on the bonnet and felt the faint trace of heat from the engine. They weren't too far ahead.

He scanned the car park, looking for a bus stop or a taxi rank. They might have stolen a car, but he doubted it. Cars were only left in supermarket car parks for short periods of time, so if they took one it would be spotted quickly. He looked along the line of stores – a supermarket, a DIY shop and a McDonald's. He looked over at LePoux, pointed at the McDonald's and started walking. He'd rather stay in the rain than get back into the rugby changing room smell of the car again and he'd left the keys in the ignition. He pulled his phone out as he walked, opened the text Belloq had sent them and typed a reply.

'Found the car. No one inside but they're close. We'll find them.'

And he would. Because the BMW was empty, which meant that, wherever they'd gone, they still had the Bluetooth tile with them.

78

Marie-Claude could feel herself sweating though it was air- conditioned almost to the point of chilly in the Hertz office. A driver's licence that wasn't Marie-Claude's lay face up on the desk and she was forcing herself to stay calm while the perfectly coiffed and painted young woman went through the paperwork. Léo was playing with a water cooler in the corner, squirting water into a plastic cup. Ordinarily she would tell him to stop but today she was grateful for the distraction.

'OK, I just need to take a card for payment,' the woman smiled, red-painted lips stretching across whitened teeth.

'Cash!' Marie-Claude said, a little too forcefully.

'Excuse me?'

'I'd like to pay cash.'

The perfect make-up cracked for an instant before the smile returned. 'Cash is fine for payment, but I'll need to swipe a card for the security deposit and excesses.'

'Right.' Marie-Claude opened the bag they'd found in the back of the BMW and rummaged around inside, trying to hide the fact that it contained five phones and seven purses. She found the one the driving licence had come from and almost gasped in relief when she discovered a credit card inside. She handed it over with a stiff smile.

'Thank you, madame.'

They had taken a taxi from the supermarket to the nearest car-hire place while Solomon explained what she needed to do. He had convinced her that the driving licence belonging to someone called Julie Dreyfus looked enough like her to work and he'd been right. But he hadn't prepared her for all this additional stuff that was now making her want to run screaming from the building. She would make a lousy criminal. She didn't have the nerve for it. Only the fear from what had happened at the rest stop and the screaming instinct to run had driven her to even attempt it.

The card terminal seemed to be taking an age and fresh panic rose as she wondered if the card was about to be declined. What would she do if it was? Try another card with someone else's name on it? Run? As she turned to check how close Léo was to the door, the machine beeped and spat out a curl of paper. The woman handed it to her and the panic returned as Marie-Claude stared at the blank space on the bottom and realized she needed to sign it. But what was her signature? She knew what Marie-Claude's signature looked like but she had no idea what *Julie Dreyfus* might look like written down. She took the pen, wrote a J, a D, followed by a side-to-side movement that crossed everything out, and put the pen down.

'Thank you, madame.' The woman ripped off the paper and handed over the bottom copy without even checking the signature against the card. 'That's for you. Now it's two hundred and twenty euros for the car hire and twenty for the child seat.'

Marie-Claude handed over five fifties, took her change

and followed the woman outside to a blue Renault Scenic. She snuck a quick look at the back of Julie Dreyfus's credit card. The signature looked nothing like the one she had done and she felt slightly annoyed that it had been so easy to commit card fraud.

She inspected the car in something of a daze, nodding when the woman pointed out slight defects. Once she had signed and initialled the documents wherever the perfect nail pointed, she strapped Léo in and drove away, convinced that the woman would come chasing after her waving the fake signature. But she didn't.

Solomon was waiting round the corner at a bus stop and he smiled as she pulled over. 'See?' he said. 'Told you it would be easy.'

'You're lucky I stopped for you,' she growled, feeling angry and relieved. 'Don't ever make me do anything like that again. Now get in before I change my mind.'

79

Jean-Luc Belloq stared out at La Place 26th Aout from the high windows of the private dining room above his café. He finished briefing the Leader about how they'd found the BMW but not the people inside and waited for his response. For a while only the sound of his breathing could be heard. Outside, the men constructing the stage for the seventieth-anniversary celebrations had stopped for lunch.

'They're getting too close,' the Leader said finally. 'There's too much at stake, it's too close to the election. This man they're travelling with . . .'

'Solomon Creed.'

'Who is he?'

'We don't know. The police don't either, but they've elevated the search alert for him in light of what happened in Vierzon.'

'We need to change that.'

'How?'

'The police are primarily looking for him in connection with the murder of Josef Engel, correct?'

'Yes.'

'We need to make that murder charge go away. If he is no longer a suspect, the police will stop looking for him quite so energetically, leaving the way clear for us to find him ourselves and discover exactly what his connection to all this is.'

Belloq shook his head. 'Making the murder charge go away won't be easy. We have greater control over the investigation now the original lead officer has stepped down, but we can't rule Creed out as a suspect without good reason.'

'You have another suspect in custody, correct? An Arab?'

'Yes, but there is no real evidence against him.'

'What if he confesses? If he confesses to the murder, Solomon Creed will no longer be a suspect.'

'But the Arab didn't do it. We framed him to create a smokescreen. How can we get him to confess to a crime he didn't commit?'

Belloq heard the rasp of the Leader's breathing before he answered. 'Plenty of people take their own lives. Consumed with guilt for the things they have done, they leave a note confessing their crime before committing suicide. He's just another Arab, after all. We want them out of France anyway, does it matter whether they go on a boat or in a box? It's all the same to us. Let this one do something useful for the cause.'

IX

'This is a glorious page in our history that has never been written and shall never be written.'

Heinrich Himmler
Speech to SS Group Leaders on the subject
of the mass extermination of Jews
4 October 1943

Extract from

**DARK MATERIAL – THE DEVIL'S TAILOR: DEATH
AND LIFE IN DIE SCHNEIDER LAGER**

⚜

By Herman Lansky

When I heard I was not the only survivor of the slaughter
at Die Schneider Lager, I wept. It felt like a great victory
of life over death. I wanted to travel back to Mulhouse
to meet the survivors, but I was too far away and I had
important work to do.

I had been seconded to a unit called the KRO, named
after a popular brand of rat poison in America called 'Kill
Rats Only'. The KRO was a Nazi-hunting unit made up
of Jewish soldiers fuelled by a deep hatred of what the
Germans had done to our people, the full horror of which
was rapidly coming to light in the wake of their retreat.

I was in the unit's temporary HQ in the captured
town of Karlsruhe when I heard the news. The town had
been almost destroyed by Allied bombing and the roads
around it were virtually impassable. Getting in had been
difficult, getting out again almost impossible, so travelling back to Mulhouse was out of the question. Also, at
the same time I received news of the Mulhouse survivors, my unit got a report that Artur Samler had been
pinned down with a pocket of Nazi fugitives in a barn
to the north of us. This was a journey I could take.

We headed out as fast as the broken roads would allow and arrived at the half-collapsed barn with the Germans trapped inside. The unit commander, Sergeant David Goldman, spoke in German through a loudhailer, explaining how the barn was surrounded and they had one minute to come out with their hands on their heads. We waited. My role was to identify captured Nazis because I'd seen many of them up close. I was both afraid and enraged at the prospect of seeing Artur Samler again.

The explosion made all of us drop to the ground, a dull thump that blew out the one remaining window in the barn and shook snow and loose tiles down from the roof. Another followed, then two more, then nothing. The KRO troops started to move closer, crawling over the snowy ground, their rifles trained on the silent building. The point man had almost reached it when a bloodied German soldier staggered from the barn, one arm raised above his head in surrender, the other missing. He stumbled forward, tried to say something but his face was a bloody pulp and it came out as a gurgle. He slumped to his knees and died right there, the white snow turning red all around him.

The point man entered the building and I waited in the jeep, shivering from more than the cold. I kept thinking there would be more gunfire, that it was a trap and Samler would walk out of the barn with a platoon of storm troopers at his back because, to me, he was inhuman, a devil who could not be killed.

After a while, Sergeant Goldman walked out of the barn and headed over to me.

'They're all dead,' he said. 'We think Samler is one of them, but we need you to try and identify him.'

I nodded and followed him back to the barn, past the bloody mess of the dead German, wondering why Sergeant Goldman had asked me to 'try' to identify him. I knew what the Devil looked like well enough, and if by some divine miracle he was inside that barn I would recognize him as surely as my own face.

We stepped into the barn. It was dark and smelled of blood, and smoke, and scorched flesh. Sergeant Goldman took a hurricane lamp from one of his men and led me towards the rear of the building, the lamp throwing a circle of light around us that lit up the carnage as we passed. The Germans had committed suicide by grenade, pulling the pins as they huddled, clutching them to their chests until they exploded and ripped out their hearts. It was a mess of scorched uniforms and bloody meat, but I felt nothing. No pity. No disgust. If anything, I was disappointed that they had not suffered nearly enough.

Sergeant Goldman led me to a horse stall and held the lamp high to cast its circle of light. The body of a German officer lay inside, propped against the wooden walls, and I saw why Sergeant Goldman had asked me to 'try' to identify him. His head was entirely gone, along with most of his neck and his hands. The stall walls were a wet mess of blood with bright fragments of bone embedded in the wood. He too had taken the coward's way out, but instead of clutching the grenade to his chest he had put it in his mouth. I had seen Samler execute people the same way. The first victim was a Russian prisoner who had stolen some food destined for the officers' mess; Samler had made him eat a grenade 'for dessert', but the grenade had fallen out of his mouth, rolling away and only maiming him when it exploded. Samler's dogs had been dispatched to finish the job. The next time he executed someone this way, he'd made the prisoner hold the grenade in place. He wanted to see the head explode, like this German officer's head had done.

Sergeant Goldman asked me if it was Samler. They hadn't found any identification on him, and clearly dental records or fingerprints weren't going to help, which meant it was down to me to pronounce the monster dead. I remember looking at what was left of the German officer. He was wearing the right uniform, the black tunic and trousers of a Hauptsturmführer with three silver pips on what remained of his collar, and the Totenkopf Death's Head insignia on the remains of his cuffs. His body seemed right too: a little soft and going slightly to fat round the middle. I so wanted it to be my words that proclaimed the monster dead, for myself and all those he had killed.

'It could be him,' I said.

But I wasn't sure. I'm still not sure. Artur Samler was a monster, inhuman, and I don't think monsters can ever really die. Not entirely.

80

The Renault Scenic pulled off the main road past the sign saying '*Myosotis-La-Fleur*' and followed the private drive that wound through trees and over low bridges for about a mile until it reached a small car park and a series of low buildings arranged in front of a high wall. The wall stretched away in both directions and had security cameras mounted at regular intervals along the top. Solomon felt a fleeting sensation of recognition, as though he had been here before or somewhere very similar. 'It feels like a prison,' he murmured. 'Which would explain why they were less than helpful on the phone.'

'I think it looks weird,' Léo said from the back seat. 'I don't like it.'

Marie-Claude pulled to a stop and switched off the engine. 'Well, we're not going to turn around and go home because you two have "bad feelings" about it.' She opened her door and the smell of damp woodland and hot engine oil billowed in.

Solomon stepped out of the car and watched one of the cameras slowly turn to point right at them. The presence of several parked cars, plus a picnic table and benches to one side of the main building, confirmed there were people around. Solomon breathed in and listened, trying to catch more scents and sounds of the place. He could smell cigarette ash coming from a well-used ashtray by the picnic table, and cooked meat and disinfectant and a faint underlying medical smell. Again there was a flicker of recognition, something similar to the sensation he experienced in cars; a sense of creeping confinement and unease that made him feel tight.

'Come on,' he said, moving towards the main building. 'If we're going to get kicked out of here, we might as well get it over with.'

The reception area was small with uncomfortable-looking sofas around a low table covered with stylish books and magazines. The medicine smell was strong in here and Solomon could hear the rumble of voices and movement in the rest of the building. A severe woman in a dark trouser suit regarded the three of them as they approached the reception desk, her face as impassive and blank as the outside cameras.

'Can I be of assistance?' she said in a flat tone that suggested the answer was almost certainly 'NO'. Her name badge identified her as Madame Roche.

'You have a man staying here,' Marie-Claude replied, 'Otto Adelstein. Would it be possible to talk with him?'

'Are you on the visitors list?'

'No. Monsieur Adelstein was an old friend of my grandfather, who recently died. He wanted me to pass something on to him.'

A door opened behind her and a man in black overalls emerged, bringing the noises and smells of the building with him. Madame Roche ignored him. 'If you give . . . whatever it is to me, I will ensure Monsieur Adelstein receives it.'

The man in overalls glanced over at them at the mention of the name.

'I have to give it to him personally,' Marie-Claude insisted, 'and I'd like to ask him some questions about how he knew my grandfather. They were in the war together.'

'In that case, you will need to make an appointment.' Madame Roche picked up a clipboard and handed it to her. 'Write down your details and the nature of your request on the form and we will submit it to the residents' committee. They will contact you with a time and a date, if your application is successful.'

Marie-Claude looked at the form. 'How long will that take?'

'They normally get back to you with a decision within seven working days.'

'Seven . . .! But we drove here specially. We've been driving all day. I brought my seven-year-old son with me because he wanted to meet his great-grandfather's old war buddy.'

Léo looked up with big, incredulous eyes at her blatant lie.

'What is this place?' Solomon asked.

'A private care facility.'

'What kind of care?'

She gave him a moment of silence as her answer before turning to Marie-Claude. 'I'm sorry, madam, but we have very strict protocols in place here, specifically for the well-being of the residents.'

'And you can't make an exception for a little boy who has travelled halfway across the country to shake the hand of the man who fought beside his grandfather in the war?'

'No exceptions.'

The man in overalls took some forms from a stationery cupboard and did his best to feign ignorance of what was going on, but Solomon could tell he was listening.

'Is there any way you could get a message to Monsieur Adelstein?' Solomon said. 'Purely to tell him there are people here who would like to talk to him about Josef Engel, about Die Schneider Lager, about *Die Anderen*.' He spoke to the woman but his attention was on the man, watching for the tiniest hint of a reaction to any of the names. He reacted to all of them.

'As I said before,' Madame Roche replied, 'we have strict protocols regarding resident interaction. Now if you wish to formally apply . . .'

'No,' Solomon said, grabbing Marie-Claude's arm and steering her towards the door. 'It's OK. Thank you for your help.'

The moment they stepped outside, Marie-Claude twisted out of his grip. 'What the hell was that?'

'We were wasting our time in there. The only thing that woman was going to give us was a form.'

'And you fibbed,' Léo said, his eyes fixed wide at the memory.

'It was only a tiny fib – and it didn't work, which means it doesn't count. What do we do now? Fill in dragon lady's form and hang around for a week?'

'We wait,' Solomon said, heading over to the picnic table.

'For what?'

'For a creature of habit to show up. Why don't we sit and eat some of those fine snacks you bought at the petrol station.'

'Can we?' Léo asked.

'I suppose,' Marie-Claude said. 'Anything's better than getting in that car again.'

She fetched the bags of snacks from the car and was handing out crisps and fruit when the side door opened and the man in black overalls appeared, fitting a cigarette into his mouth.

'Creature of habit,' Marie-Claude murmured. 'But how did you know he'd come here for a smoke?'

'I could smell smoke on him in the office and I spotted nicotine stains on his fingers. Anyone who smokes enough to stain their fingers can't go too long without a hit and I spotted the ashtray on our way in. Stay here. I'm going to have a little chat with him.'

Solomon stood and moved over to the man, smiling the whole way. 'You know him, don't you?' he said, studying the man's face. 'Otto Adelstein.'

'I might.'

'You know him and you like him too.'

The man took a deep pull on his cigarette and blew out smoke. 'He's no bother, not like some of them. Tells good stories.'

'Stories about Die Schneider Lager? About *Die Anderen*?' Solomon caught the flicker of recognition in the man's face. 'What's your name?'

'Renan.'

'What kind of work do you do here, Renan?'

'Bit of maintenance. Bit of chaperoning. Whatever needs doing.'

'Does it pay well?'

Renan shrugged. 'It's OK.'

'Ever do any guided tours?'

He smiled and shook his head. 'It's not that kind of a place.'

'What kind of a place is it?'

'You don't know?'

'I can guess, but I'd rather see for myself. Here's what I think, Renan. I think you and Otto are friends and you've heard him talk about all those things I mentioned and you know he'd love to talk to someone else who knows about them too. I also think you don't get paid nearly enough for the work you do here and I'd be willing to pay handsomely for a guided tour of this facility that included Otto Adelstein.'

Renan sucked the last bit of life out of his cigarette and stubbed it out in the ashtray. He looked up to check where the cameras were pointing. 'How handsomely?'

'Handsomely enough that you'll let my two friends come too.'

Renan shook his head. 'Men only, I'm afraid – no women no kids. It's one of the rules. Women get hassled by the residents, it causes too many problems.'

Solomon glanced back at Marie-Claude and could imagine how she would take that news but he couldn't see a way round it. 'OK, fine. How do we do this?'

'Let's define "handsomely" first.'

'Is five hundred euros handsome enough?'

'Not as handsome as a thousand.'

'OK, a thousand euros.'

Renan sucked the last bit of life out of his cigarette and crushed it out in the ashtray. 'There's a delivery gate on the far side of the wall, almost exactly opposite where we are now. If you drive along the main road, you'll see it. A truck clipped the camera there last week and they haven't replaced it yet. If you go there now, I'll let you in.' He checked his watch. 'Be there in twenty minutes. And bring the cash.'

81

Madame Roche studied the video screens. She couldn't see the people any more but their car was there. If they weren't gone in five minutes, she'd send a security team to escort them from the premises.

She opened a filing cabinet and removed a folder with '*M. Otto Adelstein*' written on the cover. There was a note in the back of every resident's file giving details of who to contact if anything unusual happened. Part of the duty of care at Myosotis-La-Fleur was to keep relatives well-informed. Because of the nature of the place and the residents there, they regularly had journalists turning up. Madame Roche prided herself on being an effective gatekeeper and always sent them away with nothing. She found a contact number and dialled it while checking the video monitors again and seeing nothing.

'Monsieur Hoffmann's office.'

'Hello, I'm calling from Myosotis-La-Fleur. May I speak to Monsieur Hoffmann, please. It concerns Monsieur Otto Adelstein.'

There was a brief pause before someone else came on the line, the voice old and breathy. 'This is Monsieur Hoffmann, is everything all right?'

'Yes, sir. Monsieur Adelstein is in perfectly good health. However, he just had visitors – a man, a woman and a young boy. They wanted to speak with him and when I informed them of the correct procedure, they left. I thought I'd better inform you.'

'You did the right thing. What did they look like?'

She touched the screen showing the feed from the reception camera and dragged her finger backwards, shuttling through the footage until the three people appeared again. 'I can email a picture of them to the address we have on record, if you like.'

'That would be most kind, thank you. When did they leave?'

'They're still here, oh, one moment.' She looked up as the three figures appeared from the side of the building and walked back to the car. 'They're leaving right now.'

'And what car are they driving?'

'It's a blue Renault Scenic. I took the liberty of making a note of the registration plate. I'll include it in my email.'

'Thank you, madame. As usual, your service is beyond excellent.'

Madame Roche smiled and felt a small swell of pride as she put the phone down. She knew she was good at her job but it was nice when other people noticed.

She watched the car drive away then closed Monsieur Adelstein's folder and filed it away, along with the four hundred other files recording the strictly confidential details of the residents of Myosotis-La-Fleur.

82

'Why can't I go in?' Marie-Claude gripped the wheel and stared at the road in fury.

'He said women disturb the residents.'

'What kind of misogynistic bullshit is that?'

Solomon finished counting fifty-euro notes and put the lid back on the shoebox. 'I think he's telling the truth.'

'Why?'

'Because I think all the residents of Myosotis-La-Fleur have Alzheimer's disease.'

'What makes you think that?'

'In English, the Myosotis flower is called a forget-me-not. I think this facility is a high-class oubliette, somewhere to put relatives who have lost their minds through dementia. I could smell Donepezil floating on the breeze as well as the ammoniac whiff of old people.'

Léo wrinkled his nose. 'I'm glad I didn't smell it.'

'Men with Alzheimer's often lose their inhibitions and start being sexually aggressive towards women. They can get violent. I would imagine all the orderlies working here can take care of themselves.'

'I can look after myself.'

'But what about Léo? Who'd look after him?'

Marie-Claude went silent for a minute. 'You're telling me I drove all this way for nothing?'

'No. Your main reason for coming was to warn Otto Adelstein he was in danger. As it turns out, he lives in a high-security compound, which means he's probably more secure than we are.'

'That wouldn't be hard. That wasn't the only reason, though. I wanted to ask him about my grandfather too. About the war. About *Die Anderen*.'

'I'll ask him for you.'

'Not the same. My grandfather's history is my history too. It feels wrong to learn it through an intermediate.'

'I don't see any way round it. However, there were four survivors. If Otto Adelstein has the list of their names or can tell us where to find it, you can still trace the last survivor and talk to him. Pull over there –' He pointed at a service road leading to a large pair of steel doors set into the wall ahead.

'There's a camera,' Marie-Claude said.

'Not working, according to my new friend.' Marie-Claude pulled off and stopped short of the gates. 'Come back in an hour,' Solomon said. 'Go somewhere public, a restaurant or a supermarket. You'll be safer in a crowd.'

Marie-Claude looked panicked. 'What if someone finds us, like in the rest stop?'

'They won't. No one knows where we are, and Julie Dreyfus is driving this car, not you. Just don't turn on your phone. You'll be fine. Trust me.'

She nodded but he could feel her reluctance to leave. 'What do we do if we come back and you're not here?'

'If I'm not here in an hour, call everyone you can think of and tell them everything you know. Call the Shoah

Foundation, the press – your friend Amand, if you think you can trust him. Use one of the phones we found in the BMW and ditch it as soon as you've made your first set of calls. Keep moving. Use the Dreyfus ID and pay for hotel rooms in cash until you can figure this thing out. Someone wants to keep this secret, so make as much noise as you can, otherwise they win.' Her eyes glazed in panic. Solomon smiled. 'Alternatively, pick me up in an hour and I'll tell you what Otto Adelstein had to say for himself.' He got out of the car. 'Léo will look after you anyway. He can spot the bad ones a mile away, right?' Léo nodded uncertainly. 'Now go, before someone spots us.'

Marie-Claude put the car in gear and he watched her drive away. When he looked up at the high walls, he felt a hollowness in his stomach at the prospect of walking into confinement. One thing he had not shared with Marie-Claude was the possibility that Otto Adelstein was suffering from such severe dementia that he might not remember anything and the whole trip might have been for nothing. Marie-Claude's past wasn't the only thing riding on this visit.

A clunk sounded inside the door as if someone had hit it with a rock, then a small section opened and Renan peered out.

'You got the money?'

Solomon held out the bundle of fifty-euro notes. Renan took it and opened the door.

The delivery area was large and cavernous, big enough for a lorry.

'Wear these,' Renan said, handing Solomon a set of black overalls and a black cap. 'Put the cap on to hide your hair, don't talk to anyone unless they talk to you first, and try and ignore the weirder stuff you see in here. The whole idea of this place is to behave as if everything that happens is normal, that way the residents don't feel confused or weird – even though they are. Our job is to maintain that illusion. I'll take you straight to Monsieur Adelstein, but the moment he gets upset we leave, understand? Even if all you get to say is "Hello". I said I'd take you to him and that's what I'll do, but I'm not risking my job any more than I need to.'

'Understood,' Solomon said, pulling the overalls over his clothes.

As soon as he was ready, Renan moved to another door, tapped in a code and pushed it open into a driveway surrounded by thick, well-kept woodland.

'Welcome to the land that time forgot,' he said.

83

The same two gendarmes who had arrested Madjid Lellouche came to his cell at dusk. They asked him to stand against the wall, handcuffed his arms behind his back then led him out into the rough-walled corridor.

'Where are you taking me?' Madjid said.

'Le Petit Bastille in Gaillac,' the taller one replied. 'You need somewhere to sleep and our cells don't have beds. You'll be more comfortable there.'

'What about food? I haven't eaten since I've been here.'

'They'll feed you,' the gendarme replied. 'Free meal, free accommodation. Who says crime doesn't pay?'

'I didn't do any crimes.'

'That's what they all say.' The gendarme pushed him up the stairs and out back where a car was waiting. 'There's some journalists out front, so keep your head down,' the tall one muttered as he pushed him into the back seat.

Madjid did as he was told, keeping low until Cordes was well behind them before rising up to watch the vineyards sliding by. The driver had his window open and Madjid breathed in the loamy, chalky smell of the land. The sun had dipped below the hills and the sky was peach and indigo and heading into night. He couldn't remember the last time he had spent a working day out of the sun. There were still people in the fields, squeezing the last few drops of light from the day. When the *vendange* started, they would work through the night and use tractor headlights to see by. He needed to be in Bordeaux by then. Everyone needed extra hands during the harvest and it would be easy to get work.

They wove through the vineyards until the lights of Gaillac appeared ahead, framed in the plane trees lining the road. Madjid didn't come to Gaillac often and he noticed the slogans sprayed on the trees, the paint new and thick, one letter on each trunk and gradually spelling out a message as the car drove by.

L-A-F-R-A-N-C-E-A-U-F-R-A-N-Ç-A-I-S – France for the French.

And another:

A-R-A-B-E-S-D-E-H-O-R-S – Arabs out.

Madjid leaned forward in his seat. 'Tonight, at Le Petit Bastille,' he asked, 'will I be sharing a cell with anybody?'

The driver shook his head in disbelief. 'You people don't want much, do you? Free meal, private room . . .'

Madjid sat back and remained silent for the rest of the trip, hugging his stomach to stop the rumbling sounds brought on by hunger and the acid burn of worry that there were people who would write such things on the trees and no one to scrub them off again.

They drove through the centre of town where people sat at café tables, enjoying the warm evening, their faces lit by flickering candles, and on to the river where the car slowed and pulled to a halt behind a red brick building. A man behind a desk in a dark uniform looked up as they entered through a side door.

'Monsieur would like a room of his own, if possible,' the tall gendarme said, 'preferably with a view of the river.'

The jailer smirked, picked up a key card and swiped it through an electronic reader to unlock the door that led to the cells. Madjid followed him down a corridor lined with metal doors with sliding hatches. Most of them were open and he could see that all the cells were empty, which made him feel better. They turned a corner into an identical corridor. 'You're in here,' the jailer said, swiping his card to open a door halfway down the row. There was a loud buzz, a metallic bang as a bolt shifted and the door opened.

The cell had a narrow metal shelf with a fixed, thin mattress on it, a tiled area in one corner with a hole in the centre that smelled of the sewers, and a small window set high in the wall with bars across it. Madjid was pushed inside and the door banged shut behind him. He slid the hatch open and called after the jailer. 'Monsieur! They said I could have some food. I haven't eaten today. Monsieur!'

The jailer ignored him and disappeared round the corner. As Madjid stared into the empty corridor he noticed a pair of eyes framed in the hatch opposite, a tattooed tear beneath the left one.

'Bonsoir, monsieur,' Madjid said.

The eyes continued to stare as if the man who owned them was about to curse or spit, then the hatch slid shut with a loud bang that echoed down the hallway. Madjid gently slid his own hatch shut and walked to the bed. He wasn't going to get any food tonight, that was clear, but he would rather go hungry than share a cell with the man opposite with the hate in his eyes.

He stood for a moment, trying to work out which way was east so he could pray to Mecca. He took off his boots and knelt on the painted concrete floor to say the *Salah*. When he was done, he lay down on the narrow bed, adding an extra prayer that tomorrow would bring better fortune. He fell asleep whispering his words of hope.

84

Solomon followed Renan down a road that curved away through thick trees to quickly hide the gates and walls. After half a minute's walk, the road straightened again and he saw buildings ahead, a collection of modern, single-storey blocks arranged around a market square. The houses were plain and neat, their shutters painted a variety of bright, cheerful colours as if children had designed them using crayons. They drew nearer and Solomon could see stalls in the market selling bread and cheese and vegetables. It looked like market day in any village in France, except the stall-holders wore black overalls and there was one old man who was diligently inspecting the aubergines and putting every one into a basket that already overflowed with them.

'Monsieur Lanois,' Renan whispered. 'Made a fortune as a commodities trader.'

'Old instincts die hard,' Solomon murmured.

They entered the market square and a thin elegant woman appeared from the door of a house, dancing to some unheard tune. She floated up to Solomon, smiled and spun away, moving to the tune in her head.

'Madame Chambord,' Renan whispered. 'One of the heirs to a great fashion house. Started as a model and ended up running the whole of the European division. She has dined with kings and presidents, lived a life most of us can only dream about, and now she remembers none of it.'

Solomon watched her dance around the stalls, the other shoppers smiling at her as if it was perfectly normal, while the men in black overalls maintained a cold scrutiny. 'There's a lot of security here,' he observed.

'It's to protect the residents. We ignore abnormal behaviour as far as we can, but sometimes it gets out of hand, or one of the other residents gets angry or upset and we have to step in. Take Monsieur Lanois and his aubergines; if he were doing this in a normal market, he would be stared at, whispered about, probably challenged and questioned, which would make him feel confused and vulnerable. Here, we let him fill his bag as if it's perfectly normal. We let them do what they're comfortable doing, no matter how crazy, as long as they're not harming anyone else. You'll see what I mean at Monsieur Adelstein's house. It's the one with the pale-blue shutters.'

The house was set apart from the rest with no other houses beyond, only green fields and more trees hiding the distant perimeter wall. Solomon heard a steady rattling sound coming from the back of the house and felt suddenly nervous at the prospect of finally meeting someone who might know him. They reached the door and Renan turned to him. 'The moment he gets upset, we leave, OK?'

Solomon nodded and Renan knocked once before opening the door. 'Monsieur Adelstein,' he said. 'You have a visitor.'

Solomon followed him into a room that was like something from a fairy tale. Lengths of striped cloth were draped over every surface and pooled on to the floor, and at the centre of it all stood an old loom, clattering away like a wooden spider, with the weaver hunched over it. He was old, his body crooked from long years bent over the loom, and his skin loose and leathery. He had large brown liver spots on his bald head and a long white beard that trailed down into the warp, as if he was weaving himself into the cloth. But his eyes were sharp and his legs moved on the treadles with the fluid grace of a dancer, and his fingers were nimble too, constantly plucking and separating the threads, spacing them out, tamping the weft down as the transports moved up and down in time with his footwork and the shuttle flew back and forth. He seemed radiantly happy, as if a light was shining out of him, and Solomon wondered what Léo would have made of him had he been here.

'Monsieur Adelstein,' Renan repeated, stepping further into the room and placing his hand gently on the weaver's shoulder. 'Your visitor.'

The old man blinked like he was waking from a dream and the machine slowed to a halt. He turned and looked up at Solomon with a look of pleasant surprise that froze the moment he saw him. 'You!' he said, rising from his stool, eyes wide. '*Der bleiche Mann. Je pensais que je vous rêvé.* I thought I dreamed you.' The different languages tripped over each other, revealing the shifting currents in the old man's mind. 'Are you a dream? Am I dreaming now?'

Solomon looked down at the old man, barely taller now than when he'd been seated. He had hoped he might recognize Otto, but the man standing before him was a stranger. 'I'm here,' he said, extending his hand. The weaver flinched. 'Take my hand,' Solomon said. 'You cannot take hold of a dream.'

Otto Adelstein looked at Solomon's hand for a long while before slowly reaching out and taking it. A smile spread across his face. 'You are here,' he said, running his fingers over Solomon's hand and the surface of his jacket. 'I thought you were only in my mind, and my mind is slippery. Things come, things go. Dreams and memory, they all seem the same to me.' His smile faded and he let go of Solomon's hand. 'Why are you here?' He looked around the room. 'Where is this place?'

'This is your atelier, Monsieur Adelstein,' Renan stepped forward, smiling. 'This man has come to see you. He's come to see your work.'

The old man looked around at the swathes of striped cloth. 'My work. Yes. Of course.' He moved over to a pile of the material and picked up an armful. 'I kept my promise to you,' he said, studying the irregular stripes as if reading. 'The names are all here, like you asked.' He let the cloth run through his arms and down to the floor. Then he looked around in confusion before his eyes found Solomon again. 'I know you, monsieur. I *know* you.'

Solomon smiled at him, his heart hammering in his chest. 'Who am I?'

'You are *der bleiche Mann*,' Otto said. 'The pale man. You came back. You said you would and here you are.'

'What else did I say? How do you know me?'

The weaver frowned. 'The camp. You were there at the camp, Die Schneider Lager, you were there at the end. You came when we thought we were lost. You said there was a way out, that if we gave you our names, you could save us. You told us to write our names down somewhere they could be seen but where they were also hidden, and that this was how we could be saved, by being visible and invisible at the same time. He said we had to keep the list of names with us always. We were frightened and didn't understand, but nothing made sense in that place. It was Max who figured it out. He said we should speak to the Golem and make you a suit. And that's what we did. I spoke our names to the Golem, the ones you took from us and the ones you gave us back, and the Golem whispered them back in the language of threads.' He held up the cloth. 'The cloth remembers. The cloth is the list of the saved, and also of the damned.' He pointed at Solomon's suit. 'You took the jacket and we kept the rest – the waistcoat, the lining and the trousers. But you have the waistcoat, which means Josef is dead.' Tears began to run down the creases of his face into the white cloud of his beard. 'I'm frightened of you, pale man. I'm afraid of why you are here.'

'I'm here because I have forgotten who I am,' Solomon said. 'I was hoping you might help me remember. I came looking for Josef Engel, but I was too late. He left a note that led me to you. That's why I'm here, asking you if you can help me. Can you tell me who I am?'

'You are he,' Otto said, backing away from Solomon, his voice cracking with fear. 'You are the dark fire in the night, the stealer of souls.' He bumped up against the wall and slid to the floor. 'I don't want to die. I kept my promise. I kept the names.' He buried his face in the striped material to muffle his broken sobs.

'Time to go,' Renan said, grabbing Solomon's arm and pulling him towards the door.

'Who am I?' Solomon said. 'What's the Golem? Who's Max – is he the other survivor?'

'Please don't take me,' the weaver sobbed. 'I don't want to go where you might take me.'

'Monsieur!' Renan pulled Solomon backwards out of the door.

'Who's Max?' Solomon repeated, but Renan closed the door before the old man could answer.

'He'll be fine in a second,' Renan said. 'The residents often get really upset or confused, but they forget all about it in seconds. They're a lot like children.'

Solomon stood outside the door listening to Otto Adelstein weeping and begging for pity and pleading. The encounter had left him frustrated and confused; he was convinced that the weaver knew more, much more. He wanted to kick the door down and shake it out of him, but the brand on his arm flared in pain and he closed his eyes and focused on that instead to help him calm down. Inside the house, the loom started up again, the shuttling sound mingling with the old man's sobs.

'Can we go back in?' Solomon asked.

Renan shook his head. 'I'm not risking it. He still sounds pretty upset. If he sees you again, he might get worse. I let you in, you've seen him, now you have to leave again – that was the deal.'

'Can we wait a little longer, to see if he calms down?'

'No, we can't.' Renan started walking away and the burn in Solomon's arm flared in pain as he thought about how easy it would be to break his neck, hide him in the bushes and slip back inside the house to force the old weaver to tell him more. He gripped his shoulder and sucked air against the pain. The old man had been afraid of him, terrified, and Solomon was afraid too. He was afraid of who he might have been, and who he might become again. He didn't need to terrorize the old man to find out who he was because if he took that path he would already have his answer. Instead he walked away from the door, the heat of his pain steadily fading to nothing as he followed Renan back through the calm green of the dappled woods.

85

The Renault Scenic was parked outside when Solomon emerged from the loading bay and he saw the look of relief on Marie-Claude's face when she spotted him. He got into the passenger seat and smiled at Léo. 'How long was I in there?'

'Just under an hour.' Marie-Claude handed him a cheese baguette and a bottle of Badoit. 'We've been having a fun time walking slowly round a supermarket.'

'It was boring,' Léo said from the back.

'It was safe,' Marie-Claude replied, 'nice and boring and safe.' She pulled away while Solomon was strapping himself in and winding his window down. 'Well? Did you talk to him?'

Solomon nodded and twisted the cap off the bottle of water. 'He was very confused. Spoke in fragments and riddles. He seemed to recognize me, but I couldn't remember him. He had a loom in his house where he spends all his time weaving a striped cloth with irregular lines on it, the same pattern over and over. He said the cloth was the list and the names were written in it.'

'Oh my God. Did you get a sample of it, a picture?'

'I didn't need to.' Solomon unbuttoned his waistcoat. 'You

said when you asked your grandfather for the names of the other survivors he gave you this.' He opened the flap and showed her the striped lining. 'This is the pattern Otto Adelstein spends all his time weaving. So he did give you the names.'

Marie-Claude stared at the waistcoat, shook her head and turned back to the road. 'No, he didn't. He must have known what kind of place Monsieur Adelstein was living in and that I'd probably not get to see him. I think all he wanted was to get that waistcoat to him and I was his best option. He never wanted to help me. This is just another one of his rejections.'

Solomon thought back through his meeting with Otto, replaying their conversation word-by-word. 'I think you're wrong. Your relationship with your grandfather was obviously difficult, but that note he left you drips with emotion and pain. I think he was annoyed and perplexed by your determination to learn about his past, but impressed by it too. His note suggests to me that he dearly wanted to tell you but was worried for you and was also bound by his sense of honour and responsibility to the other survivors. Don't forget, his secret was Otto's secret too. You're right, he would have known what kind of facility Otto was kept in, but that also means he must have known about Otto's fragile memory. I think he knew that sending you here with this waistcoat would trigger his memory and he would tell you what he could. And he did. He revealed what the list is.'

'Yes, but what good is it if it's in code?'

'Otto also mentioned someone called Max. He said he and the survivors had to write down their names and keep them hidden in plain sight, that's how they would be saved, and it was Max who figured out how to do it. He said he whispered the names to the Golem and it spoke them back in the language of threads. Does any of that mean anything to you?'

Marie-Claude frowned. 'I came across plenty of Maxes in my research, but I'd have to go back through them all to start narrowing it down. It's a start, I suppose. As for the Golem, I've never heard of it before, not in relation to the camp, at least.'

'The Golem is one of Nick Fury's Howling Commando Monsters,' Léo suggested.

'It's also a figure from Jewish folklore,' Marie-Claude said. 'An inanimate object in the shape of a man, brought to life and controlled by a master. A kind of monster really. There were plenty of monsters in the camp, most of them of the human variety. Maybe the Golem was one of those.'

Solomon nodded as fresh information flooded his brain. 'The most famous Golem story is about the Golem of Prague, built in the sixteenth century to protect the Jews from anti-Semitic attacks. Golem stories are always about Jews under attack, so the narrative is consistent with the Nazis' reign of terror. Maybe Otto was speaking symbolically when he said he whispered the names to the Golem and it spoke the names back. Or maybe there was something in the camp, something the inmates used to keep secrets from the guards.'

Marie-Claude nodded. 'If you're right, I know who we can ask.'

'Who?' Solomon asked.

'John Hamilton, the man who found the survivors. He retired to Mulhouse and is writing a book about the camp. He works at the museum part-time as a guide. We've swapped notes a few times and he's helped me with my research. Before you went, you said I should call someone I trusted if you didn't come back and he was the person I thought of. He's as passionate about telling the true story of the camp as I am and if anyone would know about any Golem legend inside Die Schneider Lager it would be him. Mulhouse is only a couple of hours' drive from here. If we don't hit any traffic we can be there before dark.'

86

The jet landed at the Basel Freiburg EuroAirport in a plume of spray from the recent rain and taxied to a stop by another black Range Rover with tinted windows.

'Is this some kind of OCD thing you have going on?' Amand said as he followed Magellan down the steps to the waiting car.

'It's the same hire company every time,' Magellan said. 'I guess they have a fleet of these things. They probably come bullet-proof as well, if you wanted.'

Amand nodded and wondered again exactly who Magellan was working for. He turned on his phone and checked for messages. He had five missed calls – four from Henri and one from Parra – as well as three voicemail messages. He got into the Range Rover and listened to them as they drove out of the airport. Henri's messages were all the same – no more news about Marie-Claude and questions about Amand's whereabouts and when he would be back in the office. Parra wanted to know where he was too. He thought about calling Parra back and asking about the case. He wanted to find out if the bloody cane had been found and sent to the labs in Albi, and if it had, whether Madjid Lellouche remained in custody. In the end, he decided to leave it. He wasn't on the case any more and he liked the idea of being off the grid. It made him feel freer and more secure and, strangely, less stressed. He switched the phone off and took the battery out as an added precaution.

'Feeling paranoid?' Magellan asked, nodding at the phone.

'Maybe. What's that saying? Just because you're paranoid doesn't mean they're not out to get you. I shouldn't be here and I know how easy it is to track phone signals, so . . . paranoid is fine for now. How far is it to Mulhouse?'

'Thirty kilometres. What's your plan when we get there?'

'My plan is to wait.'

'For how long?'

'Until someone shows up or we get news that someone else has found them.'

'And how are you going to get any news with your phone switched off?'

Amand looked down at his phone. 'I'll figure that out while we're waiting.'

87

Madjid Lellouche woke suddenly in his cell and it took him a few moments to remember where he was. He had been dreaming of fields where the vines were all healthy and the grapes heavy and plump. It had been a good dream, but something had woken him from it. A sound.

His hip was numb from lying on the thin mattress and he wondered how late it was. The lights were off but they'd been on when he'd fallen asleep. The street lights cast a long rectangle of yellow on the ceiling, the shadow of the window bars clearly defined. He looked up at the high window. There was some light in the sky, so it couldn't be that late. There was also a thin slash of white light coming from somewhere else and Madjid glanced at the door, wondering if the jailer had brought him some food after all and left the hatch open, but it was shut. It was the door that was open.

Madjid sat up in bed, remembering the buzz of the unlocking door and realizing it was this that had dragged him from sleep. He listened for more sounds outside in the corridor but everything was still: no noise, no movement.

He stood and felt the cold concrete beneath his bare feet as he made his way over to the door. He stopped. Listened again, ready to dash back to the cot if anyone was coming. He heard the muffled sound of distant voices from the entrance, but they didn't seem to be getting any closer. He peered through the thin gap into the bright corridor beyond, then slowly opened the door, checking the door opposite and remembering the hate-filled eyes that had glared at him through the hatch. The door was open. All the doors were open.

Madjid stood for a moment, frozen in doubt about what to do next. The burble of voices was louder with the door open but no one seemed to be coming. He wondered if he should go back to sleep. Surely they would discover the doors were unlocked sooner or later and as long as he was in his cell nothing would come of it. He looked at the cell door opposite again. But what if the owner of those hate-filled eyes woke first? What if he came into his cell? He moved into the corridor and headed towards the murmuring voices, deciding it would be best if he told the jailer what had happened.

He felt exposed in the corridor but he noticed the cameras and realized it was too late to go back. He stepped round the corner and the burble of voices grew louder, two men talking to each other. He could see the reception area through the bars of the gate but it was empty, no sign of anyone except for a half-eaten sandwich on the booking desk and a small radio, tuned to a sports channel, the source of the voices. He reached the gate and pushed it. Locked, and no handle on the inside. He thought about banging on it to draw the jailer's attention, but that risked drawing the attention of others, and he didn't want that, so he waited, glancing back nervously down the corridor, waiting for him to come back. Except he didn't. Time ticked on. The rugby match on the radio went to half-time. Still the jailer did not return. At one point he thought he heard something behind him, like something ripping, but the radio was too loud for him to hear it properly and he didn't hear it again.

He looked up at the camera, the cold black eye of its lens pointing right at him, and thought about what it would look like, him standing here all this time. He had left his cell intending only to inform the jailer that the doors were unlocked. He had not planned on standing out here all this time. It would look bad, him lingering by the door like this, like maybe he was trying to escape. After one last look at the empty reception area, he started back up the corridor, figuring he would listen out for the end of the game and come back when he heard the radio go off. He reached the turn and peered round to make sure the corridor was empty before hurrying back to his cell, anxious to return to the small, dark room. He reached his door, stepped inside, and breathed again.

It was dark in the cell after the brightness of the corridor. He closed the door and the cell grew darker, apart from the slash of light leaking in through the gap. He wanted to put something against the door to make it close all the way and went to pick up one of his boots. That's when he noticed the bed. It was shredded, the rubberized surface material torn away in long ragged strips, leaving tufts of grey stuffing sticking up. He took a step towards it and something looped over his head and bit hard into his neck. He grabbed at it with his hands but it was thin and tight and he couldn't get his fingers behind it. He tried to turn and face his attacker but he was kicked hard behind his knee and his leg buckled and he crumpled to the concrete floor, his weight making the noose round his neck cinch tighter. He fought for breath but couldn't breathe. Tried to shout but couldn't summon a single sound. A hand grabbed his shirt from behind and dragged him across the floor to the high window, then the noose went tighter as he was hauled upwards.

Madjid clawed at his neck, drawing blood with his nails as he fought to release the rope. He was standing on tiptoe now, his vision starting to tunnel as his brain became starved of oxygen. He was aware of a figure in the dark, leaning back on a length of knotted rope made from strips of the heavy-duty plastic cover from his bed. He looked around for something to grab hold of or use as a weapon and saw something written on the wall by his head, Arabic script scratched into the paint:

I'm sorry, it said. *I confess. I killed the Jew.*

Madjid kicked out at the man with the last of his strength when he realized what this was, not an opportunistic act of violence but a carefully orchestrated set-up. His vision was almost entirely dark now, only a small circle of light at the end of a long tunnel. He looked at his killer, his face lit by the yellow street lamp and framed in blackness, the single tattooed tear beneath an eye burning with hate.

He wanted to plead with him and ask him why, but the noose was too tight and the tunnel was closing all around him, the light at the end of it getting smaller and smaller until it condensed to a single, bright point and everything went dark.

88

Marie-Claude drove into Mulhouse as night drained the last drops of colour from the day. Léo was asleep in the back, his head rocking with the movement of the car. Solomon breathed in the smell of the place through his open window, a mix of nature and man: sweat, yeast, earth, water, rot. But there was something else here, microscopic and almost lost, a smell like graveyards and ancient tombs, of bones become dust.

'I'm going to have to turn my phone on,' Marie-Claude said. 'Hamilton's number's in my contacts.'

'Not yet.' Solomon pointed at a sign saying *Musée de Guerre*. 'Let's head there and get a feel for the place first.' He watched the town slip by, the stain of war still evident in the street names and the squat houses that lined the road, not one more than seventy years old. 'Ugly place,' he murmured, looking up at the closed shutters that made the place feel deserted. 'Makes you appreciate the wisdom of what they did in your town.'

'What do you mean?'

'Capitulation. Non-violent surrender. All those pretty stone buildings left intact.'

Marie-Claude bristled. 'Not everybody capitulated.'

'No, but the people who counted did: the community leaders, the police, the politicians. You've got to admire the pragmatism of that. Instead of destructive and bloody armed resistance against a superior military force, they simply waved the white flag, altered the menus a little to accommodate a more vinegary German palate and waited it out. And when the Allies drove the Germans away again, they simply changed the menus back and shaved the heads of all the women who'd shared the enemy's beds in a token display of indignation. And your town survived intact. The land doesn't care who lives on it or what language they speak or whether they're kind to each other or not. The notion that people can betray a country is an emotional conceit as abstract as the notion of "country" itself. "Country" exists only in the minds of men, the land itself is indifferent.'

'Not everyone surrendered,' Marie-Claude said, as she followed the museum signs out of town. 'Not everyone betrayed their country.'

They continued in silence, leaving the town behind them until the signs for the museum pointed down a curved side road leading through a forest that hid whatever lay beyond it. Marie-Claude turned off the main road, her headlights sweeping through the darkness of the trees and lighting up an evening mist that was rising from the damp ground like hordes of spectres. The curved road straightened and emerged from the forest and Marie-Claude slammed on the brakes, bringing the car to a crunching halt that jerked Léo awake. He looked up through the windscreen at a distant cluster of dark buildings surrounded by barbed-wire fence. 'Is this the bad camp?' Léo whispered.

Marie-Claude stared at it, tears brimming in her eyes and dripping down her cheeks.

'Yes,' Solomon answered. 'This is where Grampy was during the war. This is Die Schneider Lager.' He reached out to Marie-Claude and wiped a tear away with his thumb. 'Don't you want to go closer? Don't you want to see it?'

She blinked and shook her head. 'I didn't expect it would hit me like this. I've seen pictures of it before, but . . .'

'Pictures can't capture the soul of a place.' Solomon looked at the camp lying at the end of the road, the darkening sky making it seem shadowy and indistinct. There was a large cleared area in the centre of the compound with a couple of tanks on display, their guns angled up at the sky, and a large, grey marble monument beyond, carved into a huge curve like a solid wisp of smoke. The buildings were in darkness and the gate was secured with a chain and padlock.

'It's all locked up,' Marie-Claude said, turning the car around in a hurry. 'We can come back tomorrow. We should head back to town and find out where Hamilton lives.'

'I think he lives up there,' Solomon said, pointing above the treeline at a group of stone houses clinging to the valley on the far side of town.

Marie-Claude stared at them. 'How do you know that?'

'Educated guess. Let's drive up there. If I'm wrong, you can turn your phone on and call him.'

Marie-Claude looked at him like he'd lost his mind, but she did as he suggested and took the main road back into town, glancing up at the old houses and trying to figure out what it was about them that made Solomon think Hamilton lived there. They had almost reached them when she finally gave up. 'OK, what makes you think he lives in one of these houses?'

'He's a historian, so the age of these houses would appeal

to him – they're the oldest things around here apart from the church, and I doubt he lives there. Also, he's English.'

'What's that got to do with anything?'

'Everything. I think he lives in that one –' Solomon pointed at the first house.

Marie-Claude pulled over and studied it. Warm orange light spilled from the windows, making it seem cosy and welcoming. There was a hand-painted sign by the front door showing that the house had rooms to rent, and a flagpole at the entrance to the driveway with a *Tricolore* flapping violently at the top. She turned to Solomon. 'Why would an Englishman fly a French flag?'

'With this view, why would he not?' Solomon opened his door and stepped out into a cold wind. Marie-Claude and Léo followed him. She looked down at the town of Mulhouse spread out below them. She could see Die Schneider Lager too, like a dark stain on the landscape. 'What has the view got to do with anything?'

'You can see the whole town from here, which means the whole town can see us. If he flew a Union Jack, he'd never get fresh bread again. But it's the windows that give it away. Let's go and say hello.' He started walking up the drive towards the front door.

Marie-Claude followed, studying the orange glow coming through the windows, still none the wiser. A little hand curled into hers and tugged at her attention.

'It's the shutters,' Léo's tiny voice piped up. 'They're open.'

Marie-Claude smiled as she realized he was right. No French person would leave the shutters open, especially when it was this cold out.

'A German could live here,' Marie-Claude said. 'We're pretty close to the border.'

Solomon pointed at the painted board by the door saying: *Cottage for Rent, Gîte à Louer, Haus zu Mieten.* 'A German wouldn't write a sign in English first,' he said as he knocked on the door. 'Neither would a Frenchman.'

Footsteps sounded beyond the door, locks rattled and it opened, spilling heat and orange light on to them. A solid-looking man stood before them, his bald head making him seem ageless and his toothbrush moustache as neat as the knotted tie peeping out from the V of his sweater.

'John Hamilton?' Solomon asked, extending his hand.

'Indeed,' the man replied, looking shocked but shaking the hand anyway. He stared at Solomon for a long moment then looked at the others, his eyes finally settling on Marie-Claude and widening in surprise. 'I know you. But why are you—' He seemed to collect himself and the surprise turned into a warm smile. 'Come in,' he stepped aside to let them enter, 'we're letting all the warm out here. Let's go sit by the fire. I'll open a bottle of wine and you can tell me exactly what brings you here.'

89

Hamilton's home smelled of woodsmoke that leaked from a freshly lit fire in the living room that slowly overcame the evening chill. Léo curled up on the sofa in front of it and quickly fell asleep while Hamilton poured wine and listened as Marie-Claude told him everything – about her grandfather's murder, about the note he had left that had led to Otto Adelstein, about how he'd woven the names of the others into cloth.

'He said he whispered it to the Golem,' Solomon said. 'He spoke the names and the Golem whispered them back in the language of thread. Though Monsieur Adelstein also suffers from dementia, so maybe he was confused.'

'No,' Hamilton said, his face serious. 'The Golem is real. Do you have the cloth?'

Solomon took off his waistcoat and laid it on the floor. Hamilton knelt beside it almost in prayer and ran his fingers along the irregular lines. 'The list of survivors,' he whispered, the firelight dancing in his eyes. He took his phone and photographed it. 'I never knew their names,' he said. 'They were transported from the camp before I had a chance to talk to them. After the war I tried to find them, but Europe was a mess. Finding anyone was almost impossible, especially if you didn't even have a name to go on. So they disappeared, became something of a legend, almost as if they never existed. But I knew they did,' he looked up at Marie-Claude. 'And you did too.' He grabbed the waistcoat and rose stiffly from the floor. 'Come with me.'

He headed across the hallway and into a small study with piles of paper and open books everywhere and lists of names covering walls dotted with photographs of skeletal men in striped uniforms. Hamilton laid the waistcoat on the desk and started flicking through the pages of a guidebook until he found what he was looking for and held it open at a page filled with photos of a large, antique textile loom. 'This is one of the exhibits in the museum,' he said, 'an early programmable loom from the nineteenth century. The prisoners at Die Schneider Lager restored it in 1943 when the factory began producing striped material for all the death camps. Each camp had its own pattern, and they programmed the loom to weave different stripes using this control panel.' He pointed to two rows of buttons along the front of the loom that looked like stops on an organ, each with a symbol next to it.

'That's Hebrew,' Marie-Claude said. 'Léo and I have been learning it.'

Hamilton nodded. 'The loom had twenty-two settings, the same as the number of letters in the Hebrew alphabet, and they assigned each button a letter. Sometimes the programmes for different patterns formed words, and because they were bringing this huge inanimate thing to life using Hebrew, they named the loom after the old Jewish legend: the Golem.'

Marie-Claude stared at the irregular lines on the waistcoat lining. 'If we can work out what letters produced this pattern, we can recreate the list and find the name of the missing survivor.' She turned to Hamilton. 'Can you get us into the museum?'

He nodded. 'I can get the keys from Guillaume Carrièrre, a friend of mine, though we won't be able to gain access until morning. The whole complex is on a timed alarm that can't be overridden. They had to upgrade the security after too many break-ins.'

'Who would want to break into a death camp museum?'

'Oh, you'd be surprised. There's been a huge resurgence of far-right politics, not only in France but also across the border in Germany. Some people see the Third Reich and Hitler's ambitions as a missed opportunity. There is a particularly nasty cult surrounding the most infamous Nazis, Artur Samler being one of them. They break in and try to steal things that belonged to him – or they did until we ramped up security. There are also the treasure hunters. They used to break in too.' He picked up a map from his desk and handed it to Marie-Claude. It showed the town and surrounding area and various trails with swastikas marked along them. 'They stay in my *gîte* sometimes, convinced there are undiscovered hoards of looted Nazi treasure around here somewhere. I give them these maps, but I think they're wasting their time. If there ever was any Nazi loot it will be long gone; too many Nazis escaped justice after the war for it to remain here. There are rumours that it was Samler who came back to claim it. Since he was the senior officer here, he'd certainly have known where any loot was hidden, *if* he survived.'

'Do you think he did?' Solomon asked.

'Well, his death was never properly confirmed, and I have discovered plenty of instances through the course of my research where people have claimed that he survived and changed his name and appearance so he could start a new life using gold stolen from the teeth of the people he murdered.' He turned to Marie-Claude. 'Maybe he was behind your grandfather's death. He would be too old now to do it himself, but his son could have killed him, or someone else loyal to the Samlers – the cruel nature of the murder and the slogan on the wall certainly fits.'

'*Das zuende bringen was begonnen wurde,*' Solomon murmured. 'Finishing what was begun. But why now? If it is Samler's son, he's had seventy years to track down the survivors and murder them.'

Hamilton shrugged. 'Maybe it's the seventieth anniversary picking at old wounds. Or perhaps the killer only recently learned the identities of the survivors. The museum has only been open for the last ten years, and during that time it has brought to light all kinds of archival material that had been lost for decades. But whoever the killer is, and whatever their motives, we need to find the name of the last survivor and warn him of the danger he's in before they do.'

Solomon nodded. 'What time can we get into the museum?'

'The security system is deactivated at six in the morning. We can do nothing in the meantime, so I suggest the sleepy young fellow next door has the right idea and we should all get some rest. You can stay in the *gîte*, there's no one there at the moment – there rarely is these days.' Hamilton picked up a key and moved across the hall to a door by the main stairs. He unlocked it and switched lights on to reveal another set of stairs. 'I separated off a section of the house to rent out and supplement my pension. Hasn't been quite the success I'd hoped. Thank God for the deluded treasure hunters and war freaks, without them it would be empty all year round. Anyway, you'll be quite private in there: the communicating doors to the main house have locks on with the keys on your side. There are two bedrooms with beds made up, so you can arrange your sleeping arrangements however you like. I'll wake you before six and we can go to the museum and see what names the Golem may whisper to us.'

90

Jean Baptiste sipped bitter coffee from a paper cup. LePoux smoked and drank beer from a can like he was holding a grudge against it. They were sitting in the car next to a fluorescent service station close to Bruère-Allichamps, the town at the exact centre of France. Baptiste figured it was as good a place as any to wait until they got another hit on the Bluetooth tile. So they sat, hooked on to the free Wi-Fi, like a spider at the centre of a giant, silent web waiting for a twitch.

A little after ten, a police alert pinged into the email account informing them that Madjid Lellouche had been found dead in his cell in Gaillac, apparent suicide, a confession note found at the scene. Ten minutes later the search alerts for Solomon Creed, Marie-Claude and Léo were downgraded from a 1 to a 3 – still active, but no longer urgent. No one would be looking for them that hard any more. No one but Baptiste and LePoux.

They found them a few minutes after eleven when the service station was closing. Baptiste was semi-dreaming of living in a house surrounded by fields with a cherry tree and a swing in it, and a bike lying on its side beneath it like the one he'd seen behind Marie-Claude's house. It was a nice dream, a dream of his possible future. The beep snapped him out of it and the screen on his laptop lit up the inside of the car as the map zoomed out showing a new blue dot way to the east of them, right by the German border.

'Where are they?' LePoux asked, throwing his cigarette out of the window and leaning in to look. Baptiste checked the location and distance. 'Place called Mulhouse,' he said. 'Three, maybe four hours' drive.' He watched the dot for ten more minutes, until the service station closed and the Wi-Fi cut out. 'Looks like they're settled somewhere for the night. Let's get going. We can get there while they're still asleep.'

X

*'The arc of the moral universe is long,
but it bends towards justice.'*

Martin Luther King Jr

Extract from

DARK MATERIAL – THE DEVIL'S TAILOR: DEATH AND LIFE IN DIE SCHNEIDER LAGER

⚜

By Herman Lansky

I stayed with the KRO into the spring of 1945. There were a couple more Samler sightings that turned out to be dead ends, but there were a lot of rumours flying around at the ragged end of the war. Lot of people chasing shadows.

The war in Europe officially ended on 8 May 1945 and the KRO was disbanded. I was finally free – and I had never felt more elated or more wretched in my life. Everyone I had ever known was dead and my home town of Łódź was gone, occupied by the Red Army, who had seized all of Poland in the end, not just the Eastern half promised by Hitler. Since I had nothing and no one, I decided to try and find the other survivors of Die Schneider Lager, the ones known as The Others, my brothers in tragedy. All I knew was that they had been transported away from the camp by an American unit. After that, they disappeared amid the chaos of post-war Europe. I didn't even know their names, but I searched for them regardless. I search for them still.

I moved to London, where some old business contacts were kind enough to offer me work and a friend found me a small flat in Hampstead, close to where he lived and overlooking the Heath. I have a job I enjoy, money of my own, and no one asks for my papers on my way in to work, no one points guns at me or makes me witness inhuman atrocities on a daily basis. And every day I try in my own small way, through my designs and my clothes, to make the world beautiful again.

It would be easy to give in to these gentle rhythms, let the past fade and the flow of my new life wash away my ugly and terrible memories. But I cannot. I must not. To have remained alive despite the evil that conspired to end me and my kind must have meaning and reason. As a survivor, I have a duty to honour the life I still have and remember those lives the Nazis stole. I have a voice when many do not, and I must speak for them, and remember for them – because they can do neither. And that is why I have written this memoir, to record what happened while it burns fresh in my mind, to ensure it can never be forgotten. For those of us who survived have a duty to remember and to guard against this ever happening again. We live because others died and suffered – and if we forget that, it will happen again.

It haunts me that there were other survivors of Die Schneider Lager whom I cannot find. It seems from the research I have undertaken that they do not wish to be found. Though I understand their desire for privacy, I believe they need to tell their story, or at the very least let me tell it for them.

It also haunts me that I was never completely sure if it was Artur Samler lying dead in that barn near Karlsruhe. It bothers me greatly that there were sightings of him afterwards, and also of his son, Günther. I feel it as a deep truth that, until I can be absolutely certain they are both dead, I cannot rest. So I search for them too. For if the root of the poisoned vine is not pulled out and burned away, if the seeds are allowed to scatter, the plant will grow again.

✢

91

Marie-Claude woke with a start. She was lying on a bed in a dark room with a slash of light spilling through a partially opened door. Léo lay next to her, his breathing deep and steady. She listened to the silent house, gradually remembering where she was, and how Solomon had carried Léo up the stairs and laid him on the bed, and how she had tucked him in and lay on the bed next to him for a second and that was the last thing she remembered. She looked over at the window to see if the sky was getting light but the shutters were closed and the room was deep in darkness.

She sat up, careful not to wake Léo, and spotted her backpack lying on the floor next to the bed where she'd left it. She reached over and felt around inside for her laptop and froze when she felt something else. She pulled out the object and held it up to the light coming in through the door. It was the gun Solomon had taken from the big man at the rest stop. It was heavier than she thought it would be. She turned it over in her hand, noticed a small lever by her thumb set to 'safe', and aimed at a chair in the corner of the room. She closed one eye and shook her head, dropped it back in the bag and pulled out her laptop instead.

The screen lit up when she opened it. She tapped a key

to notch down the brightness and squinted at the time. A little past five: too late to go back to sleep, too early to wake Léo. She closed the laptop and looked out at the hallway. She could hear something, a faint noise outside somewhere in the house, and wondered if it might be Solomon. She swung her legs off the bed and headed out into the bright hallway.

A staircase led down to the ground floor and up to another storey with a landing and two doors. One had a key in it, the second was slightly ajar and showed a dark bedroom beyond. She moved up the stairs and listened at the open door for the sound of breathing then pushed the door open to spill a light into the room. The bed was empty and un-slept in and she felt a twinge of disappointment that Solomon wasn't there. He was such a strange contradiction of a person – distant but intimate, apparently disinterested yet incredibly observant, like the way he'd spotted the open shutters from across the valley and realized what they might mean. She liked how he was with Léo too, the way he didn't talk down to him, the way he was interested in how he saw the world and celebrated his uniqueness – something she often struggled with.

She heard the sound again, a faint tearing sound, coming from the bottom of the stairs. He must be down there, looking through Hamilton's research. She followed the sound down the stairs and through the connecting door into the main house. There was a light on in Hamilton's study and the noise was definitely coming from there. She could smell something too, something sharp and chemical and getting stronger as she moved across the hall. She reached the door, looked into the office – and froze.

A strange man was by the desk, grabbing paperwork and

throwing it on to a huge messy pile on the floor. There was a fuel can next to it, the cap removed, and a shotgun propped against the desk. The man turned with a handful of paper and saw her. 'Where's the list?' he demanded.

Marie-Claude recognized him. He was one of Jean-Luc Belloq's cronies.

'The list,' LePoux repeated. 'Tell me where it is.' He reached for the shotgun and Marie-Claude's mind flared in fear. She ran. Across the hallway and back through the door to the *gîte*. She slammed it shut behind her and twisted the key to lock it just as something heavy crashed into the door on the other side. She leaped back and scrambled up the stairs, back to the bedroom where Léo slept.

Another bang echoed up the stairwell as LePoux kicked the door. He had a shotgun but she had a gun too. She remembered how it had sat heavy in her hand as she sighted on the chair. She had to get to it. Get the gun and drag Léo to the floor, hide behind the bed and wait for LePoux to come. She would have to fire the moment he appeared; he wouldn't expect her to have a gun, which meant she could take him by surprise while he was framed in the doorway. She didn't know if a mattress could stop shotgun pellets and couldn't afford to give him the chance. She had to get the gun, get down and shoot first. She burst through the door with all this running through her mind, ready to grab Léo and shake him awake if he wasn't already. But Léo was already awake. He was sitting up in bed, eyes wide and frightened. A man with a gun sat next to him with tears in his eyes. He held Léo tight and stroked his hair.

Jean Baptiste. Reunited with his son.

92

Solomon walked the dark, silent streets of Mulhouse. He had tried to sleep but his mind wouldn't let him. It kept returning to the camp. There was something familiar about it, something that tugged and niggled until it finally pulled him off his bed and into the night, drawing him on until he stood once again by the gates of Die Schneider Lager.

He studied the darkness beyond the barbed wire. The wind had dropped now and there was a stillness to the place. It felt colder here too, a steady breeze at his back flowing steadily into the camp, and he recalled something Lansky had written in his memoir:

. . . there was someone else there on that final day . . . He wore a beautiful pale suit, perfectly cut, and I remember thinking he must be some high-ranking officer and that his arrival must mean the end was close – either surrender or evacuation. It was neither.

Solomon focused on the memory. Tried to think himself into it and summon one of his own. He laid his hand on the locked gates and they shifted and rattled, creating ripples in the darkness beyond the fence as if something had been disturbed by the sound and was now swirling and eddying into form as the chill breeze at his back thickened, like it was the cold memory of all the souls who had flowed into this place.

He could see the buildings now, sketching the shape of the camp on the surface of the night: the guard houses and the loom sheds and a vast empty space where the main factory had stood. Beyond it, piles of rubble showed where more recent excavations had taken place and a new memory surfaced along with a sharp pain in his arm as Solomon realized what it was. They were digging where the cellar had been, the place where The Others had been found. And there was something there, he was sure of it, something hidden away and waiting for him to come and reclaim it.

Rain started to fall, a soft sighing in the night, and Solomon moved along the fence, searching for a way inside. He reached the foot of a guard tower and the night exploded into brightness. He turned to the light, shielding his eyes against the painful glare of twin headlamps, and saw a figure move in front of them, a gun visible in his hand.

'Marie-Claude and Léo – where are they?'

Solomon recognized the voice. 'Commandant Amand,' he said. 'You're a long way out of your jurisdiction.'

'I'm still in France, which means I have more authority than you. Where are they?'

Solomon nodded back down the road. 'In town.'

A set of handcuffs thudded on the ground at Solomon's feet. 'Put those on and take us to them. And by God if they are hurt or distressed in any way I'll shoot you myself and save the cost of a trial.'

Solomon picked up the handcuffs, snicked them over his wrists and stood with his arms crossed in front of him. 'You said "take *us* to them". Who else is with you?'

He heard a car door open and the headlights shifted

slightly as someone got out. Solomon tilted his head back, sniffing the air for a hint of who was there and caught something beneath the smell of rain and ancient bone, something hard and metallic and chemical. 'I know you,' he said, and the mark on his arm flared in sudden pain.

The other figure stepped in front of the headlights and Solomon squinted at the silhouette. He couldn't see the man's face but his outline was familiar, the bulk of him, the way he moved – ursine, bear-like. 'Magellan!' he said, and the pain in his arm doubled at the mention of his name.

'You remember me,' a voice answered, deep and low and familiar.

'Doctor Cezar Magellan,' Solomon murmured and his feeling of déjà-vu shifted away from the camp and on to the dark figure in front of him. He remembered being in a situation like this before, with Magellan silhouetted by a different light, and pain, great pain, not only in his arm but deep down in his core, like something was being burned out of him. 'You took something from me,' he said. 'I remember the pain of it. I remember wanting to get away, as far away from you as possible.'

'And you did,' Magellan replied. 'But now it's time to go back again. I can help you remember who you are and return what you have lost. I can give you back what you seek. Your identity.'

93

Jean Baptiste stared up at Marie-Claude with eyes that were cold despite the tears that glazed them.

'Where's the boyfriend?' he said.

Marie-Claude looked at Léo, captive in his father's arms. Where was Solomon? Where was Hamilton? Surely someone must have heard all this noise? 'He's not my boyfriend,' she said, trying to reassure Léo with her eyes. 'I don't know where he is.'

'Bullshit. Don't you protect him.'

'Or what? What will you do, beat me up in front of your son again? Shoot me?' There was a splintering sound below as the door gave way. 'Let him go. Let Léo go, you're frightening him.'

'And why is that? Why is he frightened of his own father? What poison have you been telling him about me?'

'I haven't been telling him anything. What am I supposed to say? I don't know you any more.' She stared at Léo, his eyes huge even without his glasses on. He hadn't made a sound the whole time and his silence brought back painful memories. 'Did you know that Léo didn't talk for two years after you beat me?' she said. 'The doctors said it was PTSD. What you did to me gave your two-year-old son such a severe psychological trauma that he shut down for *two* years. I don't need to tell Léo anything to poison him against you. You did it yourself. When you broke my bones, you broke this family too.'

Baptiste pulled Léo closer, his hand flexing around the gun. 'I didn't break the family, you did, with your lies. But I can fix it. I'm not having some Jew whore fill his head with shit about me or how the world works. A boy needs a father. He's coming with me.'

LePoux appeared on the landing behind her. 'There's no one else here,' he said. 'I say we burn the place down and get out.'

'What about the list?'

'Fucking place is full of lists. The big man said bring it back or destroy it. I say we torch the place and maybe the fire will flush the others out from where they're hiding. Kill two birds with one stone.'

Baptiste nodded and continued to stroke Léo's hair. Marie-Claude could imagine what he was thinking. If they were going to burn the place down, they could easily do it with her inside, like Lansky's flat all over again. That way, Baptiste would be Léo's only surviving parent. Without proof that he was involved in her death, he'd probably get custody. And there would be no proof. Baptiste was an ex-cop, he knew how to get rid of evidence. She looked at Léo and thought about grabbing him and running. Then she heard the car, coming up the hill and getting closer. Baptiste heard it too. 'Someone's coming,' he said. 'Could be the old man or the boyfriend. Turn off the lights, let's wait and see.' He put his hand over Léo's mouth to keep him quiet and looked up at Marie-Claude. 'I hope it's the boyfriend. Him I would really like to meet.'

459

LePoux flicked the switch in the hallway and plunged them into darkness.

Me too – Marie-Claude thought, remembering what she'd seen Solomon do at the rest stop – *I'd love for you to meet him too.*

94

Solomon sat in the passenger seat of the Range Rover, a confusion of thoughts and feelings churning inside him and clouding his mind. The short chain of his handcuffs was threaded through the seat belt. Amand was in the rear, his service pistol pressed into the back of Solomon's seat. Magellan drove.

Magellan.

The name had risen in Solomon's mind along with the mark that continued to burn on his shoulder at his presence. He had assumed it was another half-memory surfacing, a clue that might lead him back to remembering who he was. And yet now he had found him he felt an instinctive fear towards this man – fear of what he might tell him, fear of what he had already done – and his urge was to get away from him again, as fast and as far as possible.

They turned on to the road leading up the side of the valley and Solomon stared through the rain and wipers at the distant line of stone houses. There was a dark stillness to Hamilton's house. And there was something else.

'That car,' Solomon said, 'it wasn't there earlier.'

Amand peered at the car parked on the street. 'Maybe someone came home late.'

Solomon studied the way it was parked, the steam on the windows, the grime around the wheels. 'I don't think so. Look at the registration plate.'

Amand leaned forward, saw the Cathar cross above the number 81 on the right-hand side of the plate. It was a Cordes plate, not a Mulhouse one. 'Pull up behind it,' he said. 'And switch off the headlamps.'

Magellan did as he asked and they cruised to a standstill a few metres back from the car. Solomon listened through the low moan of the wind and soft patter of rain for any sound coming from inside the house, but heard nothing. He breathed in, trying to catch a scent of the place, but the wind was in the wrong direction.

'Which house are they in?' Amand asked.

'The one with the flagpole. Who else is looking for them?'

Amand stiffened. 'Did Marie-Claude say something?'

'No, but your reaction did. It's Léo's father, isn't it?'

Amand didn't reply. 'I'll go ahead and check it out.'

'No,' Solomon said. 'Let me. I've been inside. I know the layout.'

Amand shook his head. 'I've spent most of today chasing you, I'm hardly going to let you go again that easy.' He turned to Magellan. 'If I'm not out in five minutes, call the local police.' He got out of the car and the wind gusted in, bringing the snapping sound of the flag and the smell of the night – woodsmoke and rain. Amand closed the door softly and moved towards the house, leaving the smell of the night in the car. There was something in there, something small and chemical and Solomon focused on it as he watched Amand draw closer to the house. He paused by the front door, pulled a bottle from his pocket and popped something into his mouth before heading round the back, disappearing from sight just as Solomon's mind lit up with a single word identifying the scent. 'Call the police,' Solomon said, turning to Magellan. 'Call them now.'

Magellan looked at him in a strange detached way, like Solomon was a horse he was considering buying. 'He said to give him five minutes.'

'That's because he doesn't know that whoever's in that house brought petrol with them.'

95

Léo breathed heavily against the hand clamped across his mouth. It was dark in the room with the lights off, but he could still see the colours, swirling in the dark like paint on black card: deep green and yellow for his mama, angry and scared; blues and reds for his father, good colours smeared with bad; and muddy, gloomy greys for the man with the shotgun. There was no brightness in him at all and Léo was frightened of him the most. He was like a vulture, a death creature with dull, greasy feathers.

He heard a noise. Downstairs. Léo wanted it to be Solomon, wanted him to come and save them again like he had on the motorway, but he knew it couldn't be him. Solomon wouldn't make any noise at all. The man with the muddy colours stepped out into the hallway and disappeared and Léo felt panic rise in his chest. He wanted to call out and warn whoever was downstairs that someone was coming but the hand on his mouth was too tight. He knew that the muddy-coloured man would kill whoever was down there, because his colours revealed his darkness. And if Léo didn't warn that person, his death would be partly Léo's fault. He had to try something. He opened his mouth and bit down as hard as he could and the hand jerked away, enough for him to snatch a breath, and he let out a shout, loud and short. Too short. The hand grabbed him by the throat and threw him on his back, his father's face appeared, so close that Léo could see the fury in his eyes. His colours were black now, black and red. He grabbed his father's wrist, his two small hands not even big enough to go all the way round, and tried to pull the hand away. But he was too strong. He could feel the hand squeezing his throat and there was nothing he could do to move it. Then a light came on, sudden and blinding after the darkness, and his father looked up and something hit him hard in the face, throwing him backwards and jarring his hand away from Léo's throat.

Léo gasped for air and looked over at the door expecting Solomon to be standing there, but saw his mother instead, holding a broken chair in her hands. She staggered to regain her balance, lifted the chair again, but his father kicked out and caught her knee and she screamed in pain and crumpled to the floor.

Baptiste was on top of her almost before she hit the ground. He pinned her down and started hitting her, his colours blooming red. Léo looked up at the door but there was no sign of Solomon, no sign of anyone. It was happening again, the nightmare happening again, but no one was coming. No one would save them this time. He had to be the one. He had to become the superhero.

He looked around for a weapon, anything to stop his father beating his mama, saw her backpack on the floor by the bed and reached for it. Behind him his mama cried out but the dull thud of another punch silenced her. Léo saw the gun the moment he opened the backpack. It was heavy in his hand but he knew how to do this, he'd seen it a million times in comics and in movies – two hands to keep it steady, aim at the centre, squeeze the trigger, don't jerk it.

He swung the gun round and saw his father sitting up and looking down at his mama. Léo steadied the gun in a two-handed grip and saw what his father held in his hand. 'No!' he screamed.

His father looked up, his gun whipping up to point at Léo.

The flash of a gunshot lit the room.

96

Amand was in the study, holding his arm across his face against the smell of petrol, when he heard the cry, short and high-pitched, like a child. It set him sprinting out of the study and into the darkened hallway, leading with his gun. It had come from above, somewhere on the far side of the house. There was a door ahead, set into the wall by the stairs, and he surged towards it, pushed it open and swept the small hallway beyond.

There was a door directly opposite and another set of stairs leading up. The door was open slightly, the room dark, and there was a light on in the upstairs landing. He could hear sounds too, like a struggle. He knew he should check the room on the ground floor first to make sure it was clear, but he was on his own and the sounds of the struggle were coming from above him. Then he heard Léo scream 'No!' and he leaped up the stairs as a gunshot rang out above him and he sensed movement behind. Instinct made him drop and the shotgun blast tore up the wall around him and turned the bannisters to splinters. He heard another cry from above, Marie-Claude this time, but he stayed focused on the bottom of the stairs, firing blindly back through the smoke, three shots grouped at the spot by the door where the shotgun blast had bloomed in the dark.

He slid down the stairs on his side, blood blinding him in his left eye from a head-wound. He fired again, two more shots, the muzzle flashes lighting up the smoky dark. He came to rest in a pile at the bottom of the stairs, his brain screaming orders but his body not responding. It was darker after the brightness of the gunshots and he couldn't make out much through the smoke and blood that stung his eyes. He blinked to get his night vision back and tried to breathe deeply, but the tightness in his chest felt like it was expanding, trying to split him open from within, and pain lanced through his left arm, spreading through his shoulder and chest. Verbier had warned him this would happen if he didn't take it easy, but what choice had he had?

The pain continued to spread and he raised his gun and pointed it through the smoky darkness at the doorway, waiting for his heart to burst or someone to fire at him. The smoke cleared a little and he saw something lying on the floor in front of him, a body. The light filtering down from the landing picked out the outline and Amand recognized who it was. LePoux's sightless eyes stared up at him. A shotgun lay on the floor beside him. He had two holes in his centre mass and his shirt was drenched in blood.

Amand flexed his left hand and looked down at himself. His jacket was shredded and his chest was wet and stained red from multiple wounds. He looked up the splintered staircase at the light above him, tried listening out for any new sounds but his ears were ringing from the gunshots. He needed to get up the stairs and make sure Léo and Marie-Claude were OK, only his body didn't want to move. He could feel it shutting down as the pain grew out from his arm and chest. But he had to move, somehow he had to. Because if LePoux was here, he knew that Baptiste would be here too.

97

The gunshot snapped Marie-Claude to attention. She looked up at Baptiste, straddling her and pinning her to the floor. He had a gun in his hand and was pointing it into the corner, the corner where . . .

'NO!!'

She exploded in rage and fear, bucking against the floor and battering Baptiste with her arms to get him off her. The bed was in the way, blocking her view of the corner where Léo had been, where Baptiste had been pointing his gun. She thrashed harder and Baptiste tilted backwards, offering no resistance. She wriggled out from under him and clambered up the side of the bed and sobbed in relief when she saw Léo, standing against the wall, staring at Baptiste. The gun looked huge in his tiny hand. He blinked and looked at her and she saw a flicker of pain in his eyes as he saw her beaten face.

'I remembered what to do,' he said, sounding dazed and distant. 'They always thumb the safety off before squeezing the trigger. I remembered.'

Marie-Claude scrambled across the bed and hugged him tight, reaching for the gun and pulling it from his fingers. She turned back to look at Baptiste. He was slumped on the floor and against the wall, clutching at his chest where blood ran thick over the hand that still held the gun. She could hear the wheeze and whistle of his breathing. Baptiste looked up at her, his eyes filled with hate. He tried to lift his gun but only managed to raise it a few inches before it dropped back down again.

Marie-Claude looked past him into the smoke-filled hallway. She had heard the gunshots coming from downstairs. LePoux was out there and he had a shotgun. She remembered the pile of paper in the study, the open can of petrol next to it. Her instinct was to hunker down and stay quiet, but they couldn't. They needed to get out of here.

'Come on, Léo,' she whispered, her mouth stinging where her lip was split. She scooped her rucksack off the floor and slid it on to her shoulder. She listened out for any noises in the house, but all she could hear was the wet sucking sound of Baptiste's breathing. She looked at the gun clutched in his hand and thought about taking it from him, but it was covered in blood and she didn't want to touch him or go anywhere near him. Instead, she grabbed Léo's hand and pulled him after her, switching the light off before stepping out into the smoky corridor, leaving Baptiste alone in the dark with the awful sound of his own breathing.

98

Solomon turned to Magellan at the first gunshot. 'We need to help them.'

'No,' Magellan said, 'we really don't.' He switched on the engine and started to turn the car round.

A shotgun blast shook the night, followed by the crackle of more gunfire. 'But there's a woman and young boy in that house. He's the reason I'm here. I need to save him.'

Magellan shook his head. 'A fantasy. This quest you think you're on, to save people and discover who you are, is an invention, a narrative to frame your delusions. You don't need to save anyone to find out who you are. I can tell you who you are.'

Pain burned on Solomon's arm. 'Turn back,' he said. They were picking up speed now, racing along wet roads towards the town centre.

Magellan glanced at him. 'You'd rather go back there and help those strangers than find out who you are?'

Solomon did want to know who he was, had walked thousands of miles to try and find out, but there was something stronger compelling him, something bigger than himself. 'We need to go back,' he repeated.

Magellan shook his head. 'A neighbour will have heard the gunshots and called the police by now. We can't risk it.'

Solomon knew he was probably right. He was a fugitive from the French authorities so it was safer for him to get away. But his own safety wasn't important, not as important as his responsibility to Léo, the burning pain in his shoulder told him that much, and he trusted that more than anything Magellan told him. 'Tell me one thing,' he said. 'How is it that I know many things yet nothing of myself? How can I know the phone number for an obscure address in France, or what fear smells like, or that if you hold your finger against your wrist while putting on handcuffs you leave enough of a gap to be able to escape?'

He held his right hand up, free from the cuff, then moved, fast and fluid, unclipping Magellan's seat belt with one hand while he grabbed the steering wheel with the other and yanked down hard.

Magellan stamped on the brakes but it was too late, the front dipped savagely and their momentum flipped them over. The interior exploded with dust and noise as airbags deployed. The car rolled down the road three times before skidding to a halt on its side in a shower of sparks and shattered glass.

Solomon unclipped his belt, battered airbags down and wriggled out of the broken side window. He heard a moan and Magellan's face appeared among the deflating airbags, a large cut above his eye dripping blood on to his face. He looked up at Solomon and tried to unclip his seat belt but some internal injury sent agony lancing through him and he cried out in pain. 'Help me,' he said, through gritted teeth. 'Only I can tell you who you really are.'

Solomon saw something in amongst the wreckage. 'I'd

rather find out for myself,' he said, reaching inside for the file with his photograph clipped to the front that had spilled from Magellan's briefcase.

Then he turned and started to run, cutting across driveways and gardens to take the most direct route up the hill and back to Hamilton's house.

99

Marie-Claude listened through the silence, her eyes wide against the dark. The shotgun blast had come from downstairs so they couldn't go that way.

She heard a car starting up outside and driving away. Maybe LePoux had left, scared away by the gunfire, but she couldn't risk it. Pulling Léo after her, she set off up the stairs, keeping away from the bannister in case the *vigneron* was lurking below, pointing the barrel of a shotgun up and waiting for movement.

They reached the top landing and she pressed her ear to the connecting door for a moment before twisting the key to unlock it. The door creaked open, revealing the dark upper landing of the main house. She pulled Léo through the door, locked it behind them and left the key in the lock. She listened again, hoping for a friendly sound, a voice calling out for them, Solomon or Hamilton, but all she heard was the thump of her own heartbeat and the hiss of blood in her ears.

Marie-Claude looked down at Léo, pressed her finger to her lips as she moved to the stairs and they started to creep down, one step at a time, listening the whole way. She could smell a burned salt odour that reminded her of Bastille Day fireworks and she gripped Léo's hand tighter as she realized that the gunshots must have happened here and that whoever fired them might still be around. She could see the front door now, across the hallway from the stairs, and she swept the darkness with the gun, ready to fire at anything that moved or stood in her way as she moved towards it. The doors to the lounge and Hamilton's study were both open, the rooms beyond dark, and she caught a new smell, like paint or petrol, and her lizard brain lit up with the urge to flee.

They reached the door and she turned back to the hallway, pushing Léo behind her and fumbling with the lock. She heard a noise, like something being dragged up the *gîte* stairs, and panic rose up as she considered what it might be. She twisted the handle and the front door thankfully opened, bringing a blast of cold night air into the house. She saw movement, over by Hamilton's study, and she whipped the gun towards it. The door creaked a little then settled.

Only the wind. It was only the wind.

She backed out through the door, closed it behind her and leaned back against the stone wall of the house, allowing herself to breathe for what seemed like the first time in hours. She looked down at Léo, smiling in an effort to reassure him that they were safe.

'Find the car keys, Léo,' she whispered, handing him the backpack. She scanned the driveway, the shadowy garden, the street beyond, keeping guard until Léo held the keys up with a tiny jingling sound. 'Good boy,' she said. 'Let's go.'

Marie-Claude forced herself away from the solid re-assuring stone wall of the house and moved across the drive, heading back to where she'd parked the car. She pressed the electronic key fob and the indicator lights flashed, too bright in the darkness, and opened the back door for Léo, dropping her backpack on the floor and strapping him in out of ingrained habit.

She didn't notice the shutter on the first-floor window swing open, or the gun appear and point down at her, wavering slightly in the darkness.

100

The gun felt heavy in Baptiste's hand and it took every grain of his dwindling energy to keep it steady.

He could feel the blood filling his lungs, drowning him breath by breath, his strength leaking out of him with every heartbeat. The journey across the bedroom floor to open the shutter had been a pure effort of will, every inch a tiny victory. One single thought had driven him on, acting like a light in the growing dark:

Léo had done this to him. His own son had shot him.

He could see him now, tiny and distant in the back seat of the car, coming in and out of sight as Marie-Claude strapped him in. She had done this. She had turned his son against him.

He took a breath to try and steady his aim and his chest wound sucked and gurgled. He was waiting for Marie-Claude to stand up and move away from Léo, but she was taking too long. What kind of stupid bitch worries about seat belts at a time like this? He took another breath and felt the gun get heavier.

She had ruined his son. Poisoned him. But he knew he could fix him again. It wasn't Léo's fault that he'd shot him, it was her fault. He would make him see that, in time. He just needed to get her out of the way. He held the gun steady, the sights wavering around the distant figure of his ex-wife.

He closed one eye. And fired.

101

The car window exploded and Marie-Claude dropped instinctively to the ground then remembered Léo, trapped in his seat and now fully exposed. 'Get down,' she shouted, and slammed his door shut.

The gunshot had come from behind her and she felt the tickle of something on her face. When she touched it, her hand came back bloody.

Jesus. She'd been shot.

She jackknifed in panic, scrambling across the road surface to the driver's door, desperate to get away before the shooting started again. Maybe she hadn't been shot. Maybe the flying glass had cut her.

She wrenched open the driver's side door. 'Léo,' she hissed as she crawled inside. 'Speak to me, Léo.'

'I'm OK, Mama. I'm keeping down. I took my belt off.'

'Good boy. Stay down.'

She got inside, staying as low as she could, dropped the gun in her lap and fumbled for the ignition. She looked back at the house. Saw the open shutter on the first floor, the bedroom they had been in, and realized what must have happened. She should have taken Baptiste's gun but she had been too afraid and now they were in danger. She needed to get out of here fast because if she could see the window it meant he could see her. She fumbled for the ignition but couldn't find it and panic rose again until she remembered that the hire car had a start button that worked when the keys were close. She found it on the dashboard, pushed it and muttered a silent prayer when the car started first time.

New movement in the house caught her attention, an orange light flickering in one of the downstairs windows. Hamilton's study.

Where was Hamilton?

His car was here but there was no sign of him. No sign of Solomon either. She needed to get away and call the police. She had no choice. As soon as they were safely away, she would call Amand and tell him everything.

She put the car in gear and a fresh gunshot flickered and cracked in the upper window. The loud bang on her window made her scream.

102

The bullet caught Baptiste in the shoulder, twisting him round as he fell. He took a slurping breath and frowned when the smoke cleared and he saw who was lying on the floor with his gun pointing at him.

'You lost weight,' Baptiste wheezed.

'About thirty kilos,' Amand said, struggling for breath after his climb.

'You look good on it.' Baptiste smiled, then something cruel crept into his eyes. 'You always wanted to be . . . alone in a bedroom with me . . . didn't you, you fucking faggot? You had to go and shoot me . . . to finally . . . make it happen.'

'I never wanted you,' Amand said. 'Not you. I don't know who you are.'

Baptiste felt pain in his shoulder where the bullet had hit him. The weight of his gun was pinning his hand to the floor. The idea of lifting it seemed impossible but he had to. He wanted to put a bullet right in Amand's earnest, queer face. 'How come you decided . . . to shape up?' he said, his shallow, wheezing breaths fracturing his sentences. 'You trying to muscle in . . . on Marie-Claude and Léo . . .? Fags don't normally get to have families, do they . . . only if they steal . . . someone else's.'

'They're my friends,' Amand said. 'And you love your friends as much as family. You look out for them.'

'You didn't look out for me.'

'You're not my friend. Not any more. I don't know what you are. Do you?'

Baptiste smiled and took as deep a breath as he could manage. 'I know exactly who I am,' he said. 'I'm a fucking patriot.'

He hauled his gun up from the floor and gunshots lit the room.

103

Marie-Claude jerked away from the window, fumbling for the gun in her lap. She found it and twisted towards where the bang had come from. Hamilton was standing by the car, his face creased in confusion as he looked between the gun in her hand and the fire rapidly taking hold of his house. 'What happened here?' he muttered.

Marie-Claude reached into the back and opened the door. 'Get in. Some people came. There's been shooting. Solomon's gone. I didn't know where you were either.'

'Couldn't sleep,' Hamilton said, his eyes staring at the flames growing brighter. 'I went to my friend's place to get the keys to the museum.' His face glowed orange as the fire took hold. 'I need to go in—'

'No, it's too dangerous. They're still in there. We need to get away and call the police and the *pompiers*. I smelled petrol inside.'

Hamilton shook his head. 'It's like Herman Lansky all over again. They want to destroy all the evidence of what happened here. They want us to stay silent.' He clamped his jaw shut and some steel returned to his eyes. 'Let them try. They can burn my research but they can't take away what's in here.' He tapped his head and pulled his phone from his pocket. 'We should go to the museum, make sure they don't destroy the Golem too. My car is parked down the street. I'll call the police and the *pompiers* on the way to see if they can save what's left of my house. You head to the museum. I'll meet you there.'

104

Solomon vaulted a fence and saw flames flickering ahead of him. He ran on, across several gardens, on to the road and up the hill, the cold night air razoring his lungs. He could see Hamilton's house now, fire framed in the ground-floor windows. The hire car had gone, but the one with Cordes plates was still there.

He ran straight up to the house, dropped the Magellan file by the door and burst into the hallway, ducking beneath the thick smoke filling the upper part of the hallway and swirling up the stairs. The study was an inferno, paper curling and twisting in the updraught and sending glowing embers floating through the smoke-choked air.

Solomon moved to the door leading to the *gîte* and saw a body beyond, dead eyes staring upward. He recognized the man from the vineyard and flexed his hand at the memory of his cane. He wondered why the man was here and how his story threaded into his own, but didn't have time to stop. He could smell more blood up the stairs, coming from the bedroom where he had last seen Marie-Claude and Léo.

He took the stairs three at a time and saw Amand lying on the landing, half-in and half-out of the door. The bedroom beyond was dark and reeked of blood. He moved closer, watching for movement but saw none. He reached the door, raised his hand to the hallway light-switch and flicked it on.

Light flooded the hallway and bedroom and Solomon listened for a response – an intake of breath, a tightening of a hand on a gun – but heard nothing. He peered round the doorframe and saw Baptiste slumped against the far wall, two bullet-holes in his chest and one in his left cheek. The shot to the face had killed him, blowing out the blood vessels in one eye and turning it a deep red. Solomon scanned the room. No sign of Léo or Marie-Claude. The backpack had gone too. He knelt by Amand and felt for a pulse in his neck. He was bloodied and unconscious but alive. He slapped his face until his eyelids flickered and hauled him to his feet, threw one arm over his shoulder and half-carried, half-dragged him down the stairs and out of the smoke-filled house.

'Where are they?' Solomon said. 'Where are Léo and Marie-Claude? Who took them? Where did they go?'

'I don't know,' Amand replied. 'I heard a car drive away. I think it was them. Baptiste was shooting. I had to stop him. Had to . . .' He grimaced and clutched his chest.

Solomon remembered something from earlier, felt in Amand's pocket and found the pill bottle. He took one and pushed it into Amand's mouth. 'Put it under your tongue,' he said. 'It will ease the pain until an ambulance gets here.'

Amand nodded and looked up. 'Where's Magellan?'

'Gone,' Solomon said, looking at the car with the Cordes plates. 'Can you drive?'

Amand shook his head. 'I don't think so.'

'OK, don't move.' Solomon got up and ran back to the house, using his arms to shield his face against the flames and heat now pouring through the study door. He returned to LePoux's body and patted him down, his eyes stinging from the smoke. He found some cash, a phone and a key fob before running from the house, gasping for air and blinking away smoke. He scooped the Magellan file from the ground, pressed the button on the key fob and the indicators lit up on the car with the Cordes plates.

The inside of the car was littered with food wrappers, empty bottles and cigarette butts, and smelt of men and long miles. There was also a bag with a laptop. Solomon sat in the driver's seat, placed the Magellan file on the seat next to him and opened the laptop. He squinted at the sudden brightness and saw a map on the screen showing the streets of Mulhouse with a logo saying 'GeoTracker' above it. The map widened and a small blue dot appeared to the northwest of him. This was how they had found them – not through car registrations or security camera footage but using some other device. It was still tracking them. He studied the map, realized where they were and ran back to Amand. 'I need you to drive to the museum,' he said, but Amand was unconscious and his pulse was weak and erratic. A siren wailed in the night, urgent and getting closer. He patted him down, found a pen and a notebook, scribbled a note in it before running back to the car.

He sat behind the wheel and stared at the dashboard but nothing seemed familiar, no memories came flooding back. He found the slot for the key and twisted it to start the engine. He had sat next to Marie-Claude for long miles, casually observing her driving, and yet his mind could not conjure one single practical memory that might tell him now how to do it. All he got was a jumble of half-remembered things that swarmed and shifted the more he concentrated on them.

He forced the car into gear with a horrible crunching sound and the car lurched forward and stalled. He turned the key again and the car hopped forward with each cough of the engine. He pulled it out of gear, got the engine started again and pressed one of the foot pedals down. This time the gear went in smoothly and he pressed another pedal that made the engine race. He raised his first foot and the car lurched forward and stalled again. Outside, the sirens grew louder and a new thought surfaced in his mind:

Your journey is not supposed to be easy, it whispered. And he knew it was right.

He pulled the keys from the ignition, grabbed the Magellan file from the passenger seat and ran from the car and the burning house.

105

They followed Hamilton's car down the rain-glossed streets of Mulhouse, cold night air blowing in through the shattered window, until Die Schneider Lager slid into view again, framed by the tunnel of trees. Léo felt frightened at the sight of it. He'd been glad earlier when his mama had not wanted to go closer. Places didn't usually have a colour but this one did, all purple and dark, like something bad and unhappy and secret, squatting in the middle of the forest.

The car ahead of them pulled to a halt in front of the gates and the old man waved them over.

'Park there,' Hamilton said, pointing to a loading bay and handing his mama a set of keys, one large one small. 'The big one disarms the alarm,' Hamilton explained, 'the control box is by the gate. Turn the key to the right and the red light should go green. The smaller key is for the padlock on the gate. We'll go on in my car because the security cameras won't recognize your registration plate and it'll set the alarms off.' He turned and smiled at Léo. 'You want to hop in, little man?'

Léo looked at his mama, feeling panicky at the thought of being separated from her.

'It's OK, Léo,' she said, 'I'll only be a moment. And it'll be warmer in Monsieur Hamilton's car.'

Léo opened his door and bits of shattered glass tinkled to the ground. He stepped out into the cold and across to the back seat of the old man's car, which smelled like woodsmoke and hospitals. He watched his mama drive away, park their car and start fiddling around with a white box fixed to the fence. He could see she was scared from her colours. He was scared too. The only person who seemed calm was the old man. His colours were calm too, pale green and blue as the sky, although there was also something else there, something he'd never seen before, a dark patch, small and black, that shifted through the blue like a crow or a raven in flight. Hamilton reached over to the glove compartment and a small black feather floated to the floor as he opened it and began searching through the pill bottles inside. 'You're sick, aren't you?' Leo said, realizing what the old man's dark spot must be.

'Yes.' Hamilton turned in his seat to face him. 'Yes, I am. Why do you think that?'

Léo bit his lip and thought about making something up, but figured someone who was really sick wouldn't want to be fibbed to. 'I can see people's colours,' he said. 'Everyone has them. Yours are mainly blue, but you also have a piece of black in it.'

Hamilton smiled. 'You can see that in me – the egg?'

Léo frowned. 'It looks more like a bird to me.'

'No. It's an egg,' Hamilton said, leaning in closer, 'and it contains something wonderful. Would you like to see what's inside it?'

Léo pressed back in his seat, a little scared by what the old man was asking. He didn't want to see what was in the egg, not at all, but before he could say anything the dark circle exploded, driving the pale blue away until all that was left

490

was a complete and rustling blackness that Léo recognized. He had seen it before, outside his house, trying to get in.

He opened his mouth to scream and warn his mother that the shadow was here but a hand clamped over his mouth and something sharp jabbed into his leg and the world began to melt all around him. He tried to bite the hand, like he had bitten his father, but his body was going slack, like someone had let the air out of him, and all he could do was stare at the blackness, so close and huge that it blocked out everything, until his eyes flickered shut and the darkness swallowed him entirely.

106

Marie-Claude twisted the key in the alarm panel, her hand shaking from cold and adrenaline. Seeing Baptiste again had lit a bonfire of fear inside her. She had spent years of therapy extinguishing and scattering all the flammable emotional material of what had happened to her until she'd finally felt safe and in control. Then there he was, sitting on a bed, holding their son, and the whole inferno had roared back into life again.

She moved across to the gate, unlocked the padlock and pulled the chain free with a loud clatter that echoed away into the darkness. The camp was silent as a graveyard. It *was* a graveyard. There was no one here – no lights, no sounds. So where was Solomon? He'd said he was here to save Léo, but in the end she'd done it, and Léo had shot Baptiste to save her. She felt her face, the cold tips of her fingers soothing against the bruising and cuts. It wasn't that bad. She'd heal. She did the last time.

She turned and looked back down the road, half-convinced Baptiste might be shuffling towards her out of the dark, un-killable and unstoppable, but the road was empty. Nothing there. She started to walk back to Hamilton's car and saw him, turned around in the driver's seat, leaning over Léo and shaking him.

She started to run. Léo was slumped in the back. Eyes closed. Hamilton holding his arms and trying to shake him awake. She grabbed the handle of the rear door and yanked it open. 'What happened?'

'I don't know. He said he felt hot, then had some kind of seizure.'

Marie-Claude slapped his face to try and rouse him. 'Léo, baby, wake up.' He didn't feel hot but he was floppy and unresponsive. It had to be shock. Hardly surprising, after he'd been forced to shoot his own father. 'We need to get him to a hospital,' she said. Something sharp stung her neck and she flinched away from it. Coldness spread out from the sting and she felt her whole body going slack and heavy. She slumped down in the seat, tried to get up but couldn't. She looked up at Hamilton and saw the needle in his hand and the black scarf around his neck that he was pulling up over his face.

'No doctors,' Hamilton said. 'No distractions. You must help me decipher the list, then it will all be over.'

Marie-Claude felt like she was falling away from the world and Hamilton was talking to her down a deep well.

'You need to help me,' he said, his words growing faint and distant as the world around her went dark. 'You need to help me finish what was begun.'

107

The fire truck pulled up in front of the burning house and steel-helmeted *pompiers* ran from it, pulling high-pressure water hoses behind them. The trained medics clustered around the body lying in the driveway as water arced through the night and hissed against hot stone.

Louis LeVay stepped from his car and pulled his police cap on to his head. The house looked lost, fire roaring out of an open upstairs window as well as lighting up the whole of the ground floor. He moved over to the *pompiers* manning the hose. 'Save the neighbours' houses,' he shouted above the roar of the fire, 'this one's finished.' The man nodded and switched the jet to the wall of the neighbouring house closest to the inferno.

LeVay moved over to the medics. 'He OK?'

'He's had a heart attack,' the medic replied. 'We found this on him.' He handed LeVay a notebook.

LeVay angled the book towards the flickering light of the burning house and read the old-fashioned handwriting:

This man is Commandant Benoît Amand, Cordes police.

Two more dead in the house.

'He's police,' LeVay said nodding at the man on the ground. 'Get him to hospital fast.' He moved away from the medics and pulled his phone from his pocket.

One down and two dead. It was a mess and he felt angry that it had come to his town. He had come straight from a car wreck on the main road with no sign of anyone involved. Things like this did not usually happen in Mulhouse. He looked at the burning house. He knew who lived here and felt no love for the Englishman, raking up history that he would sooner the town forgot, but he wouldn't have wished this kind of end for him if he turned out to be one of the bodies inside the house. Or maybe he wasn't dead. Someone had written the note. Maybe one of the people mentioned in the private text he had received earlier that evening. He opened it now and dialled the number included with the message. It rang twice before someone picked up.

'You have news?' The voice sounded old and dry and LeVay felt a swell of pride as he realized it was the Leader himself he was speaking to.

'Those people you're looking for,' he said. 'They're here.'

108

Marie-Claude woke slowly.

She could smell dust and mould, like old clothes, and her body felt numb and cold. She tried to open her eyes but her eyelids were too heavy. Every part of her felt heavy. She tried to remember where she was and a single thought surfaced along with screaming fear.

Léo. She had to save Léo.

She forced her eyes to open, grunting with the effort of it. Her eyelids flickered and the world appeared, murky and skewed. She was still in Hamilton's car. The door next to her was open and they were parked inside a hangar of some kind. Weak light threw shadows across a rough brick wall and a large industrial machine made from cast iron. She braced herself for another mighty effort and managed to turn her head a little. Léo was on the seat next to her, his face turned away. She couldn't see if he was awake or not. He seemed so still and she tried to move closer, but if opening her eyes had been hard this was impossible. It felt like her body was disconnected from her mind. Something shifted in the light and she looked across, as far as her eyes would reach, and saw Hamilton hunched over a series of buttons set into the side of the great machine. He was lit by the glow of a laptop displaying a detail of Solomon's waistcoat. A large ledger lay open next to it revealing different striped patterns as Hamilton turned the pages. The machine had to be the loom the prisoners had dubbed the Golem, and Hamilton was deciphering the list of *Die Anderen*, looking for the last name.

She looked back at Léo and focused all her energy on trying to move her right arm. Her fingers moved slightly as the feeling slowly returned and she started to sweat despite the cold. Then the light changed and she looked across to find Hamilton standing by the car. He wore a black scarf around his face and a black hat on his head, leaving only his eyes visible. He was staring right at her.

'It was you,' she said, her voice sounding muddy, her tongue feeling too large in her mouth. 'You killed my grandfather. Why?'

Hamilton held up a notebook. 'I need you to translate these names for me,' he said. His voice sounded strange, like someone else was speaking through him.

She looked at the Hebrew letters and names began to form as her brain automatically translated. She looked away again. 'I'm not helping you. Why would I help you?'

'Because the amount of Propofol I gave your son was probably too much for his size. I'm used to dealing with adults, you see, and I had to improvise. Which means he'll probably die unless he gets a save shot.' He held up a syringe loaded with clear liquid. 'Translate the names and I'll give it to him.'

'Give him the shot, then I'll translate.'

Hamilton shook his head. 'That's not how it works. Please understand, I do not *need* you to translate. I could easily figure these names out for myself using the internet. I want you to translate it because I want you to understand. You wish to learn your family history? Translate these names and you will. Your grandfather should have died in this place. He was a mistake of history. My mistake. Translate the names and you will understand.'

Marie-Claude looked back at the notebook and spotted her grandfather's name among the Hebrew letters. She frowned as she read further. 'There are more than four names here,' she said. 'It looks like there are . . . eight.'

Hamilton nodded. 'Eight names, but only four people. Give me the last name, the last of the Jewish names.'

Marie-Claude scanned the letters and spotted a name that was familiar to her, not only from her research but also from the fashion magazines her grandfather had always subscribed to. 'Max Hoffmann,' she said, her eyes returning to Hamilton. '*The* Max Hoffman?'

Hamilton let out a deep sigh. 'Hoffmann,' he repeated. 'There have always been rumours of how he started his fashion empire after the war, but nothing was ever proved. It seems money and success buy protection. Not any more, though. Not now I have proof of who he really is.'

Marie-Claude looked at the names, one German name for each of The Others. Max Hoffmann was a legend in the fashion industry. She'd had no idea her grandfather had even known him, let alone survived this place with him. She hadn't known they were the same age, though Hoffman had had so much plastic surgery it was hard to tell how old he was. 'The shot,' she said. 'Give Léo the shot. You promised.'

'I did,' Hamilton said, moving over to the workbench and picking up the laptop. 'I promised I would help you understand.' He moved back to the car and placed the laptop on the seat beside her, where she could see it. 'And now you shall.'

Marie-Claude looked at the screen and saw her grandfather's bruised and bloody face staring back at her. 'Please,' she said, 'give Léo the shot.' She could feel movement returning to her arms and legs but not nearly fast enough.

'I didn't get his full confession,' Hamilton said. 'Not like Saul Schwartzfeldt. But he said enough for you to understand.'

'I already understand,' Marie-Claude said, tears of anger and frustration dripping from her eyes. 'I know who you are. You're Günther Samler. Artur Samler's son.'

Hamilton shook his head. 'No. Günther Samler did survive the war, but after Herman Lansky vowed in his memoir never to give up looking for him, Samler tracked him down in order to silence him. He showed up at Lansky's flat with a gun, mocking his efforts to find *Die Anderen* and taunting him with the truth of who they were. But Lansky was prepared. Fearing someone from his past might come for him, he always carried a knife. There was a struggle. A fire started. Lansky was shot and wounded, but Günther was fatally stabbed. It was Günther Samler they found in the burned flat, not Herman Lansky. I lived in the next street to him, I was the one who'd found the flat for him when he first came to London. So he came to me, bleeding heavily from his wounds. He told me everything before he died, about Samler, about *Die Anderen*. He didn't know their new identities or where they'd gone after the war, but he knew what they were and he shared the truth with me. Before he died he asked me to find them all and make sure justice was carried out. He also made me promise to keep the real details of his death a secret so that *Die Anderen*, wherever they were, would think he'd died before talking to anyone and would therefore feel safe from his investigations. I did what he asked and buried him in a bomb site in the East End of London, another nameless victim of the war, and started my search for The Others.

'For decades I searched and found nothing but rumours and dead ends. Then you contacted me and told me your grandfather was one of them. I helped you, of course, hoping your family connection might flush them out from hiding. I hoped you might find them all before I exacted justice, but fate dealt me a death sentence of my own.' Hamilton tapped the side of his head. 'Brain tumour. Inoperable. No time left. I had to try and speed things up. That's why I needed confessions. Your grandfather was not Josef Engel. I'll let him tell you who he really was.'

He tapped the space bar and the clip started to play. Marie-Claude tried to concentrate, but her mind was screaming from what she had been told and because Léo still hadn't been given the antidote to the anaesthetic shutting his little body down.

My given name is Josef Engel . . .

Her grandfather's voice was slurred like hers, but his eyes were sharp and full of sorrow.

. . . My real name is Fritz Heissel. I achieved the rank of SS-Oberschütze in the third division of the Army of the German Reich. I was a guard in the Arbeit Lager designated as Mulhouse A, also known as Die Schneider Lager . . . This is my confession . . .

'A mistake of history,' Hamilton whispered, stepping forward and plunging the hypodermic needle into her arm instead of Léo's. 'The progeny of evil. You should never have been born, but now I can put that right. Your grandfather never wanted to talk about the war, did he, about his time in the camps? You thought it was because the memories were too painful, but in truth it was because he wasn't a Jewish prisoner. He was a German guard. He cheated death by putting on prisoner's clothes and caving a cellar in on top of himself to ensure he wouldn't be found until he was starved enough to pass for the skeletons he had been guarding.'

Marie-Claude's vision swam and her eyes began to close. She could feel the drug spreading through her like a chill, dragging her down into the dark. The door closed and she heard the engine start and felt the car move, out of the factory and into the night. 'You will be with your son soon enough,' Hamilton murmured in the voice that didn't sound like his. 'Your son and your grandfather both.'

109

The gates to the camp were wide open and Solomon felt an ominous sense of déjà-vu as he ran through them. He had been here before, he was certain of it, and he was anxious and afraid of what he might remember. For there was nothing good here, he knew that much, only pain. The air felt thicker inside the fence, and cold, like the ghosts of the place were crowding round him. Solomon pushed on through the cold, legs burning and lungs bursting from the sprint from Hamilton's house, heading towards a dim light shining through an open door in one of the loom sheds. He slowed as he approached it, listening as best he could through his laboured breathing for signs of anyone inside.

He reached the door and peered in. The huge loom stood silent and impressive, no sign of anyone around except for a large ledger of pattern samples lying open next to the control panel. Solomon walked over and flicked through the pages, studying the patterns, his photographic memory matching some to the pattern of his waistcoat. He could smell exhaust fumes in the shed and something subtle and sweet and chemical; he followed the smells back outside and over to the far side of the camp where a car was parked next to a large pile of rubble. The engine was warm beneath the bonnet but there was no one inside. Solomon could hear something now, so low it kept getting rubbed out by the gusting night breeze. It sounded like the voice of an old man and he wondered if it was one of the ghosts that thickened the air, whispering something to him from the cold, dark past. But he knew this place, knew where he was standing and in the fugue of half-memory and familiarity he looked at the pile of rubble and realized where the voice must be coming from. Solomon moved across the ground, following the shifting voice until he found the entrance to the cellar. It had only been partially cleared and he picked his way down rubble-strewn steps, the voice growing louder as he sank into the dark earth:

. . . he told us he could save us if we gave him our names . . . Der bleiche Mann . . .

Solomon reached the bottom of the steps and saw a pale light flickering at the end of a short corridor. He moved towards it, feeling his way along the rough wall and listening to the old man's voice as he went:

. . . he told us to write down our names, our old ones and the ones he gave us, and told us we had to keep them in plain sight . . .

Solomon reached the end of the corridor and looked round the corner and into the cellar. Plastic sacks of rubble were stacked by a broken doorway alongside a pile of pick-axes and shovels. The light was coming from a laptop, a video clip playing on the screen showing the bloody face of Josef Engel. Three bodies lay on the ground in front of it – Marie-Claude, Léo and Hamilton – arranged like corpses in a crypt. Solomon hurried over, dropped the Magellan file on the floor and checked each for a pulse as Josef Engel continued his sorrowful confession.

. . . it was Max's idea to use the Golem to record our names. We made a suit for the pale man and wove the names into the lining – in plain sight but also hidden, like he said it must be. The other list, the one we all had to sign, we took with us into the cellar . . .

Solomon hit the space bar to stop the clip. He needed to concentrate, and the old man's story was too distracting. He could listen to it later, when everyone was safe.

'Marie-Claude,' he said, lightly slapping her cheek. 'Come back to me.'

He rolled an eyelid back with his thumb and her pupil reacted to light but she remained unconscious. He checked her airway, rolled her on to her side, then moved over to Léo. He pressed a finger to his neck and it took him a few moments to find a pulse. It was slow and dangerously weak. He leaned in close and sniffed him, picking up scraps of the day's accumulated odours – from the car, from Hamilton's house, from the cellar floor. There was also the same sweet chemical smell that Solomon had caught in the loom shed, something heady and organic. An opiate. He rolled Léo's eyelid back but his pupil barely responded to the light. He was sinking too fast, dragged down by the drug he'd been given.

Information roared in Solomon's brain about opiate overdoses and how to treat them. There were drugs to combat it, but he had none of them. Léo needed emergency care fast and he needed to be prevented from sinking any deeper into his chemical sleep.

'Léo!' Solomon shouted, slapping him hard across the face. He picked him up, threw him over his shoulder and ran from the cellar, jostling him violently as he headed back to the loom shed. He lay Léo down on the cold, hard floor, put him on his side in the recovery position, and looked over at the huge beast of a machine. He needed to make as much noise as he could to keep Léo's senses active and his mind guided him to a large throw switch beneath the control panel. He pulled it up and the Golem clattered noisily to life, shaking the ground and walls of the factory as it built up speed and the shuttle flew back and forth across the loom. Solomon looked around and saw a phone by the entrance and his mind plucked the local emergency number from deep in his memory as he ran to it.

'State your emergency.'

'I need an ambulance immediately,' Solomon shouted above the din of the machine. 'Address is Rue de la Reine, Mulhouse.'

'Die Schneider Lager?'

'Yes. I have a woman, a child and an elderly man in induced opiate coma. The man and the woman's vital signs are steady, but the boy's are weak. He is seven or eight years old. Tell the ambulance to prepare for an immediate Lipid Resuscitation and possible adrenaline shot on arrival. He's in the main factory building, the only one with a light on. The gates are open. Tell them to hurry.'

He hung up, ran from the building and scooped cold rain-water into his hands from a puddle in the yard. He ran back inside and flung the water into Léo's face, then turned and ran back to the cellar because there was nothing else he could do for him.

Josef Engel's frozen image illuminated the cellar, his bloodied face staring out at the place where he had nearly died. Solomon leaned over Hamilton first. He was the eldest and weakest, and therefore the most likely to crash from the overdose. The sickly smell of opiates seemed stronger on him and came with a vague undercurrent of honey. Solomon thumbed back Hamilton's eyelid and his pupil reacted normally.

'Monsieur,' Solomon said, slapping his face a little.

He felt the hand flying out of the darkness more than saw it, a shift in pressure, a creak of tensing muscle. Solomon twisted away, caught the hand and diverted the stabbing needle it held into Hamilton's chest, banging his fist on the end of the syringe to empty it. Hamilton gasped as the opiates flooded into him.

'It's you,' Hamilton said, his voice already slurring as he began to slip under. '*Der bleiche Mann*, the pale man. I thought you were a story. They all said you would come back. And you did.'

'But I don't understand,' Solomon said. 'You saved these people once. Why kill them now? Why kill the woman and the boy?'

'Evil must meet justice.'

Solomon shook his head. 'The woman and her boy are not evil.'

Hamilton glanced at Engel's image on the screen. 'But they came from evil.'

Solomon thought of the long hours he'd spent with Marie-Claude and Léo. He thought of the gentle love and compassion they'd shared and the selflessness they'd displayed in seeking to travel so far to warn an old man of the danger he was in. 'Good can come from evil,' he said, and he looked down at Hamilton with a mixture of pity and disgust. 'Just as evil can come from good.'

Pain and hate twisted Hamilton's features. He tried to get up but the drugs had hold of him now. His eyes rolled up into his skull and he fell back down to the dusty floor, banging his head hard on the flagstone floor.

Solomon searched him quickly, looking for an antidote to the opiates but finding nothing. He pulled the almost empty syringe from Hamilton's chest and slipped it into his pocket. Outside, he could hear the sound of a siren getting louder above the rumble of the loom. He should go and meet them, direct them to Léo and Marie-Claude, but they were still a few minutes away and he had business here, he could *feel* it. Hamilton had called him the pale man, as Otto had done earlier. But he couldn't be him. It wasn't possible.

He hit the space bar on the laptop to restart the clip and Josef Engel's voice murmured in the room:

. . . the pale man told us to strip off our uniforms and throw them with our identity cards on to the fire. He gave us prisoners' uniforms to wear but they were new, not soiled and filthy like the ones we were used to seeing. The pale man smiled and said we would look right by the time we were found. Then he led us to one of the outbuildings, a storage hut with a concrete cellar beneath it . . .

Solomon looked around the room, something like memory leading his eye to a spot in the far corner where the rubble had yet to be cleared. He felt like he had been here before but he couldn't have been, he couldn't be the pale man, and yet the story Josef Engel was telling seemed familiar – like he could almost remember it, like he knew what he would describe next. Shifting the laptop so the glow from the screen lit the rubble on the far wall, he grabbed a shovel from the pile and started to clear it.

. . . there were thirty-four of us in that cellar, but only four of us gave the pale man our names. I was young and scared and didn't want to die so I gave him mine. He told us to write them on a sheet of paper and bury it at the site of our rebirth in an envelope he gave us with something heavy inside. I didn't see what

it was because Max sealed the letter. The pale man locked us inside the cellar and told us to wait . . .

The shovel caught something on the floor and Solomon dropped down and brushed dust away from a square slab set into the floor. He ran his finger round the edge of it and thumped it with his fist and heard a slight hollowness beneath.

. . . some of us panicked a little when the door was locked. It was like we had been in a trance and the bang of the door snapped us out of it. Within moments the ground shook with explosions and we heard masonry fall against the door and we knew we were trapped. That's when the panic really took hold . . .

Solomon grabbed a pickaxe from the pile, drove the point into the gap and leaned back to lever up the slab. Beneath it was an old tin with a picture of sewing needles on a rusted lid.

. . . If we'd known how long we would be in that cellar and how bad it would get, I think maybe we would have ended it then and there. I was scared of dying and have lived a long life since, but it has come at a great cost. It has been a life of hiding. A lie . . .

Solomon picked up the tin and prised it open. Inside was an envelope. He picked it up and felt the air thicken around him, as if ghosts were crowding around to see what was inside. There was something heavy and thin in there, and Solomon wanted to see what it was but was also afraid of it. He was connected to what had happened here. Maybe even responsible. He didn't understand how, but he felt it, he *remembered* it, and it made him feel wretched and sick. There was so much pain in this place, chilling the air and sinking it into deep shadow with a darkness more than night. And some of that pain was his. He had history here and he was afraid to learn it.

. . . I often wish I had never gone into that cellar or given the pale man my name. But when I look at my granddaughter and her son, I think that maybe it was worth the price after all, if only to see what shining good can grow from the darkest of places . . .

Outside, the wail of the siren cut out, telling him that the medics had arrived. He had information that might help them. Solomon scooped up the Magellan file from where he'd dropped it and slipped the envelope inside. He hauled Marie-Claude over his shoulder and picked up the laptop, shutting off Josef Engel's voice as he closed it. Finally he walked out of the cellar leaving Hamilton alone in the dark with the disappointed ghosts.

110

Blue lights from an ambulance and two police cars flickered in the night, lighting the dark buildings of the camp and the uniformed medics hurrying into the loom shed with their emergency equipment.

'Another one here,' Solomon shouted above the din of the loom.

One of the medics looked over and ran to help. Solomon carried Marie-Claude straight into the ambulance and lay her on a stretcher, tucking the laptop beneath her.

'They've been overdosed with this –' He took the syringe from his pocket and handed it to the medic. 'It's very fast-acting. Paralytic and narcotic. Something like Propofol.' He held his hand to the side of Marie-Claude's face, still beautiful despite the cuts and bruises, then turned as Léo was carried into the ambulance. 'Do you carry Naloxone or Naltrexone?' The medic nodded. 'Give him some. His vitals are dangerously low. His name's Léo.' He looked back at Marie-Claude. 'She's Marie-Claude, his mother. Her signs are fine. There's another one in a cellar over there. He's pretty old and will probably need the Naloxone too. I'll show you where he is.'

Solomon took one step out of the ambulance and stopped

when he saw the gun pointing right at him. 'Hands where we can see them,' the gendarme holding it said.

Solomon raised his hands, still holding the Magellan file.

'What's your name?' the gendarme asked.

'Solomon Creed.'

'Well now, Monsieur Creed, consider yourself under arrest on suspicion of murder.'

'The man you want is over there,' Solomon said, nodding in the direction of the piles of rubble and Hamilton's parked car. 'His name is John Hamilton.'

'John Hamilton, whose house is currently on fire?'

'Yes. I would imagine he probably did that too. The woman in the ambulance can confirm it all when she wakes up. So can the police officer you will have found unconscious on Hamilton's drive.'

'That man is in a critical condition in hospital. Heart attack. And until we can talk to someone who is actually conscious, I'm going to lock you up.' Another gendarme stepped forward with a set of handcuffs in his hand and two more stood behind him, their hands resting on their sidearms.

Solomon was cuffed and bundled into the back of one of the police cars. 'Stay with him, Thierry,' the man in charge said. 'The rest of you, follow me.'

LeVay headed across the courtyard towards the parked car, flashlights needling the dark and picking out the jagged edges of broken masonry. He hated this place, not only because it gave him the creeps but because it was a constant and unwelcome reminder of the past. When the party got into power and France was free again he hoped they would bulldoze the place and finally unchain his town from the anchor of what had happened here. His interest was in France's future success, not its failed past.

They found the steps to the cellar and he led the way, searching ahead with his torch. They found Hamilton near a pile of recently disturbed rubble. While the medics went to work on him, LeVay moved over to a hole in the ground and nudged the empty tin lying next to it with his foot. The leadership had told him to look for some kind of list. The empty tin suggested that maybe Solomon had found it. He remembered the file he had been holding in his hand. It was in the car now. And so was he.

The medics finished their checks and loaded Hamilton on to a stretcher. LeVay followed them out, glad to be back in the air and out of the cellar. He knew all the stories about the camp, including the one about the four survivors they'd found. If they bulldozed the place, those stories would fade away and everyone would be better off. He followed the medics back to the ambulance and the night fell silent as someone finally shut off the loom.

'Over here, Chief,' a voice called out.

LeVay walked to the ambulance and found the woman semi-awake and propped up on the stretcher. 'Léo,' she murmured.

'He's safe, madame,' LeVay said. 'They're treating him now. Can you tell me what happened here?'

'Hamilton,' she replied. 'He injected us with something. He murdered my grandfather.'

'And how is Solomon Creed involved?' LeVay asked.

She frowned. 'He saved us.'

LeVay nodded. 'Let's talk when you're more rested.'

He stepped out of the ambulance and lit a cigarette. He wouldn't be able to hold Solomon for long with the woman vouching for him. But it was the list the leadership seemed most interested in and he could give them that. He took a long pull on his cigarette, filling his lungs with smoke and night air as he walked over to the police car. He could see Thierry sitting behind the wheel, facing front. He couldn't see Solomon. He reached the car and stared into the empty back seat. 'Where is he?' he hollered, throwing his cigarette to the ground.

Thierry blinked and looked up at him. 'Where's who?'

'The prisoner? Where's the prisoner?' Thierry continued to look blank. LeVay turned and scanned the dark compound, looking for signs of movement. 'Come on, he can't have gone far. You lost him, you can help me get him back.' He pulled his gun and moved away from the car but stopped when he realized Thierry wasn't following. He turned back and glared at his sergeant, still sitting in the car and frowning at the steering wheel. 'Get out of the fucking car and help me look for him!' LeVay hollered.

Thierry continued to frown at his hands. 'I can't,' he said. 'It's my hands. My hands are stuck to the steering wheel.'

111

'Léo!!' Marie-Claude woke with a start, wrapped in the smell of hospitals.

She'd been dreaming of home, walking through Cordes and looking for Léo, running down darkening streets and calling his name.

'Mama?'

She turned her head and there he was, lying in the next bed with tubes in his arm. He looked so tiny.

'Léo.'

'I'm OK, Mama.'

She smiled at him and wanted to go over to his bed and get in and squeeze him until he clicked, but she had tubes in her arms too and a clip on her finger monitoring her heartbeat, so she stayed where she was.

She looked around the white room, trying to remember how she got there and recalling hazy fragments of Baptiste and Hamilton and a video clip of her bloodied grandfather playing on a laptop. The laptop was on a chair next to her, lying among a pile of her clothes. She wondered how it had got there and how long she had been out. She looked over at the window. It was still dark outside.

'Where's Monsieur Creed?' she asked.

'The doctor said a man called the ambulance and told them where we were and what to do to make us better. He said if he hadn't called, I'd most likely be dead.'

'Léo, a doctor would never have said that to you.'

'OK, he didn't say it exactly, but his colours were all dark and serious while he was talking, and I could tell that's what he meant. It was Monsieur Creed, wasn't it, the man who called the ambulance?'

'I think so, yes.'

Léo smiled and fell silent for a moment. 'Where do you suppose he's gone?'

'I don't know, *chéri.*'

'Do you think he'll come and see us?'

Marie-Claude shook her head. 'No, I don't think he will. I think he came to help us and he did – and now he's gone.'

'You think maybe he's gone to help someone else now, like superheroes do?'

Marie-Claude smiled and nodded. 'Yes,' she said. 'Like a superhero. Monsieur Creed is exactly like a superhero.'

The door opened and a doctor came in with two policemen behind him.

'You're awake,' the doctor said, checking her pulse. 'How are you feeling?'

Marie-Claude glanced at the gendarmes. 'Tired.'

'We wondered if we could talk to you,' the older of the two gendarmes said. 'About what happened to you tonight.'

Marie-Claude nodded. 'Of course. But could you maybe give me a few more minutes to wake up, I'm not sure I'm thinking straight yet.'

The gendarme nodded, glanced at the laptop. 'Of course. Shall we come back in, say, half an hour?'

Marie-Claude smiled. 'Thank you. And could I have

515

some water, please, my mouth feels like it's got cotton wool in it.'

The gendarmes left and the doctor poured water from a jug and shone a light into her eyes to check her pupil response while she drank it. He did the same for Léo, wrote some figures on a chart, and left them.

As soon as he was gone Marie-Claude took the laptop and opened it. The desktop was unlocked and was filled with folders and video files. She connected to the hospital Wi-Fi network, opened her Gmail account and looked over at Léo. From the moment he was born she'd spent her life trying to do what was best for him, helping him to understand who he was and where he fit into the world and all the while protecting him. She saw now that her grandfather had done the same with her. He had always warned her away from learning the truth of what had happened in the camp and now she understood why.

But she could guard the secret, like her grandfather had done; she could protect Léo from it, as he had kept it from her. She remembered what Solomon had said to her in the car, about how he believed he was here to do exactly that, to protect Léo from the knowledge of his past. To save him from it. To be his Sin Eater. And yet, when it had come down to it, he had left the laptop behind in the full knowledge of what it contained. He had left the decision to her.

She looked over at Léo, looking tiny in his hospital bed with his big knowing eyes that saw the world in such a magical way. She had seen such strength in him through all of this, such wisdom she hadn't known was there. He was magical, and Solomon had seen it. Magical and strong.

She opened up a new email and started filling the address field with all the contacts she could think of – people she knew from the Shoah Foundation, press contacts she had made through her research. Next she went online and started looking up names of national and international news outlets – TV, print, online, radio – adding the email addresses of editors and political columnists to her growing list.

'What are you doing, Mama?' Léo asked from his bed.

'Let me finish this, Léo, and I'll tell you.' She went through political sites next, adding the press office contacts of all the major French political parties to her list. When she was finished, she started to upload the video of her grandfather and Saul Schwartzfeldt's confessions to her YouTube account and wrote an email explaining everything – about Hamilton, about *Die Anderen*, finally getting to tell the story she had spent years chasing down. She had always believed the story needed to be told and, now she knew the truth, she believed it even more. Despite what she had learned about her grandfather and what he had been, she knew that he had also become a father, a grandfather, a great-grandfather. His legacy was made up of more than whatever he had done in the war. She was his legacy, as was Léo. She finished her email and wiped a tear from her cheek as she read it through. Then she attached the links to the YouTube clips, paused one last time as she considered what she was about to do, and pressed *send*, checking the time anxiously as she waited for it to go, aware that the email was large and the police were due to return any minute. A whooshing sound announced that it had gone and she breathed again, closed the laptop, sat back in her bed and looked across at Léo with his huge, expectant eyes.

'What are my colours like, Léo?'

He frowned, unused to being asked this by his mother. 'They're orangey-green. Normal. They were darker when you were working on the laptop, but now you've stopped, they've gone light again.'

Marie-Claude smiled. 'I need to talk to you about something, Léo.'

He nodded. 'Is it about Monsieur Creed?'

'No, Léo. It's about Grampy and the bad camp. It's about where we come from and who we are. It's about us.'

112

Max Hoffmann locked himself away in the bunker of his basement office, monitoring what was happening in Mulhouse through his network of spies. It was a mess: people missing, people dead – though the woman was still alive, Josef Engel's granddaughter, the Jewish bitch who had caused all this trouble. At least she was in hospital and not in full health. People died in hospital all the time. Hamilton was already as good as dead, lying in a coma he would never recover from, according to LeVay, after a huge brain embolism had turned him into a vegetable. That was one bit of good news, at least. The madman who had been hunting them down and who had killed Saul and Josef had not managed to finish off him or Otto.

He thought of Otto now, working away at his loom, his mind almost gone. He envied him sometimes, envied the luxurious oblivion of being able to forget, the lightness of it. His burden was much heavier and he carried it alone and in secret. He had often dreamed of a time, after his party had taken power, when he could finally reveal who he was. He imagined how his story might take on the dimension of legend in a new France, the tale of a man who had carried the flame of nationalism, kept it buried deep in his heart as he built a fortune from the ruin of his life and poured all the money into rekindling that flame on a grand and proper scale. He imagined they might name cities after him as part of the restructuring of a newly energized Europe, once the misguided experiments of liberalism and socialism and democracy had failed. All he had to do was stay hidden for a few more weeks, until his party had won the seats they were predicted to win as they rode the wave of dissatisfaction and racial tension he had helped cultivate. The elections were only three weeks away. Three weeks left to wait after seventy years of waiting. Nothing could stop them now. He would make sure of it. He would wait until the police had interviewed the woman and find out what she knew from LaVey. Then he would decide what to do with her. If she had to be silenced, so be it. In the meantime, he would stay locked in his mansion surrounded by the memories of his secret life – the Nazi uniform he had worn as a guard, the striped prisoner uniform he had worn to escape justice, the political posters and campaign literature of the party he had slowly built over seventy patient years. He was safe here.

But Hoffmann's mind kept drifting to the stranger, the man who had evaded every attempt to capture him, the one named Solomon Creed. The name meant nothing to him but his description did. He had read it now on several police reports, variations on the same distantly familiar theme – pale, tall, thin, white hair and skin. One of the reports had gone further, describing the clothes he wore as '. . . *resembling an incomplete suit with jacket and waistcoat but mismatched trousers*'. Hoffmann glanced over at one of the display cabinets, the soft light illuminating the mannequin inside and the pale, tailored pair of trousers with high waist and tapered legs, made to measure for someone tall and thin. It couldn't be him, the man who had saved them in the camps, the man who had asked them to make a suit but never returned to claim it. Had he come back now, after all these years? So many years. And why save them then only to hunt them down now? It couldn't be him. He just needed to keep his nerve. Wait it out, down here in his bunker, safe and secure, where nothing could reach him.

The phone call that finished him came shortly after dawn. Maria, his secretary, patched it in from the upstairs office. He had told her he wasn't taking calls, but this was from Yves DuTronc, managing editor of *France Today*, the most popular and right-leaning of the print dailies and a huge party supporter.

'I just got an email,' DuTronc said. 'It contains documentary evidence proving that you are a Nazi fugitive who escaped justice by masquerading as a Jewish prisoner.'

Hoffmann felt his blood flash hot in his veins. 'Delete it,' he said.

'The same email has been sent to the editor of every newspaper and news media outlet in France, England, Germany, America as well as to key members of the French National Assembly.'

'We can spin it,' Hoffmann said, his heart hammering against the thin walls of his chest. 'Say it's a smear. I'll threaten to sue anyone who runs it. It's too close to the election, we can't let this get out.'

'I've looked through the evidence and forwarded the email so you can see for yourself. It's too compelling to ignore. I think denial will only pour petrol on the flames.'

The email pinged into Hoffman's account. He opened it and skim-read the contents, saw his name listed alongside Josef Engel, Saul Schwartzfeldt and Otto Adelstein.

. . . these are the ones known as The Others, the message said.

. . . aside from Herman Lansky, they are the only known prisoners to survive the liquidation of Die Schneider Lager. But they were not prisoners. Two of them recorded confessions of who they really were.

Hoffman clicked on one of the video links in the mail and stared at Josef Engel's bloodied face. He started the clip playing and listened to his old friend's voice, slurred with sedative and pain:

My given name is Josef Engel. My real name is Fritz Heissel. I achieved the rank of SS-Oberschütze in the third division of the Army of the German Reich.

There it was, their great secret exposed and shared with the world after seventy long years of careful hiding. Hoffman's mind flitted around in panic, looking for a way out of this. There was always a solution, he could always see a way through, but this time he came up with nothing. 'What can we do?' he asked DuTronc.

There was a deep sigh. 'A large part of our energies have always been focused on distancing the party from any neo-Nazi accusations. This revelation that you, its chief architect and donor, are actually a former Nazi guard who posed as a Jewish prisoner to escape justice undermines all our credibility. It will kill us at the elections. There's nothing we can do. It's done. I was only calling out of courtesy, to warn you. We have no choice but to run the story. It's too big to ignore. I'm sorry.'

Max Hoffmann put down the phone and turned to the map of France. His party was leading in the polls in over three hundred of the five hundred and seventy-seven circonscriptions. They were going to win the election, there was no question. The people of France had already decided.

Even if this story did break, the people would vote for his party. The party was bigger than him now. Much bigger.

His phone rang again and he snatched it up. 'There are police here,' his secretary Maria said, her voice sounding stretched. 'They're asking for you.'

'Tell them you don't know where I am.'

Her voice lowered to a whisper. 'They have a warrant to seize all documents relating to the party. All party assets have been frozen, pending a thorough investigation of its finances and practices.'

'What?! No. They can't. We can't campaign with no finances! The election is only three weeks awa—'

'Monsieur Hoffmann,' a man's voice cut him off. 'We know you're in the building. Please surrender yourself. Do not make me come and find you.'

Hoffman hung up. Panicked. His heart hammering painfully. He grabbed his Ledger – the Ledger of the Loyal – all the names of the party faithful throughout France, contacts, positions. He had to get rid of it. If they found it, they could trace his entire network and make all kinds of unwanted connections, not least in regard to the Josef Engel murder investigation. He moved over to the fireplace and began to tear out pages, throwing them into the grate until it was full. He took a match and lit the edge of one of the pages but the paper was thick and damp from being locked away in the basement and the flame smouldered then snuffed out.

A loud hammering on the door made Hoffman drop the book. They were outside. The door was thick but they might make Maria give them the code. He looked around in panic and hurried over to the drinks cabinet. The bottle of cognac clinked as his shaking hand took it from the rack. He uncorked it and sprinkled the smouldering pages with the amber liquid.

There was another bang on the door and muffled voices. Marie was out there, he could hear her talking. They would make her unlock the door. He had to be quick. He poured more cognac on the crumpled pages, struck a match and dropped it into the fireplace. There was a whoosh of blue fire as the flame caught the alcohol fumes and exploded from the grate. Hoffman closed his eyes against the wave of heat and staggered backwards. He opened his eyes and saw that the pages were burning now, but the heat was still on him. He looked down and saw blue flame on his hands and arms. He beat at them, trying to put them out, but the sleeves of his jacket were soaked in cognac.

Hoffman staggered backwards, beating at the flames in panic. But his hands were on fire now, and all he did was spread it. He hit the wall and slumped to the floor, batting at the fire that covered him with burning hands. His instinct was to call out to Maria for help, but the ledger was still half full of pages. He had to burn it. He was unimportant now. The party and its survival were all that mattered.

He pushed himself to his feet, the flames all over him like a suit of fire. Behind him, flames spread up the wall where he'd leaned, across the map of France and the posters of all the party candidates, burning away their smiles, Jean-Luc Belloq included.

The hammering on the door intensified and Max Hoffman focused on the ledger, the pain of the fire all over him now. He dropped to the floor beside the book, tried to pick it up but his burning hands wouldn't work so he fell on the book instead, clutching it to his chest with burning arms as the door burst open and uniformed bodies surged in.

He heard Maria scream and it reminded him of a time seventy years earlier when he had stood by a burning factory, listening to similar sounds amid the smell of smoke and burning flesh. He clutched the book tighter as the photographs of party candidates behind him curled in the heat, filling the air with glowing embers and smoke.

Figures swarmed around him and Max Hoffman died wondering if they were real or ghosts, the dead come to claim him at last from the cold forgotten ashes of his past.

EPILOGUE

Solomon sat on the banks of the Rhine and watched the river flow while the sun slowly rose in a hazy sky. He'd crossed over to the German side because he needed to rest and think, and because it was nice to be in a country where the police weren't looking for him. He could hear the sound of distant sirens on the opposite side of the river, carried on the shifting breeze, and he thought of Marie-Claude and how, by helping her resolve the mystery of her past, he had raised some dark questions about his own.

He picked up the file he'd taken from Magellan, and looked at his own picture on the cover. He wanted to know what it contained but was afraid of it too. Afraid of what he might discover. Afraid of who he might be. He shook out the envelope he'd found in the cellar and turned it over in his hand. It was blank and mottled with age and he could feel something hard and flat inside it. He slid a finger beneath the flap, tore it open and tipped a folded sheet of paper and a sliver of silvered glass into his hand. The paper was as mottled as the envelope with faint words printed on a surface that had been scoured away with sand or grit, leaving only traces of the original text behind. Solomon studied what remained, translating the dry German in his head. It detailed the process of prisoner selection and appeared to have been torn from some kind of prison manual. But what had been printed on the page was unimportant, it was what was written on it now that made Solomon's mouth go dry. It was a contract, written in the same dark brown ink he had seen on a similar document in Arizona. The wording was familiar too:

We the undersigned pledge our sacred and immortal souls in exchange for liberty from this place and a long life thereafter.
Signed,

     Manfred Schiller (Max Hoffman)
     Fritz Heissel (Josef Engel)
     Wolfgang Lutz (Otto Adelstein)
     Karl Schmidt (Saul Schwartzfeldt)

Solomon stared at the words and the names written in blood.

In his memoir, Herman Lansky had described a pale man arriving at the camp on the day it was liquidated. Josef Engel had talked of him too, said he'd asked for their names:

. . . our old ones and the ones he gave us . . .

Solomon looked at the torn page and the names recorded on it. Had *he* told them to do this? Had he taken their souls in exchange for their salvation? The camp had seemed so familiar to him – and yet he can't have been the man they all remembered. It was impossible.

It's you, Hamilton had told him, *der bleiche Mann, the pale man. They all said you would come back. And you did.*

Otto Adelstein had said it too. He had been afraid of Solomon. But Léo had not. The boy had seen something else in him. Something good. He said that he shone, like a child shone, like something pure and innocent. Was he really the pale man? Had he been somehow reborn? Rebirth, transmigration, reincarnation – it was known by many names in many different cultures, but the idea was always the same: one soul living many lives, gradually perfecting an existence and making restitution for past mistakes to ultimately move on to another plane. Was that what this was? Was he revisiting his own past and putting right what another version of himself had once made wrong?

He opened the file he had taken from Magellan and scanned the documents inside – police reports summarizing what had happened in Arizona and a variety of psychological studies. They were drawn from two different facilities but were for the same patient – James John Huffam Hawdon.

Solomon said the name out loud, tasting it on his tongue. It was familiar. Sweet. Was this him?

He started to read, turning the pages so fast he tore them as he soaked up the story of the poor, genius rich boy rejected by his family who'd butchered his mother and brother. He found himself wanting it to be true, even with everything it implied, but it wasn't, not entirely. Some of it felt wrong, it tasted wrong, like bread with no flavour. Other parts he knew to be false, like he knew the mark on his arm had not come from surgery because he remembered how it had happened, by the side of an Arizona road, along with the name of a man and a conviction that he must save him somehow. And when he had saved that man, and burned the contract that recorded his name, the mark had changed again, from a I to a II. He had *seen* it happen. He was sure he had.

He could test it, prove to himself that he had not imagined it. The letter from the cellar was of the same kind as the one he had burned in Arizona, an implied bargain written in blood upon a scrubbed page. And he had felt the same sense of duty towards Léo, that he was there to save him, which meant he needed to destroy this contract too and free him from the curse of his grandfather's bargain.

Solomon picked up the letter from the cellar, shrugged off his jacket and shirt to reveal the brand on his shoulder, two parallel lines of raised flesh. He had stolen a lighter from the police car anticipating this moment and took it now, sparking a flame and touching it to the edge of the page.

Pain seized his arm the moment the contract started to burn, a heat rising like lava inside his flesh. He dropped the letter and bit down against the searing agony and watched the skin redden and bubble around his brand as the II turned to a III and a new word burned into his mind:

Furst.

He repeated it, searching it for meaning as the page burned then curled to ash and was extinguished. Solomon rubbed his hand over the new mark on his arm, a III now where the II had been, repeating the word that had come with it.

Furst.

He knew that name. He had just read it.

He picked up the file again and found a copy of a report from a forensics lab in Tucson that had been marked as 'Archived'. It recorded a corrupted match for a sample sent to the lab regarding a suspect in a murder enquiry. The suspect's name was listed as Solomon Creed. The DNA match was from a hair found in an archaeological dig in Melek Mezar, Turkey. The sample had been marked as corrupted because Carbon-14 tests had dated the hair as belonging to a man who had lived around four thousand years earlier, which ruled it out as a possible match. Except the test strips were also included in the document and they did match. Exactly.

The white noise of information in Solomon's head switched to new details plucked from this information:

Melek Mezar – Turkish for 'Tomb of the Angel'.

Believed to be the resting place and shrine of a powerful, Messianic prophet who lived two thousand years before Christ.

Excavated in the year 2000 by a Dr Brendan Furst. Born Dublin, 20 March 1968. Studied Classics and History at Balliol College, Oxford. Disappeared on his birthday, 2004. Current location unknown.

Solomon picked up the sliver of mirror and looked at his reflection. His hair had darkened to a silvery grey, shot through with stripes of black. He took out the second shard of mirror, the one he had found in Arizona, another fragment of something bigger. Was he reclaiming himself piece by piece with each new step on his journey, colouring in the empty man he had been at the beginning? He thought of Magellan and what part he was playing in all of this. He'd said he knew who Solomon really was. And it was he who had put this file together, the truths and the lies, he who had pursued him from Arizona to France, his name that had surfaced in his mind when he had burned the first contract. He thought of him as he had last seen him, lying in the wreckage of the crashed car.

Only I can tell you who you really are, he had said.

And Solomon believed him.

He heard the sirens again, floating on the wind, and wondered if Magellan was caught up in what was now happening in Mulhouse. He doubted it. Magellan had showed no interest in working with the authorities or playing by other people's rules. He would be in the wind, like Solomon was, location unknown like Dr Brendan Furst.

Solomon stared at the river flowing by, thinking about what to do next and which direction he should go. He wanted to find Magellan, on his own terms this time, and find out how much of the psychiatric notes had been fabricated and why. He wanted to discover what truths he was hiding, and learn how much of the story of James Hawdon was his. He needed to find Dr Furst too, save him from something unknown and reclaim another lost fragment of himself in the process. And then there was Jefferson Hawdon, casting his long shadow over everything. James Hawdon's father. Maybe Solomon's father too.

Three possible directions to travel in. One direction to make.

And the river flowed on beneath Solomon's gaze, reflecting the trees and the brightening day as it had done for century upon century. It flowed on still when the man rose up and walked away, buttoning his shirt and jacket as he disappeared into the woods, and back into the shadows.

ACKNOWLEDGEMENTS

This book was hard to write, not just technically but also because of the subject running like a dark bass note beneath the story. The Holocaust is a truly terrible subject to take on and I thought long and deep about whether it was a suitable element to include in, what is primarily, a piece of entertainment. But, as with all my books, I always try and explore some deeper, underlying theme through the action and suspense and in this case the recent political shift towards a nationalistic Right suggested that the wheel of history was turning back in that dark direction. Britain voted to leave the EU while I was writing this book. Donald Trump was elected president of the United States. Marine Le Pen solidified her popularity in France with a party not a million miles away in political intent from the one I invented for this book. And all of these political shifts were fuelled by the same kinds of rhetoric of intolerance and fear that brought the Nazis into power and all that ultimately came with that. This is largely a book about memory and the importance of remembering, even the difficult stuff – especially the difficult stuff. And there is nothing more difficult, or important, to remember than the Holocaust.

I spent a lot of time researching the death camps because,

even though I was constructing a fiction, I felt it was my duty to get the details of what happened right. Die Schneider Lager never existed but camps exactly like it did, and everything I described happening there happened too, to real people. To list all the resources I used would fill too many pages and actually the most useful and powerful research I found was the recorded testimony of real survivors. So if you're interested in the genuine stories behind my woven one I've uploaded a research document on the page for this book on my website (www.simontoyne.net) with links to the online sources I used, including those interviews with survivors from various death camps as well as the Łódź Ghetto.

A large part of this story is set in a town called Cordes-sur-Ciel in France. Unusually in my books, where I tend to make places up wholesale, this is an actual town and is pretty much as described here. The majority of this book was written there too, which would make you think that all descriptions should be one hundred per cent accurate. In truth I have taken small licences here and there for the sake of the story, and, in these instances, I apologize to my French neighbours, particularly the local gendarmes who aren't anything like the ones in this book. Cordes is a beautiful and magical place and I owe it a huge debt for giving me inspiration and a quiet place to write. If you look on my website you'll find plenty of pictures of that too (www.simontoyne.net).

I also want to thank all the unsung heroes behind the scenes who helped shape this book in various forms. These include Alice Saunders, Julia Wisdom, Lucy Dauman, Finn Cotton, Hannah Gamon, Adam Humphrey, Kate Elton, all at ILA and everyone else at HarperCollins UK. In the US I want to thank David Highfill, Kaitlyn Kennedy, Chloe

Moffett, and also Joel Gotler who introduced Solomon to Leonardo DiCaprio. I also owe a huge thanks to all those bloggers, reviewers, booksellers, readers, Tweeters and Facebookers who continue to help spread the word about my books and are always great to chat to online and sometimes even in person when I should really be writing. Feel free to join in with the chat on Twitter (@simontoyne) or Facebook (www.facebook.com/simon.toyne.writer) – I always accept every new friend request and reply to every message.

Finally, and most importantly, to Kathryn, Roxy, Stan and Betsy, who are always (amazingly) still there whenever I emerge blinking from the dark cave of whatever book I've been writing. They're the best.

Simon Toyne
Cordes-sur-Ciel
January, 2017